Sacred

SACRED
BRIDE

David Hair & Cath Mayo

CANELO

First published in the United Kingdom in 2019 by Canelo

This edition published in the United Kingdom in 2019 by

Canelo Digital Publishing Limited
Third Floor, 20 Mortimer Street
London W1T 3JW
United Kingdom

Print ISBN 978 1 78863 850 0
Ebook ISBN 978 1 78863 281 2

Look for more great books at www.canelo.co

David: I dedicate this book to my writing partner in this series, Cath Mayo. It takes a special person to accept having someone else blundering into your vision of your favourite hero and mythos, as well as the ability to share one's talents and knowledge so freely and brilliantly. It's been an absolute pleasure and a fun ride.

Cath: And to David, a tower of inspiration and skill, bringing drive and a deep understanding of the genre to all our books. One plus one is far more than two.

to the
AXEINOS SEA

EPIRUS Mt Olympus▲
■ Dodona THESSALIAN
KINGDOMS   ■Troy
THESPROTIA   ▲Mt Ida   HITTITE
              LOCRIS   EMPIRE
AETOLIA   AEGEAN   LUWIAN
PHOCIS ■Pytho   SEA
■Thebes   ■KINGDOMS
Cephalonia   ■Athens
        ELIS
     ■Corinth
Pisa■ Mycenae■
     Argos■■Tiryns
IONIAN
SEA   Pylos■ Sparta■   Delos
        ■Kranae
                              Kos
                        Syme
        Cythera   ○Rhodes

ACHAEA,
the AEGEAN   CRETE   MEDITERRANEAN
and ASIA MINOR   SEA

Part One: Tears of a Seeress

1 – The Caverns of Dodona

> 'There's a place, Hellopia … And Dodona was
> founded there, on its furthest border, and Zeus loved it
> and made it his oracle, one revered by men.
> And from this place mortal men bring back all oracles.
> Whoever comes there questions the immortal god and
> brings gifts and returns with good auguries.'
>
> — Hesiod, *Catalogues of Women*

Epirus

7th year of the reign of Agamemnon of Mycenae (1287BC)

Sheer cliffs rise around us, bleak and barren under sullen winter skies, the rock grey and forbidding as we edge through a narrow ravine, with icy water surging past us just a few feet below. It's teeming with rain and treacherous underfoot, so we're roped together – though by now I'm worried we're doubling the risk, not halving it: if one of us goes, we probably both will, and Ithaca will lose her prince – and my sister's worthless husband will be king when Laertes dies.

I refuse to let that happen.

Bria's leading the way, a lean form blurred by the torrential rain, and the river's rising by the moment. We need to get through this section of the ravine before we're engulfed. It's madness to be traveling in such conditions – which is why we're doing it: no one will dream we're here. The plan seemed audacious, brilliant even, with a real chance of disrupting our enemies' schemes – but right now I'm thinking it's my worst idea ever.

'You… all right?' Bria's high-pitched shout reaches me in broken snatches. I nod back as I grip the rock wall with bloodless, frozen fingers, clinging to water-polished crevices and ledges, hunched over against a fierce headwind as we round a spur. And there the ledge ends, the floodwaters boiling at our feet and the rock face upriver undercut and smooth as polished bronze. With no other choice, we're forced to climb. We struggle upwards, lugging our packs, muscles straining and skin numbed by cold. After what seems an eternity we reach the top of the cliff, and exchange weary looks before slogging on.

From here the going is easier, if clambering steeply uphill through dense undergrowth choked with fallen tree trunks and hidden boulders counts as an improvement. Above us, gaunt pines sway and moan in the howling wind. Eventually the forest gives way to deep, mushy snow, through which we plough, soaked and bone-weary, until we crest a barren rise blasted by driving sleet. Even now there's no time to rest. Belting our thick winter cloaks more tightly around us, we descend into the valley. It's dusk by the time the snow-covered scree yields to tangled scrub and forest, and dark when the pines give way to gnarled oaks girded with drifts of rain-pocked snow and icy mud. The occasional wink of light ahead tells us we're getting close.

We're moving slowly now, every nerve at screaming point – we've risked much to reach this place undetected and it would be a bitter reward for our labours to be discovered.

Suddenly, halfway up a shallow incline, the ground drops away into a hollow almost hidden by branches and we find ourselves at the mouth of a natural cave, where someone once carved an icon to Hera, the Mother Goddess, on a boulder. Someone else has defaced the icon and kicked the withered offerings aside, but the cave's dry.

'Thank the Goddess,' Bria exclaims – and she doesn't mean Hera. She and I are both sworn to Athena, who isn't exactly a bosom friend of Hera's, right now. 'Odysseus, where's that flask?' she adds, draping a rain-soaked arm around my shoulder.

I give the daemon – Bria's a body-jumping spirit – a grumpy look and remove the arm: I'm having difficulty dealing with 'her' just now. It's not that we've had a new falling out; being pissed off with each other is our natural relationship. It's just that, right now, in this body, Bria isn't a woman.

She's warned me that sometimes she inhabits men, usually if she's going to war. But she's never done so in my presence before. Whatever body she's in, though, Bria's still Bria: she swears, she's bitchy, she's irritating, and she chases men like an insolvent hooker. That's annoying enough in a woman's body, but in a male body, it's profoundly unsettling.

I'm aware of some men who wouldn't mind the advances of a slim, late-adolescent boy, and though I'm not one, I accept such desires in others. But our Achaean society, with its ancient, rigid traditions of manly honour, isn't so forgiving – and right now this is a distraction I don't need.

I shrug off my cloak to rummage in my pack and pull out a flask of potent liquor to buttress us against the cold. 'Not too much,' I tell... her... him... *Bria*. 'That body you're in mightn't be used to drink.'

Bria puts hand to hip, downing her mouthful in one gulp and smacking her lips. 'Darling, thanks for the concern, but he's got more body mass than most of my female hosts, even though he's only sixteen. I bet he and I could drink you under the table, any night.'

Perhaps that's true: despite his youth, Bria's new host, Damastor, is taller than me. That's not a high hurdle, though it doesn't bother me overly – I have other qualities. In addition, he's well-muscled, with a frame that promises genuine physical power in the future. A warrior in the making – if he survives Bria's inhabitation: not all her hosts do.

'How much further?' I ask, getting us back to the matter at hand.

Bria flickers her fingers and kindles a torch in a stone receptacle behind the icon, lighting the stark cave in flickering orange light. 'Rejoice, O Prince of Ithaca,' he-she drawls. 'We've arrived.'

My skin prickles, and not just at the chill lodged in my bones. 'This is Dodona?'

Dodona is an oracular site deep in the north-western mountains of Achaea, and such sites can render extraordinarily valuable prophecies. There's a new crisis looming over Achaea, and we have pressing questions for the oracle. However, its priests are likely to be hostile to us, so we're not going in through the front door.

'Told you I'd get you here,' Bria says smugly. 'The shrine is on the top of this hill – and this cave leads to the chamber beneath.'

The haunted chamber. I give a little shiver, then pretend it's the cold.

'Good point,' Bria chuckles. 'We should put on dry tunics before we go in. I feel like a used mop.' Instantly, he-she strips naked, bar leather leg greaves and boots, brazenly displaying a bronzed body sculpted from muscle. 'Oh look, one of those!' Bria mock-exclaims, peering at Damastor's penis. 'Hey Odysseus, have you ever wanted to—'

'No.'

'You're no fun, Ithaca.'

'You've finally worked that out? Took your time.' I wring out my long red hair, pouring a cascade of water onto the cave floor and disrobe under her over-solicitous gaze. By now I'm freezing, my bare skin bristling with goose bumps – Epirus in winter is not for the faint-hearted – and bundle myself into my spare clothes, testing the blade of my xiphos before slinging the scabbard strap over my shoulder. Bria does the same, after fiddling with her newfound cock like – well – a teenage boy. 'I

5

can never get the thing to sit comfortably,' she mutters. 'Bloody annoying, but brilliant for pissing on the run.'

'How deep does this cave run?' I ask, my exhaustion making my bones ache. This journey has only lasted three days, but we've barely stopped, even to sleep, and it feels like forever.

'It's over a hundred paces to the inner chamber,' Bria replies. 'It's blocked off, of course, but that's nothing we can't handle.'

'How do you know?'

'Because I scouted it six months ago, after the Theban war, idiot.'

Fair enough. 'The big question is, have we beaten the Trojans here?'

That wipes the smirk off Bria's face. 'I bloody hope so,' is the growled response.

We were coming here anyway, but just as we were about to beach our ship we saw another group land and set off inland. Their warship was Trojan, and they landed some thirty warriors. We're not openly at war with our eastern neighbours across the Aegean, but we know too much about their ambitions to call them friends.

Immediately, I changed our plans, deciding to not only gain the prophecies we so desperately need, but also make sure the Trojans get nothing. So we have to be here first. Not such an easy task as it might sound: they took the main road, and our route, though more direct, forced us to navigate rugged mountain country and deep canyons, the last of which almost undid us when the rain began.

'You know what really pisses me off,' Bria goes on. 'We, good loyal Achaeans, are having to sneak into this fucking hole, while those eastern bastards will be welcomed by the priests with open arms.'

'That's how things are,' I reply grimly, no happier about it than her. 'This shrine belongs to Zeus now, and the Skyfather prefers Trojans to Achaeans these days.' I can't keep the betrayal from my voice as I speak. 'And you and I will be top of Zeus's shit-list for what we did in Thebes last year. Come on: if we have made it here before the Trojans, it won't be by much.'

For years now, the oracles have claimed that war between Achaea and Troy is inevitable, and that Troy will be victorious and crush Achaea into the dust of history. To see whether that is still foreseen was my original reason for coming here.

What I don't voice is the question that's been haunting me from the moment we first saw that alien ship dragged up on the beach three days ago. Is *she* with them? *My Kyshanda*. How could she not be, if it's prophecy they seek? My heart twists in my chest as memories of her face, her scent, fill my imagination. And yet... is she still my friend, my lover? Or my most deadly enemy?

I thrust such thoughts aside while I check I have everything I need – a weapon and my little pouch of useful things. 'Are you ready?' I ask.

'I'm always ready, honey,' Bria says, doing her female sashay-thing. It looks very odd in Damastor's male body. 'The real question is, are you?'

She's right. This oracular site is one of the most potent in Achaea, and it's not a place for the unready. I have some advantages though, and I remind myself of them now: I'm a theios, one of the god-touched who are blessed with divine blood and therefore I possess an extra edge. My divine sire is my secret great-great-grandfather, Prometheus – his great-grandson Sisyphus seduced Anticleia, my mother. It's a heritage that is both my greatest treasure and my deepest shame.

But through it, I've gained much. Theioi can be one of four kinds: champions, blessed with extra speed, strength and stamina; sorcerers, able to warp the laws of nature; seers, able to divine the future; and even avatars, who're able to channel the spirit of their patron deity. From Athena and Prometheus, my patron and my sire, I have a touch of all four of these gifts, though I'm still learning the laws and the limits, under Bria's acerbic guidance.

If anyone can walk the secret hollows beneath Dodona, I tell myself, *it's me.*

It's a good thought to cling to, as Bria hefts the torch and leads the way into the depths.

Once we've passed the cave entrance, it's clear that this isn't a natural passage, carved through the surrounding limestone by water alone —it's been tooled and cut. As Bria warned, we're only a hundred yards or so in when we come to a blockage. The roof hasn't collapsed, though: it's a man-made wall of boulders that with great labour have been lugged here, stacked up and roughly plastered over. The outside face is covered with inscriptions, etched by the priests that tend the shrine; pleas to their patron, Zeus, to keep the dead within.

'I'll never forgive this,' Bria growls. 'Even though they were priestesses of that cow-faced bitch Hera.'

We both know what happened. Two years ago Zeus, seized control from the priestesses of Hera, the Earth and Mother Goddess who is also patron of Mycenae, seat of the High Kingship of Achaea, claiming that the oracle at Dodona was losing its prophetic voice. Zeus's priests, supported by armed men, overran the shrine, then walled up the priestesses in the caverns below, to 'refresh' the oracular spirits that linger there, and renew the potency of the prophecies for which Dodona is famed.

'Are Zeus's priests still putting their ears to the ground to listen to the voices, as Hera's followers did?' I ask.

'So I've heard,' Bria answers. 'Though they've been getting mixed results – the spirits are still not as potent or reliable as Pytho. But Zeus's people brag that they're improving.' She sniffs. 'We'll soon see if they're right.'

I remember Pytho with a shudder – my secret parentage was revealed there, almost destroying my family. 'How do we get past this wall?' I ask.

'Through spells,' Bria replies, then grins even wider. 'And hard manual labour. That's why I brought Damastor as my host.' She-he flexes his-her biceps with a certain relish.

8

I find this statement a little unconvincing – Bria usually borrows the muscular bodies of Hamazan women, any one of whom could heft a boulder as well or better than Damastor, athletic physique or no. But maybe she's running out of likely candidates – two of her recent Hamazan hosts met grisly deaths, and the third was impregnated not so many months ago by the Smith God Hephaestus. Genia, her name was. She must be nearing her time…

We get to work, which is no small challenge: once we've scraped off enough plaster to gauge what we're up against, we estimate the blockage to be several boulders deep, hard-packed with smaller rocks, and we can't afford to use tools. It's crucial that we make no noise, for the shrine must be almost directly above us.

But we are at an oracular site, one of those places where the walls of the natural world are thin, and this gives people like Bria and me some advantages. Since I was awakened as a theios, I've gradually widened my repertoire as a sorcerer, and now that I'm somewhere that's receptive to magic, I can do things I can't elsewhere: like mutter spells that loosen stone.

What can be made with magic, as this wall was, can be unmade the same way. 'Spirits of earth, unbind this stone,' I murmur, and those spirits hearken.

It's still damned hard work – we break fingernails and bruise toes, and our whole bodies are screaming by the time we've created a crawl-space at the top of the blockage, just a couple of feet high and twice as wide. We take turns working at the face, the other person clearing what's been loosened, while the air grows muggy and stale from our breath. I find myself doing the bulk of the heavy labour while Bria chivvies me on – it turns out she's as lazy as ever, no matter the body. So it's me with my skin chaffed and bleeding, headfirst and face down in the grit and stone of the crawl-space, and dizzy from lack of fresh air, when we come to a place that makes my flesh crawl.

It's the temperature that changes first, becoming much colder. I'm finding I'm struggling to breathe, the atmosphere drier and tighter, like the aftermath of a lightning bolt. If I were an ordinary man, I wouldn't have been able to go any further. It's not just the weight and bulk of stone, which would be impenetrable to most. Now the rock seems to resist the commonplace spells I've been summoning up, as though they are being frozen into place by a force that is actively resisting me.

I reach deep inside myself, finding fresher, stronger spell words and slowly the solid rock crumbles as I prod and push. Soon I've loosened the last boulder and rolled it back past me for Bria to remove, before wriggling snake-like through the gap and down into an empty space. 'I'm through,' I call softly back through the gap.

Crouching on the stone floor below, my sweat icy-cold on my skin and fear mounting in my heart, I raise my right hand. 'Great Sire, Champion of Fire, be with me,' I murmur. In answer, a tongue of flame kindles, warm but not searing, on the tip of my forefinger as I look around.

The chamber walls are rough-hewn, as if a natural cave has been enlarged. Pungent-smelling fumes seep in thin tendrils from cracks in the floor. There are cracks in the roof too, allowing the fumes to escape, and letting a little clean air creep in. Words in a script I don't know are etched into the stone walls, some carved with tools, but others more lightly scored. Random scratches surround the inscriptions, wild marks as if incised in a frenzy of anger or desperation.

A dozen bodies, desiccated flesh clinging to bones and clad in crumbling fabric, are lying huddled on the ground, together or singly, about the edges of the chamber. I can almost deduce the order in which they died, from posture and position. The eldest and weakest died first and were laid in a row there. Later the surviving women were too weak and despairing to care about arranging the bodies, and sought comfort in their goddess or each other haphazardly.

Who are they? Priestesses of Hera, walled up in here to die and feed their energy into the oracular prophecies of the shrine.

Who did it? Zeus's priests. Am I disgusted? Absolutely, even though I already knew what I'd find.

Bria wriggles through, with both of our belt pouches in his-her hands, slithering to the ground in a cascade of dust. She straightens and looks round, conjuring pale light within her fingertips, like small suns. 'Poor wretches,' she says in vengeful tones. 'Hades, grant them rest.'

Knowing Hades, God of Death, I'm not counting on it. He's a vindictive deity, and other gods' acolytes are among his favoured victims.

'They'd have died from lack of water before they starved,' I note grimly. 'It's faster.'

'It's torture. And to think that Hera and Zeus are so *happily* wed,' Bria says sarcastically.

Despite the tales, gods and goddesses don't marry. They're disembodied spirits, and mostly they loathe each other. Some collude, so that their priests and priestesses declare 'marriage' but they can still hate each other even then. Half the gods of Achaea, led by our 'Holy Father' Zeus himself, have been siding with Troy ever since the oracles began prophesising their victory over Achaea, spreading their worship eastwards as a means of surviving the cataclysm – because gods die when their worshippers are all gone.

But some deities, like Hera, Hermes, and my patron Athena, are too tied to Achaea to do this: they're faced with extinction and will sacrifice anything and anyone, even their champions – like Bria and me – to avoid this fate. *No, not fate; because I've learnt a crucial fact: that prophecies aren't cast in stone.* They're a best guess, by the oracular spirits. A calculation of probabilities based on a profound knowledge of our world that no mortal can possess. But their gaze isn't infinite. Troy's ascent might feel inevitable, but maybe it's just really, really highly *likely*…

Everyone loves an underdog, I tell myself, gathering my thoughts. *But the underdog needs the occasional bone, to survive.* That's why we're here, why it's so important that we succeed this time.

I pull out a clay jar, bound in cloth to protect it, and unseal the wax and then, going to the middle of the room, trickle a stream of red dust into a large circle, careful to ensure it is complete and doesn't run across any of the cracks on the floor. Then I daub a wet paste along the tongue of my sword, and dust that paste with the same powder, as a precaution, before setting it down beside me, unsheathed. Meanwhile Bria performs the unpleasant task of breaking off a finger-bone from each corpse, then placing them inside my circle in a grisly pile.

As we work, the air seems to grow still and watchful, and I fancy I can discern whisperings, sibilant and hostile, at the very edge of hearing. These grow as Bria removes a living thing from her pouch, a drugged bird that stirs when she whispers to it: a cuckoo, the sacred bird of Hera.

'How appropriate, when Zeus lays his eggs everywhere but in the nest,' she sniffs. She places the cuckoo in the circle, where it perches on the pile of finger bones, looking up at her with a gleaming, mesmerised eye. 'Whenever you're ready, Ithaca.'

I close my eyes, and open my inner vision to the world of the gods. Winds rise in my skull, licked by flames, and I catch a glimpse of a tormented man, howling in agony as an immense eagle clings to his body, raking his abdomen with its beak. But even in the midst of such agony, his eyes open and flash to mine. *Prometheus, my forebear.* There's recognition, and even warmth, until the agony takes him again and our gaze and our minds spin apart. But I carry his sacred fire with me as I pour my awareness back into the chamber, and the finger-bones ignite.

The cuckoo shrieks, streaking upwards like a comet as it immolates. I regret the death, but the spells we wield give us no choice. As the flames roar, it seems that smoke is flowing *into* the fire – from the corpses of the priestesses.

And there in the centre of the circle, within the leaping flames, clinging together, are the gauzy forms of twelve women. Fury at this desecration fills them and they snarl, drawing back grey lips over broken teeth, raising hands with long, taloned fingernails.

'Priestesses of Hera,' I greet them. The sorcery is draining, but I keep my voice steady and purposeful. 'I come in peace, to hear your words, and to set you free.'

The ghosts greet my words with a menacing hiss. One tests my powdered circle, shrieking as though stung and recoiling when she touches it. Then one of the women steps to the fore, her shadowy robes a little more ostentatious, her manner more queenly.

'Who are you, intruder?' she breathes, in a voice like an icy wind through dead trees. Behind me, Bria is prowling about, alert for hidden dangers.

'Who I am makes no difference,' I respond, because Prometheus and Athena aren't good names to bandy around hereabouts. 'Grant me the boon of prophecy, and I will release you, to go forth to Hades's Elysian Fields and drink the waters of blessed forgetfulness.'

The ghosts respond with quivering intensity, their eyes lighting up like distant stars, and I sense an internal dialogue. Then the spokeswoman turns to me again. I've never met her, but I know her name from Bria's briefings: Charea, who was once head priestess here.

'What gives you the power to grant such a gift?' she asks, while her sisters begin to hurl words at me:

'Do you come from Pytho?'

'Are you sent from Mycenae?'

'What gods do you serve?'

'Release us.'

'Don't make us do this, I beg you...'

This last sentence catches my ears. 'Why not?' I question the speaker, a wispy girl, younger than the rest.

'The spirits are hungry,' she whispers. 'They devour a little of us, each time.'

I shudder at that, but harden my heart. Athena needs whatever information they can give us and, by extension, so does Achaea.

'I bind you, by the powers of Moon and Sun, Fire and Ice, Earth and Air,' I recite. 'Give me your knowledge and I promise you release.' As I speak, the powdered circle ignites, burning a deep peacockblue which spreads to the finger-bones and the flames cloaking the priestesses. They scream, and suddenly the earth quivers and the air moans.

Then Charea steps forth again, and stamps her foot. With a sudden, horrifying crack, the very floor convulses. Bria and I are hurled to the ground, crying out in alarm, even as a line snakes across the floor, a new fissure that cuts my circle in half, tilting the stone on each side to send the burning powder down into the bowels of the earth and overwhelm my magic.

'*Kopros!*' Bria shrieks, scrambling back like a fleeing crab, in a wild attempt to get to the tunnel. 'Get out, get—'

Then a flash of pale mist streams out of the crack and envelops her. Damastor's body goes limp and falls to the ground, his face suddenly empty. I step in front of him, aghast at this sudden reversal.

Bria's bailed out on me… She's fucking gone!

The ghosts of the priestesses reform in a ragged line, cutting me off from the tunnel. I snatch up my xiphos – our only hope now – and stand over Damastor, blade raised as he stirs. He looks up at me, frowning. 'Who are you?' he stutters. 'Where…? What's happening…?'

Then he sees the spectral shapes in front of us and he goes rigid in terror.

I don't respond – all of my attention is on Charea, whose decayed face is hungry as a thousand wolves. 'Now,' she rasps, 'let's see who's going to dance, and who is going to pipe the tune.'

2 – Wraiths of the Oracle

'It is a sweet thing, too, to divine which signs are clear and sure, from all the possibilities – both fearful and good – which the immortal gods have doled out to mortals.'

—Hesiod, *Melampodia*

Dodona, Epirus

I have one remaining chance: lifting my xiphos, I conjure a tongue of flame and touch it to the powder I'd earlier pasted to the blade. Foxfire crackles along it as I hold it in front of me. As the wraiths close in, I flash the fiery blade across their paths and they recoil, snarling furiously.

I have won a brief reprieve… to get out or turn this around. One good thing has happened – their retreat has left our escape route open.

Just.

At my feet, Damastor clings to my leg – he's probably a brave enough lad, but Bria had obviously shut down his awareness while she was inside him, and he's woken into a living nightmare.

'Get up,' I tell him. 'Climb out that hole.'

He looks up, sees the crude opening in the wall and lunges for it – then to his immense credit, throws me a look over his shoulder and asks, 'What about you?'

'I'll be fine,' I lie. 'Just go!'

Mercifully he does, scrabbling in head first and plunging into the dark, his feet disappearing as dust and stones rattle down. I'm thankful, but he's cost me precious seconds, and the ghostly priestesses are closing in again, nothing but hate in their pale eyes.

Charea bares her teeth. 'We're going to devour you, mortal,' she rasps. 'This is the sacred shrine of Hera-Dione and no man may enter.'

I extend the blade at her face. 'But they *have* already, haven't they – those accursed *men*. Zeus's priests thrust you in here to die, and every day now, they walk above you.' As if in answer, a horn blows somewhere above us, the sound muffled by the rock. The Trojans must have arrived: I'm running out of time. 'What are you, but their slaves?'

The women vent a kind of keening, whining fury at my words, but they're flinching as well, because the words are true. Two years ago, I heard Zeus himself boast of walling these women up, to make Dodona's prophecies more powerful.

'At this very moment, the new seer of Dodona is preparing to receive a new party of supplicants,' I tell them. 'They're from Troy, the enemies of both Achaea and your goddess. They're going to make you prophesy for them, to further the conquest of Achaea.'

'Nooo,' some of the dead priestesses moan, as their misery and hate is redirected to the men above – their murderers.

Even Charea is doubtful now, as she narrows her eyes, considering. Then, 'Whom do you serve, Man?' she demands, in an imperious voice,

I glance at my xiphos; the powders are burning low, but I sense I may still have a chance of turning this situation around. Calmly, I pull out my flask and add some of the remaining powder to the blade. It re-ignites, filling the chamber in a blaze of light. 'I serve Athena,' I proclaim, 'whose worship is centred here in Achaea, and who will fight the Trojans to the end, alone if she must.'

My words echo round the chamber. Hopefully they're too busy up in the shrine welcoming their new visitors for any of the Zeus priests to their ears pressed to the stone, listening.

'What will it be?' I demand. 'Will you prophesise for me, and then allow me to free you forever? Or will you bite the hand that offers you succour, and continue your slavery?'

They're hearkening, even Charea. Though their despair remains, all the hunger has gone from their voices as they murmur amongst themselves. 'If you can release us, release us now,' one moans. 'Why must you also use us?'

'Because Achaea needs one last vision from you, to see if there is a way to resist the oncoming storm of war.' I focus on Charea. 'You channel these prophesies, surely you can put them into words? Please, grant me that, a final gift to the enemies of Troy – and of Zeus.'

She stares hard at me, while her fellow priestesses mutter sullenly. Then she gives a deathly sigh. 'Give me your true name, and we will grant you what you wish.' She holds out her hand. 'Let me touch you, while you speak.'

I understand: this will give her insight enough to know if I lie. And if I play them false, they will destroy me. Even if, by some miracle, I escape the cave, they will curse me in their next oracular vision to Zeus's priests, and I will stand condemned forever.

I hold out my left arm, feeling the brush of her hand on my wrist like the touch of a spider-web. 'I am Odysseus Sisyphiades, Prince of Ithaca.'

'The Man of Fire,' she groans, as if in pain.

Her followers hiss in consternation at the epithet. Charea has understood my secret identity instantly – Laertes is known as my father, in the eyes of the world, but in fact I am the bastard son of Sisyphus and the last scion of Prometheus, who gifted fire to mankind. And the 'Man of Fire' has been showing up more and more in the prophesies as an enemy both of Troy, and of Zeus and his cabal of Olympians.

'I am he,' I confirm, watching Charea carefully. The flames licking my blade are burning low again. 'I give you my word that I'll release you, once we're done.'

She considers, as orange light flickers through their bodies and my blade dims. I'm in their hands now, my chance to flee gone; but I don't flinch. I need them to see my determination.

She releases my wrist. 'What do you wish to know?' she asks.

I let out my breath as gently as I dare. She has consented, and I will get the information Athena so badly needs before I silence their prophetic voices forever.

The ghostly priestesses form a circle, facing inwards with joined hands. Charea calls out, in a high wailing voice and the fumes that had drifted from the cracks at their feet thicken, filling the chamber with a dense, pungent aroma. Then she turns her head to me enquiringly.

I recite my first question. 'Since the fall of Thebes, who in Achaea still aligns themselves with Troy?'

The wraiths raise their linked hands, and whisper invocations in a language I know a little of – the speech of the spirits, an ancient tongue now all but lost. I've been studying it under Bria's tutelage, but this is the first time I've heard someone other than the daemon speak it. I try to follow but I'm quickly lost. What I'm witnessing, though, is the working of this shrine. Here in Dodona, the ghosts now intermediate between the priestly seer above and the spirits below – an extra link in the chain, and therefore a further margin for misinterpretation and error.

The chamber falls silent, and then harsh voices rattle and click in the air around us, like the rustle of dried oak leaves in the autumn wind, uttering sounds that are even more a mystery to me.

The priestesses stir, then Charea raises her voice and they all follow, so that the prophecy they utter, thankfully in Achaean this time, is spoken in unison: '*The Lion lurks in his den, waiting for the Third Fruit. The Wolf crouches in his lair, slavering over his mate. When the Stallion rears, both shall bare teeth.*'

The hairs on my arms prickle. I'm longing to interpret the references, but I don't dare: I need to concentrate on committing it all to memory before I frame my next question: 'What do the divine allies of Troy purpose next?'

I wait again, reciting their previous answer over and over until it's imprinted, then hearken to the next response.

'*The Sky caresses the Earth with light, planting dreams. The stones listen, the soil awakens, gazing at the blood-red dawn with new hope.*'

That one's obvious, and I file it away uneasily. 'What hope is there for Achaea?'

'*Swift comes the storm, striking the forest. Branches break, lightning sunders the trunks and they fall. Withered the vines that bound them, gone the leaves that caught the wind, scattered the branches, broken the Crown.*'

That one's even worse. My next question is a direct reaction to it, not one Athena had scripted. 'How may the crown be made whole?'

There's a *long* wait for the next response.

'*Golden eggs of the cuckold, caged birds born to sing together. Possess the twain and rule. But beware the tongue of flame that consumes, burning all that it touches.*'

I grimace, because I can see exactly what people are going to make of any flame references – *me*. I go to speak again, but I suddenly realise that the priestesses have almost burned themselves out. The smallest gives a hideous moan and her pale ghost flows like a wisp of smoke back to her bones. One by one the rest do likewise, until only Charea remains, turning to face me with a grim face, as the chirping, crackling rasp of the spirits fades.

'*The storm comes,*' she intones, though her voice is weakening. '*Caught in its path, the animals twist and turn, dart hither and thither, but the wind will find them, Man of Fire. There is no hiding from the Sky! Fast comes the temptress; far is the island of solace. Flame for passion, cloth for comfort… Be the vine, forge the crown…*'

Then she's gone too, with one final, whispered imprecation: '*Honour your word.*'

I catch my breath. That last part of the prophecy wasn't in response to any of my questions. It was a spontaneous prophecy, the most potent kind. I repeat it, making sure I've remembered all the others as well. The last flames on my sword gutter and die and I'm left in the dark.

I do keep my word.

It's not enough just to have opened an escape route out of this prison – the priestesses' corpses and the energy released in death bind them here. So I drag the desiccated remains of the women into a single pile, scatter the last of my powder over them, then reach deep into the sorcery I've been gifted by my Promethean father. Combining it with the magical powers of this liminal place, I summon a new and even more powerful flame. In moments the fire has caught, propelled by my incantations, and as it begins to blaze, I hear women's voices, like distant echoes, crying out in both agony and relief. The chamber is choked with smoke, some of it disappearing into the cracks in the rock ceiling but most of it pouring out through the hole in the wall.

I sheath my xiphos and follow it, coughing and retching as the fumes bite at my throat and sear my lungs. Bria had jammed the torch into a rock crevice beside the wall and I grab it, blundering along the tunnel towards the exit, utterly exhausted by the sorcery I've summoned, as though the magic has devoured my life's blood.

I find Damastor – not Bria – waiting by the cave mouth, ashen faced, crouched just out of the rain, which is heavier than ever. When I appear through the clouds of smoke, he gives a soft squeal of alarm and then relief.

'You... you made it,' he pants, rising.

'I did indeed.' I give him a weak smile. 'Do you know who I am?'

He shakes his head. 'I don't... I can't...'

'Call me... Xenos,' I tell him – 'Stranger'. It's safer, if we're captured, that he knows as little as possible. It occurs to me that he may not even know about his host. 'What do you know of Bria?'

His eyes light up. 'Yes, yes, Bria. She… I…,' he stammers, struggling to convey who and what Bria is to him. He probably thinks I'll either condemn him as a madman, or as some kind of lover of evil spirits.

I take pity. 'I understand Bria,' I tell him. 'I don't condemn what she does.' *Not as much as I should.* 'I'll get you out of this, I promise.' *And then*, I add silently, *you might want to re-evaluate your choices.* Most people who let Bria into their lives end up dead, in my experience. Or pregnant, though he doesn't face that issue, at least.

Damastor seems to take heart from this. He stands, trembling both from the cold and his recent ordeal, but he sets his jaw. 'What happened in there?' he asks. 'Why am I here? Where's… where *is* Bria?' His lower lip begins to tremble again.

I grip his arm, make him look at me. 'She had to go.' *For whatever reason – I'll get that from her when I see her next.* 'Don't worry – I'll look after you, but we must leave. People will be realising that something's wrong, and they're going to be really, violently angry.'

To put it mildly.

'Oh.'

'Don't worry, I piss people off every day.' I clap his shoulder. 'Follow me.'

We heft our packs, abandoning whatever we don't absolutely need to save weight, and don our cloaks over the top. The wool is cold and clammy to the touch, but the cloth is rubbed full of lanolin, which will help shed the worst of the rain. And once we get moving, we'll soon warm up. I lead Damastor up out of the hollow, alarmed at how weak my legs feel. Sorcery always takes its toll, but I've slowly adapted to it, so that my recovery is faster than it used to be. Even so, what I've just done is far greater than anything I've attempted before, and at the very least it will be a while before I can use my magical powers again.

It's pitch black under the trees and I have no idea how long we've been underground – the powers that rule the liminal space on the fringes of the other world and beyond pay scant attention to time. But out here in the real world it's clearly still night.

Behind us, where the shrine must lie, I can hear raised voices, an incantation cut off by a curse, followed by angry shouts. The horn sounds again, more urgent than before. We have no time to lose.

Despite the hazards of the flooded ravine, it offers the only chance of escape. The Trojans have horses and they would soon ride us down if we took the main road. We can't risk being seen so, with regret, I extinguish the torch, praying that dawn won't be far off. I lead the way, using my enhanced theios ability to see in the dark, with Damastor clinging to a fold in my cloak as he blunders after me.

All goes well while we're in the forest, bar the odd stumble, but as we start to climb up out of the valley, I hear dogs barking behind us, and as we labour up the slope, we see torches winking in the forest below. I silently curse my stupidity – the rope and the sopping clothes we left on the cave floor will have given those hunting us our scent.

The flooded ravine is now doubly our best chance. It will throw the hounds off our trail, provided the water level hasn't swamped the ledge, so we press on. Dawn comes in a flurry of sleety rain as we reach a low gap in the ridge between squalls and spy a line of men straggling up the mountain below us. They're closer than I'd expected and they see us too, judging from their cries.

Down we plough, towards the forest above the ravine, in a flurry of wet snow. I'm praying that our enemies are as tired as we are, that the tangled undergrowth under the pines will mask where we chose to climb down the cliffs, and that the engorged river below us might have receded a little.

At last we're standing at the top of the cliff, the thunder of rushing water now the only sound we can hear, louder even than I remember when we left it. The reason becomes evident once we've clambered over the spur at the bottom of the climb and reached the water's edge. The river is now lapping at the ledge Bria and I traversed when we came up the gorge, and the torrent is raging, with fallen trees and debris swirling by. All it needs is one surge of water and we will be swept away.

'It's impossible!' Damastor cries, his voice thick with dismay. I'm inclined to agree.

If it's this bad up here, what's it like further downstream?

I glance back, assessing our options. 'We'll try and find another way,' I tell him, bellowing in his ear to be heard. He bites his lip, panic in his eyes. But there's no point hiding my concern. I don't know these lands – Bria's the expert. We go back over the spur and I plant my feet on the first footholds when movement catches my eye and I look up…

There's an armed man just ten yards above us, harnessed in leather and bronze, his head clad in the conical helm of the east. His features are swarthy, and the sword in his hand is curved. There's half a dozen more behind him, rain-drenched and surly.

Trojans!

The lead man does what any brave soldier would do, when confronted by an enemy weighed down by a pack and with his sword sheathed. He roars a battle-cry and hurls himself down the rock face, extending his sword as he leaps.

I back up, go for my xiphos but realise he's too damned close. As he lands in front of me, I abandon the draw and duck under his full-blooded lunge. As the bronze blade flashes by I seize his arm, wrestler style and pivot, using his momentum.

My boots slip on the stone, and I crash to the ground as the Trojan hurtles past. Damastor throws himself out of the way – and the easterner vanishes into the torrent, his frantic cry cut off by a splash.

I lurch to my feet, the pack unbalancing me awkwardly, as the next man approaches, but this one's more wary, pausing before he leaps and I manage to whip out my blade, yelling over my shoulder, 'Damastor, head downstream. Over the spur and along the ledge! Go!'

I can only trust that he hearkens, for all my attention is focused on my attacker's blade as he jumps down, the way his feet flash into position as he lands for an overhand slash. I deflect, two-handed, then drive my blade into his belly and hurl him into the floodwaters. As I do, I see more men appearing above me, two of them with spears at the ready. This wasn't a good place to be to start with, and it's suddenly a whole lot worse. I retreat over the spur but by the time I've scrambled down to river-level, there's a man at the crest of the spur, with a narrow coronet round his plumed helm. The rain-drenched feathers are limp as a dead chicken, but I know his face: Skaya-Mandu, prince of Troy.

And he knows mine. 'You!' he snarls, in his own tongue, one I know well. 'Take him! Take him alive!' he yells over his shoulder.

If there's one man I daren't be captured by, it's Skaya-Mandu. As his soldiers charge over the spur I retreat backwards, down towards the ledge. I need to get rid of the pack, which is hampering me badly, but it's under my cloak. I pull my dagger out of my belt with my left hand, cut a shoulder strap, manage a tricky duck, turn and spin as the first Trojan slashes wildly at me, plunge my xiphos into his guts as his guard opens up and cut the remaining shoulder strap. It could have gone badly, but I nail it, impaling the next Trojan's groin, back up in a whirl of blades, kick the pack into the river then dash for the ledge, darting a glance behind me. That's how I see the spear that should have taken me full in the back, and swerve aside.

No sign of Damastor. Hopefully he's well down the river by now. Or washed away, but I've no time to worry about that now. Once I'm on the ledge I run, water spraying from my feet as the Trojans close in behind me. Skaya-Mandu's roaring my name, the frontmost pursuer is lining up a thrust between my shoulder-blades, and the path is narrowing by the second…

I drop and rake my legs into the front runner, taking him out at the knee and sending him shrieking into the torrent. I'm back on my feet in time to block an overhand cut from the next man, stab him through the base of the throat then kick the third Trojan in the balls as he heaves his comrade aside. He yells in pain, fumbles his sword stroke and takes my xiphos in the shoulder. I wrench it out as he folds in a gush of blood, alive but out of the fight, and extend the xiphos toward his fellows, who're properly afraid of me now. I edge my way backwards along the ledge, which is well under water now, feeling my way with my feet. The crumbling bank is only a few fingers' span to my right – any misstep and I'll be swimming.

There are two men between me and Skaya-Mandu and neither of them wants to come near me, but he's got more soldiers behind him. He snarls at me from his position of safety, and urges his men forward. Like me, he's a theios, but despite the fact that this gives him an edge over ordinary men, he has a habit of getting others to do his dirty work. Like, now.

The surly arrogance that permeates his otherwise handsome, almost pretty face, contorts into hatred as he stares at me – hate that I must say I've richly earned: during the last two years I've beaten him to his knees, thwarted his people's schemes twice and seduced his twin sister. Or did she seduce me?

So he absolutely *longs* to gut me. Last time we met, he almost succeeded.

'Don't you know it's rude to attack a man unprovoked?' I call, as I try to work out how I can escape without drowning myself.

'Unprovoked?' he sneers. 'You're an affront to the gods, Ithacan. The oracle has gone silent. I listened with the priests when that evil smoke appeared, and we heard your voice – I recognised your foul mouth instantly.'

'Is your sister with you?' I ask – to rile him, but also because I really, really want to know.

His eyes flare. 'Kyshanda spits at the mention of your name,' he shouts, which doesn't answer the question.

'I'm sure she's better mannered than that,' I respond, feigning a casual air which I certainly don't feel. The two men in front of me seem to be gathering their courage – they'll attack at any moment, and the space behind Skaya-Mandu, at the base of the spur, is filling up with more Trojans, a dozen at least. Some have bows.

The Trojan prince glances over his shoulder. 'Archers, prepare,' he orders.

The new arrivals give him doubtful looks – it's pouring with rain again and their precious bowstrings are going to be ruined – but they obey: you don't question an eastern potentate.

'Send Kyshanda my warmest regards,' I call. 'Tell her that my heart still beats for her.'

This is true, unfortunately, though another part of me still believes she might be planning my betrayal.

The Trojan archers are almost ready, stringing bows and uncovering their arrow quivers, while their two comrades duck down out of the way. At this range, even with sodden strings and fletching, they can't miss.

'Aim for his legs,' Skaya-Mandu orders them, in his own tongue. 'I want him alive… for a while.'

I don't wait – as the archers raise their bows, I sheath my xiphos, spin on my heels, and propel myself off the narrow ledge into the raging flood.

–

The first few seconds are the worst – the icy plunge into the torrent, battering against rocks beneath the surface, clawing at the cauldron of racing water while branches rake my torso and limbs, gashing my shoulder as I try to reach the surface before the air in my lungs is gone, my cloak weighing down my every movement. I'm spun head over heels through the tumbling blur of white, blue-green and darkness, all but helpless.

But I've not just thrown myself into the river blindly. I have a plan. There was a large tree coming downstream as I conversed with Skaya-Mandu, and the purpose of our wee chat was mostly so I could wait for it to reach us. I see it close by as I break the surface again, kick towards it and grasp a branch as it surges through the gorge, then duck and come up on the far side of the trunk, gasping for air. I grab onto it and look back.

An arrow flashes past my face, ragged cries echo down the gorge, and I see Trojan archers running along the ledge. But with each second the gap widens: in their heavy armour they can't run easily, and the rock is awash and murderously slippery. Even as I watch, one loses his footing, goes in and doesn't come up. More arrows rip by, and two bury themselves in the trunk of my tree, but in moments my pursuers are a bend or two behind me.

So far, so good, but this water's freezing, cold enough to kill me, and the tree could flip on top of me at any moment.

I overtake Damastor a few bends later, roaring his name until he works out who's shouting – *the idiot clinging to a tree in a torrential flood, that's who*. He waves then runs alongside, unencumbered by armour, loping gracefully along and shouting something encouraging. By now I'm thinking that we've got away with this.

At least until Skaya-Mandu manages to get his men downstream, and we float into their midst…

'Next bend,' I shout, as the terrain becomes familiar. I'm pretty sure there are some shallows coming up, where this tree will hopefully catch on the riverbed and I can wade ashore. 'Next bend!'

Damastor's face breaks into a grin, he waves an arm… and then the *bloody fool* trips, cracks his head on a jutting rock and plummets into the river.

Cursing in disbelief, I clamber over the tree trunk, which immediately begins to roll, and leap feet first into the torrent where I think he might be. He's not there, so I come up again, swallow a lungful of air, and plunge under the surface once more, almost braining myself on a submerged boulder. I kick myself out of danger just as I glimpse a dark shape being swept downstream under the lee of the ledge. While I'm not tall, I'm powerfully built and a strong swimmer; even so, the torrent is such that each yard sideways towards the bank is a monumental effort.

I grasp his arm just as we're propelled over a waterfall into a deep pool. Somehow I cling onto him, wrenching his pack off, wrapping my arms around him and pulling him to my chest. I gulp another mouthful of air as soon as we break the surface, but go under again immediately. Just when I think we're done for, my feet touch bottom. I wade to shore, my legs numb with cold, drag him out onto the gravel and collapse beside him like a beached whale as the rain turns once more to sleet.

It's bitterly cold. Other men might have died of that alone. But Prometheus is all about fire – heat and energy. I conjure a little warmth into my bones, and come to my knees, slide my arms under the unconscious Damastor and with an almighty effort, lift him with me as I rise to my feet.

We've washed up on the far bank from the ledge, and that suits me very well. I glance back up the gorge and find it empty – though as I watch, one of the Trojans comes over the falls, and floats unmoving, face down, as the current pushes him through the pool. A moment later, another arrives, as dead as the first.

Any tracker with a brain will figure out that if our own bodies are not found here, the chances are high that we've escaped. Knowing Skaya-Mandu, he'll not take my death on trust. We have to get away from here and fast, before the remaining Trojans catch up with us.

For once though, luck might be with me. My scabbard is still slung over my shoulder and – even more miraculously – my xiphos is inside the sheath. I bind Damastor's head wound as best I can, stemming the blood with a strip cut from the hem of my cloak, heft him over my shoulder and stumble up the bank. Almost immediately, I find a series of goat-trails, rising up into low hills. All the while the rain's pouring down like the Flood of Deucalion, washing away my tracks, a small blessing. Despite the wet and cold, I'm beginning to feel genuine relief, though I'm very worried about Damastor's head – the young lad still hasn't regained consciousness.

I take the track that looks the least travelled and stagger along it, managing Damastor's dead weight as best I can on the slippery ground. After a while, I find another path, marked by a shred of cloth, deliberately tied on a small twig. I rip it off, drag a broken branch into the mouth of the path to hide it, and set off, the track winding up through dense forest. Eventually I find a crofter's hut in a small clearing, broken-doored and empty.

Perfect. My energy is still depleted after the sorcery and our gruelling journey since, and I feel a wave of gratitude – to the gods or plain luck, it doesn't much matter which.

I get Damastor inside, scaring off a pair of nesting crows. The thatched roof is in bad shape and the hut's been ransacked, but the hearth is sheltered from the rain and there's an old byre in the corner, half full of dry straw. I break up the wooden frame of the byre and kindle a small fire, for light as much as for warmth, then I examine Damastor's head wound. It's a nasty gash and he's bled a lot, despite my bandage: his pulse is thin, his breathing shallow and his skin deathly cold.

One thing I haven't learnt yet is the magical art of healing. His life hangs by a thread and one mistake could easily kill him. But at least I can stop the bleeding. I cut another bandage from my cloak and bind the wound more tightly. That done, my first instinct is to put him as close to the fire as I can, to warm him up. But then I remember some old soldiers talking as we sat round the campfires outside Thebes: ice is the way you treat a head wound, they'd claimed. We younger ones had argued, but the veterans said they'd seen men die from being kept too warm. One had a story about having to abandon his badly injured mate in the snow, only to have the man walk into camp the next morning, bloody head and all.

So I undress Damastor, lay him on the straw in the corner, and wring as much water as I can out of his clothes. Then I ease his heavy woollen tunic back on him and cover him with his cloak, leaving his head exposed. Once that's done, I wring out my own clothes, wrapping myself in my cloak after draping my tunic over the rocks surrounding the hearth, where it lies steaming.

We have no food – the little we had is in our packs, somewhere at the bottom of the river – but there's plenty of water outside. Occasionally I go to the door and cup my hands until they fill, and drink. In between times, when I'm not checking on Damastor, I sit staring into the fire, my xiphos beside me, huddled in my cloak and reflecting on all we've gone through.

I've just silenced the oracle of Dodona. I don't know how these things work, but it may never speak again. Or maybe they'll just find other victims to wall up beneath it, and normal business will resume. Either way, I have the priestesses' last words, and the Trojans have come all this way to Epirus for nothing. If I can survive long enough to get back to the coast and my waiting ship, this will have been a very successful mission indeed.

On the other hand, I'm now stranded somewhere in the mountains of Epirus with my most despised enemy searching for me, using who knows what sneaky sorcerous methods to track me, and I have an innocent youth to safeguard. We're not away clean, not by a long shot.

Night is falling, and the world is turning a very sullen grey. I try and stay awake, but the gathering warmth of the fire and my exhaustion are too much for me and my eyes close...

-

I wake to find my cloak snatched off me and a sharp metal point beneath my chin. A mule whinnies somewhere outside and in the faint light of the embers I can see a dark, cloaked shape standing over me. I gaze up the blade, and realise it's curved. I grope for my own sword but it's gone.

'Odysseus of Ithaca,' a voice drawls, speaking Achaean in musical eastern tones. 'Naked and at my mercy. Praise to all the gods.'

3 – Conflicting Loyalties

> 'Have I missed my target, or have I struck it truly, like an archer? Or am I a false prophet, a beggar knocking from door to door, an idle babbler?'
>
> —Aeschylus, *Agamemnon*

Epirus

It's a voice I know.

'*Kyshanda?*'

I go to rise, but she doesn't move the scimitar, and I have to flop back or slit my own throat.

'Uh, uh,' she says, in a sultry voice. 'Did I say you could get up?' She glances at Damastor's prone form on the other side of the hut. 'Is he…?' she asks.

'Unconscious,' I tell her, my mind reeling with amazement, lust, doubt and fear in equal measure. 'Concussion… Kyshanda, what are you—?'

'Shh,' she purrs, sliding her left hand down her belly sensuously, though the sword blade hasn't moved far from my throat. She's wearing the strange attire of eastern males: tubed leggings instead of good Achaea kilts and tunics. She deftly unknots her waistband one-handed and steps out of her leggings before my disbelieving eyes, her taut, coppery legs gleaming in the light of the embers. Then she straddles my torso while I watch, too thunderstruck to move, slowly squatting over me then dropping to her knees and pressing her darkly-thatched pubis against mine.

Her angular, equine face is blessed with big, luminescent eyes that fasten on mine. She plants her left hand on my chest, giggles as she teasingly draws her sword back and forth above my throat then – to my immense relief – places it to one side and kisses me. Her mouth tastes of cloves and cinnamon. I empty my mind of the doubts that have assailed me over the last months, too overwhelmed to resist her, drinking her in while my hands grope for the ties that bind up her hair and let them loose, so that her hair cascades down on either side of her face like a lustrous shroud.

'Ye Gods, I've missed you,' I breathe, and she sighs into my mouth, grinding herself against my thickening cock. She tilts and rocks her hips, riding her moist cleft back and forth along the underside of my tool while we devour each other's lips and tongues.

'I've been dreaming of this ever since Delos,' she answers in a whispery moan. Her vaginal opening is soaked with her juices, and my cock is now as rigid as it can get. 'Don't move,' she tells me, then she reaches down, grips my penis and slowly feeds it into her hungry sheath, moaning as I fill her. 'Stay still – let me ride you,' she pants, sitting up on my hips and peeling her tunic off. Her breasts are small, high and firm, with dark aureoles that quiver as she begins to grind again, groaning as she rubs her clitoris against my pubic mound.

I'm more than happy to be her mount, gazing up at her in rapture as her tight belly undulates, her breasts sway and her mouth falls open, her eyes rolling back every few seconds as pleasure claims her. Her movement isn't so much out and in, rather she contains my rod, the muscles of her vagina clenching around it, so withholding my climax is effortless. Long, long passages of bliss ensue as she builds toward release, at times catching my gaze, other times lost inside her own senses, until her movements become ever more urgent.

'I'm coming,' she suddenly blurts, her face going through pleasure to an agony of pent-up need. Then she orgasms, in the longest most drawn-out climax I've ever witnessed, her face flushing and her breath ragged then almost ceasing as she vents a drawn-out cry. 'Urhhh… unnnn…ahhh…oohhh…' Tears start in her eyes, running down her cheeks as she sobs and then unleashes a high guttural wail as her belly quivers and her hips spasm. I pull her shoulders down, holding her head in the nape of my neck as she convulses through her final ecstasy.

The legendary seer Tiresias, who spent parts of his life as both man and woman, told Hera and Zeus that a woman's orgasm is tenfold that of a man; but I think he under-counted. Kyshanda's face, as I draw it up to study it, is filled with rapture. It's a vision of Elysium, a moment to take to my grave.

'Now me,' I breathe, sliding my hands down her side over silky skin, gripping her hips and then clenching my back and buttock muscles, thrusting up into her, jolting her whole body. We're of a height, but I'm much stockier, much stronger, and I feel huge inside her. I have myself under control, enabling me to bring us both to a heavenly plateau where we linger, ready to take the final plunge.

I roll her over and enjoy the vision of her wondrous face, hair spread beneath like rays of a dark sun. Her legs lock behind my back as she opens herself wider. 'Yes,' she groans as I move harder and faster, plunging in and in and in, the weight of my need now flooding my loins, until I can't hold back and expend myself in her in a series of furious thrusts, knocking the breath from my lungs. And she's coming again, clinging to me through her pleasure.

Perfect… perfect… a dream made flesh.

Gradually we subside, moaning, sighing, kissing, and the most wonderful sense of serenity fills me, something I've never felt before. For a long time we're too spent to talk, just lying there woven together as our sweat mingles. I realise suddenly that there's tears on her cheeks and touch them with my fingers. 'Are you sad?' I ask. 'Why—?'

She giggles. 'No, my eyes sometimes leak, during a big one. I'm sorry, lover, but you need to get off me. There are stones under my arse and they're horribly uncomfortable.'

How is it that women can be so damn practical *after making love?*

I slowly, regretfully, pull out of her, and she rubs her small behind ruefully, sweeps the earthen floor clear beneath her then rolls over and faces me, teeth gleaming through smiling lips. 'Greetings, Achaean,' she breathes, with mock formality. 'How nice to see you again.'

'It's indeed a pleasure to reacquaint with you,' I tell her, matching her manner. 'How did you find me?'

'Please,' she says smugly. 'I'm the daughter of Hekuba. I could find you blindfold in the Labyrinth of Minos.'

'But Skaya-Mandu…?'

'It seems he went the wrong way after he lost you in the gorge,' she says lightly. 'He'd forbidden me to join the hunt, of course. So I just waited in the shrine until everyone else was gone, then gave my guards the slip and set out. Our horses are not fit for such mountainous country as this, but Dodona has plenty of mules.' She throws a glance over my shoulder, at the still unconscious Damastor. 'Who's that?'

'A local guide,' I lie. I don't know if the Trojans know who or what Bria is, but it's not my secret to divulge, and for all our passion, Kyshanda is still an enemy. Officially. And, despite what has just happened, she may be my enemy unofficially as well. In the aftermath of such purity of desire, the world begins to intrude, despite my wish that it just go away and leave us to enjoy this, only our second time together. 'Delos was the happiest day of my life,' I tell her, truthfully. 'And this is the best night.'

She looks pleased at that, kisses my hand then places it over her left breast. 'My heart is yours,' she whispers.

This should be music to me, but since we parted last, I learned something, from a source I don't even know I can trust – the very same Tiresias of Thebes who spent part of his life as a woman. With his dying words, he told me that Hekuba, Queen of Troy, had commanded her daughter Kyshanda to seduce me to the Trojan cause. And Kyshanda has several times exhorted me to forsake Achaea and come to her homeland. That's why I don't know whether I can trust her, and that poisons everything. *Is she driven by politics or love?* Or even both – some combination that I could possibly live with? But I'll go mad if she's just playing me for a fool.

'So, my lover,' she says, as if there's no doubt in her mind. 'I believe you've silenced Dodona? As if you didn't already have enough enemies!'

I start to tell her of the plight of the ghost priestesses, but she interrupts.

'I know,' she whispers, 'and you did well.'

I'm surprised, and warmed by her assertion. We can all recognise cruelty, but so often we tolerate it when it's perpetrated on our so-called enemies. But she's always vowed that she wants peace between our peoples.

Albeit a peace in which Troy is preeminent.

'I was in the upper chamber with Skaya-Mandu, when the Zeus priests realised the spirits were speaking unprompted,' she goes on, arching an eyebrow. 'They were speaking to *you*, weren't they? I thought I heard your voice. You asked something before you set them free...?'

Suddenly I'm wary – and I wouldn't have been if it wasn't for *blasted* Tiresias.

She senses my hesitation, and reaches out, mirroring the placement of my hand over her heart. 'Look at me, Odysseus,' she says sadly. 'We're on the same side, dear love.' Then her voice rises, with increasing vehemence. 'I don't want a war between us. I want us to be like this, together. I want passion and madness and every curtain ripped aside and every sense explored and I want everything to—'

She stops, her voice cut off, as if she's caught herself from falling. She's got tears in her eyes again.

I'm reminded that Kyshanda recently spent a season serving Persephone, who's not entirely sane. Crossing the border of life and death can distort anyone, and it makes me wonder what Kyshanda gained, and what she lost. Filled with pity, I shift my hand, placing it over the one she's rested on my chest, and squeeze.

Maybe I'm a fool, but I believe her.

'Yes, I questioned the spirits,' I tell her. 'I haven't even had time to think about the meaning of what they said.' It pains me to be coy about this, but dammit, I *can't* say more… *May Tiresias rot forever in the very lowest levels of Tartarus and may Hades conjure up the very worst torture he can devise for him…* 'What news of Troy?' I ask her, stalling while I try to measure what I can trust her with.

She sighs, her face showing her hurt as she recognises the game I'm playing. This for that, as a substitute for total sharing. But she's a princess, well versed in the courtly art of intrigue. 'Troy prospers,' she tells me. 'Our new harbour is thriving and there are ships there all the time. My father King Piri-Yamu levies a toll and we're richer now than ever before. The Hittite Emperor sends us felicitations, and encourages him in his efforts to strengthen our alliance. My brother Heka-Taru is currently visiting their capital city, Hattusas, negotiating a military treaty, a precursor to trade talks.'

'And what about Trojan plans for Achaea?'

'You know the answer to that,' she says sadly. 'My father the king speaks of conquest, by spear and gold. The destruction of his prospective ally, Thebes, has changed nothing. He seeks new treaties with our neighbouring kingdoms to further this. It's a slow process – there are many ancient quarrels to overcome – but we make headway.'

None of this quells my unease. As a prince of Ithaca, whose lifeblood is the sea, for both fishing and trading, I spend a lot of time talking with sailors and sea-merchants. I know the prices as well as any merchant, and that many goods have become far more expensive since Troy's new harbour opened, especially the strategically vital metal, tin, which is blended with copper to make bronze, the hardest known alloy and the foundation of military power. The strangulation of Achaea, long prophesised, is well underway. The only question is whether they'll be content to slowly crush us, or whether they take the faster, more ruinous path of outright war.

'There's no need for either a trade war, or one of violence,' I comment forcefully. 'Jason – an Achaean hero – founded the tin mines on the eastern shores of the Axeinos Sea. They belong to our people.'

'They belong to whoever can hold them,' she counters, and though it vexes me, she's right.

'To attack us would be madness,' I tell her. 'I've studied how your people fight: on open ground, flat plains, chariots and light infantry. You can't find enough flat ground in the whole of Achaea to fight like that. If Piri-Yamu thinks numbers are everything, he's a fool.'

'My father's not a fool,' she says defensively. 'Why do you think he and Mother send us here so frequently? We're learning you too. He knows that any invasion would be costly and difficult. But you must understand that no kingdom placed where we are, on the edge of the Hittite Confederacy, can afford to be anything but strong! You speak of plains and flat land – the hinterland, the barrier between us and the Hittites, is mountainous but the coastal plains are wide, fertile and rich in copper, gold and silver. It's a long way for the Hittites to march an army, but not too far for an empire as strong as they are. The mountains are the *only* deterrent there is for them not to crush us, should they choose. The Hittites are aggressive, with designs of conquest, into even such faraway places as Egypt. To avoid being seen as tempting prey, we *must* grow stronger, and we can only look north and west – especially west – for new opportunities. If Achaea surrendered sovereignty to us, we could protect each other.'

It's a depressingly familiar tale – when the Hittites are divided, as they have been in previous generations, torn by internecine fighting, we can all relax. But when they unite, it makes trouble for everyone. I've heard all this from merchant captains many times. 'Tell me something I don't know,' I murmur.

She pulls her hand away, turning a little sulky, but then she meets my eye again. 'Parassi has returned to Troy. It's a secret for now, but he's going to be formally introduced to court.'

'Parassi,' I breathe. 'Wasn't he just some random shepherd?' *But I had my suspicions even when I first saw him, up on Mount Ida.* 'No, of course he wasn't.'

My first mission in the service of Athena was to act as her bodyguard at a meeting of the gods – in which Parassi 'just happened' to be picked out by Zeus to adjudicate on who best exemplified ideal womanhood: Earth Mother Hera; coldly practical Athena; or sexy and seemingly-subservient Aphrodite.

'He's my *half*-brother,' Kyshanda says meaningfully. She too attended that farce.

'*Half?*' I exclaim. Now this *is* news, and sharing it is a genuine show of trust from Kyshanda. 'Piri-Yamu has a bastard he's prepared to acknowledge? But he's got several official wives and dozens of legitimate children!'

The fecundity of Queen Hekuba, in particular, is legendary – fifteen children and still going.

Kyshanda looks troubled. 'No, Parassi is Mother's.'

'*What?*'

'Every equinox, as High Priestess of Kamrusepa, our goddess of feminine magic—'

'Akin to our Hecate,' I interject.

'Yes, they are aligned in purpose if not worship,' she replies, before going on. 'Every equinox our queen ritually mates with the high priest of our neighbours, the Dardanians, during a secret ceremony to bless the new season. This cannot be avoided, even if the queen is fertile. She took precautions, but those failed. For a long while, Father was wrathful and wouldn't have the boy raised among us, but he's relented, at the behest of the priests.'

Fascinating. Has Piri-Yamu changed his mind because Parassi was singled out by Zeus on Mount Ida? 'How will Parassi be presented to your father's court?'

'Mother's concocted some impressive-sounding nonsense about omens and secret propitiations of the gods,' Kyshanda mutters. 'He's older than Skaya and even Heka-Taru, and he's a *theios*, of course. My full brothers despise him – he's too pretty – and though he can shoot a bow as well as anyone, he barely knows which end of a sword to hold.'

'And what do you think of him?'

'I think he's a snake.'

I guess a half-brother's never going to measure up in her eyes, especially if there's a chance Hekuba might somehow contrive to elevate him before Kyshanda's full brothers. 'Where does he fit in the succession?' I ask.

'In our lands, the successor can be any recognised son, nominated by the dying king,' she replies. 'It keeps my brothers on their toes.' She strokes my chest and looks into my eyes. 'I have one more, very important thing to tell you, but first… What *did* the oracle reveal, my darling? Surely you can remember the words, at least?'

It's a moment of truth. Do I trust to love, or to the dying testament of the greatest prophet of the age?

Love, every time. Tiresias was a murdering scheming, treacherous liar.

I take a deep breath, then recite it all.

'"*The Lion lurks in his den, waiting for the Third Fruit. The Wolf crouches in his lair, slavering over his mate. When the Stallion rears, both shall bare teeth.*

'"*The Sky caresses the Earth with light, planting dreams. The stones listen, the soil awakens, gazing at the blood-red dawn in new hope.*

"'*Swift comes the storm, striking the forest. Branches break, lightning sunders the trunks and they fall. Withered the vines that bound them, gone the leaves that caught the wind, scattered the branches, broken the Crown.*

"'*Golden eggs of the cuckold, caged birds born to sing together. Possess the twain and rule. But beware the tongue of flame that consumes, burning all that it touches.*'"

She's a trained sorceress and seer; I watch her pretty face frown in concentration as she commits it to memory. She'll know the references better than I. When she's got it, she chuckles drily. 'All right, clever man... what were the questions?'

'Those you have to earn,' I tell her. We share a smile, and I reach out to stroke her breast, her hip and then cup her mound, and she shivers. 'Gods, I'm still battered,' she groans, but she has a twinkle in her eye, as she artfully rolls over and wriggles her behind into my groin. 'This way?' she suggests. 'Be gentle,' she adds, looking over her shoulder with a lascivious smile, 'but not too gentle.'

I press myself to her back, aroused once more.

And that's when her mule whinnies again. We freeze, straining to hear any sound over the steady drumming of rain on the ground outside. There's a crack – a breaking branch, still some distance away. And then another, a little closer...

–

We curse, rising swiftly and hauling on our clothes. I heft my blade while she darts outside.

What's she doing? Is she planning to ride away and leave Damastor and me to our fate?

I stop at the door, peering out into the gloom. The wind is strong, the rain still steady and the night sky pitch dark, but I can see three men weaving up the path through the forest, each bearing a fiery torch to light their way.

Kyshanda is just outside the hut, standing beside her mule and clutching a bow and quiver. I sheath my xiphos, snatch the bow from her and string it, then reach for an arrow.

'Please,' she says, laying a hand on my arm. 'It's my brother. I didn't think he could find me, but he's been growing more skilled. Let me talk to him, before you shoot.'

'Will he believe you, if you go to meet him and say no one's here?' I ask.

She meets my eye. 'No. But it'll give you time…'

Skaya-Mandu… there's no reasoning with that prick anyway. And I have Damastor to worry about as well. I shake my head. 'He's going to kill me, and probably you too. He'll guess immediately what we've been doing.'

Her face fills with despair, because she knows I'm right. In his eyes, she'll have just lowered herself to something worse than a whore. 'I have to try,' she says bravely.

'No – it's a waste of breath,' I tell her. 'And if it comes down to him or me, I know who I'm choosing.'

I brush her hand away and snatch the quiver, nock an arrow and aim at the approaching torches, sighting along the shaft.

'Can't you just run?' she pleads.

I set my jaw. 'I can't abandon Damastor.'

She clutches my shoulder, her face fervent. 'Odysseus, there is a way out of this – without bloodshed. There's another thing I was going to share with you: Mother supports the offer I once made you: *Marry me.*'

This confirms what Tiresias has already told me. But in one essential way, the prophet was wrong. Or lied – it comes to the same thing. Now I'm certain Kyshanda's offer comes from her love for me, not from any political calculation.

'Come to Troy,' she continues to plead, 'take an oath to Father and Mother, and we can be as one. Just say yes, and Skaya can't touch you. No one can. We will be together forever.'

I can marry the woman I love? A princess of Troy?

My mind reels. I've been longing for her, dreaming of her, but I've always known that she's as far above me as the sun above

the earth, that our one dalliance on Delos was a chance alignment of the stars, something that could never happen again.
This night has been a miracle, lightning striking the same place
twice.

To marry her, and make such joy a permanent part of my
life: it's my dearest desire.

But to bind myself to Troy is unthinkable. I would be
swearing away my loyalty to Achaea, and therefore to Athena,
to my family, to Ithaca – to everything and everyone I hold
dear.

But perhaps I could be Achaea's agent in Troy… I could work
for Achaea, to maintain peace and protect my people from their
enemies…?

'I… I…,' I stammer, caught in utter indecision. Then I
finally blurt, 'I love you…'

Her whole face and body lights up.

'But I can't marry you,' I finish, in a wretched voice. 'My
people are Achaean, and I cannot betray them.'

Her face collapses, but she doesn't give up. 'Odysseus, in our
tales, Troy was an Achaean colony, in an earlier age. That's why
our gods are so aligned. We're nearly the same…'

'No – you're of the east, we're of the west.'

'You're wrong! Why must you see difference? This isn't
conquest my father purposes but reunification. Please, you and
I can still fight for peace, but from the inside. Please my love!'
She drops to her knees in the mud. '*Please.*'

'I can't,' I groan, and then my temper rises, because surely
she knows this is impossible. *I've got three men coming to kill me
and she says this now?* 'Here's my counter-offer: marry me, and
become a princess of Ithaca.'

Her lovely face twists in agony. 'You know I can't do that.
It's impossible. My parents would never consent. They'd send
an army to bring me back.'

'Let them come,' I snarl, returning my attention to the
oncoming men. 'It's no more impossible than trying to turn

me into a Trojan.' Then I say the most *stupid* thing I've ever said in my life. 'If you truly loved me, you'd come back with me to Ithaca.'

I hate myself, the moment the words are out there. And then *fucking* Skaya-Mandu gets close enough to call out, and all chance to deny my words is gone. 'Sister!' he shouts, from behind the leading soldier. 'Is that you? Who are you with?'

Kyshanda's still kneeling, looking up at me with a look of betrayal on her face, mingled with indignation. 'I do truly love you,' she says in a hurt voice. 'I love you, but I can't go to Ithaca. It would be stupidity and it would bring the whole world down on us.'

She's right again, and that just makes me angrier – with life, with manipulative kings and gods, with greedy Hittites and conniving Trojans and most of all, right now, with my stupid self.

And her damnable brother…

I turn away from her, sight again and shoot: my arrow takes the first Trojan in the middle of the chest, and he slumps to the ground. I'm already aiming again, as the other two burst into motion. I glimpse Skaya's narrow, snarling face and I fire…

…but he's a blasted theios, and he lunges sideways. Luckily for him: not so great for the man directly behind him though – he takes the arrow in the throat and collapses in a heap, his torch hissing and dying as it falls in a puddle.

But Skaya-Mandu's charging straight at us. He's on me before I can nock another arrow and draw, his scimitar slashes down and all I can do is raise the bow, while Kyshanda screams at us to stop.

The bow is cloven in two, but the blow has been absorbed. I toss the ruined weapon aside, lunge for my xiphos, barely grasping it before he batters me against the hut's wall, almost breaking my arm. I see his sword flash and parry – just – and his next blow strikes my xiphos squarely, breaking my blade a hand's length from the hilt. I'm thrown sideways, straight into Kyshanda as she's coming to her feet, shrieking at us to stop.

Skaya-Mandu aims another blow, which I've no chance of blocking or evading.

I do the only thing possible, and seal my fate. Our fate.

I throw my left arm around Kyshanda's shoulder and twist her round in front of me, placing the broken blade against her throat and shouting, 'Stop, or your sister dies.'

Kyshanda screams, 'No, don't—' and I jam my forearm into her mouth to silence her. I don't want her to betray what we've done. I want her blameless in his eyes, if the worst comes to the worst.

But Skaya-Mandu's spits derisively. 'You're not going to kill that slut,' he jeers. 'You're too much in *love* for that.' He scowls at his twin, his voice turning to venom, an outpouring of what to me sounds like jealous rage. 'You think you're the only one, Ithacan? She fucks a different man every night at home, like a common whore. She rents herself out to brothels, and couples with dogs in the alley.' He jams his torch into a gap in the hut's walls and raises his blade. 'You're not going to kill her, you swine. But I'm going to kill you.'

4 – Mercy

'I've got some nasty plans for him: hit him with both fists, knock every tooth out of his jaw onto the ground like a pig that's been rooting up the crops…'

—Homer, *The Odyssey*

Epirus

He's absolutely right – I can't kill Kyshanda and I never intended to. As he hurls himself at me, I fling her aside, hating myself for manhandling her but an instant later his blade slashes through the space she occupied – and slams into my broken blade, smashing the rest of it and leaving me weaponless. Instead of trying to dart from reach, I do the opposite: stepping in, grabbing at his sword-arm and slamming my forehead into his face.

It would have worked better if he wasn't wearing a bronze and leather helm with a nose-guard. I gash my brow on the guard, but his head rocks back and I slam a fist down onto his wrist, and jolt the scimitar loose. As it drops into the mud, I batter my knee at his groin while trying to hook my other arm around his, and wrench.

Had the ground been dry, I'd have had him pinned – but my standing foot slips in a puddle and gives way. Instead of him crashing to the ground beneath me, we both flail for balance, and he's able to backhand me away, while his left hand grasps his curved dagger, unsheathing it in a flash and sweeping it toward my throat.

'Stop!' Kyshanda shrieks, her voice snatched away by the wind and rain. But I can't take my eyes off Skaya's blade, as he darts at me and slashes with vicious speed. I'm forced to give ground, almost tripping on the abandoned arrow quiver, dropping to a crouch and hurling my now useless sword hilt at his face, while grabbing a handful of arrows and blocking the knife blow, trying to close on him again.

He's good, damn him – he pirouettes away, flashing a blow at me that I have to contort to avoid, only to realise he's switched dagger-hand. The weapon slices across my chest and I reel back. He snarls triumphantly as lightning cracks overhead and Kyshanda wails, grabbing at her brother's shoulder just as he aims another blow.

'No, Skaya!' she screams.

That she still wants to protect me is heartbreaking.

But Skaya-Mandu batters a forearm across his twin sister's chest and knocks her back into the mud, barely losing an instant. But that tiny respite gives me a chance to regain composure, though my chest is gashed and my tunic splattered with blood. I've got to get that dagger off him, and fast. He's taller than me, and he's a theios of the Hittite war-god Ishtar, and armoured in leather and bronze. So mere fists aren't going to hurt him.

He attacks again in a blur of slashing metal, and I must give ground. I duck round a thorny bush and leap onto a handy boulder, switching half the arrows to my left hand while leaving the rest in my right, stabbing at his face as he comes into reach, forcing him to pause. Not for long – he comes on again as I retreat, drawing back my right arm and hurling a cluster of arrows at his face. Most fly wide, but one rakes his pretty face and he yells in fury. He recovers quickly, leaping at me, as I push my foot into another load of mud, slither and drop my guard.

Deliberately.

His dagger rips at my throat, but instead of trying to duck away I throw myself into him, my left arm coming up under his blade hand and striking the wrist while my right fist drives into his face, smashing into his cheek and almost lifting him off his feet. He staggers and I spin and slam the rest of my arrows into his right forearm, hard enough that his hand splays and the dagger spins away.

He strikes back, slamming a fist into my jaw, and we both reel. But I'm more solidly built, and can take a blow. I go for him, striking with my fists, elbows, forearms and feet, and then hammer into his torso and we both crash around in the morass of mud we've churned up, fighting with all our bodies.

In Achaea, we have a sport we call the pankration: it's a form of unarmed combat in which almost *anything* goes. In Troy, they just fence, box and maybe wrestle. So though he's taller than me, it's now a handicap for him – being low-built and compact, I have more leverage, and I hit him like a runaway chariot, mauling him with fists and kicks and headbutts, careless of my own body as I seek to break his. He panics, flails at me and I duck beneath, lunge in like an eel, grip his helm and rip his head aside, then slam him face down into the mud and bludgeon his pretty nose into the ground.

His next breath is full of water and mud. He thrashes and tries to throw me off, but I wrap my arm round his throat and slam my knees into the small of his back. Bronze and leather aren't enough to stop me knocking the breath out of him and I do it again, and yet again, while I hammer his face into the ground until he goes limp.

'*Nooo!*' Kyshanda howls, grabbing at me. '*No!!! He's my brother, my twin!*' Her mud-splattered face is a tortured mask, her big eyes pleading. '*Please, Odysseus!*'

Absurd as her concern for him seems, after he called her a whore not so many moments ago, it's enough to make me pause. I relax my grip, but even as she thinks me done, I haul up his head and smash my fist into his jaw once more, hopefully breaking it, and knocking whatever shreds of consciousness he has left into tomorrow. That done, I haul him onto his side as she claws at me, still shouting at me to stop.

He doesn't look nearly as pretty as he did. I roll him back on his face and stand.

'I have stopped,' I pant. 'I just needed to make sure he was out cold.' I grab her flailing arms and pull her to me, pinning her arms to her sides. 'Shh, I'm done, I'm done. I won't kill him, I promise.'

I see anger, relief, terror and betrayal on her face. She's bedraggled, her dress is soaked in mud and half-torn, and she's gasping for air and shaking like a leaf. Skaya's as motionless as his two dead guards. The rain is easing a little, thankfully, but I'm utterly soaked, the blood from my chest wound mingling with the water and running down my leg greaves in red streaks.

'He wasn't going to stop,' I tell her. 'Did he hurt you? Let me look—'

Her head quivers in denial, or refusal. 'Let me go,' she sobs, but she doesn't pull away, instead collapsing against me and bursting into tears. For a long time we just cling to each other.

And then I hear a distant shout. Down on the forest path, a trail of lit torches gleam in the night.

No, I groan. *Give us this moment! Give me time to think!*

'It's Parassi,' she sobs, grabbing at me again. 'He's here with us. Don't run! Stay! I swear to you, we have Mother's blessing, and Parassi knows. He won't let his men harm you, I swear. Skaya... he lost control. It won't happen again.'

I'm struck mute by the choice.

By every god, I want her so much. The passion we share feels all-embracing. I love her mind, I adore her body, our souls share the same vision and the love we made just moments ago makes everything she does seem enchanted. Even soaked and bedraggled I've never seen anyone so beautiful. I don't want a life without her.

But I also know that to Queen Hekuba, I'm not Odysseus, the lover of her daughter – I'm the *Man of Fire*, the one person who in the oracles consistently comes up as a fly in the Trojan ointment. Hekuba doesn't want me as a son, she wants me neutralised, and she's prepared to use her daughter to enable that.

I trust Kyshanda, but I don't trust any other member of her family.

And even if it's a genuine offer, I don't wish to enable the triumph of Troy over my people, however peaceful the process might turn out to be. The thought of seeing them crush Achaea sickens me. I try to imagine some arrogant Trojan prince like Skaya-Mandu installed over my father; or lording it in Mycenae or Sparta, and it fills me with loathing. And when I think about all my enemies among the servants of Zeus, Ares, Aphrodite and the rest, so smugly confident of their eventual triumph, I want to spit.

I will not join them.

'I'm sorry,' I tell her, pushing her to arm's length. 'I love you, but I can't accept.'

'*But, my love—*' She goes to protest, but she chokes it back, seeing something in my face that tells her not to try. Instead she hangs her head. 'I can't come to Ithaca. It would be madness.'

The torchlight is coming closer. 'I know,' I whisper hoarsely. 'I'm sorry I insulted you by insisting. I can be a complete idiot sometimes.'

Her big eyes melt my heart. I seize her face and we kiss – fiercely, longingly, imparting all that could have been into a one last stolen heartbeat of time. Then I tear myself away and run to the hut. Damastor is still lying motionless in the corner. I roll him up in his cloak and heave him into my arms. By the time I come out, Kyshanda, bless her, has untied her mule and is offering me the reins.

'May your gods go with you,' she murmurs.

Beyond the encircling mountains, the first hint of dawn is stirring as I ease Damastor over the beast's neck, before donning my own cloak and clambering up behind him. There's a faint trace of another track at the far end of the clearing and I urge the animal towards it. With luck it will take us up into the hills. The rain is easing and there's just enough light to help me see my way.

My last sight of Kyshanda shows me a heartbroken wraith, rain-soaked and weeping, crouched over the grave of our hopes and dreams.

–

Sunrise finds me wandering the jumbled foothills of Epirus, somewhere east of the gorge we came inland by, leading the mule with Damastor still slung over its back. I have no idea where we are – the clouds are still too thick to guess at the sun's direction. I could be going east, north, south or west. Thankfully the rain has eased a little, and I just continue on, pausing occasionally to check my chest wound – now bound as tight as Damastor's head, eat from the mule's saddlebags, and drink from the occasional stream. I keep looking back but there's no sign of pursuit.

Has Kyshanda somehow managed to hide the mule's tracks? She's an experienced and powerful sorceress, with skills far beyond mine. Who knows what she has been able to achieve? And will Skaya-Mandu fly into another murderous rage when he wakes to find me gone. Has he killed her already?

I'm wracked with fear and doubt. Have I made the right decision? Or is Achaea's only real chance of surviving the Trojan expansion to have a prince working from within the Trojan camp, as Kyshanda believes? I can't decide. All I know is that the only woman I've ever truly loved is now lost to me forever, and I am utterly wretched.

I've been tending to Damastor as best I can. Around midmorning, he stirs, groans and opens his eyes. 'Oi, Ithaca,' he says, sharply. 'What have you done to me, you kopros?'

Clearly, Bria is back.

I help 'him' slide from the horse's back. 'What happened?' I demand. 'You left me – and your precious host – in a death-trap.'

Bria takes in my matted hair, mud-soaked and ripped cloak, my clotted bandages and blood-splattered tunic with a critical frown. 'It wasn't my fault. Those ghosts knew what I was, and they cast me out. I had no choice.'

I wonder about that, but I don't know enough to say whether she's lying or not. I don't owe her the benefit of the doubt, but I let her have it anyway. 'You might have warned me that they could do that.'

'I didn't know.' She gives me an assessing look. 'What have I missed?'

I bring her up to date with a selected version of what happened – the prophecies and the freeing of the priestesses, our retreat through the forest and over the mountains, and the Trojan pursuit into the ravine. I leave out the presence of Kyshanda and Skaya-Mandu entirely, telling her merely that we'd lost our gear when I rescued Damastor from the river, and then been surprised by a Trojan patrol and had to abandon our overnight refuge. I let her believe the mule was stolen during our escape from the hut.

Bria gives me one of her soul-piercing stares, though I've made that last bit sound as plausible as I can. Regardless, she returns to the most important matter – the prophecies. 'So you managed to question the Dodona spirits, and then disable the site? That's good work, Ithaca,' she says, a little grudgingly. 'What did they tell you?'

I give her the words – questions and answers – in case we're separated and only one of us gets back to safety. She shakes her head as I speak but offers no comment, which pisses me off a little. No doubt she'll come up with something, when we have more time to talk. Right now, we need to work out where we are and get as far away from the Trojans as possible.

Luckily Bria knows these hills well enough to lead us south and westward, towards the coast. We're supposed to take turns riding the mule but Bria contrives to have a headache most of the time and claims the lion's share – my chest wound doesn't rank. Otherwise, despite the usual jibes and teases, we get on as well as can be expected.

Two days later we're overlooking a small inlet, where a stream discharges into the Ionian Sea and my ship awaits us. Our galley is beached, and the men are watchful – this is the Thesprotian coast, and half the fishing villages are prone to piracy. We've still seen no sign of pursuit – if the Trojans are looking for us, they're not looking in the right places.

Eurybates, the keryx or herald of my father, King Laertes, comes to greet us, a broad smile on his dark, clever face. He's part-Egyptian, around thirty-five years old with a wily head on his shoulders. In many ways he's been more of a father to me than close-mouthed, belligerent Laertes, and I greet him like kin.

'No troubles?' I ask.

'Just boredom,' he laughs, looking me over. 'And you?'

'Trojans, ghostly priestesses, and an irritating and frankly useless companion,' I tell him.

'Useless?' Bria says sourly. 'You'd still be wandering about lost in those hills if not for me.'

Eury is aware Damastor is Bria, though the rest of the crew don't know the tall, slim lad beside me is anything other than he looks. He gives me a wink. 'What happened to your gear?' he asks.

'Most of it is at the bottom of a flooded river. No point asking "Damastor" about that – he slept through it all.'

Bria pulls a face, but can't exactly deny it. Instead she changes the subject. Typically. 'Our mistress needs to know what we learned—'

'What *I* learned,' I correct her.

'Yes, what *you* learned, O wise and brilliant Odysseus,' she grumbles. 'I must commune with Athena, but I can tell you already – she'll want to confer with you in person. Set sail for Corinth.'

Eurybates looks at me questioningly – Ithaca, our home, lies not so very far to the south of the inlet, and Corinth is a long way out of our way, at the far end of the Corinthian Gulf. The lads will be wanting to get back to their families, not sail any further than they have to. In winter, every sea voyage is a gamble. But in this case, I concur.

Except on very rare occasions, Gods can appear only through an avatar – a rare theios or theia with the power to channel their chosen deity through their physical body. I've seen Bria take this role on two occasions now, but it's becoming clear to me that either she's reluctant to act as an avatar herself because she's a daemon; or that Athena prefers to use human avatars, who are more dedicated to the task. We will need to travel to the nearest of these avatars, and if she happens to live in Corinth, then it's to Corinth that we must go.

'I'll take auguries on the weather,' I tell Eury, and then drop my voice, so we're not overheard. 'I don't like it either, but I think Bria's right.'

Bria and I go down to the shoreline alone, where I carve some lines in the sand, close my eyes and face the sea. Ever since Prometheus opened doors in my mind, I've been chipping gently away at the knowledge I've been given access to. Bria is my guide, but I've got this spell mastered now.

'Spirits of Poseidon,' I call softly, invoking the spirits that inhabit the seas and coasts, using an old tongue Bria's been teaching me, one that the spirits know. As I speak I breathe on the little flame inside me that Prometheus lit, and it flares up. 'Eyes of the Sea, show me the waters from here to Corinth.'

It pays to keep things simple with the spirits, I've learned. They're beings of pure awareness rather than intellect, and what they see is not what mortals perceive. But the easier the task, the more reliable the results, and this one's straightforward. A wave comes in, higher than the rest, and for a few seconds it's glassy, and I see what I need in its depths; a flowing vision of rocky cliffs and jagged promontories, taking me round the shores of Thesprotia, Acarnania and Aetolia, and through the Corinthian Gulf, soaring over waves of sour metalgrey under leaden skies.

There are dark clouds to the south over the Peloponnese hinterland, heavy with snow, but there's a northerly wind blowing, which will hold the brooding storm at bay and aid our journey. A window of opportunity, if we seize it.

I call the lads together, and give them the bad news; they're Ithacans, an argumentative lot, so they don't just accept it unquestioningly: I'm bombarded by complaints and questions, but I'm their prince, and they know me well enough to understand I don't do this sort of thing lightly.

We drag the galley back into the water, catching that promised north wind, the Boreas, which fills our sails with its icy-cool breath. Eurybates wants to talk, and Bria's giving the bandage over my chest wound meaningful looks – presumably she thinks I should change the dressing, which is untypically caring of her. But for a moment I just want to be alone.

To grieve.

I still can't believe the journey I travelled that night: from the heights of ecstasy to a desperate fight for my life, from a beautiful consummation of love, to a rejection of the chance to be with my beloved forever. I ache to see Kyshanda, to explain myself fully, to beg her forgiveness, to tell her that if she waits for me, I'll wait for her, that there will be a way through this labyrinth. But logic tells me that such an outcome is impossible, and that I'm being a fool.

Even if I was welcomed by King Piri-Yama and Queen Hekuba with open arms, married to Kyshanda in their most sacred temples, Skaya-Mandu or another of his brothers would murder me, because I would never be worthy of her, in their eyes. I'm a pauper prince, from the smallest kingdom of Achaea, with nothing to offer her but my love… while they'd be able to eliminate the 'Man of Fire', the most major obstacle to Troy's ambitions.

For my part, I don't even know why the spirits see me as a threat. There are many theioi in Achaea, and no doubt many more in the Hittite kingdoms, and I'm far from the most powerful, skilled or knowledgeable. Yet somehow, it's my name that comes up when the spirits are asked to identify the threats to Troy's grand designs. It makes no sense to me, and it must make less to them. I'm amazed they take it seriously.

Bria has lost patience with me, for she's making her way down the central gangway, a boy walking like a woman, and drawing mutters from my crew. With an effort, I put aside thoughts of Kyshanda.

'Does Athena know we're coming?' I ask her.

'Of course.'

Though Bria is a daemon, many of her skills parallel those of a theios like me, one who has access to all four of the theios gifts. But she's not human, and her powers can take other forms. I've discovered she can also access Athena in some basic way, by communicating somehow through the spirit world. Even now, Athena's avatar in Corinth will know we're coming.

'So,' she begins, 'what do you know of Corinth?'

'Too much and not enough,' I reply. I don't really need to elaborate – last summer, we both camped outside the walls, along with the Argive army, on our way to Thebes. But due to the behaviour of some Argive thugs, we were forbidden entry to the city itself, so its streets are unknown to me.

On the other hand, my true father, Sisyphus, who seduced my mother in secret, was King of Corinth before he was slaughtered, his body left in the streets for the dogs to rip apart. Sisyphus's murderers were overthrown in turn, and Mycenae sent in soldiers to "keep the peace". Now Agamemnon rules the city from his citadel at Mycenae, with a governor to oversee it, a handy outcome for him, as it gives him free access to the Gulf and its trade routes.

'Is there anyone there who will be actively trying to kill me?' I ask drily.

'Now, wouldn't that be a novelty,' Bria drawls. 'Everyone has spies there – it's such a crossroads. We'll need to keep our heads down.'

'Suits me.'

She fixes me with a look. 'Who led the Trojans at Dodona?'

I have a white lie already prepared for this one. 'Parassi. Remember him?'

Damastor's open face doesn't suit Bria's scowl. 'I wasn't at the Judgement. But you were right – he was never a mere shepherd.'

'I'm guessing he's one of Piri-Yama's by-blows,' I comment, because I haven't worked out how I could know otherwise, without revealing my conversation with Kyshanda.

'Brave man – I'm told Hekuba's not someone to cross.'

I expect I'm going to find out all about that, now that Hekuba's first plan – to nullify me by marriage – has failed.

Bria looks me over. 'What else happened?' she asks eventually. 'You're very subdued.'

You have to be careful how you lie to Bria – she's very perceptive. 'My interpretation of the prophecies is that we're no closer to turning things around,' I tell her, which is at least being honest, if not the real reason for my despair. 'We kept the Trojans from stealing Helen two summers ago, then we destroyed their planned alliance with Thebes last year, but they still have all the advantages.'

She seems to buy that. 'You're right, it's frustrating,' she says. 'I thought too, that the death of Tiresias might change the odds, that we might see a rise in counter-prophecies. But hey, you and I know that a prophecy is just the best prediction the spirits can make, given what they know, at any moment in time.'

'True,' I say flatly. 'I just wish they'd see more cause for optimism.'

'We'll turn it around,' she tells me, with forced cheer. 'There's nothing more unpredictable than war.'

I hope she's right.

5 – The Avatar of Corinth

'…Athena, with her bright, blazing eyes, daughter of
aegis-clad Zeus … takes no joy in the works of golden
Aphrodite but loves wars instead, and the work of
Ares, fights and battles, and the making of shining
arms – she was the first to teach mortal men,
carpenters and joiners, to make chariots for peace and
for war, decorated with bronze; and she taught the art
of fine workmanship to tender-skinned maidens in
their homes, embedding it within the hearts of each
one of them.'

—*The Homeric Hymns: To Aphrodite*

Corinth

We spend the night on an Aetolian beach, and sail into Corinth
in the middle of the following day. I dye my hair a dun colour,
and take up my usual alter-persona, Megon of Cephalonia,
telling the lads that for this visit they're escorting a trader.
They're used to such things by now. I have plenty of my own
war gear stored on board – a leather vest sewn with bronze
plates and another xiphos, and most importantly, my prized
bow – the renowned Great Bow of Eurytus. But all that has to
stay on the ship – the bow is too recognisable, and 'Megon' isn't
a fighting man.

With Eurybates left in charge of the ship, Bria and I head into
the city clutching some 'samples', to find Athena's local avatar.
Bria, still in Damastor's body, takes the lead, guiding me to a

small house in a backstreet, where a grey-haired servant opens the door. 'My Lady is asleep,' she announces, loudly enough for any passer-by to hear. 'But you may enter and wait for her to wake.'

I frown, surprised and annoyed that Athena's avatar can't be bothered to stay awake long enough to greet us, but Bria just smiles as we're led through the house to a back room, furnished only with three chairs.

Then the old maid straightens, her dull raiment ripples into an illusion of finery and a bronze helm appears on her head. Somewhere above us, an owl hoots, and her face becomes smooth and timeless. Cool grey eyes regard me, as I recover from my surprise and raise my hands in supplication, Bria doing the same.

The old woman is the avatar, not her lady.

'No one really sees a servant,' Athena says coolly. I smile in appreciation of the subterfuge – which tells me a lot about how important security must be here, in this city of spies. 'Take a seat,' the goddess continues. 'We have too much to discuss to waste time on homage and chatter.'

An avatar can only contain the presence of their god for a short time, and the fewer the illusions they use to signal their presence, and the smaller the audience, the longer they can sustain it. Hence, possessing an avatar in public to boost belief doesn't really work: most present will disagree about what, if anything, they saw, and cry trickery.

Funnily enough, the more vague the omens and signs, the more they're believed: faith, it's called, and it's what these beings we call gods feed on.

They didn't make us, we made them. But that doesn't make them any less real.

'So, tell me these prophesies you extracted from Dodona,' Athena says, her voice as commanding as usual.

I sit and do as I'm bid, trying to decipher whether she's pleased or displeased by the silencing of the shrine, but I can't read her. Perhaps we've been forgiven because of my success in making the priestesses speak. 'I asked the questions you gave Bria, before we set out for Dodona.' The goddess gives me a satisfied nod. 'So, to the first one, "Since the fall of Thebes, who in Achaea still aligns themselves with Troy?" the priestesses replied: "*The Lion lurks in his den, waiting for the Third Fruit. The Wolf crouches in his lair, slavering over his mate. When the Stallion rears, both shall bare teeth.*"'

Athena takes that in gravely. 'The Lion usually means Mycenae,' she comments. 'But this time, I believe, it refers to another prophecy: as you may know, the Sons of Heracles are in Attica, planning to invade the Peloponnese again, to perpetuate one of their father's feuds. But they've been told they must delay until the "Third Fruit".'

Bria and I suck in our breath – we had indeed assumed this verse was about Mycenae. But Heracles was famous for wearing a lionskin cloak. Most people revere him, but since becoming a theios I've formed a different view: he was a brute, prone to blind rage and unbridled lust. Twenty years ago, his sons ravaged the Peloponnese, only to be driven out by a plague that followed their bloody conquests. That they plan to return is an open secret, and no one wants to face them.

'The Third Fruit?' Bria asks, her Damastor face serious. 'What's that?'

'A spontaneous prophesy received at Pytho, that spoke of a Heraclid victory,' Athena explains, 'if they attack after the coming of the "Third Fruit", but warning of disaster if they fail to do so. They're still arguing over its meaning. We'll leave that for now – I'm more interested in this new prophecy: "*The Wolf crouches in his lair, slavering over his mate. When the Stallion rears, both shall bare teeth.*" The first part speaks to me of Tantalus, King of Pisa. He's a notable theios from his mother's side, known as the Wolf by his people. And he hates his cousin Agamemnon – being the only survivor of Thyestes's brood.'

The Atreus-Thyestes feud over the High Kingship – two warring, murderous brothers fighting over a glittering crown –

is yet another of those family quarrels that we Achaeans seem to specialise in. It's into its second generation and very much alive, with Agamemnon Atreiades ruling in Mycenae and Tantalus Thyestiades lurking in western Arcadia. I'm not surprised the problem is raising its ugly head again.

'And the Stallion is Troy, obviously,' I mutter, thinking of Kyshanda and dying a little inside. 'So when Troy demands it, Tantalus and Hyllus will rise to its aid. It seems that the prophecies haven't changed, despite the fall of Thebes.' I'm disappointed – what looked to us like a crushing defeat for Troy was just a setback – the Trojans have other allies to turn to.

Since it became accepted wisdom that Achaea is doomed, Achaeans have reacted as Achaeans do – by scattering in all directions. Some deny the prophesies, others are paralysed by fear, or merely pray their little kingdom can somehow survive the storm alone. But others have sought accommodation with our enemy, and why not, when Zeus himself is doing the same? 'Zeus-Tarhum' is how he likes to be known now, as he merges his identity with Tarhum, the Skyfather of Troy, so that no matter the result of any war, he wins.

We fall silent, until Bria mutters, 'Tantalus, slavering over his mate. He kidnapped Clytemnestra, Tyndareus of Sparta's daughter, and forced her into marriage.'

'Indeed – perhaps we can use that to motivate Agamemnon,' Bria suggests.

'Perhaps,' Athena replies, looking doubtful. 'Tyndareus has been trying and failing to do just that for years. What about the second question?' she asks me.

'"What do the divine allies of Troy purpose next?"' I reply. 'The oracle responded: "*The Sky caresses the Earth with light, planting dreams. The stones listen, the soil awakens, gazing at the blood-red dawn with new hope.*"'

'And your interpretation?'

'The sky is generally Zeus and the Earth is usually Hera,' I reply. '"Caresses", "dreams" – I would suggest that Zeus is trying to woo Hera back to his side, telling her she can do as he is, and align herself with the Earth Mother deity of Troy. Dawn is always toward the east.'

'That's how I see it too,' Bria puts in. 'And the word "dreams" hints that he's lying.'

Athena accepts that, with a grimace upwards at the ceiling, as if chiding her mythic 'father' for his treachery. 'And my third question: "What hope is there for Achaea?"'

'"*Swift comes the storm*,"' I recite, '"*striking the forest. Branches break, lightning sunders the trunks and they fall. Withered the vines that bound them, gone the leaves that caught the wind, scattered the branches, broken the Crown.*" I interpret that as meaning that the attack will be soon, and deadly.'

It's clear from the silence that we all do. Even Athena – timeless goddess – looks ashen, her eyes hollow.

'You know, it may not be quite that bad,' Bria puts in. 'The thing about the spirits is that they communicate in a stream of consciousness, with little regard to past or future tenses. The grammar of their tongue differs from ours. So when you think about the last phrase, "Withered the vines that bound them, gone the leaves that caught the wind, scattered the branches, broken the crown", it might be the result of the storm, or a comment on the preconditions that make the storm so devastating.'

'So if the "vines that bound them" weren't withered, or could be rejuvenated, the trees might survive the storm?' I ask, to clarify. 'If the crown wasn't broken, if the leaves hadn't been swept away?'

'Exactly,' Bria says.

'In other words, the hope you dangle is based on the very slight possibility they're using bad grammar?'

I'm not feeling at my most optimistic, right now.

'Don't forget that the prophecies at Dodona are coming from the spirits through an extra layer, which can garble them.'

'So we have the excuse to garble them even further?' I snap back.

But Athena is nodding slowly. 'Union,' she murmurs. 'The vines signify uniting factors. Troy and its kingdom, the Troad, stand united; Achaea is a mess of feuding kings – personified by their ruling house: the High Kingship is held by Agamemnon and the House of Atreus, but the House of Thyestes contests their rule. In the same way, the sons of Oedipus all but destroyed each other, and almost ruined Achaea with them.'

'Settle the Atreus-Thyestes mess finally,' I conclude, 'and perhaps we can unite Achaea, and become too strong for Troy to push around?'

'Could I just point out that Tantalus has an army every bit as powerful as Agamemnon's,' Bria says in a joy-killing monotone. 'And it's winter. No sane man will launch war until spring, and by then, we might be too late. What if all Hyllus, Tantalus and the Trojans are waiting for is for the winter storms to blow over?'

'You may be right,' Athena sighs, making to stand up. It's clear she assumes I've given them all I have.

'Those were the scripted questions,' I say, 'but I did ask one more.'

'What was that?' Athena asks sharply, sitting down again.

'"How may the crown be made whole?"' I tell them, and Athena nods in approval. 'The oracle replied: "*Golden eggs of the cuckold, caged birds born to sing together. Possess the twain and rule. But beware the tongue of flame that consumes, burning all that it touches.*"'

Neither Bria nor Athena says anything. I hear the street noise outside, and from upstairs, a loud snoring – the lady of the house. Athena finally stirs. 'Tyndareus, the Spartan King – he's the cuckold. His daughter Clytemnestra is one of the eggs, and her sister Helen the other.'

Leda and the Swan.

'"*Caged birds born to sing together,*"' Bria repeats, as soon as Athena pauses. 'At the moment, Tantalus has Clytemnestra and Helen is in Sparta – they aren't together, and there's hatred between Tantalus and Tyndareus.'

'Tantalus has made overtures to Tyndareus, Nestra's father, many times,' I tell them. 'He insists the girl wasn't abducted – that she eloped. He's constantly sending heralds claiming they're wonderfully happy, and that he and Tyndareus should be allies, as father and son-in-law.'

'And Tyndareus is, after Agamemnon and Tantalus, the most powerful king in the Peloponnese,' Athena notes. 'If Tantalus wins Tyndareus's allegiance, they would triumph even over Mycenae's great walls.'

'And if Hyllus and his Heraclids join with them…' Bria adds.

'They'll bring down the High Kingship, at the precise moment we need to be united,' I growl. 'And then squabble over whatever scraps the Trojans leave them. But Tyndareus sheltered Agamemnon and Menelaus when they were young. He overthrew Thyestes to put Agamemnon on the throne. He'll never change sides.'

Though when I think about that, I wonder. Agamemnon is very difficult to like – he's cold, paranoid and utterly calculating, which I guess is inevitable when you've grown up fearing the assassin's blade every day of your life. Not only that, he's very difficult to *trust*. We all know of men he's ruined for fear they'll eclipse him. Gold, silver, bronze and *power* – those matter to him, and little else. Menelaus, his brother, is a good soul and I love him dearly, but he's not wily enough to be a king yet, and maybe never will be. But Agamemnon Atreiades is a king we all fear, rather than love.

Tantalus, though, has charisma and charm to match his fearsome reputation on the battlefield. Unlike Agamemnon and Menelaus, in whom the theioi blood has petered out, Tantalus is god-touched, known as a favourite of Ares.

Could he be the unifying figure Achaea needs?

I reject that instantly – Ares is in Zeus's camp: he and Aphrodite are aligning their cults with that of Ishtar, the Love and War Goddess of the Hittites. And the enmity Tyndareus bears him is surely irreconcilable. If Tantalus is to be High King, he'll do it by conquest alone – and for the benefit of the Trojans.

'Don't forget the "*tongue of flame that consumes, burning all it touches*", O Man of Fire,' Bria says, in a snarky voice. 'Perhaps it's best you stay out of this one.'

'No,' I say firmly. 'If they meant "Man of Fire" they would have said so. "Tongue of flame" is different, I'm sure of it.'

In truth though, I'm *not* sure at all. But I'm not going to allow myself to be excluded. I spent my teenage years in the house of Tyndareus, and Menelaus is like a brother to me. I'm not going to leave their fate to Bria's untender mercies.

'Best you keep it quiet then,' Bria warns. 'I'm not the only one who'll read it that way.'

'Withholding it might prevent us solving it,' Athena says, her voice uncharacteristically vague.

I clear my throat. 'There was one final telling, and it didn't come as a result of any question from me.'

Athena stares at me. 'You mean, a spontaneous prophecy?' she breathes.

We all know that such prophecies can be the most important ones of all.

'I suppose so,' I reply. '"*The storm comes. Caught in its path, the animals twist and turn, dart hither and thither, but the wind will find them, Man of Fire. There is no hiding from the Sky! Fast comes the temptress; far is the island of solace. Flame for passion, cloth for comfort. Be the vine, forge the crown.*"'

There's a long silence, which Bria finally breaks. 'The first part is just as bad as the rest,' she says. 'But—'

'But then comes the first promise of hope that we've had,' says Athena. 'And it seems to involve you, Odysseus. "*Be the vine, forge the crown…*" You *have* to be involved.'

I slump in my chair with relief – though of course it's my back the knives will go in, if I fail.

'So,' Athena goes on. 'We have a plan. Go to Mycenae in secret, and rouse Agamemnon against Tantalus. Ensure your discussions with him are kept from the priests and priestesses of Hera, Mycenae's patron goddess, now we know she's being wooed by Zeus. Strike against the Wolf, bring him down and strengthen the House of Atreus. Unite Achaea behind her High King, and perhaps the omens will begin to read differently.'

By all that's fair and lovely, I hope so.

Part Two: Tantalus & Clytemnestra

6 – The High King

'Would it not be a fine thing, if wisdom was of such a
nature that it could flow from one who was full of it to
one who was empty, if only by touching one another,
even as water in these cups flows through wool from
the fuller one to the emptier one? For if wisdom too
could travel in this way, I would be greatly honoured
to settle down beside you.'

—Plato, *Symposium*

Mycenae

Bria and I enter Mycenae quietly, and not through the mighty
Lion Gate; it's too open and obvious, when we're here in secret.
We take the lesser Postern Gate, and a narrow path through the
clustered buildings that cling to the hillside below the palace.
Eventually this leads us to a small courtyard with an altar to
an early incarnation of Hera, where Agamemnon's messenger
awaits us – just one man, sitting on a bench with a wide-
brimmed hat, the shadows concealing his face.

He spots us immediately. Thankfully Bria's back in a
woman's body, that of a girl she's co-opted – or corrupted.
And slightly embarrassingly, I've met the girl before, though I
haven't had a chance to find out if she remembers me – Bria
tells me she's blocked the girl's awareness while she's inside her.
Her name's Meliboea, or 'Meli' for short. She's a honey-blonde
maenad – a Dionysus worshipper – and I met her on Delos last

year, but this is the first I know that Bria has since recruited her as a host. Damastor is still suffering the effects of concussion, and she departed him, only to show up next morning in Meli's body.

The man waiting for us sweeps off his hat, revealing a mane of golden hair, and envelops me in a huge embrace. 'My friend, how are you?' he cries. 'It's been too long!' We pound each other's backs and burst into spontaneous laughter, just from the sheer pleasure of seeing each other.

'Menelaus, you look the picture of princeliness,' I tell him. He does indeed – six foot tall, strongly built, a face that's gently handsome and always ready to smile. My best friend, the companion of my teenage years in Sparta. There's not a tree near the city we didn't climb, a river pool we didn't swim in, or an orchard we didn't raid. 'How are things here?'

'Well. Always well,' he replies, turning to Bria. 'Lady?'

He has no idea that it's Bria, and I'm not going to tell him. Her eyes are brimming with secret humour as she clasps his extended hand: she slept with him while she was in Genia's Hamazan body, the night before the battle at Glisas that broke the Theban army. This body is lushly feminine and entirely un-martial.

'Meli,' she names herself. 'I'm a servant of the Goddess.' She doesn't bother to say which one.

And Menelaus is too much the gentleman to ask. 'Her blessings be upon you,' he replies politely, then turns back to me. 'So, here you are, still creeping round on secret missions.'

'It was all those escapades in Sparta,' I laugh. 'The ideal training.'

'Indeed it was!' he laughs. 'Come then,' he says, replacing his hat. 'Where are your men?'

'I left them in Corinth, with Eurybates. I'll send for them if they're needed. Who's coming to our meeting?'

'Tyndareus himself has come,' Menelaus tells me, 'all the way up from Lacedaemon with his sons Castor and Polydeuces—'

I groan.

'Yes, I know what you think of them, and they haven't improved, from what I've seen. They still speak against you, for that misunderstanding over Theseus and Helen, but Tyndareus swears they will respect the xenia of Agamemnon's house, and restrain their anger. Besides, you're Tyndareus's own guest friend.'

By 'misunderstanding;, Menelaus means he doesn't really comprehend what happened but he's giving me the benefit of the doubt. It's simple enough if you know the inside story, which Menelaus doesn't: Athena commanded me to help Theseus kidnap the barely-teenage Helen. And so the hero did, but for himself, not the goddess, and I had to help Castor and Polydeuces get her back. We succeeded, but in the process they found out some of my original role in the debacle and now blame me. Theseus is dead now… but he left a child in Helen's belly. I was once welcomed as family in Sparta but now the brothers don't trust me in the slightest.

'I will seek Tyndareus's forgiveness,' I mutter.

'I'm sure there's nothing to forgive,' Menelaus says blithely. 'Laas has travelled up with them – remember him? And your friend Diomedes has come from Argos, with a prince from Elis called Meges who knows Tantalus's lands well.'

'I've met Meges,' I tell him. 'He's come to Ithaca at various times with his fellow princes. He reminds me a little of myself,' I add with a wink, 'and there's few things that impress me more than that.'

Menelaus barks with laughter, while Bria snorts. 'You think Ithaca's joking,' she says drily, and Menelaus throws her a sharp glance, perhaps reminded of another woman with the same sly tongue.

Being with Bria is always complicated.

'I look forward to seeing Diomedes again,' I throw in, to deflect Menelaus from thinking about 'Meli'.

'I've been watching him practice in the yards,' Menelaus enthuses. 'I've never seen a man fight like him.'

I nod; Diomedes is damned good. 'That's everyone?'

'Well, Agamemnon has invited two northern princes – Patroclus and Elephenor. They've just been negotiating a treaty with Agamemnon, in the face of the Heraclid threat, and they're backed by a few other northern tribes. Agamemnon likes them, even if they're barbarians.'

Agamemnon might like Elephenor and Patroclus, but clearly Menelaus doesn't, I note. I hide my annoyance at Agamemnon's extended invitation – what we have to discuss is highly secret and sensitive and I don't know these two at all. But this is Agamemnon's citadel and he can do what he likes.

'And you've kept this meeting secret from the Hera priests?' Bria asks.

'Yes, Lady,' Menelaus tells her. 'Exactly as requested.' He looks troubled by this – Menelaus would rather that all things were done openly. More than this, because Hera is the patron deity of Mycenae – both the city and the kingdom of the same name – the ties between Mycenae and Hera's oracle at Pytho are centuries old. But the Dodona prophecy was clear that the cults of Hera and Zeus are exploring the possibility of working together again, after their recent estrangement, so Hera can't be involved. Especially since the prophecy hinted that Hera is being duped.

We ascend the hill as inconspicuously as we can, and into Agamemnon's palace via a small side door. The fortress itself, enclosing the palace at the top of the hill and the sprawl of workshops, store houses and lesser dwellings spread around it like a splayed-out skirt, has the strongest walls I've ever seen. People call them Cyclopean, because the locals like to say that the legendary giants, the Cyclopses, hefted the immense boulders used in their construction, though Menelaus and I both know they were built by men, a monstrous labour for the royal dynasty, over many years.

Given the history of the House of Atreus, they need all the fortifications they can build – but those walls didn't prevent

Tyndareus from driving Thyestes from Mycenae eight years ago, and installing Agamemnon as king. It's that act, more than anything else, that reassures me yet again that no matter what, Tyndareus will side with Agamemnon over Tantalus.

Menelaus shows us to our rooms himself – Bria in the women's wing, and myself in a richly-furnished suite below his own, linked by stairs. I'm not surprised by the opulence; I already know from past visits that Agamemnon lives in breath-taking luxury. Not because he's soft or pampered – with Agamemnon, it's all about prestige. Look kingly, and men will grovel.

I settle my gear and wash the travel grit from my face, then shave with a bronze razor while Menelaus chats about the doings of Mycenae. Then we follow the sound of clashing metal and rippling applause to a balcony overlooking a small training arena.

Two men are pummelling each other with heavy practice blades and shields, clad only in kilts and helms. One is tall and broad-shouldered, with thick, light-brown hair whom I recognise immediately as Agamemnon; the other is a thickset, bullish man – a stranger – blonde-haired but swarthy-skinned, with a face battered about from battle or the boxing ring, or both.

It's the High King who's barking orders, taking them both through a punishing series of combinations. I glance question-ingly at Menelaus.

'Agamemnon's been flogging himself in training of late,' he says. 'He fears being shamed in battle.'

I can understand that. The theioi are a guarded secret; those who know, know: mostly kings and priests; but ordinary people just believe that some men are naturally far better than others. The advantages are slim, in truth; an extra few yards of speed, an extra few minutes of stamina, enhanced reflexes. But we still have to train. And the bridge can be sometimes be closed by those ordinary men who have the determination to drive themselves hard.

Agamemnon knows that the divine blood of Zeus never reached his generation. He can't undo that, but he can make himself almost as formidable, with dedication. And being Agamemnon, he's willing to pay the price in sweat and blood.

'He's getting good,' I comment. 'Who's he training with?'

'That's Elephenor,' Menelaus says in a noncommittal voice, confirming what I'd already guessed. It takes a lot for Menelaus to actively dislike someone; he's the most fair-minded man I know. Then he points out a tall, lordly-looking man standing nearby, also blonde-haired, with a fur-lined cloak and a face like a demigod. 'And that's his friend Patroclus, another northern barbarian.' He wrinkles his nose. 'Makes my skin crawl, that one. He looks at men like they're women.'

Menelaus is sensitive about such things – he was once jeered by his elder brother for his close friendship to me. I didn't care, but I remember it upset him greatly, especially since he couldn't answer back.

'Where's he from?'

'Locris. They say he's the best swordsman in the north.'

The bout finishes with Agamemnon hammering away at Elephenor's guard, until the younger man slams the High King's sword aside and lashes out with a boot, tripping Agamemnon and leaving him on his back, with a blunt xiphos tip tickling his throat. 'Never over-commit,' the Abantes prince pronounces, while everyone watching sucks in their breath. I do too; Agamemnon hates to look foolish.

To my surprise, when he's climbed to his feet, he clasps Elephenor's hand briefly before stamping away with a brooding expression on his face. By Agamemnon's standards, that's losing with grace. I've seen him flog men that dared to show him up, in the courtroom or the arena. 'He's mellowing,' I remark.

'A little,' Menelaus says wryly. 'Elephenor and Patroclus are the only ones who can get away with beating him; everyone else, even Diomedes, still has to take a tumble.'

'Then maybe they're a good influence?'

'No, just a little better at reading my brother's moods.'

Better than you, I think sympathetically. Menelaus has no guile and is totally loyal. Nevertheless, everything he does is scrutinised by his elder brother for the smallest hint of treachery. Given their father's relationship with their uncle, Agamemnon's behaviour can – perhaps – be excused. But it forces my dear friend to walk a tightrope.

'And Agamemnon still shows no signs of marrying?' I ask, though it's more of a statement than a question.

Menelaus frowns. 'It's complicated. Tyndareus wants him to marry Helen, obviously. But in Agamemnon's eyes, she's tainted goods; and despite everything Tyndareus has done for us – or perhaps because of it – Agamemnon fears that he's setting himself up to be controlled by Sparta, like a puppet. The fact that she's such a gifted theia does nothing to reassure him. But he's hard to please – any other girl would need a huge dowry and impeccable lineage.'

I think about Helen; she'll be fifteen now. Two years ago, I witnessed the start of her awakening as a theia; a glorious, god-touched girl. Zeus intended her to be a prize bride for a Trojan prince, but the disastrous kidnapping by Theseus prevented that, though not in the manner Athena intended. Theseus raped her and got her with child, and that crime and its resulting progeny has meant marrying Helen off to anyone else out of the question in the short-term, even though her pregnancy was kept secret.

The baby itself must have been born by now. It seems to have disappeared, possibly it was killed, which if so is tragic but not surprising in the circumstances. I don't even know whether it was a girl or a boy.

And, by all accounts, Helen has grown into a precocious bitch. Which, given what she's been subjected to, isn't so surprising either.

Nevertheless, a few of the prophecies concerning the fate of Achaea are starting to refer to her. Marry the daughter of Zeus and you will rule Achaea, some have been interpreted to mean. As indeed our Dodona prophecy seems to have done, with the added complication of Clytemnestra. *Possess the Twain and rule…*

So Helen's not short of suitors, but so far, there are none she or her father will accept.

Perhaps the prophecies I gained from Dodona might change that?

–

Six hours later, the city of Mycenae is settling into sleep, but her ruler is wide awake.

After a solitary meal, Bria and I have been summoned to a small council chamber, high up in the palace. Those men Menelaus told me of are there already, standing around in twos and threes; Menelaus himself, with Tyndareus, Castor, Polydeuces, Laas, Meges and Diomedes, plus Elephenor and Patroclus, the two northerners. There's a long table in the centre of the room but no one may sit until Agamemnon arrives and takes his seat.

Predictably, Polydeuces – a giant of a youth who's bigger than most full-grown men – tries to smash my face in, the moment I walk into the room. He would have, too, except his blow is so clearly signalled that I duck with ease, and propel him over a bench face first, before enough people interpose to restrain him.

'I will not listen to a word this lying bastard says!' he rails, red-faced and furious, while his older but slightly smaller brother tries to get at me too. Polydeuces, like his twin Helen, is a theios; Castor isn't, but the brothers are bonded as though they too shared a womb.

'You will listen, my sons, or you will depart,' Tyndareus barks. 'Odysseus is my house guest, and I trust his version of events. So should you.'

That would be so much more heartwarming if my version of events about Theseus and Helen wasn't fabricated. Lying to those I care about brings me no pleasure. But what matters now is that Tyndareus believes me.

'Thank you,' I say to him. 'I swear, I'm here with nothing but goodwill.'

I look round the room. Laas looks no more welcoming than the brothers – but then, he was with me during the pursuit of Theseus, and the final denouement in front of Hades. He gives me a cool, appraising look, but acknowledges his king's words. 'Greetings, Ithacan,' he growls. 'This will be entertaining, no doubt.'

Then Diomedes comes forward, the tall Argive prince, already commander of the fortress of Tiryns, though he's not yet twenty. He looks like Adonis's more handsome brother, with his finely chiselled face and lustrous black curls. He embraces me – we're fellow champions of Athena. 'This man was the true victor at Thebes,' he proclaims. 'Any that question his loyalty to Achaea will face my wrath.'

It's a very Diomedes thing to say, and I see some eyes rolling, but I'm grateful nonetheless.

I'm very conscious of the scrutiny of the two barbarian warriors from the north; bullish, battered-faced Elephenor and blond, handsome Patroclus. I hear the former smirk something about 'runtish islanders' that does nothing to make me warm to him.

I already know Meges – an ordinary-looking young man with deceptive wit. The introductions are completed as Agamemnon strides in with a bald, grey-bearded man tottering behind him, wearing a garland of laurels. The old man is somewhat primitive in appearance: he has a long, straggling beard that makes him look as though he's emerged from some mountain wilderness, and his bright eyes dart around the room in a very uncourtly fashion. His robes, reaching down to his feet, are, ragged and travel-stained, and he walks with an awkward gait, as if his legs have been broken when younger, and set poorly. He's introduced as Telmius; I know the name – he's an itinerant wise-man, by all accounts, a follower of Hermes.

That immediately makes me wary: Hermes follows Zeus in the divine struggle.

'Lord King,' I say, only just managing to keep my voice level, 'I must question this man's presence here.'

Agamemnon's dark eyes glitter at my presumption to question whom he invites. 'Telmius is renowned as a counsellor to kings, and his loyalty to the House of Atreus is beyond doubt.'

I bow my head in reluctant acceptance. 'No offence was intended.'

'Your doubt is excused,' Telmius says, in a merry, lilting voice. 'You know as well as I do that all men can exercise free will, where the gods are concerned.' *Even theioi*, his eyes add. 'My counsel is gladly given, and my discretion is well-attested.'

It's a fair response, and unexpectedly, I find I'm liking this Telmius. And though Hermes is known as Zeus's herald, his worship is confined exclusively to the Peloponnese. He, too, has everything to lose from a Trojan invasion.

Agamemnon's gaze shifts to 'Meli', the only woman in the room. 'And you are?'

'Bria, of Everywhere,' she says, abandoning her false identity. 'I'm here for Athena.'

The men exchange startled glances: Bria's name is well known in theioi circles. And of course, Menelaus goes scarlet, remembering that night of pre-battle nerves outside Thebes, and how he and she relieved his tension. Bria moues at him and follows it with an ironic smile.

'Let us give a toast to the gods,' Agamemnon says, sweeping up a goblet of wine, pouring a small libation into a bowl placed at his feet for the purpose, and drinking. We follow suit, bar the libation – a messy business indoors which would have had the floor awash. That done, Agamemnon sits down at the head of the table and bids us take our places. Then he turns to me. 'Speak, Prince Odysseus. It's at your behest that we're here.'

I take them through my questions and the answers the Dodona oracle provided, with Bria chipping in with analysis, leading them along the path we want them to take. I hesitate before repeating the very last, unsolicited prophecy – it seems to favour me, which I know will be treated with derision, and perhaps undermine the credibility of the whole. On the other hand, it's the only part that strikes a note of optimism, and that last sentence: '*Be the vine, forge the crown*' can be heard as a general call to arms, rather than a personal appeal.

Which is how Bria interprets it to the room. 'In summary,' she says, 'we believe that this is the first true cause of hope that we have been given, and a sign that the fall of Thebes was a crucial development. In unity, we have a chance of resisting Trojan expansionism. Troy seeks new allies, and they've found willing ears in the House of Thyestes, and the Sons of Heracles. Deal with those threats, and the unification of Achaea under the House of Atreus will be uncontested.'

This is, of course, music to Agamemnon's ears. After a childhood spent in exile, and a fraught return to Mycenae propped up by the support of Tyndareus, he's felt the presence of Tantalus and the House of Thyestes in the west like an axe over his head. His sullen face is lit by hope as he contemplates Bria's tenuous analysis – but given that the alternative is doom and defeat, that's not really surprising.

Telmius is more critical, however – he repeatedly asks Bria and me if we're not wilfully misinterpreting what we've heard. I'm struggling to read him – is he here to disrupt or mislead, or truly give wise counsel? He's particularly concerned about the "Tongue of Flame", predictably, I suppose.

'I have been called the "Man of Fire",' I admit. 'And that term, too, is used in the prophecy – but not at this point.'

'Are you sure?' he persists. 'Do you recall the words correctly? You were the only one there.'

'I'm certain. A man is not a tongue.'

'Shame,' Bria murmurs, which is no help whatever. But at least she gets a lusty guffaw out of Telmius.

'And the other words,' I emphasise, 'were "consumes" and "burns", not "destroys". You can be consumed by something

78

noble and good, and burn with enthusiasm or courage, inflamed by the rightness of your cause.'

'I'm satisfied with the Ithacan's loyalty,' Agamemnon growls. Despite his reluctance to go to war in the past, he seems more open to a campaign this time – probably because he can see that the benefits will mostly accrue to him.

'Tantalus, Hyllus.' Bria gestures as though sweeping them away. 'Eliminate them and we are one people.'

'Yes, but how?' Laas asks, looking doubtful. 'The former is shielded by the mountains of Arcadia, and the latter by the Corinthian isthmus and the protection offered by the king of Attica. Perhaps we should wait—'

'If they act in unison, we'll all be destroyed come the spring, with or without a Trojan invasion,' I put in firmly. 'We must strike first, and eliminate one or other of them. And it has to be now, before winter's end, when they least expect it.'

It's bold, but it's common sense, so long as they accept that we are now under urgency to nullify these threats. There's hesitation – Agamemnon is naturally risk-averse, and this is a gamble like none he's made before. He sat out the war with Thebes, for fear a setback would undermine his rule. But the time for sitting on one's hands is passing.

The resulting discussion serves to eliminate the Heraclids as our primary target, not so much because they would be harder to conquer, but because we all recognise that Tantalus seems to pose the greatest threat at this point.

'But what of the second-to-last verse?' Telmius asks. '"*Golden eggs of the cuckold, caged birds born to sing together.*"' He turns to Tyndareus, who has gone red. 'My pardon, great king, but the question must be asked.'

Brave man, this Telmius.

Tyndareus is clearly humiliated – he's the cuckold, and this shame has lain in his heart for many years. Zeus, like the other gods, can possess a willing human, or even an animal, then using their innate magic to shape-change to a more pleasing form.

The whisper is that Tyndareus's queen, Leda, was found naked and post-coital with a *swan*, though afterwards she spoke of a devastatingly handsome and powerful man as her divine lover. Hence the references to eggs and birds.

I see the two northerners smirk. Tyndareus has tried to suppress the tale, but it's been out there for years, sniggered over behind courtly hands in palace corridors, or greeted with guffaws in taverns all over Achaea, where it's told with ribald humour coupled with a touch of awe. Elephenor and Patroclus are clearly enjoying both Tyndareus's distress and the bawdier aspects of Zeus's behaviour, and that lowers them still further in my eyes.

In a society so bound up with honour as ours, Tyndareus must hate this public discussion, even though he was usurped in his marital bed by the King of the Gods himself.

To me the tale is monstrous – a rape by proxy, using a beast. And the most tragic part is that Leda has never recovered – it has driven her to drunkenness and the edge of insanity. For Tyndareus, who still loves the woman she once was, this is the hardest part.

'Are the golden eggs of this prophecy Clytemnestra and Helen?' Telmius asks. 'Or Helen and Polydeuces?'

That's something I, too, have been troubled by. Nine months after Leda's seduction by the swan, Polydeuces and Helen were born. But it's not that straightforward. 'The priestesses used the feminine forms of the words,' I tell him. 'I took especial note of that. So they must mean the two daughters. Even though the girls are not full sisters, they were always close.'

That's the truth – except Helen outshone poor Nestra, like the sun and the moon, even as infants.

'My daughter Clytemnestra was abducted by Tantalus,' Tyndareus says bitterly. 'He has seeded her belly with children, but she has watched the first two die, as if being forced into his bed were not enough for evil Fate to inflict on her. As you tell it, "*The Wolf crouches in his den, slavering over his mate.*"

Slavering… My darling daughter…' His voice breaks and it's a moment before he can regather his composure. 'Without allied help, my kingdom has never had the military strength to regain her.' His eyes flash to Agamemnon, who looks away. For years now, the High King has ignored his requests to go to war with him to recover Clytemnestra, always protesting that the time was not right. 'And Helen is a daughter any man would be proud to marry,' he concludes meaningfully.

Agamemnon shakes his head. 'She's not the bride for me.' He turns back to Telmius. '"*Caged birds born to sing together*". What does that mean?'

'To me, it says that the two girls must be reunited,' I say quickly, to prevent Telmius disrupting things further. But as I speak the words, I can feel the truth in them. '"*Possess the twain and rule*". While Tantalus has Clytemnestra, she's a hostage against you both. Recover her, and the picture changes. Unite the songbirds and we're free to unite Achaea.'

Tyndareus's gaze lights up and he gives me a half-smile. 'They sang together beautifully as children,' he reminds me, before growing sombre again. 'Tantalus guards her closely. He also insults me by sending heralds to tell me how *happy* she is, and forces her to write letters proclaiming her love for him. She's just borne him another son,' he concludes bitterly. 'I'll never get her back. Unless…'

'I'm prepared to risk war,' Diomedes states, slamming his hand palm down on the table. He's all for warring, is our Diomedes.

Castor and Polydeuces make emphatic noises, especially the elder brother Castor, who's Nestra's twin. Tyndareus leans forward. 'Perhaps the time has come, if my lord Agamemnon and Diomedes will join with me? And Elephenor? Patroclus? What men can you bring? Perhaps Fate smiles at last?'

I don't believe in fate, personally – but there are goddesses of Fate, the Moirae. They're not really worshipped, but they are sacrificed – and prayed-to with great fervour, so I'm hazarding they exist. But I do know that prophecy is not an accurate foretelling of the future, just a best guess: so in that case, the whole concept of 'fate' is undermined, to my way of thinking. However, most men still believe in it, and the Moirae.

Regardless, Bria and I have prepared for this moment. 'Such a war may not be fated at all,' I put in. 'I'm willing to try and retrieve her covertly.'

That causes a stir, not least because of my involvement in Theseus's abduction of Helen.

'Not got your fill of kidnapping women, yet?' Laas growls. 'Though if someone is needed to skulk around like a thief, you're the man.'

'It's a rescue, not an abduction,' I retort. 'King Tyndareus has spoken of a newborn child – Telmius, is it not traditional for Arcadian children to be formally presented to Artemis at the first holy day following their birth?'

'Aye,' Telmius admits, looking at me with renewed interest.

'The festival of Ploistos is soon,' Bria puts in. 'Three weeks from today, on the first full moon of spring, the child will be taken to the grove of Artemis near Pisa town. Only women may enter the grove, and once in there'll only be women to stop us. We can pluck Clytemnestra out of their midst.'

'Yes,' Telmius grudgingly admits, 'what you say is true. It could be the opportunity you need. But would that not merely leave you stranded in the kingdom of Pisa? What would you do next, when the search for you is called? Tantalus commands hunters who know the lands there like they know the bodies of their lovers.'

'And how does it help us defeat Tantalus?' Polydeuces adds.

'Think about it,' I reply, keeping my focus on Agamemnon. 'If we can rescue Clytemnestra, Tantalus is honour-bound to pursue. We can lead him into a trap, if you can get a war party into his lands undetected, to back us up?'

'It's still winter,' Diomedes puts in doubtfully.

'And the paths through the Arcadian mountains are treacherous, even in summer,' says Agamemnon, 'and well-watched.'

'What about going by sea?' I suggest. 'We can get there undetected, beach our ships and move inland quickly.'

The men look at each other, hesitating. 'The Aegean's been a witch's brew this season. There've been ships wrecked up and down the eastern coast,' says Diomedes.

'The same thing is true in the south,' Laas says gloomily. 'Sudden storms, out of nowhere. We could lose an entire fleet on the spin of a coin. Especially if great Poseidon sympathises with Tantalus.'

I don't entirely disagree. This is the major weakness in our plan. 'I'm willing to take my galley round the coast,' I insist. 'I would risk my own men for this.'

'We'd need at least six ships, if we're to get enough men into Pisa to make a difference,' Agamemnon replies. 'And the king of Elis will warn Pisa of our approach, if we sail south from the Corinthian Gulf.'

'Aye, that he would,' says Meges, joining the conversation belatedly. 'As an alternative, I could show you paths down through the northern mountains, but they'll be badly snow-bound, with the added risk of avalanches if we get an early thaw, and I couldn't guarantee we'll get to Pisa without loss, if we get there at all.' He makes a hopeless gesture.

'And Pylos will sound the alarm if we approach up the west coast from Lacedaemon,' adds Laas. 'Neither they nor Elis are very fond of Tantalus, but that evil bastard is too strong for them to try and counter.'

The room falls silent, most of us slumped back in our chairs looking defeated. I glance over at Bria, who is biting her lower lip in frustration.

Well, we tried…

Then, unexpectedly, Telmius speaks up, his words lighting a new fire in the room. 'I know a way through the Arcadian mountains. I can get your men to Pisa undetected.'

7 – *Arcadia*

'When he had spoken at length, he urged [them]
onwards through shadowed mountains and ravines
noisy with wind…'

—*The Homeric Hymns: To Hermes*

Arcadia

Two and a half weeks later, we're climbing up a winding trail
into the heights of the Arcadian mountains, laden with packs,
dark-stained leather armour and our weapons. The two kings
have allowed Bria and me to take the lead in this, with Telmius
as our guide, and with Diomedes and Laas along for their
prowess as warriors. In addition, we have four theioi champions
from Mycenae, and though two owe allegiance to Ares, all
of them are sworn to Agamemnon, who claims they are as
loyal as any men he has – crop-haired Agrius, lean and lanky
Philapor, and the Ares lads, dour brothers Ceraus and Pseras.
Agamemnon put forward the two northerners, Elephenor and
Patroclus, but I outright refused to have them. Thankfully Laas
backed me up, and his word swung it.

Despite a certain reserve between us – we serve several
different gods and there's the matter of Theseus and Helen that's
still rankling with Laas – we're all working together well so far,
though Telmius remains a puzzle to me. That's a concern, since
we're putting our lives in his hands.

Despite this, I continue to like him. He's got a blithe hardiness, and laughs easily but never cruelly. He'll share a joke as readily as a sly swig of liquor, and he clearly knows the wilds. 'Forty years I've been traversing these mountains,' he tells us. 'I could tell you some tales.'

He takes a shine to Bria, flirting with her shamelessly. Of course she responds, though not with any real intent: I've seen Bria when she's serious and she doesn't just lap up jokes and flattery – she turns aggressively sexual. However, it's his baritone laugh and her fluting giggles that have accompanied us on the first part of our journey, whenever they deem us far enough away from any habitation not to be overheard.

From Mycenae we wound our way north and west, skirting the town of Orneia, up in the hills, and the fortress of Orchomenos, out in the wide plains of East Arcadia, where there are too many eyes that might sympathise with Tantalus.

We're travelling a day ahead of a larger body of soldiers, led by Agamemnon himself, with Elephenor and Patroclus with them. We're in two parties in order to make our small group easier to conceal, since our role in the plan relies so much on stealth. Hiding the passage of the fifty men who follow us may well be harder, but if they are detected, it could work as a distraction for the Pisans, masking our own advance.

Sadly, Menelaus has been left behind, though part of me is relieved that he won't be put in danger – this is not going to be a picnic. But when Agamemnon declared that he himself would join the war party, it became inevitable – it would be a foolish king that risked his heir on the same mission.

The war party is being guided by a friend of Telmius, a funny little man called Amolus who, like Telmius, wears a thick beard, against all fashion. A true Achaean man shaves, to show that he's civilised. I've heard, though, that some northern barbarians are known to let their beards grow full on more extended campaigns, and I'm vaguely curious to see whether Elephenor and Patroclus would let themselves go to that extent. This trip, however, will hopefully be too short to find that out.

Our own task is to cross the whole of Arcadia, all the way through Tantalus's kingdom to his ruling city of Pisa, kidnap his wife and then flee back the way we've come, joining with Agamemnon's force in an ambush for our pursuers. But Telmius still hasn't revealed how we're going to do it – he just speaks of 'hidden paths'.

The Hermes priest is leading the way this afternoon, and I'm next, followed by Bria. Laas and Diomedes are behind us, deep in conversation about sword-fighting techniques, with the four Mycenaeans trailing us watchfully. The two brothers, Ceraus and Pseras, are archers, and I'm bearing the Great Bow of Eurytus. Many soldiers scorn archery, or more particularly, the hours of training and practice that are required – they already have to spend so much time with sword, spear and shield.

Me, I'm just that bit more dedicated. Laertes loves to tell me that a small man has to work twice as hard as a big one, if he wants to be half the warrior: that's my oversized stepfather for you – all encouragement.

'What can we expect from here on?' I ask Telmius, catching him up.

'It may only be fifty miles from here to Pisa,' he replies. 'Trouble is, boy, it's the worst fifty miles in Achaea. Ahead of us lies some of the most rugged land known, trackless labyrinths of sheer cliffs and boulder-choked ravines. And at this time of year the mountains are still crusted with snow. If you're lucky enough to get some decent weather, the rivers turn into frigid torrents as the thaw starts. The standard route travels north around the worst of it, but it will be watched and we'll have to take a different path. Then we need to find the river Ladon and follow it downstream to the confluence with the Alpheius, which winds past Pisa. This time of year it's impossible, unless you're with folks like Amolus and me.'

'And you swear this path is unknown to the Pisans? And safe?'

'Is anywhere safe?' He wipes sweat from his balding scalp. 'I'll lead you by paths no one else treads.' It's not a comforting

answer – surely Tantalus and his hunters know every pass-
able wild goat track there is – and nor is his appraising stare.
'You come with a certain reputation, Prince Odysseus. King
Agamemnon says that you were the worst troublemaker in
Sparta as a youth, but that you have a silver tongue and can
wriggle out of any corner.'

'Agamemnon was older than us, and Tyndareus kept him
busy learning the affairs of state all hours of the day and night.
When we weren't at our lessons or arms training, Menelaus and
I ran wild. He was jealous of us.'

'So I deduced,' Telmius says lightly. 'It's a pleasure to finally
meet you – and of course, to meet the infamous Bria. She
is something of a legend among legends, if you know what I
mean?'

I do know what he means – Bria's exploits are often secret,
seldom credited and she's almost never mentioned in any tales
that slip into public awareness, but among the theioi she's more
than just a name. 'Don't tell her that, her ego's bad enough as
it is,' I say, laughing.

We make camp that night below a high tor, where I can see
that some kind of primitive stone monument has been erected
long ago – a number of huge rocks placed in a circle. Telmius
tells us it's a holy place to Hermes, and that we're making good
time.

The weather is holding, and I bless our luck. The nights
are freezing cold but there's no rain and little snow lying on
the ground where we are, and we have plenty of warm gear
to put on. As usual Telmius and Bria's lively banter lights up
the evening. The Hermes priest passes round a wine skin – I
don't know where he finds them but he never seems to run
out – and soon we're all quite tipsy. The Mycenaeans decide
we should play a game of chance, using the knuckle bones they
carry around in their wallets. Diomedes and Laas join in, but
after a brief and urgent-looking conversation with Telmius, Bria
goes off alone, claiming she needs some privacy for 'womanly
reasons'.

I give the Hermes priest a suspicious look. 'What was that all about?' I mutter.

'We were just discussing tomorrow's route. Come, let's take in the view.'

He leads me up the tor, a stiff climb, with the snow lying deep in the hollows beside the track, and we examine the stones atop the hill. They've been placed in a ragged circle, many years ago, judging by the moss that covers them.

'I was conceived at a place like this,' Telmius tells me. 'It was a tradition for newlyweds to spend their first night inside such a circle.'

'Doesn't sound very comfortable.'

He laughs. 'The couples usually managed to keep warm.'

'So which way tomorrow?' I ask, staring out from the peak at the taller, cliff-bound heights that already surround us. The land is so tangled and the ravines so deep, I can't work out which direction we can possibly take next. 'When does this secret path of yours begin?'

'Right here,' the Hermes priest says. 'On this hilltop. Bria tells me that you and she have both walked in Hades's realm, as has Laas?'

I have indeed. Telmius is not talking in metaphors: there are places outside but *adjacent* to this world. Bria calls the process 'walking inside the mind of a god'. Something in the energies of worship and belief that the great deities feed upon creates these places: they bring to life the ideals of that god, and feel as solid as this world – but they're not on any map.

I realise with growing alarm that this is his purpose – to lead us through the Arcadian mountains undetected, by taking us out of this world into the realm of Hermes. 'Aye,' I tell him, my body tense, both with fear and rising excitement: such places are a test, but they can be rewarding in strange ways. 'It's true I've been to Erebus, Hades's realm, and to the smithy of Hephaestus also. But are you serious?'

'Of course,' he says gravely. 'Tomorrow I will take you all into the Arcadia of Hermes.' He's watching my reaction carefully.

'Does Bria know?'

'She does – I told her before bringing you up here. We'll tell the others tomorrow morning.'

I try to think it through. It sounds horribly risky, not the least because I'm still not sure how closely tied to Zeus Hermes is. I stare at Telmius, my skin prickling. *Are we being led into a trap?* 'Why would Hermes allow this?' I ask. 'He's Zeus's messenger.'

'Indeed he is… but he's already having doubts, though I'm a little ahead of him in this matter – perhaps because I don't have Zeus looking over my shoulder all the time.' He gives me a piercing look. 'As you well know, a theios can have thoughts independent to those of his god. And in the case of this Trojan matter, I'm not content for my master to toady around at Zeus's beck and call, especially when there isn't a Hittite god that my master will find suitable to align with. He's an Achaean god through and through, and he's not stupid.'

He's telling me that his divine master might be biddable…

This is perhaps the best news we've had since the fall of Thebes. Though clearly it's far from a settled deal, I'm exhilarated by a sense of possibility. *Hermes on our side, but spying on Zeus? Could that work?*

But I know I'm getting ahead of myself. Way ahead. Equally, this could be a baited trap, as I've already wondered. 'So we can trust Hermes to help us?'

Telmius puts his head on one side. 'I'm not going to risk letting him know all our thoughts… No, no, don't look so worried. It's really quite safe so long as we don't draw attention to ourselves.'

'Meaning, without Hermes realising we're in his realm?'

Telmius nods cheerfully. 'That's it. I can open this gateway to let us in, and guide you through and out again, without him knowing.'

Tricky. But is not Hermes the God of Trickery? Which implies his theioi are also skilled in deviousness. I try and quell my nerves. Can the servant outwit his master?

We really are in Telmius's hands now, and rather more than I had feared. 'Then let this mission forge bonds of trust between us,' I say carefully.

He laughs merrily. 'You don't allow yourself to trust anyone, do you? You're even worse than Agamemnon.'

'I've been stabbed in the back a few times too often,' I tell him grimly. 'So has Bria. I want to believe in this, and we'll play it your way, but if there's treachery, you'll go down first.'

With that warning spoken, our bonhomie evaporates and I leave him to commune with his stones while I stalk back down the steep path to the camp. I veer into the next gully, meaning to talk to Bria, but then I see her head bobbing in the waters of a pool, one that must be cold as ice. I cannot imagine how she stands it, except that she's a daemon and can probably stand all sorts of things I can't even imagine. Hopefully her host, soft, smiling Meliboea, is oblivious to it too. I leave her to her bathing and return to camp.

Diomedes and the Mycenaeans are still knuckle-boning and drinking from Telmius's wine-skin, but I've got too much on my mind and leave them to it. Reassuringly, Laas is standing on guard duty, a little way from the fire. I tell him to wake me when he's had enough, before wrapping myself in my blanket and cloak, and closing my eyes to think, first and foremost, and then to sleep.

-

Laas nudges me awake some hours later, for my turn to keep watch,. The fire has burned low, and the other men are all snoring and venting clouds of wine fumes. I'm still half asleep as I add new branches to the flames, kick them into life and take up my post, huddled in my cloak, still caught in the tail end of a weird dream in which pipes danced over the music of the mountain streams. There's a strangely warm wind blowing from the tor above, scented with heather, and the stars and moon are glistening overhead, crystalline and remote.

Laas swiftly falls asleep, and I scan Diomedes and the Mycenaeans slumped together companionably in a tight circle round the fire. Then I look for Telmius…

I jolt wide awake, my blood going cold.

His blanket is empty. I cast my gaze about, but he's nowhere to be seen, though when I glance upwards, it's like there's a faraway star, a pinprick of light, atop the tor. A trick of the light, surely, but I'm nervous now. I come to my feet, unsure if I'm jumping at shadows or if there's genuine danger here. All seems calm, and perhaps Telmius is still up on the hill, readying the gateway to Hermes's realm?

I decide I really do need to talk this through with Bria, even if it means waking the grumpy cow up.

I don't bother strapping on my armour – it's too time consuming and noisy – so I settle for slinging my xiphos over my shoulder and stealing over to where she's sleeping.

Or where I thought she was sleeping: there's just empty ground – even her blanket is gone. For one ghastly moment I think she's been dragged off by a wolf, or worse, but then I catch sight of movement up on the tor itself and creep up the steep path towards it.

I'm nearly at the top when I catch sight of her – or what I assume is her; right in the middle of the circle, surrounded by drifts of snow, a sleeping shape with a tumble of pale hair just like Meli's protruding from one end of a wrinkled blanket. I'm debating with myself about disturbing her when someone steals out from behind one of the stones, a squat shape with a bald pate, a wild beard and bright eyes. He bends stealthily over her, reaching out…

Telmius! What's the double-dealing bastard doing…?

I open my mouth to holler a warning. But two things make the words die in my throat.

The first is that Bria stirs, just as his hand grips the edge of her blanket, and with a throaty chuckle she twists up into his arms. She's naked – I see moonlit flesh as she lets him kiss her, while his hand grasps and then kneads at her left breast.

And someone grips my wrist. 'Shhh…' a woman's voice hisses.

There's a dark shape, right beside me, and I catch a whiff of ripe, feminine body. 'Quiet,' she whispers, and something prods my back, right between my shoulder-blades. It's not sharp enough to be a sword but I'm left somehow immobile and speechless.

How could I have let myself be caught like this?

The woman directs my eyes back to the stone circle – Bria's abandoned the blanket and dropped to her knees, presenting her naked behind to Telmius. The wind has dropped to a whisper, but even so, it's freezing up here, yet she's oblivious to the cold. The priest lets his robes fall from his shoulders, and I feel as though my heart has stopped. Now that he too is naked, the reason for his odd gait becomes clear: he's got the hairiest legs I've ever seen, and they're *backward jointed*, ending in large, shaggy hooves, which have previously been hidden by his boots. Bria doesn't seem to notice or care, and I realise that this isn't the first time he's gone to her. *So much for thinking she isn't interested in him…* She arches her back and moans in pleasure as he enters her.

I look away again, at my captor.

In the dim light, she's a feral thing, dirty-faced with a mane of dark hair and honey-coloured eyes which the moonlight fails to bleach. Her hot breath is fruity and sweet, and her teeth pointed and oddly bright. I don't feel imperilled though; there's just a strange sense of dislocation, as if this is happening to someone other than me. I realise that all that she's pressed to my back is her finger.

But I'm paralysed anyway, even when she runs her free hand down the front of my tunic. Without warning the memory of

Kyshanda overwhelms me, and I choke on a wave of misery and despair. The wild girl goes still, peering at my face curiously before leaning in and licking at the tears coursing down my face.

Her tongue is rough like a cat, and the shock of it – the coarse wetness, coupled with the hand massaging my crotch – takes my breath away. She kisses me, breathing through my mouth as if reviving a drowning man. The act makes my heart thud back to life, and blood gushes through my body.

Suddenly, overpoweringly, irrationally, I want her.

Kyshanda is gone, that small part of my mind that's still trying to make sense of this tells me. *Gone from your life forever.*

That doesn't mean I can't long for her, mourn her, my heart replies. *Or remain true to her memory.*

I'm appalled at what is happening, appalled that my body can be so much at odds with my feelings, but the urgency of need, an overwhelming madness of the senses, has taken over. I let the woman drag me down onto the ground and pull up first my tunic then hers: in the moonlight her skin is bronzed, her hips narrow and her pubis thickly haired. She's clearly already fully aroused and has no time for pleasuring, pulling me down onto her and moaning as I penetrate her wetness easily, and for several moments we grind and thrust, until her eyes bulge and a low groan escapes her.

It's then that I realise that, in the midst of our passion, her forehead has sprouted horns, and her eyes are lit with yellow light. Whatever she is, she's not human. But I don't care. All I want to do is to use her to forget Kyshanda. Caught up in my need, I pound her until release floods me, a hot rush of pure lust that sweeps all thought, all the pain of my loss away for a few blissful seconds.

Then the reality returns, and I'm lying, entangled with a stranger who's not even human. I wrench myself away, filled with self-loathing and stagger to my feet as she looks up at me with a puzzled, hurt look. But I can't stand to be here a moment longer. I pull down my tunic, wrap myself in my cloak and flee, stumbling down the steep path and battering my toes against the rocks, all but oblivious to the pain.

I've betrayed Kyshanda. I'm a piece of shit…

–

Dawn finds me on a low rise below the camp. It's still freezing cold and the sharp, ice-glazed rocks I'm sitting on, huddled over and clutching my misery to me, are stabbing through my tunic into my behind. My cheeks are crusted with tears and my eyes are swollen from weeping. The only time I've ever felt so wretched was the day I found out I was a bastard child and was cast from my family – but that day wasn't my fault. This last night was.

I'm supposed to be in love; aren't good people supposed to do *everything* for love? Yet I've betrayed Kyshanda, the most wonderful woman in the world, a woman to die for. It was only a month ago that we shared the most astonishing lovemaking. But as soon as temptation arose, I stuck my cock into a half-animal… I'm utterly disgusted at myself.

The crunch of footsteps behind me is the last thing I want to hear. I can tell who it is from their tread but I'm too numb to turn.

'Fuck off,' I mutter.

'Poor Ithaca,' Bria says, plopping herself down beside me. 'Forced to have sex with a being of wild nature and magic, when all he really wants to do is sulk,' she adds, without a trace of sympathy. She drapes an unwanted arm round my shoulder. Her hair is wet and she smells freshly washed. I most certainly don't.

'Why don't you tell Big Sister Bria what's the matter?' she coos.

I go to push her away – but then it occurs to me that I *do* need to talk about this, and if not to her, then to whom? She's the only one who knows – not conclusively, but she does – that I'm

94

in love with Kyshanda, and she also understands the intricacies of the theioi world. If anyone is going to understand, it's her.

'Very well. You guessed right, Kyshanda was among the Trojan party at Dodona. Damastor and I managed to escape Skaya-Mandu in the gorge, but when Damastor fell and knocked himself unconscious, I found an abandoned hut in the hills for us to hide in. Kyshanda found us – she came alone, without her brother's knowledge. We made love, and she offered me the chance to go with her to Troy. She swore I would be safe, and that Queen Hekuba herself had given her permission for us to marry. If I'd said yes, I'd be in Troy with the woman I love. At this very moment.'

'But you didn't say yes.'

'Of course not! How could I? They still intend to conquer us, either by crushing our trade or by force. And Skaya-Mandu hates me. He'd murder me before we had the chance to get married, even if the queen's offer is genuine. I had to say no, but…'

'But it's broken your heart. Poor boy,' Bria murmurs, but this time there is sympathy in her voice. 'I'll not pretend I understand – I've never been in love. But I do feel sorry for you.'

I shoot her a glance. 'Never in love? What about Hephaestus?'

She shakes her head. 'No. Not even with him. I've had gods, daemons, people I wanted… needed… craved… who were snatched away from me. I've been reduced to this pitiful bodiless thing but I—' Her voice cuts off, as if she's caught herself on the verge of revealing too much. Then she sighs. 'But never love. It must be horrible.'

'What? No, it's wonderful.'

'Is it? I don't see the evidence. All that unhappiness, that agony of want. And even if you get together, it just turns to banality and babies. Pooing and fouled breach cloths and wailing and vomiting, endless sleepless nights. Ugh! Look at you, crying on a hillside in the middle of nowhere! Great advertisement for love, you are.' Her voice takes on her more familiar, practical tones. 'All's not lost, Ithaca. Your fate and hers seem intertwined. You've refused Troy, but you can still use her. Turn her to our side.'

'Impossible... and I'll not *use* her – I *love* her.'

'Well, she is a prize piece of eastern fanny, I'll grant you that,' she says, with deliberate callousness. 'Contrive to see her, give her some of that Ithacan whatever that she seems to like. And tell her this: that the only chance we have of a peaceful solution is if she works with us. See if she bites.'

'That's disgusting. I will not pervert or betray our love! It's... it's dishonourable.'

'Dishonourable? Since when is the survival of our people a matter for honour?' Bria snaps. 'And what about trying to lure your enemies to your side with your body, like she does? How honourable is that, O Noble Prince?'

'*It's not like that!*'

'Isn't it? Maybe not on her part, but her bitch mother is happy to suggest it.' Bria claps my shoulder. 'Look, maybe you and she can still be together, if we win this secret war. Unlikely, but who knows? Isn't that worth fighting for, instead of just giving up and crying your balls off on this fucking freezing mountainside?'

I stare at her in amazement. '*Win* the war? Is that possible? I thought the most we can hope for is Achaea's survival.'

'Of course it's possible. You have to believe, Ithaca. Without hope, no one achieves anything.'

I hang my head, wondering if I can do this. *Perhaps I can... and surely it's worth trying?* 'But that girl... satyr... nymph thing... Kyshanda will hate me...'

'Why, are you going to tell her or something?' Bria snorts. 'You alone, you were bereft, and that horny little nymph caught you at a weak moment. From what you're saying, neither you or Kyshanda have considered yourselves together since

Dodona anyway. So really, all that happened was that a nature spirit wanting some carefree rumpy-pumpy caught you with your guard down, and you obliged. Big deal.'

'You don't understand.'

'No, *you* don't. Harden up, Ithaca.'

'She wasn't even human.'

'No, she was *more* than human – a creature of magic from Hermes's realm, who came through the hilltop gate looking for some fun. Sadly for her, all she found was misery-guts you.'

We fall silent, as I reflect on what she's said. Yes, it does feel better to have talked, and I do feel somewhat less guilty. That doesn't mean I'm feeling good about any of it, but maybe there are things I can forgive myself for.

'So, you and Telmius?' I sigh, eventually. 'Clearly it wasn't the first time.'

'Ha ha, horny as a goat, that old man,' she chuckles. 'We've been screwing every night since we left Mycenae. Dirty bastard can't help himself.' There's absolutely no embarrassment on her face at all.

'He's a satyr!'

'Mmm. And *everything* you've heard about them is true.'

I roll my eyes. 'Why does no one know that?'

'Who says no one does? He was born when Hermes possessed a he-goat, reshaped the body to a gorgeous man and seduced an Arcadian shepherdess. It's the kind of thing that happens in Arcadia all the time. Hermes might look like a skinny weakling when he's fawning round Zeus, but out here he's the alpha wolf, gifted with all the wildness, the fecundity, the elemental power of nature this place can bring.' She gives a little shudder, clearly remembering something that I have no desire to know about. 'Anyway, it's something Telmius's closer friends turn a blind eye to. He's valuable, and he's fun to be around.'

'So I see,' I grumble.

'Don't worry, it's just fucking,' she snorts. 'You know me, I'm a heartless bitch and nothing distracts me from the real job at hand.' She stands. 'Come on, the others will be waiting.'

I bite my lip, then stand, and before I can prevent her, she gives me a hug. 'If we can put a knife into Tantalus, things will improve, Ithaca. The prophesies will change, Troy won't look so scary, and your girlfriend might become a whole lot more accessible.' Then she pulls away and wrinkles her nose. 'On the way back, take a quick splash in the pond – you smell of nanny-goat.'

She peels with laughter and sashays away.

–

An hour later, we're back atop the tor with our packs, among the stacked piles of stone. Telmius has traced two inter-locking triangles, to form a six-pointed star linking every stone. Diomedes is pale beneath his tanned Adonis face, Laas is fidgeting, the journey into Hades's realm in search of Helen clearly on his mind; and the four Mycenaeans are exchanging nervous glances. Agrius is wiping sweat from his close-cropped pate, Philapor is praying under his breath, and the two brothers are muttering to each other. Only Telmius and Bria look calm.

And me, I hope.

Philapor draws his xiphos, and Telmius gives him a sharp look. 'No drawn blades, not even an arrow,' he snaps. 'I told you before.' He beckons us all closer, so we don't miss anything he says. 'Remember, this is another world we're entering, adjacent and akin to ours. It will seem peaceful to you, but there are dangers. The woods and pools harbour entities that will seek to take you and devour you, and the berries are not for the likes of you, and nor are all the streams safe. It's best to keep anything with a blade sheathed, and to consume nothing but what you bring with you, unless I tell you it's safe.'

'Will the rivers poison us?' Pseras asks anxiously.

'Some, yes. Others will leave you longing to return here, losing all will to go on in our world. That's why I've told you to fill your water skins. Remember this – the fairer something seems, the more dangerous it likely is. Especially beware any women you see.' He looks at Bria and laughs, 'Even you.'

'I'll try to keep my legs crossed,' Bria snorts.

'And finally, you are entering this world without Hermes's knowledge. Keep close behind me and behave as inconspicuously as you can. Do nothing against my will.'

The Mycenaean champions don't look happy at all: Philapor prays even harder, and Ceraus and Pseras press their foreheads together, willing themselves on. Not all theioi have seen as much as I have of the supernatural world, even though I'm relatively new to the game. Athena doesn't have as many theioi as the other gods, so we have to pack more in, I guess.

I glance at Diomedes, who sets his jaw. 'My love for Athena will anchor my soul,' he pronounces. He's speaking literally: the poor fool really is in love with Athena.

Telmius raises his voice, stepping to the centre of the stones, and begins to chant.

'*Oh great Hermes, child of Zeus and Maia, ruler of Arcadia with its many flocks of sheep, willing envoy to the immortal gods whom Maia bore, that nymph, that modest goddess with beautiful hair who lay coupled in love with Zeus...*'

As his voice rises, it seems to resonate around the stone circle, as if we're inside a rock chamber or a throne hall, not standing on a windy hilltop. The warmer breeze I caught an echo of last night becomes stronger and more prevalent, blowing the cold wintery mountain air away and replacing it with pastoral scents that tease the nostrils. Merely breathing becomes a pleasure, filling our lungs with wholesomeness.

'Take me to thy realm, Great One,' Telmius cries, going from stone to stone with his teetering gait, striking each with his staff. 'Open the way!' Six times he calls, and then he returns to the middle and strikes the ground. Light courses from stone to stone, and we gasp, staring about us.

At his final blow, the world changes. The mountains surrounding us remain the same shape, but only the peaks are snowy, and the lower slopes become a soft verdant swathe. The skies are clear and blue, heat envelops us and we're instantly bathed in a light sheen of perspiration. Birds call, swooping around us, calling out their joyous songs.

'Blessed Hera,' Philapor groans, his eyes going wide.

'Be silent,' Telmius snaps. 'Do not call upon her name in this realm.' He's red-faced from the unseen exertions of working this magic, leaning on his staff and panting, though with a satisfied look on his face as he gazes about him.

'Welcome to my homeland,' he says grandly.

I look round, savouring the air, and studying the terrain – it looks a whole lot friendlier now, though we still have a maze of rock to find our way through. 'What's the plan from here?'

Telmius smiles broadly. 'Through meadows green and forests fair, across merry streams and sombre glades, ever onward, ever glad,' he says, probably quoting something. Bria smiles fondly, and they exchange a satisfied look.

'If you old people are done with nostalgia, we've places we need to be,' I suggest. Now that Bria has talked some sense into me, I'm anxious to be going, to strike a blow for a future with Kyshanda, one that might be unlikely but is still worth fighting for.

Telmius squeezes Bria's hand, then totters down the far side of the tor, on a slope that seems far easier than it appeared yesterday. We all follow him, along a goat-path… or satyr-path, I suppose… that descends in a sweeping arc until we're heading broadly west into a valley full of flowers that takes us further into the mountains. Telmius has already told us we've not shortened the distance to Pisa by doing this, but that paths otherwise blocked by snow or flooding will be open to us, and the weather will remain clement. It's a boon beyond price.

The day passes in idyllic conditions. After the long, fertile valley, we climb a high steep trail to a ridge that in our world would be covered in snow and ice, but here is clear, the going rugged but manageable. Even Laas relaxes a little, and as we descend toward a glade where Telmius announces we'll camp, the taciturn Spartan theios addresses me, for the first time since we set out.

'So, I thought we'd meet again,' he says in his gruff voice. 'I've still not made up my mind about that damned Theseus affair, but I'll give you some rope.'

We look each other over – he's a little heavier-set since I last saw him, his hair thinner on top and greyer at the temples, with a touch of sadness around his eyes. 'How do you fare?' I ask him.

'My son died,' Laas says flatly. 'A boar hunt that went wrong.'

I have a boar's-tusk wound on my thigh, a wound that would have killed me had not Athena and Bria intervened. 'I'm sorry for your loss,' I tell him, sincerely. 'Do you have other children?'

He shakes his head. 'Only a daughter. And my wife died, giving birth to her. The Goddess has not been kind.'

He means Hera, Queen of Childbirth, busy with other things that were obviously more important to her while Laas's wife haemorrhaged to death.

'I'm sorry,' I say again. We share an awkward silence.

'So, that prick Theseus got his due,' he comments, eventually. 'Thrown from the highest rock in Athens by Menestheus's men, eh? Good riddance.'

'I don't disagree,' I tell him, honestly. Theseus was a great hero, but he'd turned rancid. 'Nor does Athena.'

'And you restored Helen to her family,' he goes on slowly. 'Pregnant, though I'm sure you know that.'

I do, but I prick up my ears. Laas is a close confidante of the Spartan King, and likely to know more about how Helen and her child have fared than others.

'So I've heard,' I say.

He gives me a sharp look. 'Then you know more than most – her father has worked hard to keep it a secret. To the outside world, Helen's still a virgin, a most eligible bride.'

'Very eligible,' I agree, wondering where this is leading. Neither of us need to count the months off on our fingers to know she will have birthed the child by now. 'Boy or girl?'

'A girl. King Tyndareus told me. Keep that to yourself, though.'

I'm relieved – a boy would almost certainly have been dumped on some mountainside for the wild animals to feast on. 'What's happened to the baby?'

'They've not let her keep it – which makes sense to me. She didn't cope well with having it – well, what would you expect, when you've been raped? But the king has found a home for it, being his first and only grandchild to date – that's on the quiet too, mind. Makes me think,' Laas adds, after a moment. 'I need a new bride, even if I'll be too old to see my sons grow to men. And I've done well for myself in south Lacedaemon. I'm governor there now, with a new-built fortress town called Laos, named by the king for me, with a strong war band and more than a few ships. I'd make the girl a fitting husband.'

Helen's a poisoned cup, I go to tell him, but pause. Perhaps something like this would be a good solution. Marrying her off to a lower-ranking man like Laas, a man Tyndareus trusts and someone tough and experienced who could learn her moods, might be a waste of her undoubtedly prodigious theioi gifts, but better that than her ending up in Troy. One day, she might shake worlds – you don't get the blessing of every Olympian god and goddess and remain a nobody. But in the meantime, while the Trojans are such a threat…

'It sounds a reasonable hope,' I tell him. 'But why tell me?'

He looks at me squarely. 'Because you're the Man of Fire.' When I demure, he laughs grimly. 'You weren't contradicted, by Telmius or anyone else, at Agamemnon's council. And you're the cleverest prick I've ever met, and Tyndareus listens to you.'

It's strange to think of Helen with this taciturn man, so much older than her. Nonetheless… 'For what it's worth, I'll speak for you,' I tell him. 'I promise. Once we've got this Tantalus business resolved.'

He nods his thanks, and we stride on until we reach a flat stretch, a beautiful glade of mountain pasture where Telmius breaks into a lolloping run. We all follow suit, enjoying the change in pace and the sense of freedom it gives us, despite the weight of our gear, our strength buoyed by the magical energy of this place. We burst through a copse, and a herd of wild deer look at us then scatter, and I swear I glimpse a creature akin to the legendary centaur among them, a deer body with the torso, arms and head of an antlered man. They flash into the trees as we hurry past, while butterflies of extraordinary size and colour rise from our path and swarm about. Brightly-coloured birds glide over us, as if curious, then dart away.

Telmius takes us next through a narrow defile, alongside a rushing stream. I glimpse men and women on the far bank, among the trees, but when they see us they bound away, goat-legged satyrs and fleet-footed nymphs leap up the slope and into the pines. One horned girl looks back at me and I realise it's *her* – from last night – but a moment later she's gone, to my relief.

We pause at a ford, a few hundred yards downstream, and I gaze around. It's beautiful, is Hermes's realm. I'm more relaxed now, soaked in the tranquillity and the gentle sunlight that kisses everything and makes it glow. But the feeling isn't shared, especially by Philapor, who's mumbling a prayer to Hera.

'I told you, before! Be silent!' Telmius admonishes him. 'Someone will hear.'

'My Lady, the Queen of Olympus, will hear,' Philapor retorts.

Telmius shakes his head. 'Perhaps. But other ears are closer, and less friendly.'

That only makes the Mycenaean warrior pray all the harder. '*Who* will hear?' I ask Bria. 'Hermes?'

'I don't know,' she mutters, scowling. 'Oi, Philapor, shut your stupid mouth.'

Good old Bria, always one to defuse a tense situation.

The Mycenaeans give her an evil glare. All four of them are on edge, and eager to find someone or something to lash out at.

Agrius puffs out his chest and steps toward her, fists bunching, and his mates crowd in behind him. I step in front, a placating palm pressed in either direction. 'Tact, please Bria,' I tell her, before turning to face the four angry theioi, as Diomedes joins me. 'What she means is, this is the realm of Hermes – anyone calling out prayers to Hera is bound to attract attention from someone they might not want to annoy. Pray, by all means, but do it silently.'

The four Mycenaean champions don't look mollified, but they're probably reluctant to start a brawl on hostile territory and Bria does have a somewhat lethal reputation. So they accept my words, backing away while giving Bria their most belligerent stares, just to let her know she'd better watch herself.

'My hero,' Bria breathes in my ear – sarcastically, of course. She turns to give Diomedes a slap on the shoulder. 'You too, darling,' she says, rolling her eyes. 'I'm so helpless on my own.'

Diomedes frowns. 'Next time, you will be on your own,' he grunts.

'We're all done playing?' Laas growls. 'Good – let's move on.'

We follow the stream down to another river, then climb again, weaving to and fro along a winding path that makes little sense. I swear at times the rivers are running uphill, and the sun moves round willy-nilly as if it can't decide what time of the day it is. But the landscape is breathtaking – giant outcroppings like spearheads, natural arches and trees like great towers, pools so clear you can see the fish swarming far below. It's teeming with life; lizards, snakes, birds and beasts. We see spiders the size of cats weaving massive webs, and glimpse faces carved on tree trunks, whose eyes follow us as we pass. Reed pipes trill among the trees.

All day, Telmius leads us through paths no one else could have found, the most obscure clefts in rock faces opening out into wide trails, while seemingly obvious tracks lead to dead ends. Although we're constantly watchful, the extraordinary beauty seems to be soothing even the Mycenaeans' tension, and by evening we're all talking like old friends. I walk mostly with Diomedes, who for all his stalwart singlemindedness and naivety, is maturing fast. It's easy to forget he's only nineteen – or so say I, only three years his senior.

Having helped him and his extended Argive family gain their revenge against Thebes, I'm interested in his family news. 'King Adrastus still reigns in Argos, but he's lost all interest in the kingdom,' he tells me. 'Thersander rules Thebes, but the populace have fled and the city is in ruins.'

'Your army burned it down,' I remind Diomedes.

'We forgot in our anger that someday we'd need to rebuild whatever we destroyed,' he admits. 'But our biggest worry is Alcmaeon. He's drinking heavily, ever since the priests of Pytho took away his war prize, Manto.'

I pretend I don't know this already, ironical given that it was my idea, though I'd hoped they would kill the meddling sorceress. 'I thought he was going to execute her?'

Manto is the daughter of Tiresias, and possibly the old seer's equal in power and cunning. She hates the Epigoni… and me too, for my role in the fall of Thebes, and the death of her father.

'She's in Pytho as a prisoner,' Diomedes says defensively. 'The Pythia demanded that she help the oracle undo the work of her father, and Adrastus agreed. He was worried Alcmaeon was losing his heart to the woman.'

'Losing his heart'. *More like addicted to her body.* I fume silently, because as I understand it, Manto has beguiled the priests and priestesses of Pytho as well. If the Pythia thinks she can control Manto, she's being dangerously arrogant. But that's another day's problem.

We continue our winding, oblique journey until the sun meanders towards what I assume is the western horizon, and the sky turns a stunning rose-gold. Telmius halts us as the light dims and we make camp.

'Is it safe to light a fire here?' I ask him, as we settle ourselves in a lush clearing, with a dancing stream burbling past. 'Do we need to set a watch?'

Telmius's face crinkles into a grin. 'Hermes is a patron of hunters, Odysseus. This place is nature in all its facets, the placid and the merciless. Fire is permitted so long as it is controlled and we use only fallen branches. And yes, it is better we post sentries. Our idylls are behind us – from now on, we must be wary.'

I take that to mean he and Bria won't be slipping away tonight. We draw up a roster, two men every two hours, leaving Bria free to get some beauty sleep. I've drawn a straw for the first watch and settle down with a still-grumpy Agrius, though after I give him a swig from my liquor flask – an aniseed spirit Eurybates brews from an Egyptian recipe – he perks up considerably, and by the end of our two hours I know his entire family history. Then we rouse Pseras and Diomedes, and I settle into my blanket while Agrius goes to the stream for a drink.

The Mycenean champion is kneeling at the water's edge as I go to close my eyes. Suddenly the water in front of him takes on a faint luminescence. He makes a small, choked sound as an arm shoots out of the river – *which is impossible because that spot is only a few inches deep.* It's a thin greenish-skinned arm with a webbed hand that grasps Agrius's throat and wrenches him face down into the water.

I leap to my feet, shouting the alert as he thrashes, legs kicking frantically as he's hauled towards a deep pool.

Diomedes is already halfway there, drawing his xiphos as he runs, and the rest of us close in, yelling in alarm. The big Argive prince grips Agrius's collar and wrenches, lifting his blade to hack down at the exposed arm of the river creature.

Suddenly there's a brilliant flash of light, the air around us seems to explode and a figure appears in the midst of the blaze, throwing Diomedes aside like a toy. A pulsing force hurls us all off our feet and I land flat on my back, staring as the newcomer kicks Agrius out of the river, freeing him from the grasp of whatever creature had seized him and knocking all the breath out of him in the process. He stands over Diomedes and places one winged sandal on his throat.

Hermes – for it is none but he – is a tall but deceptively slender figure, clad in a glowing, rough-woven kilt, with sharp features and a winged cap over unruly golden hair. His gleaming eyes shift through a rainbow of colours as he stares around him. The wings on his sandals are small and golden-coloured – perhaps more decorative or symbolic rather than practical, to my eyes. But this is his realm, where he can do and be anything he wants.

I don't move a muscle, but my eyes scan the glade, the darkness lit up by Hermes's divine radiance. Satyrs, centaurs, nymphs and dryads are rising from the pasture and the water on every side; perhaps as many as a hundred wild looking creatures emerge, each of them in semi-human form.

I also notice one of our party has not been knocked flat. It's Telmius. Hermes turns to him. 'Well done, faithful servant,' he says.

'You bloody bastard…' Bria starts. Then her voice trails off, because she's not stupid.

Except that we are – all of us. Stupid as newly-born babes. We've walked into this, blindly, and there's every chance we're not walking out.

8 – The Herald of Zeus

'From the heavens, Father Zeus himself ordained …
that glorious Hermes should have charge especially
over birds of omen and fierce lions and white-tusked
boars, and over dogs and sheep, as many as the broad
earth breeds, and dominion over all cattle.'
    −*The Homeric Hymns: To Hermes*

Hermes's realm, Arcadia

Telmius gives Bria a solemn look, with perhaps a touch of
apology, then raises his arms in supplication. 'Divine Father,
Herald of Zeus, Great Hermes,' he calls out, 'I have led these
men to you, as you asked me to do when you espied them here,
but I pray you hearken to them, before passing your judgment.'

Hermes looks at him sternly. 'Why should I listen to tres-
passers, wayward son?'

'Because I tricked them into coming here,' Telmius replies,
avoiding our eyes.

I grip the hilt of my xiphos but find I can't pull it free.
So much for promising Telmius the worst if he betrayed us,
worthless piece of kopros that he is…

Hermes arches one eyebrow. 'Why would you trick them,
my son?'

Why indeed?

I stare, my mind racing, and then it starts to dawn on me.

Telmius told us he thought his father and patron was wrong
in his allegiances; perhaps he's been looking for a way to bring

this home to Hermes, and he sees us as that chance. In that case, he may have led us here, right into Hermes's clutches, expressly for us to state the case for Achaea over Troy. I can almost forgive him his lies… I might even have done the same. But if we can't persuade Zeus's herald to betray the Skyfather, we're all dead, and I'm not so forgiving about that.

Telmius's response confirms my suspicions. 'Divine Father,' he says, in a nervously obsequious voice, 'these men – and this woman – travel on a matter of vital import, for the safety and security both of Achaea, and all those people who give you worship. They sought the paths of your realm to evade the winter, at my suggestion.'

Hermes is listening intently, his eyes shifting in hue from blue to green to gold. 'To what purpose?' he asks, in a voice of soft menace.

'To rescue a woman abducted from her family, and forced into marriage to another against her will. And to bring that miscreant to justice.'

But that's not our primary purpose. And why should Hermes care about one abducted girl? Why doesn't Telmius speak more to the point?

But Hermes does appear moved by the tale. 'A heinous crime indeed,' he says, nodding thoughtfully. 'And yet, not uncommon. How does this rescue safeguard my worshippers?'

Telmius mops his brow. 'The man who perpetrated this crime is in collusion with the enemies of Achaea, and his fall would greatly weaken them.'

It's a convoluted way of drip feeding Hermes the necessary information, but I can see what he's doing. Engaging Hermes's sympathies for Nestra's fate could make the Herald-God think more kindly of us and our cause. But now he's frowning, as he begins to see Telmius's purpose.

His strange, motley minions murmur and chatter as they listen, straining their ears and eyes to take in their master's words. I doubt that's a coincidence either: Telmius must have made sure they'd be here, to witness the decision if it goes our way. I'm stunned at his audacity, but if he's misjudged, he won't be a 'favoured son' much longer.

'And the name of this criminal?' Hermes asks slowly, glancing around the clearing. He's probably come to the same conclusion as I have, and it doesn't seem to be pleasing him. 'Speak clearly, Telmius, for I am not happy to be disturbed by intruders in my own realm.'

'Great Father, the miscreant of whom I speak is King Tantalus, who has stolen Clytemnestra, the daughter of King Tyndareus of Sparta. It is to Pisa these men go, to rescue her.'

Hermes's face becomes ever more thunderous, and his people shiver and take a backwards step. I glance carefully about to check on our party. Diomedes's eyes are closed, but I can see his chest rising and falling. Agrius is bent over his own belly, winded and scared to do aught but snatch at his breath. Like me, Laas, Bria, and the other three Mycenaeans are still lying on the ground, gaping wide-eyed, their limbs rigid.

'Who speaks for these intruders?' Hermes asks reluctantly.

'I do,' I say, before anyone else can. I know my gifts of oratory, and though Bria might know more about the nuances of this place, she's just as likely going to piss everyone off. 'I am Odysseus of Ithaca.'

Hermes's glittering eyes turn my way, settling on me like molten stone. 'The Man of Fire,' he says coldly. 'I have heard your name spoken, but always in tones of mistrust and contempt.'

I test my limbs and find I can rise – I do so, but only to one knee. 'Great Hermes, you have perhaps only heard my enemies speak of me. Why would they not condemn me, if they fear me?'

I can't see any point in doing this half-heartedly.

Telmius winces, but his master gives nothing away. 'Why would you assail my loyal servant Tantalus, who gives due and reverent sacrifice to me, and instructs his people to do the same?' Hermes demands. 'The King of Pisa has created a bastion for me, and I regard his people as my own children.'

He glares at Telmius as he utters that last word, clearly not well-disposed to this particular child of his, just now.

'Great Hermes,' I reply, 'Tantalus abducted and raped Clytemnestra. Her family claim restoration and revenge, but he boasts falsely of her happiness. That in itself is enough for war. But he has thrown his hand in with the King of Troy, and with Hyllus, son of Heracles, in a plan to aid the Trojan invasion of Achaea. How can his worship of you sit well with a plan which will destroy the homeland of your worshippers?'

Now Hermes's quicksilver face changes again, this time to anger. 'Hyllus, son of Heracles,' he growls. 'That is not a name to conjure lightly. Arcadia and all of the lands of the Peloponnese still remember all that monster did. Every beast of war did he unleash, from famine to plague to bloody massacre.' He moves toward me, covering a dozen yards in an instant, and I confess that my heart almost fails me. 'What proofs do you have of this *alleged* conspiracy?' He seizes my face with an icy hand and stares into my eyes. '*Speak...* and I will know if you lie, mortal!'

His eyes grip mine as strongly as his fingers on my jaw. I feel as though my soul is a parchment he's reading, and my heart is laid bare. What he sees inside me, I dread to think – from Kyshanda, to Sisyphus, to the abduction of Helen... I try and focus my mind on the key prophecy Charea and her priestesses gave me.

'This is what the oracle of Dodona told me,' I stammer: "'*The Lion lurks in his den, waiting for the Third Fruit. The Wolf crouches in his lair, slavering over his mate. When the Stallion rears, both shall bare teeth.*" All expert interpretations agree – the Lion is Hyllus, whose father wore a lion-pelt; and Hyllus has received a prophecy about the Third Fruit. The Wolf is Tantalus, who indeed is slavering over his mate – Clytemnestra. The Stallion is Troy, home of fabled horse-breeders, who commands both to war.'

I can scarcely breathe for fear, as the god's eyes burn into mine, changing colour yet again. His cold hand still clamps hold of my chin, and I'm petrified he'll twist it, and break my neck.

'Dodona is silent,' he hisses. 'You silenced it, the only oracular shrine I have access to, since Hera denies me the voice of Pytho. I'm not the only one angered by this – there are great rewards offered for your head over that crime.'

'The priestesses gave me those words, before I released them from entombment and slavery,' I reply, as boldly as I dare. 'Is it a crime to release the shades of those murdered women, when they are the holiest servants of Hera? If they had been servants of Hermes, would you not have demanded their release?'

His grip on my chin tightens even further, and his eyes go black. 'Do not question me, mortal.' Those ebony orbs penetrate right through me, his hand quivers with tension, barely restrained... and then his gaze fades to pale green, and he says, 'You were at the Judgment of Parassi, and know my politics. Zeus is the All-father, the King of Olympus. I am his loyal servant, now and forever.'

This is not going well...

'But is not a King the servant of his people?' I reply.

Hermes snorts with mirth. 'A bizarre thought.'

I gather my courage and press on with my argument. 'What kingdom thrives when its king does not act to preserve it, and what is that kingdom, but the people and the land? Zeus seeks to bind himself to Tarhum, the Hittite Skyfather, turning his back on his many worshippers in Achaea, for the sake of many, many more in the east. You know this. Perhaps it's all very well for him, but you're an Achaean God. Your people are here. Who will pray and sacrifice to you, when they're put to the sword by Hyllus or by the Trojans?'

His eyes swirl, like clouds in a tempest. 'You don't understand anything, mortal. I am eternal.'

To my surprise, Bria speaks up. 'I thought myself eternal also,' she says in a voice of echoing sadness.

Only now does he look away, surprise creasing his features momentarily as he glances across at Bria. The air quivers around us.

A moment later he's holding both of us by the throat, me in his right hand and her in the left. 'And who in Tartarus are you?' he says to her, in a voice like glass breaking.

We're being held so that our tiptoed feet can barely keep us upright, and our windpipes are half-crushed, but somehow even as she goes puce, she gasps out, 'I'll tell you, but not in front of him.'

A moment later I'm sprawled on my back on the grassy sward, winded and clutching my bruised neck, trying to force air into my tortured lungs. Through dizzied eyes I see Bria whisper something, and the god's eyes glisten like trapped stars, then he goes still and his visage turns calculating. Slowly, he lowers her to the ground and releases her throat, and then he smiles as she sinks down to clasp his knees, as if her giving him homage pleases him greatly.

'So... *Bria*... why does that mortal speak before you?' he says, gesturing contemptuously at me.

'He's difficult to shut up,' she says offhandedly. 'He's right, though. Zeus demands your loyalty, but there's nothing in the treasure chests he promises you but extinction. I know his kind all too well.'

Finally, I see a crack in the god's composure, a hesitation that betrays all the seething uncertainty beneath and behind. 'Zeus has promised me that Hyllus will never despoil my beautiful homeland again,' he says, in a voice that catches, for just the slightest moment, on the world *despoil*.

'But you've just heard from Zeus's own oracle that he will.'

The watching centaurs and satyrs and other demi-human creatures of this unworldly landscape whisper as they watch their lord and god *waver*. He realises belatedly and with a gesture of his hand they vanish, as if they were never real, never here. Such is his power in his own realm.

I look round the clearing. Diomedes is stirring; Agrius is lying on his back, eyes wide but too scared to move; Laas, too, is motionless as a statue; Philapor is whimpering, too terrified even to pray to here – a merciful blessing; and the brothers Pseras and Ceraus are now curled in a foetal position. Telmius is still standing, arms raised, his jovial face pale and his balding head gleaming with sweat as he watches his gamble unfold. Or unravel.

'I can't think with your damned racket,' Hermes suddenly says, and flicks a finger at Philapor. The Mycenaean's lips seal together, he panics and turns red then purple until he remembers he has nostrils, at which point he subsides into a twitching heap. 'Hera can't hear you here, fool,' the god says venomously, before turning back to Bria. 'I should take you directly to Zeus's throne,' he snarls. 'He'd give me whatever I ask.'

'More empty treasure chests,' she sniffs. Then she leans forward. 'What would it cost you, to let us through? No one's going to know, and if we succeed, you'll see exactly how Zeus stands on the question of Hyllus.'

'How so?'

'Because the first thing he'll do is vow to unleash the Sons of Heracles on the Peloponnese once more.'

'He's sworn he will never do that,' Hermes says again, but there's clear doubt in his voice now.

'What better way to find out?' Bria says, her voice casual, but I know her well enough to see how stressed she is, even in this less familiar body she's wearing.

'Perhaps,' Hermes says, waving a hand at her in a gesture of delay, as he walks to the kneeling Telmius. 'You set this up, didn't you, my conniving, faithless son?' He grasps at the man's forehead and horns appear, one of which he grasps and wrenches, making Telmius cry out sharply. 'Why should I not reward infidelity with death?'

'Because a son may believe his father errs and seek to open his eyes,' Telmius bleats.

'You should have spoken to me, not played this charade!'

'I tried, Father,' Telmius says desperately, as Hermes lifts him bodily by the horn, making his neck bones twist and crack. 'Please, I tried! You wouldn't listen to me!'

The god raises his other hand, then lowers it. 'I cannot be seen to listen to dissenters. Zeus's people watch me.'

'I know,' Telmius groans. 'But not here. That's why I sought to confront you with this problem… to hear it from others… in your own realm. Please Father, I mean you no ill. I love you. I worship you.'

Barely perceptibly, Hermes's face softens. 'Aye, I see that you do, my recalcitrant son. I see and understand.'

Then with his left fist, he smashes Telmius across the face, releasing the horn as he strikes so that the satyr goes head over heels across the grass and lands, unconscious, at the water's edge.

To her credit, Bria makes a concerned sound and scurries to Telmius's side, speaking some words that revive him, as she cradles his head in her lap. 'Striking one who has served you in good faith, does you no credit, Hermes,' she scolds, boldly. 'Come, what is your answer? Are you a toady to the Skyfather, willing to sacrifice all that worship you in the hope of reward? Or do you stand with free Achaea?'

'I cannot stand openly with your mistress,' Hermes hisses.

'No, but you can stand with Zeus, while secretly aiding us,' I put in.

He turns to me, his expression incredulous. 'You ask me to *spy* upon the all-knowing King of Olympus?'

'I do.' Never let it be said that I hold back when the going gets tough.

'Zeus isn't actually all-knowing, is he?' Bria chimes in. 'If he were all-knowing, my mistress and all those others that defy his wishes would already be dealt with. Thebes would never have fallen, and Troy would rule us now. He's a god, with all that implies, but he's not omniscient and he's not omnipotent. One day, he could even be as diminished as me.'

By Hades, who was *she?*

Her words seem to have struck home, for Hermes groans. 'But you cannot ask…'

'Help us, and you stand to gain if we prevail – and if we fail, deny, deny and deny again, and reap whatever false promises Zeus has made to you. An obol both ways, Hermes, that's what we're offering you. You can be a winner no matter the outcome – assuming Zeus doesn't do what I know he will and betray you. The only thing you'd need to do is not get caught.'

'You think that's easy?'

'You're a smart lad,' she says, somewhat condescendingly, making Telmius and me wince again. 'The God of Thieves and Trickery, I've heard.'

'Great Hermes,' I throw in, 'let this mission be a matter of faith between us. We will never disclose your involvement – I swear that, on behalf of us all. All you need do is let Telmius guide us onwards, and take note of the outcomes. From that, you'll know who to trust.'

The glade falls silent, and I notice that even the river and the wind are stilled. This place that is a living extension of the god himself, and it waits, as though paralysed.

'If Tantalus has made treaty with the Trojans,' Hermes says, after a pause that feels as though a lifetime has passed, 'then I want his head. Zeus has sworn to me that the conquest of Achaea will be bloodless, and my worship will be left intact. Prove him a liar, and I'll succour your cause in secret.'

My heart is pounding so hard, I can barely trust myself to decipher his words. But I've heard truly – he's relented – for the river begins to flow again and a light, warm breeze ruffles the grass.

'You may pass, all of you,' Hermes says, looking away. 'But if any one of you breathes of our agreement, I'll take you bodily to Hades's realm and hand-feed your entrails to Cerberus. *Am I understood?*'

We profess our agreement with all the sincerity and ardour of men making their dying testaments, which indeed we still might be doing. I for one mean every word of it, and I hope the others do too, because if not, I will help Hermes hunt them down.

'And you, my son,' Hermes adds, standing over the stricken Telmius, where he lies cradled on Bria's thighs. 'Let the fidelity of this group be the proving of your own.'

Then the herald-god vanishes, the night closes in on us and we can breathe again.

It takes a moment before I can summon the strength to go to Diomedes and ensure he's not too badly damaged. He has a magnificent black eye but otherwise, to my relief, he seems fine, once I have him on his feet and moving around. Then I go to Telmius and Bria and offer the satyr a hand up.

In response, he merely wriggles the back of his head deeper into Bria's lap. 'I'm quite comfortable where I am,' he chuckles.

'Dirty old goat,' Bria mutters, shoving him away before clasping my hand and hauling herself up. I face her, dropping my voice to a whisper. 'Just who *are* you?' I ask. 'Come on, you owe it to me.'

'Do I?' she says, feigning astonishment. 'No, I fucking don't! Now piss off and leave me alone.' She stalks away, snatches up her blanket and heads away into the darkness. 'No one follows,' she calls over her shoulder. 'Especially you,' she says, jabbing a finger at Telmius. 'I am not some piece on a board game you can just shove around.'

Telmius looks at me, eyebrows raised, but to be honest, I'm with Bria on that one. 'I also like to know in advance when my life's at stake,' I tell him tersely.

'You'd never have come this way if you'd known,' he says, with a diffident shrug. He looks regretfully at Bria's behind as it sways angrily away. 'Her loss.'

I snort derisively. And yet, I can't help forgiving him: his type of cockiness is hard to dislike. On a whim, I go to his pack, grab that wine sack of his that never seems to empty, then sit down beside him again. 'I for one won't be sleeping after that,' I tell him. 'So let's have a drink and a proper talk, eh?'

He gives Bria's back a regretful farewell, and shrugs. 'Why not? Tell me, Prince, have you ever had your heart broken? What was it like?'

I frown at the question. How much has Bria told him of my love for Kyshanda and why does he want to pry? Then I realise he is, for once, being guileless: he's genuinely curious. He and Bria are all brain and libido; neither has ever been in love, which is why they're drawn to each other.

My mother Anticleia once told me that every human is made of four things, in a mix unique to each individual: body, mind, heart and soul. But Bria and Telmius have no heart – I don't mean the physical organ, but empathy and compassion – there's nothing to warm and nothing to break.

When I think of Kyshanda, I almost envy them that lack.

–

It's evening of the next day, after a weirdly empty trek through Hermes's realm – it seems the god has decided to clear away any creature who might witness our passing. We've followed the rivers out of the mountains, criss-crossing them at need, with barely even a bird in sight, but with a sense of watchfulness. We stop for a rest on the banks of the biggest river, at a place where it spreads out wide. Out in the middle, there's a small eyot topped with low scrub and long grass, and the water on either side is shallow enough to wade.

Telmius gathers us in a circle, and tells us that his colleague Amolus is guiding Agamemnon's party along the same route we've taken, and that they're less than a day behind us, with Hermes turning a blind eye to them as well. So far, our deal is holding. How Telmius knows is sorcerer's business, but not an aspect of the art I've mastered yet.

Diomedes has only one good eye right now; the other is puffed up like a ball and completely closed, which has left him struggling with depth-perception all day. Agrius has cracked ribs, but insists on continuing – no one sane would want to be left alone here, anyway. Laas and the other three Mycenaeans are clearly impatient to be out of here, away from the oppressive stillness. The realms of the gods aren't comfortable places to be.

'This is our last chance to confer without the risk of being seen by the Pisans and having our presence reported to Tantalus,' Telmius says. 'The gate is on that eyot; we'll emerge into a landscape exactly like this, but outside Hermes's realm. Humans call this river the Alpheios; it runs swift and deep for much of its length and this is the only crossing for many miles. The crofters and shepherds will have their flocks settling for the night – the sun's already down in your world. I know a place we can camp, but we can't risk fire tonight.'

'How far are we from Pisa?' I ask.

'No more than a handful of miles,' the satyr replies. 'I can take you by a route through lowlands – woods and gullies – so you're within reach of the sacred wood before dawn. After that, it's up to you.'

Bria takes over. 'Ploistos is one of the most sacred rites of Artemis,' she tells us. 'It has many facets, culminating in music, singing and a lot of drinking come nightfall, but the day itself is solemn and sacred. The tradition that interests us is that children born in the preceding few months are presented to the goddess, in the central grove. There'll be sacred chanting and incense and other boring kopros like that. The crucial point is, no men are allowed to attend.'

'Easy pickings,' Pseras growls to his brother, and Ceraus grins.

'I wouldn't count on that,' Bria says. 'No men inside the sacred grove itself doesn't mean there'll be no guards. This is the nearest sanctuary to Pisa and Tantalus is not at all blind to the risks. There will be champions of Artemis the Huntress present, both at the ceremonies and keeping watch around the sacred wood, women who can fight, and more importantly, put an arrow through your eyeball at one hundred paces. They'll be led by Atalanta, if that name means anything to you lot?'

It does, to me and to Laas — but clearly not to the Mycenaeans, who probably don't listen to old tales from the hinterland, nor to Diomedes: the only tales he grew up with were those of vengeance against Thebes.

'She'd be getting on by now, wouldn't she?' Laas asks. 'That old Calydonian Boar Hunt was decades ago.'

Bria smiles grimly. 'She's a tough old bird, and she could still outrun you fat-arses; and plug you in the back before you knew she was there.'

'Go on, then,' Philapor says; the first words he's said for days that aren't prayers. 'Tell us the tale.'

I guess he wants to know what to pray about.

'I'll tell it,' I put in. 'My father, Laertes, was there and I've heard it many times.' Some of them might suspect that Laertes isn't my father, but they all listen in. 'It was almost thirty years ago, before my father became King of Ithaca. Back then, princes often journeyed about; it was before that bloody feud between the Houses of Atreus and Thyestes, and travel between kingdoms was easier. So when the Boar appeared, men banded together.'

'What was so special about this boar?' Ceraus asks sceptically. 'I've killed a few in my time, and they're nothing a good man can't handle on his own, if he knows what he's doing.'

'Not this one,' I respond. 'It was huge. Father says it was thrice the normal size, barely natural.'

'It wasn't natural at all,' Telmius puts in. 'It came from this realm. My father Hermes hand-reared it, but Artemis stole into this place and fed it something to drive it mad. Petty revenge for some slight, it was. She led it to a gateway out of Hermes's realm, somewhere up in Aetolia, and unleashed it into your world.'

'It destroyed a series of farmsteads, but it would vanish before the hunters arrived,' I tell them, taking up the narrative again. 'Once it became apparent this was no ordinary beast, the local king, Oeneus—'

'My grandfather,' Diomedes interrupts.

'—who was also on Artemis's shit-list, assembled a hunting party of thirty, mostly his kin; though for years after, I've heard men claim to have been there, some of whom weren't even born. Twenty-nine men – and one woman, Atalanta—'

'But isn't she a champion of Artemis?' Laas asks. 'I've always wondered why she would hunt the very creature her mistress loosed.'

'A few reasons,' Bria puts in. 'Artemis knew she was pissing everyone off, so she wanted one of her own to clean things up, once her point was made. And she wanted to tweak the noses of those that said that a woman couldn't compete in a man's world. She knew Atalanta's presence would cause arguments, and so it did.'

'It certainly did,' I say loudly, piqued that others keep jumping into my tale. 'Some refused to hunt with her; others stole the hide once it was killed. She'd wounded the boar first, and by rights it had been awarded to her. Fighting broke out and many of Oeneus's kin were maimed or killed. The hunters caused more harm to each other than the boar ever did.'

'What happened to Atalanta?' Agrius asks.

'Well—'

'She married Hippomenes, a prince of Arcadia,' Diomedes interjects. 'I remember my father telling me this! She's actually kin of mine! She and Hippomenes bore Parthenopaios, my great uncle.'

'I'm sure if you explain that to her, she won't shoot you,' I say acidly. Trying to tell this lot a tale is like trying to get the dawn chorus to shut up and listen to you sing.

'She boasted that she'd never marry a man that couldn't outrun her,' Diomedes goes on excitedly. 'But Hippomenes tricked her into picking up golden apples during the race, so he could win.'

'Aphrodite supplied the apples,' Bria adds. 'She wanted Atalanta porked, so that she'd lose some of her power as a virgin of Artemis. The whole running race thing was to prove that Artemis women were better than men, but the Clamshell can't stand virgins. Atalanta was never as strong after that, but she's still formidable.' She looks at me meaningfully. 'She's a shapechanger, she and Hippomenes both. They can turn themselves into lions.'

The four Mycenaeans – sheltered fellows that they are – scoff in disbelief, but I'm remembering the shape-changer at Pytho who almost killed me, two years ago. 'Thanks for the warning,' I tell her. 'But remind me never to try and tell a story to you lot again. Couldn't get a bloody word in edgewise. Shall we go?'

Telmius takes us across the ford to the little eyot, and sure enough there's a ring of stones there, similar to the ones on the tor. The ritual to open the gate is much the same as the previous one – as before, we don't actually step through anything; instead the world is transformed around us. Immediately the cold hits us. It's a frigid night, and after the balmy conditions in Hermes's realm, that's a shock.

We wade to the bank on the far side through the now-icy water, the river already swollen by the start of the spring melt; it's waist deep and about forty yards across, all told. Once over, we dry off, wrap ourselves in our cloaks, and set off. The night is clear and the moon is almost full. We're seven miles from Pisa, and the festival of Ploistos is tomorrow.

9 – The Rites of Ploistos

'If all the best of us were gathered together ... for an
ambush, it's then that men's bravery would be shown
up most clearly; the cowardly man and the brave man
revealed. For the coward's skin changes, now to one
colour, now another; he can't sit quietly without
trembling, or control his feelings; he shifts his weight
from leg to leg, from one foot to the other; his heart
hammers mightily against his ribs as he forecasts his
doom, and his teeth start to chatter.
But the brave man's skin doesn't change colour, nor is
he greatly frightened, from the first moment he takes
his place in the ambush, whenever that might be, but
prays to join in the grim business of fighting as soon as
possible.'

—Homer, *The Iliad*

Pisa, Western Peloponnese

The faint glow in the sky behind us announces the oncoming
dawn, silhouetting the jagged heights of the mountains. We're
crouching in a dense cluster of oleanders, not far from the
edge of Artemis's sacred grove. I breathe slowly and deeply,
preparing myself mentally for the deed we must do. If it all
goes to plan, we'll get away clean, and lure Tantalus straight
into Agamemnon's force, with surprise on our side.

But what if it doesn't go to plan? What if Amolus hasn't
brought Agamemnon's force through Hermes's realm safely?

What if we're hotly pursued, and they're not in position by the time we reach the foothills? We'll be trapped between the mountains and a vengeful Tantalus – just as the Argonauts were caught between Scylla and Charybdis.

Bria, myself, Diomedes, Laas, and the two brothers are going right in to the clearing at the heart of the grove, half a mile away; the other two Mycenaeans will stand by, just outside the grove, ready to back us up the moment we break from cover. Agrius's ribs are still giving him trouble, but Bria has applied some herbs she collected while we were still in Hermes's realm that have eased his pain and hastened the healing process somewhat, so he'll still be handy enough in a fight.

Telmius has already left us, to find Amolus and help guide Agamemnon to the agreed ambush site, a place not far upstream from the main ford and the eyot of Hermes's gate, where cliffs bound both sides the River Alpheios.

I sidle up to Bria. 'Are you ready?' I ask.

'I'm always ready, Ithaca,' she drawls. She runs a sharp eye round the group, assessing us, then leans in. 'Diomedes will seize Clytemnestra, not that she'll need much seizing. She'll be pretty desperate to be rescued from that evil bastard Tantalus. I'll grab her child, and you cover us with your bow, your eyesight being in a damn sight better state than Dio's, right now. Ceraus and Pseras close in as soon as we have them, and guard our retreat.'

I'm brought up short – I've truly not thought too closely about the baby, an heir of Tantalus but an innocent barely birthed. I'd assumed we'd just leave it behind.

'Why do we have to take the child?' I ask her.

It's a brutal fact of life that when a king is overthrown, their male children are often murdered with them. The bloodiest tales of Achaea are revenge stories, intergenerational feuds that bring kingdoms to their knees, producing the fractured Achaea of today. But surely a newborn deserves a life.

She reads me easily. 'Don't go soft, Ithaca. If we kill Tantalus, then it's up to Agamemnon to decide. If we don't, then we're going to be neck-deep in kopros, and the baby's a hostage, a bargaining point.'

I don't like what she's saying, but she's right. Agamemnon is somewhat unproven, still on the young side, but he's not merciful; this may well be the last act in the bloody feud between his father Atreus and Thyestes, and he'll have the whole weight of its history on his shoulders.

If he lets the baby live, the boy could well grow up to take his revenge in turn on Agamemnon and whatever offspring he might produce. But there are other ways to break this whole ghastly cycle. 'I will plead the child's case before the High King,' I tell her. 'He can always be anonymously adopted. It's a time-honoured solution to such matters.'

She shrugs. 'On your head. Look what happened with Oedipus.' She turns to the others. 'Come on, it's time.'

Pseras and Ceraus ready their bows, I string the Great Bow and loop it over my shoulder beside a quiver of arrows. Those of us going in for the ambush loosen our blades in their sheaths, making sure all metal is covered. Diomedes blinks in the dim light, insisting his vision is much improved, despite his swollen, blackened eye.

Philapor begins another prayer and I shush him. 'Is this grove akin to Hermes's realm?' he asks, indignant.

'It's in our world,' Bria tells him. 'But I'd still my lips if I were you; sound carries further at dawn. There'll be watchers in the wood, and we can't afford to raise the alarm on the way in. Atalanta will be on full alert, and she can smell blood a mile off. And when we run, we don't wait for anyone.'

'How do you know all this?' Agrius growls.

'Because I've been here before, obviously,' Bria tells him. 'I got myself in and out again just fine, but that time I didn't have a bunch of clodhopping men slowing me down. Now shut up and follow.'

Those encouraging words delivered, she leads us towards the grove via an overgrown gully, before ghosting through clumps of wild olives and a field of tangled vines that take us into the shelter of a steep ridge. Beyond this, she's informed us, lies the wood, with the sacred grove deep inside. She stops us with a raised hand and a finger over her lips, as though we weren't being as silent as possible already. Away to our right, a slender figure is half-silhouetted against the skyline – a huntress of Artemis.

'New girl,' Bria breathes. 'Careless.'

She leads us forward, slithering on hands and knees and sometimes even on our bellies through low scrub, past the place the sentry overlooks. Bria presses her mouth to my ear 'Note her position,' she whispers. 'On the way out, she's going to be putting arrows in our backs.'

I pat the Great Bow. 'I can shoot too.'

'Don't get cocky – you're no Artemis,' she tells me.

We're about to negotiate the short distance left between us and the grove when a strange coughing sound reaches our ears, borne by a light breeze from the west. In the growing light I glimpse movement – something large, prowling across our path. As it moves between two trees, it pauses and turns its head towards us, eyes glinting. A lioness… My skin pricks.

'It's her, Atalanta,' Bria breathes in my ear.

The boar-tusk scars on my thigh begin to itch.

I'm convinced she's going to come our way, and I stealthily remove the Great Bow from my shoulder. But we're downwind of her; she can't smell us. Eventually, she pads away to our right, and we all breathe again.

'Could just be a wild lioness,' Philapor says hopefully. He certainly picks his moments to be an optimist.

Once we're sure she's gone, we creep through the remaining scrub and move silently into the grove itself, where the scent of cat is heavy in the air. From here, according to Bria's description, the trees must stretch roughly a mile to the far edge, with the sacred clearing more or less in the middle. We're only a few yards in when we hear horses whinnying, somewhere off to our left. Bria gestures to us excitedly and we gather around her.

'Change of plan,' she whispers. 'The important women must have come by chariot from Pisa – why bother using your legs when you've got wheels? They'll have left them at the start of the main path into the grove. Those horses will come in very handy if we've a lioness at our heels, assuming we can get our hands on them. Agrius, Philanor, you work your way over to where they're tethered. Kill the attendants and ready the horses for riding, but don't make an almighty racket doing it. We'll bring Nestra to you.'

The sky has lightened perceptibly as we set off again, making it easier to avoid treading on fallen branches, but increasing the risk of being seen. The trees are mostly deciduous, and starkly bare, with only the merest smudge of pale green, here and there, to show that spring is beckoning. Their leaves are soft and rotting on the ground, deadening our footfalls as we glide from tree trunk to sheltering tree truck. The ground is undulating, rather than flat, but that's a blessing – the contours will give us more cover. The sun will be up soon, and I'm beginning to fear we've left our approach too late, when I hear a distant female voice, singing.

'Not far now,' Bria murmurs, leading us toward the sound. Then she crouches, and we all follow suit, as a thickset woman appears a little way off, stalking left to right, an arrow already nocked and the string half-drawn. 'Wait, she'll be gone in a moment.'

She's right – the sentries are maintaining a mobile perimeter, and the woman soon disappears into the trees again. Presumably there'll be another along shortly – as we get closer, the security is tightening. But though the women seem alert, I get the impression they're going through the motions – Bria says that no one has dared disturb the rites here in decades. We should have surprise on our side.

The sound of the singing swells. 'That's the nobs arriving,' Bria murmurs. 'They'll all be just over this next rise, in the dell below, a few dozen women, that's all. They're all just pampered upper-class types – it's the huntresses in the woods we need to watch.'

The next sentry stalks past, but this one's slack, her gaze turned inwards to the dell, and she's even murmuring the song. She passes from sight, as the sunlight brightens – it must have just cleared the mountains behind us, and the voices rise.

'Now,' Bria whispers, and the six of us glide forward up the rise and drop to the ground, overlooking the dell.

Below us, at the bottom of a shrub-covered slope, a circular stand of cypress trees have been planted, their trunks towering high. Among them, gathered in front of a stone altar, stand roughly forty women, clad in white; most of them holding young babies. I can see individual faces, and easily pick out the queen – she's in the middle, garlanded with winter roses and wearing a gold circlet and neck chain.

Clytemnestra is not the unearthly beauty that her half-sister Helen is. She's older, dark-haired like her father Tyndareus, with no divine theioi blood. During my years in Lacedaemon, I knew her as a quiet, stubborn girl, lacking Helen's dazzling charm. She has a fleshy face and a stocky body which is still carrying the weight of her recent pregnancy. If she was just a villager, no one would notice her. But her face is radiant as she looks down at the babe in her arms. Whatever she feels about the man who abducted and raped her, she loves the child, and that endears her to me, even as I ready an arrow and prepare for chaos.

Ceraus and Pseras remain on guard, while Bria, Diomedes, Laas and I advance down the slope, weaving through the shrubs. Diomedes and Bria take the front; I follow, my bow string drawn, sweeping the bow around, seeking a target, with Laas covering my back.

It takes a few breaths before anyone notices us, and when they do, there's a moment when Bria's presence and my bow makes them think we're part of the security. The women hush and murmur, there's alarm at the presence of men but not outright fear.

Then Laas slams a fist into the face of an archer woman who comes to meet us with a puzzled look on her face. Bria hammers a priestess in the belly and she folds to the ground, and the remaining women emit frightened gasps.

Diomedes thrusts his way through the women, right up to Queen Clytemnestra who's standing in front of the altar, open mouthed and wide-eyed, clutching her baby. 'Who…? What…?' she stammers, eyes widening further.

Diomedes has been indoctrinated to think exactly like a hero of legend, so he drops to one knee before her, arms outstretched. 'Princess Clytemnestra!' he announces. Clearly he's decided that her marriage to Tantalus doesn't count. 'Odysseus of Ithaca has led us here to rescue you!'

The women gasp then fall silent, staring intently as Bria and I arrive behind him. Babies wail, and from the woods around us I hear a horn blare in alarm.

Clytemnestra gapes at the kneeling Argive, then opens her mouth and screams her lungs out.

Oh fuck, I think. *Maybe she doesn't want to be rescued at all…*

–

I'm shocked, but Diomedes is utterly stunned. Noble soul that he is, he has no idea what's really happening, and lets the ashen-faced queen back away. There's a shout from the rise above us – Ceraus, his voice urgent. 'They're coming!' he yells.

Bria reacts. '*Move, you kopros-headed oaf!*' she shouts at the kneeling Diomedes, steps forward and snatches the baby from the queen's arms. As Clytemnestra recoils in horror, Bria lands a roundhouse punch on her jaw with her left fist, and she goes down like a sack of beets. Laas shoulder-charges a woman who tries to aid the queen, then hammers her head with his sword hilt when she doesn't heed him.

My brain catches up. 'Grab Nestra!' I roar at Diomedes, who's still gaping. 'Now!'

I step forward, spinning and aiming my arrow at face after face, as the women back off, white-faced and horrified. Laas roars abuse, spraying spittle as he waves his sword in their faces.

Horns blare again, closer now, and on the opposite rim of the dell a huntress appears, drawing her bow. I curse and shoot at her legs rather than her body – out of some manly spirit of chivalry, I suppose. Before she can loose, my arrow slams into her left thigh and she folds, her arrow spilling.

'Diomedes, come on!' I shout at him.

Finally, the Argive prince regains control. He scoops up Nestra, who is limp as a corpse. I ready another arrow as Bria tucks the baby under her left arm and whips out her sword.

'*Go!*' she shrieks. '*Go!*'

Diomedes, his face twisted with emotion, hefts the unconscious Clytemnestra over his shoulder and we run up the slope, where Pseras and Ceraus are exchanging arrows with a trio of huntresses, darting in and out of cover to shoot. One of the women sees me, but I scythe her down with an arrow in the side before she can shoot. Laas slashes another shaft from the air, snapping it in half with a miraculous sweep of his blade, and we crash into the trees, legs pounding. I let the others go ahead, spinning as I nock another shaft, catch a blur of movement and drop. An arrow slams into a tree trunk beside me, I shoot back and my shaft slams into the chest of the archer, instincts overriding my desire not to kill. I mutter a prayer, spin and run on.

From somewhere far off to my right, a lioness roars.

'*Run!*' Bria hollers, the baby in her arms now screeching its head off. '*Head for the horses! Move your arses!*'

The two Mycenaean brothers fall back to run with me, panting hard as they ready more arrows, while Diomedes lumbers along under the weight of the queen, gasping for breath despite his prodigious strength. We're heading into the sun, the sky ahead blood red as though angered at this desecration – or it's going to rain, if omens aren't your thing. The lioness roars again, already closer.

Pseras shouts, 'Watch your—'

Then his back arches and he goes down, an arrow jutting from his right eye.

Ceraus screams, and stops running, firing his arrow and slamming a shaft into the chest of the huntress who shot his brother. She staggers backwards against the trunk of a pine, but the Mycenaean doesn't stop there. He feathers her again, putting a second shaft through her groin and then a third through her left breast.

'Ceraus, run!' I shout, but he's past hearing, his face torn, bereft. I've seen it on battlefields, when loss overrides all care for self, and when I look back, there are at least a dozen women sprinting after us. 'Ceraus, come on!' I shout, firing to slow them.

But he's too far gone. He puts another arrow in that same woman's gut, even though she's already dead. He doesn't care, reaching for another arrow and finding his quiver's empty. That breaks something in him. He staggers over to his brother's body and drops to his knees.

I leave him; he'll be dead any moment now, and if I stay, I will be too.

As I catch up to Diomedes and Bria, I sense movement to my right and dart behind a tree as a shaft whistles by, turn and shoot back – wide, this time. Behind us, Ceraus's battle roar is cut off mid-cry.

Two down.

Three more arrows hurtle past me. Laas, Bria and Diomedes are well ahead now, somewhere in the trees. I send another shot round the trunk, shooting blind to slow my pursuers. I'm almost out of arrows now, so I focus on escape, racing down into a shallow gully, weaving about to avoid any shots and catching up to Bria and Diomedes as they climb out of it via a narrow cutting that gives us a little cover. I spin, sweep my second last arrow up and nock it, as the first of the huntresses tops the rise on the other side of the gully sixty yards behind – but they're wary, after the trail of dead and wounded I've left behind us. One steps from cover and I put my arrow in her right thigh, and her sisters jerk back into shelter.

I turn and sprint after Bria and Dio, dodging as the hiss of arrows pursues me. Ahead of us, I hear the horses whinny and my heart leaps.

'We're over here!' Bria shouts, and we hear Agrius shout back, some wordless response. We're close to the edge of the grove now, and the ground is flatter, but the undergrowth is thicker and more tangled. The huntresses' arrows falter – they must be scared of hitting the queen, now that they can no longer see us clearly.

We break from the trees, and there's Agrius and Philapor, already mounted, each leading a string of three more horses by their severed chariot reins. Nearby, several bodies lie prone beside the discarded chariots. The Mycenaeans have done well. I run past Diomedes, leap onto my somewhat unwilling mount and beckon to him. '*Here!*' I shout. '*Give Nestra to me!*'

Diomedes, his face distraught, heaves the still unconscious Clytemnestra off his back and across my horse's withers. Bria has the baby, purple-faced and squalling, in the crook of her left arm, her features contorted with worry as she grasps the reins of Philapor's second horse in her right hand. Diomedes hurries over to give her a leg up before swinging himself onto his own mount, sending the beast skittering sideways and almost losing his seat.

'Where's Pseras and Ceraus?' Agrius yells.

'Fucked,' Laas shouts back, his arms nearly jerked from their sockets as he struggles to control his horse.

Philapor releases the last pair of horses, those intended for the two brothers, his face ablaze with anger. 'Filthy *pornes*, bloody shit-eating whores! Hera, curse the lot of them!' he screams, oblivious in his rage to the fact that *we* attacked *them*, and we've paid the consequences.

Archers emerge from the trees as we all wheel, dig in our heels and send our steeds careering eastwards, toward the mountains, with arrows arcing into the sky behind us. But we're moving fast now, and it takes a hell of a shot or outright luck to score a hit. A few come close, but a fraught few minutes later we're belting along a wide track through scattered fields and clumps of forest, the odd early-rising shepherd or farmer staring at us gap-mouthed as we thunder past.

I draw alongside Bria. 'What in Erebus just happened?' I shout. 'Why did Nestra scream?'

'She didn't understand,' Bria calls back. 'She thought we meant to hurt her child.'

'That's not how I saw it!' I reply. 'She didn't want to come!'

'Bullshit,' Bria snaps. 'And anyway, it's irrelevant. She's ours now, and soon she'll be back with her family.'

I throw a look over my shoulder at Diomedes, who's looking miserable and confused, and Laas who is simply looking grim, as he battles to control his horse. Obviously the beast, raised as a chariot horse, isn't happy about being ridden. The two Mycenaeans are openly weeping over the loss of their two comrades, men they knew far better than I did. 'We've got a hard ride ahead,' I call back to Diomedes. 'We've got to get to the ambush spot before we're caught.'

He nods mutely, staring at Clytemnestra, who's being jolted up and down on my thighs. At the very least she's going to be a mess of bruises, by the time we're safe. But she still hasn't stirred and I'm worried Bria's done her some permanent harm. I can't spare her too much attention however – we're riding hard, and from behind us, the sounds of brazen horns are echoing across the plain behind us.

Along with the roar of a lioness, too damn close for comfort. The hunt is well and truly up, and we're the quarry.

Agamemnon, you'd better bloody be there…

I glance behind me to see a blur of gold streaking towards us. The lioness – Atalanta – has outrun the pursuit with ease. At any moment she will be on us.

10 – Tantalus

'And behind them, the dark goddesses of Doom,
grinding their white teeth, fierce-eyed, bristling,
reeking of blood, monstrous and unapproachable, were
engaged in battle around the fallen, all of them avid to
drink the dark blood.'

—Hesiod, *Shield of Heracles*

River Alpheios, near Pisa, Western Peloponnese

I have one arrow left.

I loop the reins through my belt and twist, gripping as
hard as I can with my knees as I wrestle the Great Bow from
my shoulder and nock the final arrow. She's almost upon the
rearmost horse, her muscles tensed to spring as I fire, aiming at
her head, and those blazing eyes. But even as I release the string,
she's leaping. The arrow takes her in an outstretched paw and
she falters, stumbles to the ground and limps away into cover.

I curse under my breath. I had the chance to kill her – it
was pure luck I hit her at all… but at least I've disabled her. For
now.

I should feel relief, but instead I'm faintly nauseous. *That was
all too easy…*

The horns behind us are still blaring, and when we top a
rise we see a distant knot of horsemen on the road behind us.
Tantalus is coming after us, to regain his wife and child. But
they're still several miles back…

So far, all is going to plan – except two of us are dead, and Tantalus has been quicker to respond than we'd calculated. And we have no idea if Agamemnon with his fifty men will reach the ambush point in time.

Nor have we rescued Nestra, as far as I can see. We've abducted her, which is a whole different business.

Suddenly Laas points south, across the river. There's another bunch of riders over there, converging on us fast. We're in real danger of getting cut off unless we reach the ford before them, We have to cross the river to get to the ambush spot.

Or… If Bria can replicate Telmius's spells, we could slip into Hermes's realm via the gateway on the eyot… But that assumes that we can close the gate quickly behind us again, to prevent our pursuers following, and I have no idea if or how that could be done.

And the whole case we presented to Hermes was based on rescuing Nestra, not abducting her. If she wakens, once we're in there, and reveals what we've done to Hermes, what will the god do to us?

Given that, I surmise that Hermes's realm may not be a refuge for us, but where else can we go?

'Ride!' Bria shouts, and we all urge our mounts into renewed effort. In my lap, Clytemnestra groans and writhes about, which is the last thing I need. I'm holding her as steadily as I can with my left hand, so she's pinned against my thighs, while my right grips the reins. Already I can feel my horse is labouring under the double load, unused even to carrying one person on its back. I'm slowing us all down – at this rate the men across the river will outrun us.

But what choices do we have…?

As if in response to my unspoken question, Laas kicks his horse forward to catch up with Bria. 'I'll take Diomedes ahead and secure the ford,' he yells, over the screams of the baby. 'They'll not cross before us!'

I bless him for his quick wits as the pair gallop ahead, quickly leaving us behind.

Agrius and Philapor flank me, faces red from exertion. Theioi like them are an elite – trained in all aspects of war, including driving a chariot in battle. But riding is mostly for lesser men – couriers, messengers and the like. They have enough experience to stay on a horse's back, but this mad, panicked ride is demanding all their concentration. None of these chariot horses are well-accustomed to being ridden, and we're struggling to keep them under control.

Just then poor Nestra jolts back to awareness, grabbing at my thigh and shifting her weight. We almost fall off, I shout in warning and haul on my reins, wrenching at her waist with all my considerable strength to get her back over the horse's withers.

She looks up at me with blank horror. '*Tantalus*,' she wails, '*Tantalus! Help me!*'

The horse takes fright, rearing up in alarm. I fight for control as Nestra thrashes in my grip, almost unseating us both as I cling on with my knees. 'Nestra! Nestra! It's me!' I shout. 'Odysseus! Remember me?'

'*Tantalus!*'

Somehow my mount thumps down onto all fours again, prancing about and rolling its eyes. Bria wheels her horse around and gallops back to draw close alongside, Agrius joining us a moment later. 'Watch out—' the Mycenaean champion shouts, as Nestra's arm flashes round…

…and slams my own dagger into my flank.

The thick leather jerkin saves me, coupled with her confusion and lack of strength. The blade skews off, but I'm almost too shocked to prevent her trying again, as she thrashes her legs and her arm goes back once more – but then I catch her wrist and squeeze, forcing her to drop the knife. Bria's fist crunches into her temple and she slides off the horse and crashes onto the ground, out cold again.

I leap down, clutching the reins to stop my horse bolting, and check Nestra's breathing before glaring up at Bria. The baby is screaming again, harder than ever.

'Anyone else think this isn't a fucking rescue?' I shout. 'It's a bloody kidnapping.'

'Should be right up your alley,' Agrius grunts, looking back over his shoulder. 'Get her up again, Ithacan. That lot over the river are at the ford already. And those bastards behind us are catching us up.'

He's right. I hoist Nestra back up, swearing and cursing under my breath, regain my dagger and mount again behind her. On we go. But my brain is screaming at me that we're too slow – the pursuit is too fierce, too well organised, and the ambush point is still well up the valley. And I'm losing heart for this whole, blighted escapade. But I have no choice but to continue.

The final mile to the ford seems to last an eternity, but at last we reach the Alpheios. It's a mighty river, the longest in Achaea, I'm told. There are four bodies out in the middle, tangled up in some stranded logs. My heart jolts in alarm until I espy Diomedes and Laas on the eyot midstream, with their horses huddled into the bank on this side. The two warriors are crouching behind the boulders that mark the gateway, while the surviving Pisans from the bunch across the river are massing on the far bank for another push, a dozen of them led by a beast of a man with a big war spear.

Laas has a bow – presumably taken from one of the dead Pisans. He and Diomedes have also managed to grab the slain Pisan's shields, which will help. As our horses reach the eyot, he waves us to dismount and get into cover.

'We've kept them pinned since they first attacked, but I've used up most of that bastard's arrows,' he says grimly, brandishing the bow at one of the corpses. 'Here,' he passes his last four shafts to me. 'You're a better shot. Bria, can you get the gates to open for us?'

He's been thinking along the same lines as I did. Just not as well…

'No,' I interrupt, pointing to Nestra's prone form. 'She'll intercede with Hermes and have us killed.'

'Not if she stays unconscious, she won't,' Bria growls.

'For three days?' I reply. 'You're mad.'

But Bria has turned her back on me, crouching down in the middle of the stone circle to avoid the Pisan arrows and raising her voice in the same chant Telmius used on the far side of Arcadia. '*Oh great Hermes, child of Zeus and Maia…*'

An arrow hisses past my face and I hunch down behind the shield Diomedes has provided for me, lining up my first shot.

'…*willing envoy to the immortal gods whom Maia bore…*'

A heartbeat later, the Pisans across the river lock shields and wade into the water.

We've no choice but to confront them: I leave Clytemnestra with Agrius and Bria, and join Philapor, Diomedes and Laas at the river's edge. As the enemy shuffle forward, battling the current, I take aim, seeking an opening, but my first arrow hits the shield wall, and so does the second.

'…*with beautiful hair who lay coupled in love with Zeus…*' Bria's voice is rising, edged with tension.

I curse, take better aim and lance my third arrow through a gap, and another man drops. But someone's been watching and counting, because the Pisans suddenly break formation and come barging at us through the water, roaring in fury, led by the giant with the spear.

Bria is shouting now. '…*WITH BEAUTIFUL HAIR WHO LAY COUPLED IN LOVE WITH ZEUS…*' she screams. By the sound of it, she's pounding the ground with her fist. '*FUCK YOU, HERMES!*' she bellows, abandoning the circle and joining us by the water, her face red with anger.

'Not so easy?' I mutter, making room for her in our shield wall. 'Maybe you got the spell wrong.'

'Just shut the fuck up and fight,' she replies through clenched teeth.

The Pisans are more than half way across. '*Do you even know who I am, fools?*' the massive spearman roars as he leads the charge.

138

'No,' I mutter, as I nock the last of the arrows Laas gave me and send it whistling at him. Driven by the superior power of the Great Bow, it plunges through bronze and leather, ribs and tissue, and he staggers backward before vanishing under the water. His men recoil, even as Diomedes and Laas charge, spray flying and blades slashing, bludgeoning the first men down as Philapor and I follow them in.

Philapor screeches, 'For Hera!' as the Pisans turn to run. He leaps on one man's back and plunges his sword down through the hollow of his right shoulder and they both go under, splashing as the water turns red. Laas beheads another from behind and the rest drop everything and plough their way back to the far bank, several of them stumbling on hidden rocks and falling, the river's swift current sweeping them down into deeper water, dragged under by the weight of their bronze armour.

We let them go – Bria's shouting from behind us. 'Back here! Grab your horses,' she cries.

I turn, and see what she means. The main pursuit is only half a mile away, and there's a red banner amidst the lead horsemen with some device on it that I can't make out. Tantalus's flag, no doubt. There's at least thirty soldiers so, even though we're theioi, we won't stand a chance.

'Come on,' I yell. 'We've got to ride!'

I grab as many arrows out of the turf as I can and stuff them in my belt. We mount up again, with Laas taking Nestra this time – I'll need my hands free to shoot. We're gasping for breath, our hearts pounding. Once we've reached the far bank I draw alongside Laas. 'Any idea who that moron with the spear was?' I ask.

'No,' the Spartan grunts. 'Hope it was Hyllus.'

'You think it was?'

'Nah – too short.'

'Poseidon's Balls, that's a scary thought.'

'Shut up and ride,' Bria tells us, clutching the purple-faced, shrieking baby to her chest and wincing at every wailing cry.

'This little brat has shat himself again,' she complains. 'I should have left him behind.'

Somehow, our final burst, following the path along the south side of the river, takes us to our ambush point. One moment I'm despairing, the next moment we're there, at a place where cliffs bound both banks of the Alpheios. A small waterfall plunges from the cliff on our side of the river, a torrent cascading straight into the river below, throwing up a cloud of spray.

Here the river's only a dozen yards wide, but fast, deep and swift, with no chance of crossing safely. Just short of the waterfall, there's a narrow path, wide enough to lead a horse but no more, which angles up the cliff, reaching the top some thirty feet above. Not a slope you'd want to be scaling when a crowd of archers and spearmen are above you, trying to skewer you. It's the perfect killing ground – though we have no spears and I'm running out of arrows again. But Agamemnon's men will be well-armed.

We all look up. 'We're here,' Bria cries as we rein in, beneath the cliff. 'Hello?'

No one answers. No one rises to wave. The only reply is a crow, whose cawing echoes about us.

'Telmius!' I shout. 'Amolus! Agamemnon!'

Still silence.

'Wonderful,' Laas growls. 'They aren't here.'

–

'If I ever see that bloody satyr again, I'm going to castrate him with a blunt knife,' Bria tells me.

We're crouched on the cliff top, waiting for the Pisans – there's no point trying to go on. Our horses are blown, and there are open woods on the river flats further upstream, where we won't be able to defend ourselves. We must fight here, and it's as defensible a spot as we're likely to find. The only real disadvantage with our position is that there's a steep ridge to our left which blocks our view of anyone approaching from downstream, though we should be able to hear them coming. The steep cliffs closing about the river prevent the enemy from outflanking us, without doubling back for miles – though it's possible Tantalus has summoned other forces to do so. We'll find out the hard way, I suppose, but at least for now, all we'll face is a frontal assault.

'I thought Telmius liked me,' Bria goes on in a whiney voice.

'Really?' I ask, raising an eyebrow. 'Bria, *no one* likes you.' I'm half-joking – but only half.

She looks at me solemnly. 'I suppose not… but I thought at least that he might want to screw me again.'

I cast a rueful look eastwards, where nothing and no one is coming to our rescue. 'I think he just did.'

'Hilarious, Ithaca.' She spits over the edge. 'Amolus probably led Agamemnon straight to the Gates of Cerberus.'

Then we hear the sound of hooves, and I glance left and right: the five of us are strung out along the edge of the cliff beside the falls, commanding the path: me, Bria, Laas, Diomedes and Philapor. Agrius and his cracked ribs are a little further upstream, with Nestra. The queen's awake, and tied to a tree nearby with strips torn off Laas's cloak, but we've left her arms free so she can breastfeed her infant. Agrius is there to make sure she doesn't untie her bonds, but he isn't quite sure where to look.

'We could threaten to kill her,' Laas suggests, indicating the queen.

'Tyndareus would gut us if we did, assuming we ever lived to tell him. And Tantalus knows it,' Bria replies dismissively. 'No, we either fight here or we split up and run, though that'll just give the huntresses sport, considering our horses are blown.'

'We shall stand and fall together,' Diomedes says, like a character from a storyteller's tale.

'There's a better chance we won't be taken alive if we fight together,' Laas agrees. 'Which is a good outcome. Believe me, you don't want to fall into Tantalus's hands, unless you're already a corpse. They say he's a master at inflicting pain.'

With that cheerful thought, we crouch lower as the first of Tantalus's riders appears round the outcropping that blocks our view of the land downstream – and our enemies' approach. He spots us immediately on the clifftop above, and is gone before I can fire. A few moments later, we hear horses whinnying, and the tramp of booted feet. They pause, just out of sight, and a rich and melodious voice rings out.

'Odysseus of Ithaca,' it says. 'Do you lead this infamy?'

For a moment I'm astounded. How does Tantalus know I'm here? Is that where Telmius went to, after he left us near the grove? Then I remember that Diomedes spoke my name in front of the altar, when appealing to Clytemnestra.

Before I can respond, Nestra shrieks, '*Tantalus! I'm here, my love!*' before Agrius jams a hand over her mouth.

'Nestra?' Tantalus calls. 'Don't fear, my love. We'll be reunited soon.'

'That's up to us,' I call back. 'And yes, I am indeed Odysseus.'

'How are you involved in this, Ithacan?' the Pisan King shouts. 'What offence have I ever caused to you and yours? Did you not dwell with my wife in Sparta as a youth? So why have Agamemnon and Tyndareus sent you to do their dirty work?'

'We're rescuing an abducted princess,' Bria hollers back, before I have a chance to speak, not that there's too much I can rightly say. 'There's no infamy in such deeds. That shame belongs to her kidnapper and rapist – you. You've imprisoned her for too long, Tantalus! It's time to give her up.'

'You are misinformed, Prince Odysseus,' he shouts back. 'You and your motley friends. My wife was not abducted – she ran away, and came gladly with me to Pisa. Our home together is no prison. There are no locks on the doors of our bedroom.'

Unfortunately, this is ringing only too true. I fight back a wave of guilt.

'Kill them all, my love!' Nestra shrieks. 'Kill them for me! They've got my baby!' Agrius tries to shut her up again and she bites his hand, leaving him hopping round, cursing fluently.

Holy Athena, now what do we do? I ask the skies silently. Then it strikes me: *Athena herself is the answer.* 'Summon Athena!' I hiss at Bria. 'It's our only chance.'

She stares, then swallows. 'No, never…'

'Why not?' I demand.

'Because if I die, with her inside me, we're both screwed.'

Well, that's that, then.

'Let's get this over with,' I rasp. 'Tantalus,' I call, raising my voice. 'You're a traitor to Achaea and a Trojan-loving son of a whore!' *This is rich, coming from me.* 'If you want your wife back, come and get her.'

As if they've been waiting for the invitation, a line of Pisan soldiers burst from the cover of the ridge, roaring war cries and with their shields held high. I fire what arrows I have, scoring several hits, but soon all my shafts are gone. When they realise that there are no more arrows, the Pisans shout triumphantly and come barrelling up the path towards us, with more emerging from behind the outcropping. In a trice the space below is filled with Pisan soldiers, who swarm up the slope, shields held high.

We've no spears, and we're five against at least three dozen. Apart from the shields we filched from the dead Pisans down-river, the terrain is our only friend, and even that's no more than an awkward climb. But as the first men come within reach, we all drop to one knee and hack and stab downwards. I deliberately batter the rim of the first man's shield, wrenching it sideways, and Diomedes plunges his sword into the man's exposed neck and shoulders. The Pisan gives a choked cry and falls onto the man below him, causing a small landslide of bodies. Pleading at the top of his voice to Hera, Philapor follows my lead, opening up his first foe to a slash to the throat from Laas, and another man collapses onto his friends, splattering blood.

The attack falters, but not for long. They advance again, crabbing upwards while the men below shout encouragement and curses, locking shields until – incredibly daringly –

Diomedes suddenly sweeps both his legs around and slams his feet into the leading shields with all his prodigious strength, battering them backwards down the slope while rebounding back onto the cliff-edge, evading a slashing blade as he does. Laas hacks an attacker's hand off, and he shrieks and falls away, blood spurting from the stump. Bria kicks a man in the face who's trying to flank us by scrabbling up the rough rock face; he teeters, momentarily stunned, and she slides her blade into his left armpit and skewers his heart, to send him tumbling down on his mates.

Once more they come at us, two abreast, braced against each other more tightly. Diomedes, Laas and I crouch at the top of the path with locked shields, and I repeat my earlier trick, hammering at the shield wall until a chink opens that Diomedes and Laas can exploit, while Bria and Philapor guard our flanks, battling the wave of men that edges up, up and up. More fall, more maimed than slain, but the weight of their surge is inexorable…

For the next attack, they try to take us at a rush – all of them coming on at once – turning their shields to one side and lashing out with blades as they try and gain the cliff top. I block a thrust on one side while darting aside from another and thrust straight-armed, take a man in the throat, in and out in a blinding lunge, block and stab.

Beside me, Diomedes parries three blades at once and slashes back, but Philapor takes a sword point to the arm and staggers, Laas kills one but is being driven back from the edge, while at the far end Bria shrieks a curse as someone with a spear almost skewers her face, before grabbing the shaft, pulling up on it and then slicing her blade down its length, chopping the attacker's fingers off. She hauls the spear up and then reverses it, jabbing it down into the shield wall below her, wounding another man, who loses his balance and topples backwards. But several enemy soldiers have reached the crest of the cliff…

I don't hesitate. Stepping in as my immediate foe plants a foot on the clifftop, I drive my blade down, through the collar of the man's armour and into the chest, wrenching the xiphos blade out and then sliding feet first under the men in front of Laas as they reach the top, hacking at knee tendons and hamstrings. I take three of them down in a tangle of bodies as Laas bellows and launches himself at them, cutting down another man who has grabbed me and raised his blade to kill me. I hurl him off me, down the slope and sweep two more men away – but a blade I never saw plunges into my side, below my right ribs. Philapor skewers the attacker for me and I barely feel the wound, such is my battle rage, despite the flow of blood. Diomedes weighs in, kicking another man in the face and off the cliff, and suddenly we're alone again, if only for a moment.

'You're insane,' Laas tells me. 'Look to that wound.'

'No time!' I shout back. We're dead anyway.

Then the Pisans advance again, stubborn bastards that they are, sensing victory and furious that a mere five warriors have cost them so dear. They attack in a narrow wedge, ignoring the treacherous rock slopes this time, where their footing is so precarious. I'm feeling sick from blood-loss, but I have to keep fighting. Laas, Philapor and Diomedes line up beside me and Bria draws back the spear she wrenched off her attacker. I glimpse Tantalus below now with his elite troops, directing more men up the slope, and realise that he's her target.

I'm thinking something even more suicidal – that maybe if I took a running jump I could reach him…

But then I hear a frightened yell and a low growl behind me and spin. Nestra has somehow untied herself from the tree and Agrius has dumped the baby on the ground to wrestle out his sword with one hand, while holding onto the queen with the other. They're both facing towards the woods behind us, from which an immense male lion has emerged, teeth bared and tail twitching.

Before I can cry out, the lion charges forward and leaps. Agrius lets Nestra go and lunges his sword upwards but he's too slow and the lion hurls him off his feet. Those massive jaws open, crunch shut on his windpipe and wrench.

Behind the lion, a lioness emerges from the trees and bounds over to Clytemnestra. There's a mark on her front paw – the mark where my arrow went in – but it's almost healed. *What else could I expect from a theia as powerful as Atalanta?* The lioness snarls at me as I take a step toward them, and I sense Bria turning. The other three are caught up in the fight, unable to look back.

It's all over now, a voice whispers in my brain.

I refuse to listen, lifting my xiphos and charging, as the air pulses like a sudden cold shivering, and an owl shrieks in the trees. I throw a glance sideways, eyes widening as Bria's body changes, from Spartan Meli to a tall and erect Attican virgin, pale-skinned with honey-coloured hair and grey eyes, a silver helm on her head and the stolen spear lengthening.

Bria's summoned Athena after all…

There's no time to dwell on that – if I let the lion leap at me, I'm done. So I run at it with what strength I have left, slashing at the animal as it recoils from Agrius's broken body. Clytemnestra sees me coming, screams and gathers up her baby, backing behind the lion. 'Hippomenes, kill him!' she shouts.

Part of me has already guessed his identity – Atalanta's mate, who like his theia wife has the power to shape-shift. These are older beasts, with scars on their flanks and too much intelligence in their eyes. I see the lioness – Atalanta – roar and charge at Bria-Athena, who jabs with the spear and forces the she-beast away. Then Hippomenes comes at me and my entire life contracts down to the space between us.

He claws at my front leg, twists from my slashing blade as I hurl myself away, then darts left and right, jaws snapping, paws raking but never quite in reach of my sword, trying to make me stumble, while the wound in my side sends stabbing pain through my torso, my brain finally catching up with my body. The blood's running even more freely now, soaking my tunic and thigh.

Then he sweeps round me, makes me turn, my feet tangle and I trip, his paws rip at my inner arm, my shield is torn away and the xiphos ripped from my numbed hand. Then he rears up, hot breath washing over my face as the contorted leonine face fills my sight, his immense body weight bearing down on me...

All my instincts from years of wrestling and the pankration kick in, as they did with Skaya-Mandu. I ignore the lost sword and grasp at the lion's waist, planting my feet and then wrenching with all my power. For a lion, being upright isn't sustainable, and he crashes down flat on his stomach. His legs thrash about as he tries to twist over and rake me with all four sets of claws. But I'm holding onto his scruff with one arm – the wounded one, slippery with blood, something I can't maintain for more a few heartbeats.

But my other hand grasps the dagger from my belt and I rip it out, and plunge it into the lion's rib cage. His whole body convulses at the impact, and I do it again – and again and again as his throaty snarl turns weak, and then I change grip, catch the great beast underneath the jaws and pull back then slash sideways, opening his throat.

He writhes into stillness as I hang on, drenched in gore. Then I look up.

Athena – it's wholly her now – is standing over the body of the lioness, who she's skewered on the spear, the pair of them caught in a beam of sunlight, a sight of transcendent, barbaric majesty. She turns her grey eyes my way and nods once, then turns to glare at our captured queen.

'Clytemnestra, be still,' she says in a booming voice, and the young queen goes rigid. The Goddess stalks toward her and pulls her to her feet. 'Child, listen,' she says. 'Aphrodite would say that it is better to love foolishly than not at all, but she is wrong. You're caught up in the great struggle of our time, and you have loved foolishly indeed. You must be strong now.'

The young woman just goggles up at her, awestruck and terrified.

I glance back, reeling as the punishment I've taken hits me – my lower legs have been raked with claws, my arm is torn and my side slashed, and I'm dizzy with exertion and blood-loss. I crawl from the dead lion's body as the magic that sustained the shape-change fades, leaving a naked man with grey curls and a heavy-set body dead in the dust beside a grey-haired woman with a similarly muscular frame, impaled upon Athena's spear.

Then with a choked cry, the goddess staggers and becomes Bria again, falling to her knees in the dust as the energy required to sustain the divine presence collapses. Bria finds it harder to act as an avatar than one solely dedicated to the role, and now I'm seeing the consequences. She looks at me despairingly, and faints.

I glance back to see that somehow, Laas, Diomedes and Philapor have held firm, at the rim of the cliff. But even as I register this, an arrow slams into Philapor's chest. From the trajectory, it's been fired from a position high on the other side of the river. I seize my shield and xiphos, and race back to the others. There are two women in buckskin standing on the top of the opposite cliff, and, as the second one looses, I throw myself aside and the arrow carves the air where I'd been.

We have no hope of fighting the men below us with these two able to fire on us at the same time. I rush back to Bria, hoping to save Meli's life at least, and start dragging her limp body towards the wood, as Diomedes and Laas take cover. The Pisans gain the cliff top, snarling with rage. And my theios hearing tells me there are more soldiers coming, from the east this time, the tread of many feet and the faint clang of armour approaching through the trees behind us, out of sight. We've lost control of the cliff and now we're surrounded on all sides. We're done for.

It really is all over. All I can do now is die well and hope someone bothers to tell my family.

I drag Bria with me into the bushes on the edge of the wood, as Clytemnestra lurches to her feet, grabbing up the baby. There's no one to stop her running to the cliff edge.

'Tantalus, my love!' she shrieks as she stumbles along.

She's taken in by a pair of Pisan warriors, while the rest advance on us, shields up as they fan out. They know we've no arrows left, they can see we're exhausted and they want blood, for the comrades lost and wounded. But they're in no hurry now. Diomedes, Bria, Laas and me – that's a haul for anyone to boast of.

Tantalus himself tops the cliff and strides forward to stand in front of his remaining men, removing his helmet to kiss his young wife, and to stroke the hair of his, now silent, baby. He's a darkly handsome man twice her age, with luxuriant deep brown hair and a shapely jaw.

'You abducted my lawful wife,' he accuses us. 'You endangered her and our child. You desecratedthe sacred rites of Artemis; and you have slain two of the greatest heroes of our lands, Atalanta and Hippomenes, whose names shall live long in our tales while you're rotting in Tartarus. I will give you the lingering, agonised death your crimes have earned.'

'Aye,' his men growl. 'Let's make these bastards scream.'

Even if we could run, our escape route has been cut off, and we're all too exhausted anyway. And I have no doubt he means every word he says.

I reverse the grip on my dagger. I'll not let them take Bria or me alive. Better a quick death than a slow agonising one. It's not the ending I want. Not with my heart broken, and so much still undone. But it's probably the one I deserve...

'Take them,' Tantalus growls, and his soldiers sweep forward.

11 – A Child's Life

'A man is weak-minded who puts the father to death
and leaves the sons alive.'
—Clement of Alexandria, *Miscellanies*

Pisa, Western Peloponnese

Before the Pisans can reach us, a mass of soldiers break from the trees behind us. To my eternal astonishment and relief they're screaming, 'Atreiades! Atreiades!'

In a moment a wave of Mycenaean warriors surges past us, slamming into the Pisans before they can form a solid defence line. The Mycenaeans smash through their ranks, and a furious melee ensues. I see Agamemnon himself leading the attack, joining in the fray with apparent abandon, hacking at the men of Pisa who are fighting despairingly to protect Tantalus and Clytemnestra. The two barbarians from the north, Elephenor and Patroclus, are with Agamemnon, and whatever else I might think they are, they can fight like whirlwinds – their longer swords bludgeon down the men before them, slaying the best of Tantalus's theioi, all the while whooping as if this is some great game.

The remaining men charge right round to the cliff edge to hem the Pisans in and prevent their escape. A handful of Mycenaean archers start firing across the stream, and I see one of the Pisan huntresses go down, leaving one survivor who is forced to run.

I'm so amazed, I almost collapse with relief.

Telmius hobbles out from beneath the trees, his bald head gleaming and his beard dripping sweat. He goes to Bria's prone form and wraps his arms around her, while I clench and unclench my fist.

'Where have you fucking been?' I grate.

'That confounded idiot Amolus brought them out through the wrong gate,' the satyr retorts. 'It took me an age to find them and bring them down here.'

'Where is that hairy-legged *koprologos*?' I swear. 'He just about cost us all our lives!'

Telmius gives me a wry smile. 'I don't imagine he's hanging round anywhere nearby.'

Which makes him a convenient scapegoat... Not that I have enough of a sense of humour at the moment to share the joke with Telmius.

'What happened to my Bria?' Telmius adds, stroking her temple.

'She took on Athena's spirit,' I tell him. 'To kill Atalanta.'

Telmius's eyes widen as he sees the impaled corpse over by the tree, and he hangs his head in sorrow. 'For many years there's been great friendship between Hermes and Artemis,' he says. 'I had huge respect for Atalanta. The great feud of the Atreiades and the Thyestiades claims yet more of our best.'

'That's the truth,' I sigh.

Please, all you gods, let it end today...

We look up, as a cry goes up for a truce. The Mycenaeans draw off, leaving a small group of Pisans clustered around Tantalus and Clytemnestra. Agamemnon confronts the Pisan king, panting hard, sword bloodied. 'Surrender, cousin,' he calls.

Elephenor and Patroclus join him. 'Let me take the head of this craven king,' Patroclus demands.

'Come here and say that,' a Pisan guarding Tantalus snarls.

The northerner idly points a finger at the warrior, marking him. 'That one's mine,' he drawls.

I leave Bria to Telmius and edge forward, even though I'm almost out on my feet. This moment could mark the end of the feud that's weakened Achaea so badly. Tantalus may well have more men coming – this truce is presumably to buy time. But with luck, they're still miles away; at any rate, I can't see any sign of them from here. My plan has worked, after a fashion, and this will be its bloody culmination. I need to see it.

It will also tell me much about what kind of king Agamemnon purposes to be, once his reign is unchallenged.

The High King pats Patroclus's arm and a few words pass between them. Then Agamemnon raises his voice again to address us all, in that pompous, entitled tone he so often adopts. 'It is *my* place, my *duty*, to end this matter.' He turns back to the Pisan king. 'Tantalus, we are honourable men. You and I shall fight to the death. Let the victor be the undisputed ruler of Achaea.'

I am stunned. *Agamemnon would risk this, on a fight already won? When Tantalus is a theios renowned throughout Achaea for his warrior skills, and Agamemnon is not a theios at all, whatever training regime he's put himself through…*

I can understand it a little: if Agamemnon makes a grand gesture now, he'll not just end this fight but remove all doubt about his right to claim the High Kingship. An execution would always taint his victory. He may feel he needs this to secure his reign, once and for all – and give the tale-singers something for the ages…

Everyone falls silent as they take this in, then Tantalus replies. 'Your offer is accepted,' he calls out.

Poor Clytemnestra makes a sobbing sound. 'Please, High King, I beg you!' she calls out to Agamemnon. 'We've done nothing wrong! I love my husband, and went to him willingly!' She holds her baby aloft. 'This is my father's grandchild! Have mercy on us!'

Agamemnon doesn't deign to reply. 'Help me prepare, my friend,' he says, clapping Patroclus on the shoulders. The two men turn and vanish into the trees, along with the High King's keryx.

Tantalus hushes his wife. I'm sure he believes that, other than through victory in the coming duel, he'll never be allowed to leave this place alive. Perhaps he even doubts that. Even so, he seems to be treating the offer as genuine.

I check on Telmius and Bria – she's still unconscious. Laas and Diomedes join us, stunned still over the suddenness of our rescue, and demanding answers of the satyr, leaving me to gather my thoughts.

If Agamemnon dies here, he's leaving Achaea wide open to the Trojans. And Tantalus will kill Menelaus, along with a lot of other people I care about… Including me…

It's not long before Agamemnon emerges from the trees again, with just his keryx, Talthybius. He's fully harnessed for war, his plumed helmet with its broad cheek and nose guards over his dusty, stubble-crusted and blood-smeared face. A clear circle has been created by hauling aside the bodies of the fallen, and Tantalus's men fan out round one side, with their backs to the cliff, with the Mycenaeans facing them on the other. Talthybius reminds us all of the rules of the duel – they are starkly simple: no other man may aid or hinder either fighter; and both combatants must fight with honour. Tantalus invokes Artemis and Hermes, but Agamemnon says nothing.

They close, armed with shields and xiphos only, eschewing the traditional javelin throws that usually begin such a combat, for neither man has one with him.

Tantalus is a very big man indeed, a theios and taller than Agamemnon by half a head, and it's quickly apparent that he's a fine swordsman. The Mycenaeans groan as their king is driven back and back, blades crashing together. Always Tantalus comes off better, each time calling out an invocation to his patron gods, Hermes and Artemis, as he evades Agamemnon's blows. He clearly senses victory.

So much for all Agamemnon's training sessions with Elephenor and Patroclus before we set out from Mycenae. I hold my breath as I recognise the same, slightly clumsy footwork, the same over-exertion, the same, small miscalculations…

The end comes suddenly – Tantalus delivers a series of thrashing blows at Agamemnon, and follows it with a thrust that catches the side of the High King's helm. Agamemnon staggers, and Tantalus lunges…

…and incredibly, Agamemnon arches his spine away, lets the blade scrape past him, the bronze rasping across the surface of his breastplate; but Tantalus has opened himself up and the High King slams his shield rim across his foe's face, breaking the Pisan's nose, making him stagger back.

And then, with an immaculate pirouette, Agamemnon drives his sword through Tantalus's chest.

The Pisan men moan – but Clytemnestra *screams*, falling to her knees as her husband collapses. The man supposedly warding her lets her go, and she scrambles towards her fallen husband. But before she can reach him, Elephenor grabs her, the barbarian wrapping a brawny arm round her throat, ripping the infant from her grasp and hurling her to the ground. The shrieks of mother and child fill the air.

Agamemnon wrenches out his blade, raises his fist in triumph – and then simply strides away, back into the forest. I stare, as his keryx, Talthybius, steps in front of those going to congratulate him, telling them to let him be.

'He goes to give thanks to the gods,' Talthybius says loudly. 'He will return soon.'

Possible, plausible even. Yet a foul suspicion fills my mind.

No one's paying me any attention, so I drift over to the trees then dart into their shadows, flitting deeper into the woods. I hear voices ahead, and let the sounds guide me as I move with all my well-practised stealth. In a few moments I'm behind a fallen log, with a view across a small clearing.

Patroclus is already half-stripped out of the king's armour, and handing what he's removed to Agamemnon. They're so close in build – tall, broad-shouldered – that Agamemnon's gear has clad him as though made to fit. They're both laughing and backslapping, as the northerner helps re-arm the King. I am stunned at the temerity of it; but also not really surprised at all.

I've just seen the king that Agamemnon purposes to be: devious, ruthless and unscrupulous.

I rejoin the fighting men just in time to see Agamemnon re-emerge from the woods, bareheaded and with his face freshly washed. He takes the acclaim of his men and no one seems any the wiser.

Clytemnestra is on her knees now, begging Elephenor for her baby, but he's taunting her, clearly enjoying her distress. I tap Diomedes on the shoulder and we shoulder our way through the press around them. I scoop Clytemnestra up, and confront Elephenor.

'Give her the child,' I tell him.

The northerner's ugly visage contorts in contempt. 'You don't tell me what to do, runt,' he snarls, holding the baby high in the air. Diomedes goes to grab at the boy, and in a blur of motion the Boeotian flashes out a dagger and plants it against Diomedes's throat. We all freeze.

'Heh, heh,' Elephenor chuckles, weaving the dagger about under Diomedes's chin. 'Not so high and mighty now, eh? Perhaps we need another duel, to teach you some manners?'

'Any time,' Diomedes growls.

Elephenor waves the wailing baby about, its head snapping back and forth and its limbs thrashing. 'Great King,' he calls. 'Here's the last of the Thyestiad line. Do you wish me to end it for you?'

'*No!*' Clytemnestra screams.

Agamemnon strides through the gathered throng and brushes Elephenor's dagger away from Diomedes's throat.

'There are things that must be done, Prince of Tiryns,' he tells Diomedes. 'This feud must end. May the gods grant that you are spared the strife I have endured.'

Diomedes hasn't exactly had an easy life either. Strange how everyone always values their own troubles more highly than anyone else's. And none more so that Agamemnon.

Agamemnon holds out his hands, and Elephenor drops the infant into his grasp.

'Please, please, kinsman, please,' Clytemnestra begs.

Agamemnon turns his back on her, breaks the child's neck across his knee and lays the lifeless body on the ground before the queen, who collapses in a flood of gut-wrenching tears.

'Barely a meal's worth,' Elephenor snickers, pointing to the dead child.

There's a collective sucking-in of breath. Perhaps this *suagros*, this absolute pig of a man, doesn't know of the slander spread by Tantalus a few years ago, that Agamemnon's father Atreus killed Thyestes's other sons, and tricked his brother into eating them?

But I bet he does.

I turn and walk away, dangerously close to committing a murder of my own.

My plan or not, the desired outcome or not, this is hideous. I am left bleakly certain that the gods are watching, and that one day, we will all pay for this. Especially me.

–

As soon as Tantalus was killed, the remaining Pisans fled for their lives, down the slope and away. A few of the Mycenaeans gave chase, but most of the enemy have escaped. I have no interest in their fate. I'm more concerned now with getting away from the poisonous circle of men around High King Agamemnon. Clytemnestra is being tended by Talthybius, the keryx, in the lee of the trees. She's cradling the body of her infant son, alternately keening and lapsing into a deathly silence.

Laas, Diomedes and I make our own camp beside the stream that feeds the waterfall, where Telmius is nursing Bria back to consciousness. I let her know what's happened and even she, the cold-hearted bitch, is a little appalled.

'I must go to Clytemnestra,' she says at once. 'Come on, Ithaca, let's see what we can do.' Still pale as a ghost, she limps over to confront Talthybius, who has stepped forward to block our way. 'Let me see her,' she tells him. 'She needs a woman.'

The keryx hesitates – he's probably under orders to let no one near the queen – but he clearly also has no idea how to look after her, and the dead child obviously scares him.

'Not you,' he tells me.

'He knew her as a child,' Bria snaps. 'Piss off and let us handle this.'

Faced with her burnished glare, Talthybius backs off.

I busy myself with practical matters –making sure Nestra has enough cloaks and blankets, fresh water and what little privacy we can muster; Bria does the talking, a low and continuous stream of soothing words and sounds. I don't catch all she says, as I come and go, but I do hear her repeating, 'Women are always stronger than men,' over and over again. 'We bend when they break, and we'll outlast them, I promise you.'

When the queen finally manages to speak, it's largely in broken, incoherent sentences, as if her brain can't deal with all she's seen; she leaps from thought to thought unchecked, leaving her tongue to muddle on. 'My dark magician… How could they?… The foul bastards… Poor, poor, sweet baby… Why are the gods so cruel?… Father would never let… Why isn't love enough…?' Eventually she falls asleep, her dead child in her arms.

I've been feeling completely useless, but suddenly I have the germ of an idea. I get up and walk a short distance away, beckoning to Bria to follow me, dropping my voice to a whisper, as I explain what I'm thinking.

At first she's cautious, but when I share all that I recently learnt from Laas, she gives me a terse smile and grips my arm in silent encouragement.

It might be workable… Something good might still come of this ghastly mess.

I leave her to return to Nestra and take my unwelcome self to the king's fire, where he sits with Elephenor and Patroclus, Talthybius hovering at his shoulder. Agamemnon frowns at my approach, but when Talthybius whispers in his ear, he signs for his guards to let me approach.

'Prince Odysseus, kindly join us,' he says coolly.

'Feeling better now?' Elephenor sneers.

'Had a little puke and a cry?' Patroclus snickers.

'The day I take pleasure in the death of an innocent child is the day I am no longer a man, but an animal,' I reply, looking not at the two barbarians, but Agamemnon.

Elephenor rises angrily, but the High King gestures for him to sit.

'I took no pleasure in it, either,' Agamemnon says. 'But if that black deed ends this ruinous feud, then I will account for it without remorse or shame before the Judges in Erebus, when my time comes.'

Interesting. It seems that appealing to Agamemnon's higher qualities can work – he wants to be *seen* as better than everyone else, even if his ruse over the duel proves that he's unwilling to risk himself in doing so. To him, victory justifies all.

'Your scheme worked, Odysseus,' he says, amiably enough. 'You always were clever.' He doesn't really mean it as a compliment, but I pretend he does. Cleverness is unmanly, to most men's eyes.

'Thank you,' I say, forcing a courtly smile. 'What do you purpose to do with Clytemnestra?'

'The prophecy you recited, from Dodona – that second-to-last stanza especially – still intrigues me,' he replies. '"*Golden eggs of the cuckold, caged birds born to sing together. Possess the twain and rule*". Clearly Tyndareus's daughters are the "eggs of the cuckold". Born to sing together, you say, and I concur. Tyndareus and I have the largest, most powerful armies in the

Peloponnese. It is time we formalised our alliance, through my marriage to Clytemnestra.'

I really have to school my face to not show my outrage, and I'm relieved when I find I'm able to respond evenly. 'Great King, I commend the intention, but you slew her husband and son before her eyes. Every time you touch her, she will smell the blood on your hands. For her sake, ask for Helen instead. Let Clytemnestra find peace.'

'For a woman, peace lies in marriage and children,' Agamemnon tells me, as if he knows. 'They're not like us.'

'They only care about breeding,' Patroclus puts in contemptuously. 'It's their nature.'

'Exactly,' Elephenor agrees. 'Plough her furrow a few times, and she'll be mewling for more,' His voice is crudely raucous but his eyes deadly cold as he studies me for a reaction. 'Get her with child and she'll worship you.'

Dear Gods, separate our High King from these pigs!

But what's clear is that these men have their hooks into Agamemnon already: if I, a mere companion of his younger brother, argue the point, I'll lose what little attention I can command. And my new plan is already wrecked by Agamemnon's announcement that he'll marry Nestra.

So I change tack, adjusting that plan into a new configuration. 'As you say, women put great store in their children,' I say in an agreeable tone. 'Nestra has just lost one, and her grief could make your marriage bed unpleasant. But,' and here I barely do more than mouth the words, my lips close to Agamemnon's ear, 'there's another child, an unwanted one, that might give her surcease of her sorrows, if given to her to adopt.'

From his expression, Agamemnon is already guessing where this conversation is heading.

'You're shrewd, aren't you?' he murmurs. 'Always had a glib tongue.' He sits for a moment, mulling it over. Then, abruptly, he turns to the northerners. 'My friends,' he announces. 'I must discuss a personal matter with Prince Odysseus. You are very welcome to rejoin me later.'

Once we're alone, Agamemnon studies me the way a merchant assesses goods for purchase. 'Tell me more.'

I share what I've just learnt from Bria: 'As you know, Helen returned from her abduction pregnant to Theseus. She's birthed a girl, but she doesn't want it. Theseus raped her, and she sees him in the child, even though it's a girl. They took the baby from her and fostered it out in secret – it is, after all, Tyndareus's first grandchild and he couldn't bring himself to have it killed. Meanwhile, Helen is still consumed by her trauma.'

'One reason why I won't marry her,' Agamemnon states.

That and because she scares you.

'On the other hand,' I continue, 'Clytemnestra has always craved children, from a young age. Give her Helen's daughter, to replace the son that tradition *forced* you to execute, and you will go some way to healing her. And a daughter won't interfere with the succession, when you and she conceive your own children.'

'It seems a big step, to adopt another man's child, merely to ameliorate the feelings of a woman,' Agamemnon says doubtfully. 'Especially for a High King.'

'The little girl will be a theia, and she will believe herself yours,' I point out. 'And what price can one put on a contented wife? Would you force her every night?'

He winces. For all his tolerance of the barbarians' bluster, Agamemnon had been raised to exhibit exemplary behaviour, whatever his private thoughts. 'But everyone knows I slew her only surviving child.'

'Spread a new story: that two summers ago, during the hunting season when Tantalus was away, you seduced Clytemnestra, and cuckolded the King of Pisa. Tell them the baby girl Nestra bore a year ago is hers and yours, that Nestra faked the baby's death to keep it safe from Tantalus's suspicions, falling pregnant again to Tantalus shortly after. Say that, with Tantalus dead, you and she are now able to bring the little girl out of hiding. You're the High King; your tale will be the one believed.'

Agamemnon frowns, but after a few sips of wine from is flask, he nods in agreement. 'Your prophecy… "*caged birds born to sing together*" and "*possess the twain and rule.*"… Surely that means that I must also see Helen wed?'

'Absolutely,' I tell him. 'Bind yourself to Tyndareus and Sparta through Clytemnestra; and bind another to both yourself and him through Helen. Preferably the third most powerful king in Achaea, whoever that is.' It's a matter of some debate. 'Between the three of you – yourself, Tyndareus and whoever Helen marries – you'll be able to unite Achaea.'

Against Troy, I add silently, to myself.

I have a sudden vision of our lands suddenly free of these ruinous feuds and civil wars, a united front that won't collude with the Trojans, but stand together in the face of their aggression.

'Yes, indeed,' Agamemnon muses, smiling now. 'I shall return at once to Mycenae, formalise my marriage to Clytemnestra, and adopt Helen's secret daughter. Then I shall prevail upon Tyndareus to put Helen up for marriage.' He strokes his chin. 'Let all the kings and princes of Achaea contest for her, and I'll choose the one that best suits my plans.'

Well enough, I decide, but a suspicion blooms in my mind. 'Not one of the barbarians,' I counsel him. 'You've seen and heard them – they aren't fit for any Achaean princess, nor to be married into our royalty.'

'Haven't taken a liking to my new friends, then?' he smirks. 'I know what they are, Odysseus: *savages* – but by Ares, they know how to fight, and there's a lot of the bastards. Thessaly, Epirus – all the kingdoms in the north – are jammed full of war bands led by men like Elephenor and Patroclus. The man that harnesses those wolves will have no rivals. We could crush Hyllus, and subjugate Attica as well.'

I don't like the sound of that one bit, but I know better than to say so.

The king's barbarian friends return, and I take my leave – drinking with that pair will lead to knife-fights. Rejoining Bria,

I tell her how Agamemnon received my plan and for once, she congratulates me.

'Good thinking, Ithaca,' she murmurs. 'Clytemnestra's likely to take her own life the moment we turn our backs, but Helen's child might be exactly the thing to pull her through. Gives her something to live for.'

Maybe, I think grimly. *But will… or can… Clytemnestra ever forgive Agamemnon for what he's done?*

Part Three: The Winning of Helen

12 – All roads lead to Sparta

'Indeed I would never blame anyone who weeps over
the death of a man and the unlucky lot he has drawn.
For this, above all things, is the honour due to poor,
miserable mankind, to cut off our hair and let a tear
run down our cheeks.'

—Homer, *The Odyssey*

Cranae and Sparta, Lacedaemon

Three months later, my galley rides the surf into a beach
sheltered by a small rocky island on the south coast of the
Peloponnese, a small port town called Cranae. As usual I'm in
the prow, calling the strokes as we ease our way to shore, the
white sand glistening in the late afternoon sun. The intervening
months at home have refreshed my crew, the late spring winds
have filled our sails on the journey and we're all eager for land
again.

We're not the only ones coming ashore here: there are a
dozen other ships beached already and more following. The
coastal strip in front of the town is strewn with travellers in
makeshift tents and lean-tos, a target for those who make a
living fleecing itinerants of their obols in return for overpriced
provisions and wine, and other services of a more dubious
nature.

I'm somewhat taken aback; the last time I visited
Lacedaemon, Cranae was a lazy backwater, overshadowed by

the main port of Helos a little further along the coast, which is where I had expected most if not all the suitors to head to. But Laas told me, back in Arcadia, that Tyndareus had given him governorship over this southwestern corner of Lacedaemon, and it seems he's been using the opportunity to good effect. Many of the houses in the town are new, gleaming with fresh whitewash and aspiration.

Given my unfortunate relationship with Tyndareus's twins and the uncertain welcome I'm likely to get as a consequence, I had hoped for a rather less conspicuous arrival than I'm now obliged to make. But there's nothing to be done about it. I'll just have to watch my back.

For anyone making for Sparta, Lacedaemon's ruling city, this coast is the end of a long sea journey, but provides the doorway to the easiest land approach – a gentle amble north over rolling hills to the wide central plain. Entering the kingdom from any other direction is fraught – Taygetus, a great wall of a mountain range guards the routes from the west, while the tangled mass of the Parnon mountains blocks the east. And north, of course, lies Arcadia. This means that most of the suitors for the wedding games will arrive by ship, on their way to Sparta, where Tyndareus is no doubt preparing to receive many royal guests and their retinues.

I gaze around at the crowds. There are men from Crete, and from the Aegean islands, and even a knot of Thessalian warriors, I note with a grimace. Since the word went out two months ago that the king of Sparta's astoundingly beautiful daughter is to be married to 'the best man in Achaea', every single king, prince and champion with an ego has mobilised. I'm already wondering if Tyndareus has underestimated how much interest there will be.

There's no way this is going to happen without me, of course. I've told my parents that I plan on competing for Helen's hand and they're supportive, if a little bemused. They think my intentions are genuine, and that I'm hoping that knowing Helen when she was a child might sway things. I know otherwise. I see my role as ensuring the right outcome for Achaea. Bria is with me, in the body of Meliboea, and she has similar intentions.

I've got Eurybates and my usual crew of Ithacans with me, good men if anything turns bloody. They all think it's going to be one big party, and I hope they're right. But I doubt it.

We're met on the beach by none other than Laas. The gruff, weather-beaten warrior is out of armour for a change, though there are plenty of soldiers around, and they're all doing his bidding. His new stronghold, Laos, is nearby, and he seems to be using it to maintain tight control over his patch.

'I recognised the northern cut of your sails,' he says, striding forward and offering his hand, as friendly a greeting as he's ever given me. Maybe our excursion to Pisa has warmed him to me. 'Thought it must be you.' He nods to Bria then walks with me up the beach. 'With fresh ships landing every day, it's been chaos here, trying to keep the peace and get the suitors on their way north.'

I nod toward the Thessalians. 'That's not you-know-who, is it?' I ask.

Laas spits. 'Aye, Patroclus and his clan. He arrived a day ago, and he's waiting for his mate Elephenor, then they'll ride north together.' He drops his voice. 'I'll be damned glad to see the back of them – they've been nothing but trouble. But I'll see them again in Sparta, no doubt.'

'So you're still hoping to win Helen's hand?' I ask, remembering our conversation on the mountain journey through Arcadia.

'Of course, and you've not forgotten your promise, to speak for me to Tyndareus?'

'Of course I haven't.'

He gestures about him, beaming with pride. 'Remember what a hole this place used to be? Since I took over, half the trade comes through here. Tyndareus and I have a good understanding.'

I'm still struggling to imagine Laas and Helen together, but it makes sense on one level at least: He's a decent man, a little on the rough side, but he would give his life for Tyndareus, and he's very capable. However, he's also nearly fifty and Helen's barely twenty, so I can't see this as a match she'd ask for – assuming she has any say at all.

'Of course I'll speak for you,' I repeat, hiding my doubts. 'But you might be overrating my importance.'

Laas smiles wryly. 'Oh, you're the talk of Sparta. Ever since you wrote to say you were coming to offer your suit, Castor and Polydeuces have been going round saying they'll arrest you over the Theseus plot, and string you up without trial.'

Knowing those two, this is probably true.

'A suitor is protected by the law,' I remind Laas, with a wink. 'Legally they can't touch me.'

'Legally, they don't give a shit,' he drawls. 'And you'll need to get to Sparta alive to lodge your suit formally before the law takes effect. Still, it's your balls on the anvil.' He claps me on the shoulder. 'I'll be keeping a close eye out for you, not that they'd dare piss on my patch.' He slaps me on the back. 'See you for a drink tonight – I recommend the big tavern on the far side of town – fewer beach rats, shysters and Thessalians.'

–

Bria, Eurybates and I get our lads settled into a snug camp at the end of the beach, close to the ship, then, as evening falls, the three of us head off through the township of Cranae which is squalidly overcrowded right now. Laas's men are keeping order, but I can tell, despite their apparent calm, that they're having a struggle. It's not our problem, but we don't feel altogether safe. The local lads are being crowded out by the foreigners, and there's some kind of push going on to reassert control.

Eury and I manage to look just intimidating enough that no one does more than wolf whistle at Bria as we wind our way through an area full of new stores, warehouses and bars and into an older part of the town, where there's less hassle. We find the tavern Laas recommended and order a meal – a mediocre but generous fish stew, washed down with some overpriced but decent ale.

Laas joins us, and I get the impression he's been to every tavern in the town on his rounds and been stood a drink in each – he's red-faced and a little bleary-eyed; we sit him down, and I set about trying to sober him up with what's left of the stew – and ply him with questions about what's to come.

'Make no mish— *mis*take,' he says, trying to hold himself straight. 'It's going to be a fuckin' mess. Tyndareus doesn't rightly know what he wants. *And* he's been ill, ever since we pulled little Nestra out of Pisa. Castor and bloody Poly have been riding roughshod over everything, I'm telling you. They've cooked up this scheme that every suitor has to pay a whopping great courting gift, just to be considered. No returns, no guarantees.'

Eurybates looks horrified. 'Surely not?' he asks.

I'm just as surprised. The traditions that surround wedding arrangements are old as time. The initial courting gifts are usually mere tokens, compared to the lavish gift exchanges that follow – the husband's marriage gifts and the bride's dowry – once the lucky man has been selected. These first ones, the dora, are simply to establish any prospective suitor's serious intent. What follows can occasionally vary, especially with high-class marriages; the husband's marriage gifts can be waived if some kind of competitive games are brought into play.

In this case, the games have been widely publicised. Now, it seems, the dora, effectively the fee to enter the games, is being vastly inflated. *And somehow, Castor and Polydeuces have neglected to tell me that… How strange…*

Basically, they're abusing the whole system, treating it as a get-richquick scheme.

'True as I'm speakin' to you,' Laas insists, lurching drunkenly on his stool. 'No guaran… tees, no fuckin' returns. I'm bleeding my lands dry to compete, and only because I know I've got some inside running, thanks to me an' Tyndareus being close.' He grabs my shoulder. 'You're def'nitely going to speak for me, right?'

'Absolutely,' I assure him.

'We've had at least forty wooing parties go north, between here and Port Helos, and I hear they may have as many coming again. Any prince with half a shred of ambition's goin' up there, rattling their spears an' trying to get Helen's eye. Gonna be some fuckin' disappointed buggers, an' some of them will be those northern bastards who'll cut your throat quick as look at you.'

He finishes this just as a large shape looms up behind him. I look up to see Patroclus, and he's heard every word, judging by the icy stare he's directing at the back of Laas's head. He glances at the rest of us with distaste as I stand.

'Sir,' I greet him, unsure of his title.

'My father is King of Opus, *Prince* Odysseus,' the Thessalian says coolly. Laas finally notices him and gives him a casual wave, blearily ignorant of the offence he's caused. 'Milord Laas,' Patroclus continues, 'I was hoping you would give me some guidance about the road north.' He pauses, for effect as much as any other reason. 'But you seem otherwise detained.'

''S no matter,' Laas answers. 'Join us if you like.'

Patroclus looks as if he'd just as soon not but he complies, and accepts a beer, swilling it round his mouth as if he's tasted far better before pushing it aside, while Laas gives him a rambling description of the road to Sparta. Patroclus is an unusual man for a northerner. It turns out, despite his crassness on campaign a few months ago, that he's been educated in some of the more cultured courts of the northern mainland. But there's something almost reptilian about him, an oddness I can't put my finger on.

For all that, he can be charming when he wants to be, and he seems to be trying to win me over, including me in his little asides and jests. At first I'm surprised and a little distant, but then I start to relax, even warm to him a little.

After a time though, a line of suppliants begins to form behind Laas's seat and it's clear he's needed in his official capacity, so we all rise. The tavern is getting over-full of northerners and the atmosphere is turning rowdy, so I give Patroclus a nod, wish Laas luck in whatever duties he has, and follow Bria and Eury to the door.

'Keep your back to the wall around that Patroclus, Ithaca,' Bria says as soon as we're outside.

'Really? I thought he was showing some human qualities at long last.'

Bria roars with laughter. 'Don't say you didn't notice. You're priceless!'

'Why, you think he's a backstabber and can't be trusted?'

Bria laughs even louder, and even Eurybates rolls his eyes. 'I mean,' she says, patting my behind, 'that he'd do *something over-friendly* behind your back, given half a chance. Nice arse, by the way.'

I go red. 'You mean he… Oh.'

'Didn't you see the way he was trying to give you the eye? Goodness sake, Ithaca! I thought you were a man of the world.'

'Well, it's his business,' I stammer. 'There's no law against it.' I thought I was a better reader of men than that, and I'm still not at all sure she's right. 'Anyhow, he seems a step up from that pig, Elephenor.'

Bria snorts. 'That wouldn't be hard.'

'I wonder,' says Eury, 'if either of them think they have a genuine shot of winning Helen?'

'Tyndareus isn't going to give his prize daughter to those animals,' Bria snorts. 'And I doubt Patroclus even wants her, unless she's got a wizzle hidden under her dress. But Laas is right – watch for them to cut up rough if they don't get their way.'

We're only a street or two away, when we hear shouting from behind us. Someone comes running by, hollering for the watchmen.

'What is it, man?' I call.

'It's the fucking barbarians,' he says over his shoulder. 'They're starting a fight!'

Oh, shit…

'It can only take a moment,' I exclaim to Eurybates and Bria, as we break into a run, heading back the way we came. 'Where are Laas's men?' I can guess – down at the port, where the real danger *ought* to be. We race towards the tavern and through the gathering crowd, as women shriek and men shout in alarm at the smashing of pottery and the sound of metal on metal. We have to fight our way through the press, pushing and shoving – and then a massive hand is planted on my chest, and a big shaggy Thessalian shoves me back into the crowd.

I peer around over the man's shoulder, to see Laas raging in fury, his weathered face ablaze with anger as he lifts his xiphos and stabs it at the neck of another armed man.

Patroclus.

What happens next seems to stretch ever so slowly over far too many heartbeats. Patroclus sways from Laas's easily-read blow, diverting the blade away and slashing sideways with effortless grace and precision, sending his long bronze blade crunching into the side of Laas's head, shattering his cheek bone and lodging in his skull.

The Spartan lord is dead before he hits the ground.

The Thessalians surrounding the duelling-space roar triumphantly, as Patroclus makes a show of dropping to one knee.

'No!' he shouts showily. 'No, I never meant this… But it couldn't be allowed to pass. My honour is my life.'

You bastard, I think, amazed at his temerity.

'Patroclus, what have you done?' I shout, earning another shove from his trained ape. This time I shove back, sending him staggering sideways. He goes to draw his sword, and Patroclus grabs his arm, while Bria grabs mine.

'Careful, Ithaca,' she murmurs.

171

'You saw how he was,' Patroclus says loudly. 'He was already drunk when I arrived, and the moment you left, he said something vile, the sort of thing no decent man should say – first about you and your woman, and then about me when I defended you. He drew – first. Everyone here saw.'

I look round the crowd, a sea of faces, some horrified, some stunned, some alight with a kaleidoscope of emotion, and damn him – damn them all – they're nodding to a man.

'Laas wouldn't do that,' I retort.

'Laas *did* do that,' the Thessalian prince replies, in the exact same tones. 'He came at me, murder in his eyes. I tried to disarm him, but it was him or me.'

I look down at the body, lying glassy-eyed in a pool of blood, the body of a man who I had a huge respect for, and a bleak sorrow settles on my heart. This is how the lives of warriors so often end – not gloriously on the battlefield but in meaningless brawls in squalid little towns, at the hands of murderous bastards like Patroclus.

He provoked Laas, I'm sure of it...

But I wasn't there. I can't prove it. And no one at all is speaking up for Laas. Perhaps I wouldn't either, if I was just an ordinary man and there were a dozen brawny Thessalians in my face.

Laas might never have become a close friend, but he was a decent man, loyal and generous and shrewd, and this serpent butchered him, probably only because he was an obstacle to winning Helen. I'm suddenly *very* afraid of what will befall us all in Sparta.

–

There's nothing to be done for Laas, but to grieve – and nothing at all I can do about Patroclus. He's claimed self-defence and there's a whole room full of witnesses who are backing him. The local captain of soldiery here takes charge, and the Thessalians are gone by dawn. I take my time following, because I have no desire to share the journey north with Patroclus and his men. I'm still certain the Thessalian prince deliberately provoked the fight with Laas, but I can't find anyone to break ranks from the tale that Laas was blind drunk and paid the price.

Except that I felt that he was sobering up by the time we left the tavern… But I can't prove that either.

We stay on for Laas's burial, so it's not until the morning of the following day that we too take the road, leaving a dozen men with the ship and bringing the rest – nearly forty of them, north with us. We treat it like a trek through hostile territory, with scouts before and behind us. We camp in the wilds, posting sentries all around us and don't go near the towns, which are filling up and turning as lawless as Cranae.

Finally, after three days, avoiding the increasingly crowded roads, we arrive in Sparta just as the sun sets. It's a place I know well, having spent my teenage years here, out in the middle of the plains, with Tyndareus's palace atop a well-fortified hill and the town spread along a low ridge to its south. The palace is large and luxurious, but still too small to permit all the wedding suitors and their retinues, so even great kings are having to set up their own mini-courts, either in the best houses in the town or beyond it, on the tail of the ridge or even in the fields of the plain.

It feels as though the whole of Achaea has descended upon this place, the visitors outnumbering the locals – and they're all armed to the teeth.

We've not seen Patroclus's men since Cranae, and because we've avoided contact with other groups, we haven't been able to tell whether Laas had been exaggerating about how many have come. He hadn't: there are dark-skinned Minoans with ringletted hair, and deeply-tanned islanders from as far away as Cos and Syme and Rhodes, who look more eastern than Achaean. There are richly-clad Atticans and wild-looking Thessalians, and even wilder-looking Abantes, Elephenor's people, brutal warriors from the large island of Euboea, along with swarms of lesser kings, princes and strapping theioi warriors.

And priests, everywhere you look: lordly acolytes of Zeus, imperious priestesses of Hera, muscle-bound followers of Ares, and the servants of Hermes and Athena and Aphrodite and even the eastern Apaliunas – or Apollo, as people name him here. Dancers and revellers of Dionysus flock the informal markets that have sprung up everywhere, and wary huntresses of Artemis stalk about.

They all know that Helen is more than just a bride.

My mind goes back to an afternoon, two years ago, when Athena took me to an assembly of the gods. I didn't really understand what a god was, back then – I still imagined they'd created us, that they loved us and were omniscient and omnipotent. I now know they're more like hungry ghosts, who love mankind the way a lion loves its prey.

Yet we who have a few drops of their 'divine' blood still serve them – mostly for our own ends, I suspect. I would be dead without Athena's intervention, and I will repay that debt. And hers is probably the only ethos among the gods that I can respect: wisdom and reason.

During that afternoon on Mount Ida – now referred to as 'The Judgement of Parassi' among those who were there – two significant things happened.

The first was that Helen and her brother Polydeuces were introduced incognito as children of Zeus, who invited every deity to bless them, giving them all the gifts the 'god-touched' can possess. Such bounty is very rare, and can result in madness, genius, or both. The man who marries Helen will have a wife who can twist the world around her fingers – if he lets her express her full powers. I'm sure she will someday rule us all, regardless of Agamemnon's ambitions, as will Polydeuces, when he reaches manhood in a few years.

The second major act of that bizarre afternoon was that Zeus contrived a 'beauty contest' between his wife Hera, my patron

Athena and Aphrodite, the Goddess of Love. The purpose of this farce was to put Hera in her place, and prepare the way for a new consort: Aphrodite. Gods and goddesses don't actually marry – they'd rather eat each other – but sometimes their cults grow stronger through such alliances. Zeus's purpose is to gradually disentangle himself from Hera and supplant her with a more malleable mate.

That night, his instrument was Parassi – supposedly a shepherd, though Kyshanda has put the lie to that. Aphrodite's proffered reward was 'the most beautiful woman in the world'. That person was clearly intended to be Helen, destined to be a mighty queen uniting two kingdoms, with Troy as the ruling partner, all under the aegis of Zeus-Tarhum, the east-west incarnation of Zeus. The King of Olympus is effectively betraying his own people, in favour of those of a bigger nation. That's the nature of gods, and the religion they inflict on us.

My priority though, is to get myself on the list of suitors before Castor and Polydeuces realise I'm here and make some stupid move against me. So while Eurybates settles our men into our camp, erecting tents on the fringe of the general chaos, Bria and I join the crowds trudging up the ridge toward the palace, the way lined by stalls and hawkers and, no doubt, spies. I keep a fold of my cloak over my distinctive red hair, and tell the guards I'm 'Megon of Cephalonia' – my standard alias – here to sell trinkets to Queen Leda. I have a token from Tyndareus himself, given me in friendlier days, that gets me through. Once past the gates of the citadel, I join the queue outside Tyndareus's reception hall, leaving Bria outside with my weapons to keep watch.

Inside the palace, I espy men I know, but I keep my hair covered and my face averted as we slowly shuffle forward, through the echoing vestibule and into the main *megaron*, Tyndareus's large and elaborated-painted throne room, where Tyndareus, Castor and Polydeuces are greeting those who've come to court Princess Helen. Tyndareus looks pale and tired, but his two sons are in their element, playing at being kings. This process is just a registration of sorts; the all-important gift-giving will occur tomorrow.

I see Diomedes presented – as a warrior prince of Argos, that ancient and lordly House of Perseus, he's a prime catch. Presumably his royal cousins have already arrived. Then King Menestheus of Athens steps forth. Patroclus follows, cutting a striking figure with his broad shoulders, blonde curly mane and tall, barbaric splendour. A giant named Aias of Salamis strides up, the biggest man I've ever seen. I've been lurking behind him, and no one's recognised me yet.

Now for the moment of danger. I give my name to the keryx at the head of the queue, and his eyes widen.

'Odysseus of Ithaca,' he calls.

The name silences the room. Then Castor and Polydeuces, hot-headed young giants, leap to their feet.

'Guards,' Castor begins, 'seize him—'

Then Tyndareus's voice cracks out. 'Be still! Prince Odysseus is welcome here.' He rises and comes to greet me, giving me a kiss on both cheeks while his sons watch, fuming. 'Through you, my dear daughter was rescued,' he murmurs. 'Any imagined misdemeanours are forgotten.'

'Not by all,' I note.

'But I am still king here,' he says tiredly. Up close his face is drawn and grey. He's been the bastion of Achaea, during the bloody years of Atreus's and Thyestes's feud, and it's taken its toll. 'We are honoured by your presence, Odysseus,' he says, raising his voice over the hubbub that has broken out. 'You dwelt with us as an honoured guest-friend, and it's as a guest-friend and son that I welcome you again.'

I smile back in relief. The king is still determined to cast aside the suspicions that have justifiably clung to me since the Theseus affair. I don't deserve this forgiveness, but I'll gladly take it.

'How is Clytemnestra?' I ask quietly, as I raise my arms in public salutation.

'Sad,' he says frankly. 'I don't think I will ever understand her relationship with Tantalus, and what she claims she's lost. If she is to be believed, she fell in love with her family's worst enemy. Other fathers would kill her for such a thing, but I can't. Atreus and Thyestes and their feud has crippled the lives of us all, but it's over now, thank all the gods.' He leans in and whispers in my ear. 'And she finds comfort in the infant girl – Iphigenia, she's named her. That was well-thought of, my friend.'

'Will she marry Agamemnon?'

'She already has, last week in Mycenae,' he tells me. 'He made his offer and she finally acquiesced – I wouldn't have allowed it otherwise. I was too ill to travel, and I understand Agamemnon won't be bringing her here: too soon, he tells me through his messengers. He arrives tomorrow, for the gift-giving ceremony.' He looks troubled, despite this supposedly good news. 'I fear, despite her agreement to the marriage, that she hasn't yet forgiven Agamemnon.'

'I'm sure all will be well,' I reassure him, though I don't believe that can truly be possible: as a child, Clytemnestra, for all her quiet manners, never forgave nor forgot – it was almost her defining trait.

On the one hand, it's odd that Agamemnon wouldn't want to flaunt his new bride in front of the assembled royalty of Achaea. But if Nestra is still traumatised, he can't risk her behaviour – she could easily use the opportunity to make him look foolish, or worse. And I'm glad – very glad – she can stay quietly at Mycenae with the little girl and hopefully find a way forward for them both.

With my name added to the official register of suitors, I am now supposedly untouchable for the duration of the wedding games. Castor and Polydeuces give me foul looks, but they're stuck with me. I give them a cheery wave before taking my leave.

Bria joins me as I exit, peering over my shoulder for any trouble, before tugging at my arm. 'Come on,' she murmurs. 'Athena wants to see us.'

–

We meet in a house in the town which Diomedes has managed to secure as lodgings. Bria and I enter a small upstairs room to find him and another Athena champion already present: Menestheus, king of Athens.

If there is a common characteristic among the theioi of Athena, it's that we're ruled by our heads. Even Diomedes, who isn't outwardly a thinker, restrains his emotions with rationality. But in this turbulent world, we're a minority. Most men, other theioi in particular, are ruled by the irrational forces of honour and ego.

That doesn't always make us Athena-worshippers nice people, of course. Not even his mother would claim that for Menestheus, a lean and lordly man in his late twenties, wealthy and with a reputation as a cold-hearted horse-trader. He's so reserved when we're introduced, he's bordering on disdain. I honestly can't see him winning anyone's heart, let alone Helen's. But perhaps he won't need to – his riches might be enough.

I'm puzzled why he hasn't already married, when many men don't expect to survive their thirties, but I'm guessing his ambition has caused him to wait for a better marriage than any he's considered as yet, while his reluctance to risk himself in the ugly slaughter of battle gives him no urgency to breed before being cut down.

Menestheus clearly has little time for me: an outsider from a remote island with no wealth, few ships and a tiny army compared to his. And he knows Helen despises me. He also knows I was neck-deep in the Theseus kidnapping plot. He's far more worried about being upstaged by Diomedes, who cuts a vastly more impressive figure as a warrior, is closer to Helen's age, and is devastatingly handsome to boot.

And that's us – Athena's three most eligible champions. There are others, but they don't have either the birth or the brawn to make them realistic candidates for Helen's hand.

We're joined in our meeting by an old woman from Tiryns who I met last year. Teliope is one of Athena's precious avatars – someone who can house the goddess's spirit for a worthwhile period of time. When we've placed guards outside the door and locked it, Teliope intones a prayer. Within moments, her spine straightens, her grey hair becomes lustrous and her green eyes go grey. A silver helmet appears on her head and an owl shrieks, somewhere in the night outside.

We raise our arms in supplication. Athena surveys us gravely, then indicates the chairs arranged around the walls. 'Please, sit,' she says in a cool, resonant voice.

Diomedes gazes at her with worshipful, even puppy-like devotion – he's both a believer, and madly in love with her. It won't do him any good; she's a virgin goddess. Menestheus is reverent and nervous, as though he doesn't know how to react to someone who outranks him. Bria's laconically obedient, while I'm measured and watchful. Athena knows I have another allegiance – to Prometheus – something she chose to live with when she claimed me and awakened my theioi powers.

Bria updates us. She has a full list of the suitors, and she's found out the planned program for the coming days. 'These are going to be old-fashioned wedding games,' she tells us. 'The suitors must compete in archery, running, boxing and wrestling – but not the pankration, presumably because of the danger of serious wounding and maiming – after presenting a "worthy gift" to the bride.'

'Which Tyndareus will keep, no matter what,' Menestheus grumbles.

'Running these things is expensive,' Bria says. 'Though I suspect, from what I've heard about the gifts being brought, that Tyndareus could run it for a year and never have to dip into his treasury,' she adds drily.

'It's naked greed,' Diomedes grumbles.

'But it's exactly what I'd do, given the chance,' Menestheus says seriously. At least he's being practical, though he clearly hasn't thought too hard about the potential for trouble from disgruntled suitors.

'A lot of these suitors will be too old or out of condition to run, wrestle or shoot,' I comment. 'Is this a sign that Helen will seek a younger man?'

I'm being provocative – Diomedes is twenty and Menestheus is in his forties. Although, as a king, he has to keep himself in some sort of fighting trim, he looks like the things he wrestles with most often are ledgers.

He shakes his head. 'The gift – and the wealth and power of the suitor – will be the only real measure. These games are just a ploy to distract and placate the younger men.'

He might be right.

'How are you placed then?' I say, more to provoke a reaction than to seek an answer – I know how much he's worth, but I'm curious to see how he views himself.

'Attica is a growing power. We trade all through the Aegean, and Tyndareus and Agamemnon recognise this,' Menestheus replies loftily.

I hide a smile. Menestheus might be personally rich – very rich, in fact – but Attica has a way to go before it can rival Mycenae or even Argos in trade.

'He'll only marry her to someone Agamemnon approves of,' Diomedes puts in, possibly to annoy the King of Athens. Agamemnon and Menestheus – two cold, calculating and paranoid kings – aren't the best of friends.

'That remains to be seen,' Athena says crisply. 'We must determine our approach, because this is a great opportunity to further our cause. Who are our main rivals, Bria?'

Bria has obviously been giving this a great deal of thought, because she answers crisply. 'Let's start with the champions of Zeus, and Heracles – they're working together. Their best contenders are Philoctetes, the famed archer; and Polyxenus, the King of Elis, who has plenty of divine blood and a strong war band. There are dozens of others but most of them aren't big names, not people Tyndareus would select. But the shock contender in the Zeus-Heracles camp is Iolaus.'

We all stare. Iolaus was the young companion of the mighty Heracles, until the demi-god died thirty years ago. He must be fifty by now, and the last I heard, he was advising Hyllus, Heracles's eldest son.

And he's been the driving force behind the possible Heraclid invasion of the Peloponnese. Has Zeus changed his strategy, or is Iolaus here in Sparta as the prelude for war? Is he spying or searching for potential allies, or hoping to exploit the violence that's already lurking under the surface?

'The word is that Iolaus and Hyllus have fallen out,' Menestheus comments, as if in answer to my thoughts. He should know: the war band of Hyllus is camped out in rural Attica, and Menestheus has been too frightened to do anything about them, not that he would appreciate being told that. They live like warlords, don't pay tax or indeed pay for anything at all. 'As you know, Iolaus has been wanting them to invade the Peloponnese but this cryptic prophecy about the 'third fruit' keeps delaying them. Iolaus has one interpretation, but Carnus, Hyllus's favourite seer, refuses to endorse a march.'

'Then Iolaus is the last person we desire to win,' Athena remarks, frowning. 'But is he really here to compete? Or is it a ruse – will Hyllus try to disrupt this?'

'My agents say no,' says Menetheus. 'They claim that the Sons of Heracles were shocked by the death of Tantalus – another reason Iolaus broke with Hyllus, as I understand it. He accuses Hyllus of losing his nerve.'

Perhaps... but in my opinion, Menestheus has been too eager to accept the most comforting explanation.

'Iolaus, Polyxenus, Philoctetes,' Athena repeats. 'They're not a terribly impressive trio of contenders, to my mind. I thought there would be better candidates from that quarter.'

'Meaning the real contenders are still under wraps?' I suggest. 'Trojans, perhaps?'

'*Trojans?*' Menestheus exclaims. 'They wouldn't dare!'

'I bet they would,' Bria retorts.

'Conquest by marriage,' I muse. 'But they know they can't appear here openly. So they disrupt, stall and wreck other's bids, then approach Helen on the quiet?'

'Tyndareus would never permit it,' Diomedes says flatly.

'But he's been ill, and still is, from what I just saw,' I respond. 'It's Polydeuces – *Zeus's son* – who's really running the selection process. An ugly scenario – especially when you factor in Tyndareus's rather convenient illness. Poison, maybe?'

'Investigate that,' Athena tells Bria. 'What about the other contenders?'

Bria scans her lists. 'For Ares, the top people are Aias of Salamis – that big brute of a man – and another Aias from Locris who's smaller, but a renowned fighter and athlete. Our new friend, Patroclus and his mate Elephenor, too. And Odysseus's old "friend" Palamedes is here as well, in Aphrodite's service.'

I grit my teeth. 'So many shitheads in one place.'

It's Palamedes that I'm most intent on – in Delos last year he tried to seduce the Artemis priestess, Penelope – or Arnacia as she was then – using magic, and then resorted to abduction when that failed. I've told him that if he tries anything similar again he'll face me.

'Hera has a number of candidates, but she's pinning her hopes on King Agapenor of Central Arcadia,' Bria goes on. 'He's young but already very capable. Since he's a neighbour of Tantalus, Agamemnon has backed him to take control of Pisa, lending him extra soldiers for the task. He's mature but still young, and he has a level head. A good candidate, because with him on board, Agamemnon would effectively control the whole of the northern Peloponnese.'

'He's a backwater hick,' Menestheus sniffs. The more impressive his rivals, the more put-out he looks.

'Hera's also endorsed Idomeneus, the King of Crete,' Bria adds. 'Crete is nowhere near what it used to be, though. I think this is just a favour to Poseidon – a token of friendship, to put pressure on Zeus.'

'If Hera and Zeus are considering reconciliation,' Athena muses, 'then such an overture to Poseidon could be a smoke-screen. In any case, he doesn't seem to have any candidates here – Pylos is where he has the strongest following, but King Nestor's sons are too young for marriage. But the real question for us is, how do we promote you two?'

She means Menestheus and Diomedes. 'And who do we back, if neither of you are selected?' Bria throws in, not even glancing at me, let alone rating me.

'I've just provided Agamemnon with a wife favoured by one of the most astounding prophecies in recent years,' I comment, not that it's going to make any difference. 'And helped end the worst feud in Achaean history; and given Tyndareus back his stolen daughter. At the moment, I'm the favourite son he never had.'

'Mmm,' Athena frowns. 'Maybe you can get in his ear and push him towards Menestheus or Diomedes?'

Thanks for the ringing endorsement of my own prospects, my Goddess...

'My best chance is the games, not the gifts,' Diomedes says. 'Tiryns is strong but it's not rich.'

'My focus is the gifts,' Menestheus growls. 'Backed by the prestige of Athens.'

'An obol each way, then,' Bria quips. 'Let's get Ithaca along-side Tyndareus, then see how the gift-giving plays out. If it goes well for Menestheus, we get in behind him, otherwise we shift our focus to the games, and Diomedes.'

'That seems reasonable.' Athena gives a tired sigh. Even when a pure avatar is possessed by their deity, the process is draining. 'Any closing thoughts?'

'That this could turn into a bloodbath,' I tell them. 'It's already started – Patroclus has effectively murdered Laas. Everyone is furious that Tyndareus has announced he'll keep every gift, not just that of the winning man. There are too many foreigners for the Spartan soldiers to control, and armed enemies are camping cheek by jowl with their sworn rivals and enemies. There will be violence.'

'A little violence could be twisted to work in our favour,' Bria suggests, her head on one side.

I stare at her. 'What do you mean?'

'Maybe if a few more of them can kill each other off—'

'Don't be bloody ridiculous,' I snarl. 'That's a perfect recipe for starting an all-out war – one that would consume the whole of Achaea.'

That assessment sobers everyone up.

'Read the crowd, Odysseus,' Athena urges me. 'And make sure it's Tyndareus, not Polydeuces, who has the ultimate say on all decisions. If we can guide him, we can at least prevent a disastrous result.' She pulls a sour face. 'If that means backing one of Hera's suitors over a Zeus or Ares candidate, so be it.'

'One person we didn't debate,' Bria says, scanning the list. 'Agamemnon's brother Menelaus is on the list.' She looks at me. 'He's your best friend. What are his chances?'

'I didn't even know he'd put his name forward,' I admit, my heart sinking. 'I'm not surprised, though – Menelaus sees a woman in distress and wants to rescue her. But Agamemnon wants a new alliance, or so he told me. Menelaus brings nothing that Agamemnon doesn't already command. It would double the marital bonds to Sparta, but at the expense of every other potential alliance. I don't think even Agamemnon will support his brother in this.'

Athena considers, then nods. 'I agree. He's not a contender. Anyone else of note?'

Bria shakes her head. 'There are dozens more, but they're no-names.'

'Then you know what do: Menestheus, remember to be charming, and don't stint on gifts. Diomedes, smile and flex a lot, but show no mercy in the games. Odysseus – get close to the king. And Bria – find out about the possibility of poison and whether Zeus really does have any Trojans up his sleeve.'

Her head sags, and a moment later, the goddess is gone. Teliope sits, swaying silently in her chair, until she has regained enough energy to speak.

'I heard it all,' she says, with a tired but serene smile. Avatars exist for these moments; to her she's just experienced Elysium. 'Athena be with you,' she says, with a touch of irony. 'You know your tasks, and I'll be around if you need my assistance.'

We thank her solemnly: we'll need all the help we can get.

13 – Gifts and Gambles

'Then and there, their knees were weakened, and their
hearts were bewitched with lustful desire, and all of
them prayed that they could lie down with her in her
bed.'

—Homer, *The Odyssey*

Sparta

None of the candidates want to go first, lest their rivals simply
add more to their own presents, in order to outdo them. But
someone has to start things off. It's a dilemma, and it has all the
kings and princes of Achaea stumped.

Inside the great hall, Tyndareus waits with his two sons, and
a hoard of assessors with weights and measures, ready to apply a
value to it all. The megaron is packed with priests, all declaring
omens and signs about this or that. Servants and courtiers are
everywhere, and so many strangers that the guards are having
palpitations.

Here outside the doors, everyone's got handcarts laden down
with golden bowls and two-handed cups, elaborately-woven
carpets and wall-hangings and embroidered gowns, Eastern
spices, ostrich egg goblets mounted in silver, plumes from
Egypt, ivory and ebony from Kush, finely-wrought bronze
weapons forged by the greatest smiths, and silks and fine linen of
surpassing beauty. The men guarding each cart are doing their
best to cover them over, to hide the full extent of the riches
within from other suitors' eyes.

The suitors themselves are gathered in a knot, bickering over order of precedence – not who will go first, this time, but who will come last. They all want to make the final, most triumphal appearance.

It's the sort of thing that can start a fight, and the sort of fight that can start any number of wars.

On a more mundane note, it means no one wants to enter the hall ahead of the others. We're at an impasse, possibly an insoluble one.

'Mine is a lineage unsurpassed on the mainland,' Prince Idomeneus declares. A haughty, haunted man in his early thirties and already widowed, with crinkled hair and oily skin, he claims descent from the great King Minos, whose hands were said to only ever handle gold. But Crete, his island kingdom, hasn't been a power in the region for many decades.

'I think the word "*main*-land" answers that claim,' Menestheus of Athens sneers. 'What Sparta would want with a backwater king I have no idea.'

'My palace surpasses Mycenae itself,' Idomeneus shouts. 'It's thrice the size of Agamemnon's stronghold.'

'But threadbare,' King Agapenor of Arcadia puts in dismissively.

'Gentlemen, I'll go first,' a voice says crisply, cutting like a knife across the chatter.

It's my voice.

'*You?*' they all sneer, then the smarter ones shoot me suspicious glances. '*Why?*' they demand.

I give them a confident, knowing look, and flick my hair. 'Better to catch the eye of the princess early, while she's attentive. Youth and good looks, you know. These young women have a short attention span.'

'It's wealth that'll decide this, not looks,' Agapenor sniffs. 'Not that you're overly blessed with either, Prince… umm…?' His voice trails off into a question, even though he knows *exactly* who I am.

'Oh no, this will be all about Helen and what *she* wants,' I tell them. 'I'm close to the family – I grew up with them, here in Sparta. I had quite a soft spot for Helen when she was a little child – sweet, wee thing she was – and I'm sure she remembers how kind I was to her.' *In fact we had very little contact – she was in the nursery and I was off mucking about with Menelaus...* 'Polydeuces is the one really running this, and he's devoted to his twin sister. He'll make sure she's happy first. All other considerations are secondary.'

They look at me with burning eyes, trying to work out whether I'm showing them the secret road to glory, or merely leading them up the garden path. The rest of the courtyard has fallen silent to listen, while the suitors around me suddenly decide it's vital to be among the early candidates. The whole process has reversed.

'*I'll go first,*' King Idomeneus announces, pushing me aside, and then they're all jostling for position instead of holding back, an undignified throng outside the vestibule, the giant entrance way to the throne room, kings and princes and their servants elbowing each other in a rush to get to the front of the queue.

But at least we've made progress. Tyndareus's keryx, Nassius, an older man I have known since I came here to live, has been waiting – the whole kingdom's been waiting – for half an hour for this wrangle to be resolved. Nassius throws me a look of pure gratitude, before returning to the megaron door, ready to announce us in turn.

I had no desire to be first anyway, so I seek out the best viewpoint instead, to assess the opening moves. Many other suitors decide to do the same, but I have a home advantage – I know all the tricks of sneaking around Sparta's palace, so I slip through a side door and onto the servant's stairs, which lead me up to the balcony which rings the megaron – a perfect lookout.

Menelaus is there ahead of me, and we share a grin, before settling down to watch the show unfurl. Just below us, Tyndareus sits, tensed, on the main throne, already drawn and tired. He's flanked by his sons Castor and Polydeuces on his left side – those two mountains of brash, youthful muscle – and Agamemnon and one empty throne on his right. It seems we're all still waiting on Helen, so this show can't begin after all…

Then my eye catches another familiar figure: amidst a knot of priests and priestesses of every god, lurking behind the thrones in advisory positions, is my grandmother – Amphithea, the high priestess of Pytho. I shrink back before she sees me – she's just as likely to point me out to Castor and Polydeuces.

But seeing all these priests here makes me wonder – what is Zeus's purpose in all this? Does he still intend Helen for the Trojans, or has that plan been abandoned, now that Tantalus, the Trojan's chief ally in Achaea, is dead? What other purposes intersect here?

But then Helen makes her entrance, without fanfare, from a rear door behind the thrones, catching Tyndareus's keryx unaware, so that she's already standing before her throne before he sees her. 'Her highness, the Princess Helen,' he hurriedly calls, his face going red.

Everyone goes wide-eyed at this first glimpse of the greatest prize in Achaea, the sacred bride to be.

She's slender but shapely, clad in a silk bodice and flounced skirt of dazzling peacock blue, with a gauzy veil hemmed in gold cast over her golden hair, which streams down her back and upper arms in a river of radiant curls. Her ivory-pale arms are bedecked in gold bangles and a wide belt embroidered in gold thread enhances her breathtakingly slender waist and full, curved hips and bosom. She pauses a moment, fully aware of every eye, milking their appreciation, and their desire to see her face, then slowly removes the veil and gazes out over the court, taking the weight of scrutiny with effortless ease, a playful smile creasing her perfect, slightly-parted lips.

Every man and woman present forgets to breathe, forgets that anything else exists but this one being. Their future queen, the woman who'll fulfil their dreams. A child of Zeus himself, the prize bride, a fantasy made flesh. Seemingly so vulnerable, just a slip of a girl, but she is silk draped over marble, with a presence that seems timeless. Her presence fills the throne hall, and suddenly all these kings, princes and warriors are mere shadows.

It's as if an avatar of Aphrodite and Artemis called both goddesses to their body at once. There is youthful expectation balanced with absolute poise, sensual promise wrapped in innocence. Her divine heritage glows within her like an unseen fire.

'*A tongue of flame that consumes, burning all that it touches*'... The last unexplained phrase from the Dodona prophecy leaps to my mind, and my mouth goes dry. *Is* she *the one who that's about – the flame we all want to hold, even though it burns?*

I'm less affected than almost anyone else present. For one thing, I've seen her before so her appearance isn't such a surprise. There's another thing: Helen once tried to kill me, during that damned Theseus affair – and when someone looks at you along the shaft of an arrow, mockingly recalls your shared past and then tries to put that arrow through your chest, a certain amount of empathy dies.

And of course, my heart has already been given, torn asunder and handed back to me in pieces, only too recently.

Even so, I still wonder a little how those lips would taste...

Menelaus, poor fool, is gazing as if he's never truly seen her before. *Poor fool.*

Everyone else seems stupefied by her beauty, her poise, and the promise of all she brings – divine favour, wealth and power. And for the men, there's the added allure of knowing that her gorgeous face could be the one he sees as he snuffs out the candles at night, and her perfect body the one he rides into the realm of Aphrodite.

As if all the world is merely a play for her amusement, Helen signals to Nassius, waiting at the doors, and sits down on her throne, ramrod straight. It's almost with disappointment that those present pull their eyes from her – if they can – to watch the suitors present themselves, and wonder if any mere mortal can be worthy of her.

'*Prince Idomeneus of Crete*,' Nassius booms, and the first of the candidates advances down the aisle, his face grim and lordly, like a man leading his warriors into battle. Idomeneus walks erect and proud, his waist-long hair oiled, bearing an ancient trident as a rod of office; though his true allegiance is to Hera, he retains some of the traditional emblems of Poseidon. His slaves are weighed down with bolts of finely-woven wool, the strands dyed in a startling array of colours, for Crete is famous for its flocks and the quality of its handwork.

Under the cloth lie chests overflowing with golden neck-laces and finely-carved ivory, and signet stones of beautiful, translucent agate, etched with tiny but exquisite figures and sacred images. He must have emptied his coffers to put together such a hoard, I'm thinking, which will have his nerves on edge. He comes before the thrones, makes his salutations first to Tyndareus, then to High King Agamemnon, and finally dropping to one knee before Helen, his arms outstretched beseechingly.

'I, Idomeneus of the line of the great Minos, extend my hand to thee, and offer marriage,' he recites formally. 'I bring you these gifts freely, and pray you will bless my suit with favour. Crete once ruled the Aegean and will do so again, with thy divine presence at my side, to bring us the favour of the gods.'

Ambitious, I think wryly. *And not the sort of thing to say in front of Agamemnon.* 'Nice of him to eliminate himself so soon,' I whisper in Menelaus's ear. I don't think he hears – he's still staring slack-jawed at Helen.

Idomeneus's servants busy themselves unloading the cart and arraying his gifts at Helen's feet. He stays looking up at her, and I can see him desperately looking for some sign of favour. Her eyes are shining, and after a moment of graceful pause, she extends her hand, palm down, and he shuffles onto both knees and kisses it, reverently.

Now he must move aside, his face alight with worship, while everyone else tries to outbid him.

'*King Menetheus of Athens!*'

Athena's favoured king stalks forward and doubles his rival's gift hoard, adding in a string of beautiful slave girls skilled in fine needlework and the promise of his fastest race horses. His coolly-calculating eyes glaze over as he too kneels before Helen and stumbles over his speech, all eloquence dissolving before her melting gaze. But she lets him kiss her hand nonetheless, which renders Menestheus speechless with adoration.

'*King Polyxenus of Elis!*' Nassius announces.

Like Idomeneus, he's widowed and in his mid-thirties, and with a reputation as a seasoned warrior. Elis is in the western Peloponnese, and they're traditional allies of Sparta. But it's not a strong kingdom, its wealth and strength dissipated by vicious feuds, with successive kings struggling to centralise authority. His gifts are nowhere near as generous as the preceding two kings', and everyone reads the dismissive looks on Castor's and Polydeuces's faces as a sign that he's already behind his rivals, though Helen still permits him to kiss her hand.

'*King Agapenor of Arcadia,*' Nassius calls out.

Agapenor is Hera's man, and something in Helen's shift of gaze tells me that in her eyes, he's far more to her liking than the older kings who have preceded him. I can already sense that, to her, the gifts are nothing, even though her brothers are drooling at the wealth piling up at her feet. Her eyes glint as she receives the man's booming declarations of love, and takes in his ruggedly handsome looks, deep chest and strong arms. He's a warrior-king, a fine theios too, and looks the part. As well as a staggering amount of richly embroidered cloth, a large casket of golden jewellery, and a string of slave girls even more beautiful than Menestheus's, he has brought more martial gifts – gilded blades and helms, and a decorative bow, 'because I know the Lady loves to shoot'.

Mmm, you'll have to watch that, I think wryly, remembering Helen's potshot at me, back in Erebus.

I lean in to Menelaus. 'Let's get down there,' I murmur. Eventually he hears.

We're about to leave the balcony when Philoctetes strides forward, clutching Heracles's Great Bow, the only bow in Achaea that can match my own. I want to see what he intends, so we wait, leaning over the rail to watch. Philoctetes is a prince of Methone, a northern region of Thessaly, with a highly strung, pricklish air. To my amazement, he has the cheek to pledge the Great Bow *if* and only if his suite is successful. His other gifts reflect a wild, poor region. But Castor and Polydeuces are eying up his bow greedily.

'Our terms are that all gifts must be given, verdict unknown, and will not be returned,' the young Polydeuces says loftily. 'Either you are a suitor, or you are not.'

Philoctetes flushes. 'The Great Bow is an heirloom from the greatest warrior ever known, given to me because I am alone in matching his ancient skill. It is mine in trust, only to be passed on to one who is worthy.' *Meaning a son by Helen, presumably...* He indicates the small jewellery casket he's also brought. 'These are my wooing gifts.' He bends and kisses Helen's hand, murmuring something that makes her colour slightly, then smile, which makes the whole room murmur. Perhaps he has skill with verbal arrows too.

Elephenor has already presented himself while Menelaus and I were hurrying downstairs; we join the queue at the great door into the hall as Patroclus steps forward, looking quite extraordinarily handsome in a gold-embroidered kilt and deep purple cloak that sets off his blazing blue eyes. He's armed with a load of rich furs, including a snow-white pelt from lands far to the north, in addition to looted weapons and jewellery. Once he reaches the thrones, I can't see him for the throng of heads in the way, but I hear him proudly reciting the names of the men he killed in battle to gain them, as if their shades are part of the gift hoard.

Then Aias of Salamis, a man as immense as his island kingdom is small, carries in a huge stag over his shoulder to lay at Helen's feet. Good venison, I don't doubt, but it looks very dead. His booming voice echoes round the megaron as he also promises an unlikely number of beef cattle. There's no sign of them here in Sparta however; the rumour is that he intends to steal them off his neighbours, who can't be very impressed.

I'm getting a bit frustrated now; my height – or lack of it – means I can't see a damn thing. So I deposit my rather modest jewellery cask on a table beside Nassius at the door and explain to him in a whisper that I'm not trying to jump the queue. He nods agreement and I elbow my way forward in time to see Helen making a show of touching Aias's huge biceps, and letting him kiss both her hands. *Both hands… He* has *made an impression…* Aias strides to his place beside a pillar looking like he's won already.

I cross my fingers for Diomedes, who cuts a fine figure as he strides forward and gives his lineage. As prince of Tiryns he's a decent catch, and his looks outshine everyone else, with the exception of Patroclus, enough to draw an appreciative sideways look from Helen to her brothers, though my young friend is clearly nervous of her.

After him comes a surprise contender, who wasn't on Bria's list yesterday: Prince Alcmaeon of Argos. He commanded the Argive conquest of Thebes last year, and he's a surly, malevolent figure. Last I saw him, he swore to hang me – yes, someone else that wants me dead – because we disagreed over what to do with the two Theban seers, Tiresias and his daughter Manto. He wanted to torture the former and rape the latter: I prevented both outcomes, and Alcmaeon is not the sort of man you thwart. He presents himself before the throne in all his glowering anger, and stalks out afterwards, his eyes meeting mine as he leaves.

He draws a finger across his throat. Looks like I'm not yet forgiven.

Then it's Menelaus's turn. As I watch, I'm joined by another suitor who sidles up beside me. A quick glance shows me a young man with a shifty face and dull-blond hair. As Menelaus goes on one knee before the girl he knew as a child, I wonder if he's thinking how little chance he has, even though he's Agamemnon's brother. Knowing him, he'll see her as a young woman who has suffered, and needs to be cared for, after the ordeal with Theseus and her resulting pregnancy. His noble heart burns to 'rescue' her, though I don't see a woman that needs rescuing – quite the opposite.

His gifts are generous enough to befit a man who represents Mycenae, and he's Agamemnon's heir, in the event the High King dies before fathering a son. But what he lays before Helen is noticeably less than Agapenor's gifts, and there's a reason – Agapenor is Agamemnon's first preference and the High King has been adding greatly to the Arcadian king's offerings.

'That one's weak,' the man beside me growls. 'No threat to anyone.'

'Mind your words,' I snap, looking the stranger up and down. He's another northerner, judging by his accent, with a burly but not overly tall build. He stinks of sweat and women – common *pornes*, judging by the smell, a mixture of cheap perfume and unwashed crotches. But it's his whole manner that sets my teeth on edge. 'I know Menelaus well,' I add. 'Who are you?'

'I am Aias, Prince of Locris,' he replies, without looking at me. His eyes are full of Helen, drinking her in with naked lust writ large on his face. 'Wouldn't you like to skewer that sweet piece of meat?' he drools.

'I'd keep such sentiments to myself, were I you,' I tell him, icily.

'Why? Isn't that why we're here?' Aias says, in a low, crafty voice. 'No doubt some rich pig will yoke her in the end – but meantime, we get to sniff around her fanny.'

I face him fully. 'You'll shut your face, or I'll shut it for you.'

'You? I don't think so.' His eyes flicker over me, then he looks back at Helen. 'Anyway, you're just like me –a chancer trying his luck, so you can tell your bastard grandchildren that you were here. And I bet that little wanton sleeps with her window open – she's no virgin, I'll tell you that for free. Women don't bat their eyelashes like that unless they've had a cock in them.'

Right, you dirty piece of shit…

I go to grasp his collar – and Nassius announces, '*Prince Odysseus of Ithaca.*'

Reluctantly, I let my hand drop, at which Aias of Locris snickers, 'Any time, Islander.'

'There will be a time,' I assure him, then stride, still seething, through the megaron.

About halfway across, I realise that in my fury at that Locrian pig, I've left my paltry gift box on the table outside, and that the whole court is looking at me like I'm an idiot.

Which I am.

I have a choice – to stand like a fool and ask someone to bring my little cask; or turn around and fetch it myself. Either way, the entire hall will have a laugh at my expense, and I'll have probably messed up any chance I have of influencing this event.

Or…

Bugger it, why not? I mutter, as my idea takes form. Because this whole process isn't going Menestheus's way – he's been outbid several times. Nor is Diomedes likely to shine – despite Helen's sideways glances. He's been noticeably overshadowed by Patroclus's dazzling good looks and Aias's brawn. Either this whole gift-giving larceny gets sidelined, or we, Athena's champions, have lost already.

So I stride forward, salute Tyndareus and Agamemnon and Helen, ignore the two princes because they loathe me anyway, and announce myself in a loud, proud voice. 'I am indeed Odysseus Laertiades, Prince of Ithaca, and my gift to you, Princess Helen, is my true heart, and my dedicated service, in the name of Achaea. I pray that you accept my offer.'

'No gift?' sneers Polydeuces. 'That's outrageous! Where's your honour?'

'None at all?' Castor echoes, angrily. 'How dare you mock our sister—'

'Peace,' Tyndareus wheezes, and despite his weak voice, his sons go quiet. He sits up – he still looks deathly, and he's been all but asleep for the last few suitors – but now he's interested again. 'Please, Odysseus, my ward and son of my great friend Laertes, explain yourself.'

'My King, you are as much a father to me as Laertes,' I reply, addressing him directly but burningly conscious that Helen is looking at me with piercing eyes, trying to discern what game I'm playing. 'You know me as only a father knows his son, and so you know how deeply I honour your daughter and all your family. But if my offer of love, companionship and respect is to be judged solely by the quality of my material gifts, then my honour and yours are diminished. These noble virtues cannot be purchased. And to avoid hubris and absurdity, I must tailor my worldly gifts to my prospects, which apparently are none.'

The hall is now silent, as they all try to work out what I'm saying – I've been deliberately obtuse, but hey, I'm thinking on my feet here.

Castor and Polydeuces are turning Helen's wooing into little more than a cattle auction, lowering the honour of Sparta. But do I dare say this out loud?

Tyndareus gives me an approving nod. *Perhaps he's come to the same conclusion?*

'We were invited to Helen's wedding games,' I add, emboldened now to speak for all the suitors here who are no richer than I. 'We ask no more than for a fair chance to compete for the hand of a beautiful young woman, as your invitation promised.'

Castor and Polydeuces are glaring at me furiously – in their minds they've already spent the gifts – and Helen is frowning. Agamemnon looks interested, though; who knows what labyrinthine thoughts are passing through his paranoid mind?

Then Tyndareus darts a look at Helen, whose face is now a mask. *Hiding what?* 'Your suit is of course welcomed, Prince

Odysseus, and my daughter is honoured,' he wheezes. 'And be assured, the gifts offered are not the only measure of any suitor, in my eyes or those of my daughter. And I value the sentiments you have offered, from the nobleness of your heart.' He gestures me forward, towards Helen, while the hall mutters at his words.

Those suitors that have already pledged gifts are now looking at me as though I've tricked them, as I kneel before Helen, who gazes down at me with suspicious eyes. 'I haven't forgotten a thing, Ithacan,' she murmurs, her voice like ice. 'Theseus said you aided in abducting me, until you dirty thieves fell out.'

'He lied,' I say, in a low whisper for her ears alone – *barefaced cheek on my part, given that I'm the one lying.* Up close she's flawless, her skin perfect, but she exudes – for my benefit – a glacial coldness.

'I will never marry you, you stinking fisherman,' she whispers back, while smiling for her father's sake.

'Then who will you marry?' I ask, mirroring her smile.

Her face turns sly. 'The man I want. Not some old fart my family try to foist on me.'

'Then choose well,' I exhort her, quite seriously. 'The fate of Achaea rests on your decision.'

'Whoever I choose will be victorious, won't they,' she murmurs smugly. 'So regardless, I win – and I really don't care who loses.' Her smile widens, showing her pearl-like teeth. 'Now piss off, before I change my mind about allowing you here.'

She offers her hand and I kiss it, though I'd rather kiss a cobra.

-

The rest of the gift-giving is more muted, as Tyndareus's words sink in, and people begin to think hard about the games to come. Most weddings are predestined – the guests arrive knowing who the groom will be. This openly competitive situation is very rare, and when it occurs, major gift-giving is only expected from the winning contender. And when games are used to determine who will become the husband, no marriage gifts from the groom are required at all. The only wealth handed over is the bride's dowry.

Castor and Polydeuces have broken that rule... and now their father has overridden them.

I can sense the consternation of some – the rich, non-martial kings like Menestheus – as it sinks in that their wealth may not buy them the prize. But others, like Diomedes, Philoctetes, and Aias of Salamis, will now fancy their chances.

The remainder of the suitors present their gifts – fifty-odd men in total are offering themselves today, most of them looking both angry and bitter, as they behold the greedy farce that has drained their treasuries – but few stand out as real contenders. My hackles rise as I watch the vile Aias of Locris swagger forward, and murmur something that makes Helen's cheeks go pink; and I'm still fuming as Palamedes, son of Nauplius, presents himself. He's a rakish man, a charmer with a glib tongue. When he sees me watching him, his face hardens. But he's an Aphrodite man – he won't come at me head on.

If he gets Helen alone, though, he'll use the same tricks he tried on a young priestess in Delos, a girl I helped to rescue from him. I resolve that, so far as it's in my power, that won't happen.

Eventually, though, I lose track of the contenders, studying Helen instead, trying to read her mood. So I don't really notice the slender, robed figure that arrives at my side until she plucks my sleeve.

'Hello Odysseus,' she whispers.

I turn to see the very same young Delian woman who had filled my thoughts not long before. She's wearing a pale green dress and a green veil with a pendant of a leaping deer hung round her neck. Her thick brown hair is tightly bound back, and there's a half-smile on her sharp, clever face.

'Arnacia!' I exclaim involuntarily, grinning with pleasure. 'I was just thinking of you—'

She puts a finger to my lips to remind me to keep my voice down. 'I'm called Penelope now,' she murmurs. 'Remember? Perhaps you're not thinking hard enough?'

Her words are chiding, but her smile widens as her intelligent eyes measure me. She must be here with the Artemis priestesses, a sworn virgin and a theia to boot, a seeress whose prophecies are widely sought. 'I'm surprised to see you here, pledging your heart to Helen. I thought another woman had won your love.'

She knows about Kyshanda – indeed they worked together to save my life, last year on Delos – but obviously she's unaware that our relationship has ended. I shake my head, my expression telling her what I cannot put into words. 'An Ithacan prince must set his sights upon the attainable,' I tell her.

'And you think *Helen* is attainable?' She laughs, and then touches my arm apologetically. 'I'm sorry your... er, eastern liaison hasn't worked out. You seemed a good match, in spirit if not rank.'

I'm reminded how much I like this woman, an admiration born of the adventure we shared in the seas west of Delos, in which Diomedes, Bria and I helped her escape from the rapacious hands of Palamedes and his vile father, Nauplius. I gesture toward that erstwhile prince. 'Does Palamedes still covet you, Lady Penelope?'

Her face hardens. 'I received a letter, not long after you returned me to the shrine at Delos, apologising for their "misunderstanding". Nothing since, thankfully.'

'If he comes near you, I'll gut him,' I tell her grimly, meaning every syllable.

'Thank you kindly, but I'm not short of protectors here.'

I look over her shoulder and see a knot of Artemis priestesses – including some theia huntresses who look like they'd happily put an arrow in my back. *Do I recognise any from Pisa?* I give them a cheery wave. 'I'm pleased they've let you off that dreary island,' I tell Penelope. 'I thought they'd lock you up there, to prophesize for ever more.'

She gives me a slightly sad look. 'So did I. And this is just a short interlude - we return there as soon as this is over.'

'Then I hope for your sake that Helen takes her time,' I joke. 'How do you spend your days on Delos?'

'I walk briskly around the island every day, and I swim,' she tells me, with forced cheeriness. 'I weave for hours – that's how my prophecies now come to me. And I have Actoris for company.' Her eyes twinkle. 'She remembers you fondly,' she adds in a teasing voice.

Actoris is her servant and companion, a plucky girl who kissed me in gratitude for helping her mistress, though nothing further happened between us.

'I hope she too enjoys your island life,' I say.

Penelope laughs. 'I urge her to marry, but she insists the local fishermen are all idiots. She says she'll marry when she's good and ready.' She looks at me frankly. 'I think she has dreams above her station, poor girl.'

'I know what that's like,' I sigh, ignoring the hidden meaning behind her words. 'Any new prophecies?'

'Nothing I could possibly share with that dangerous rogue they call the "Man of Fire".'

'Him? He's not so bad as people say,' I tell her with a wink, making her smile.

'He's got a lot of enemies in this room and very few friends,' she murmurs, her levity fading. 'Be careful, Odysseus. This place is like a tangled forest, infested with poisonous spiders and snakes. The gods are watching this place, and the stakes are terrifyingly high.'

'Thanks for the warning,' I tell her. 'What would Artemis consider a good outcome here?'

'I'm sure I can't say,' she says, a trace of regret in her voice that tells me that she still harbours doubts about her cult's alliance with Apaliunas-Apollo. Not so long ago, Artemis had no 'twin brother', and her mother was Achaean Hera, not eastern Leto. Penelope is a traditionalist, and her heart is with Achaea, not the East.

'Let's hope the outcome is conducive to peace and security in Achaea,' I tell her. 'Now, you be careful too. People have been watching us talk, and they'll want to know what we've spoken of.'

'The weather, and the state of the crops,' she says drily. 'It's good to see you, Odysseus. Regardless of our politics and allegiances, you will always be a friend, to me.'

She glides away, while I glow in that little moment of warmth. *What an asset she'd be for our cause.*

But I believe her vocation to Artemis to be steadfast, so that's not likely to happen. I turn my mind to more immediate matters – the last of the suitors has been presented, and Tyndareus – now exhausted and deathly pale – staggers to his feet to address the room.

'Thank you for your gifts,' he tells the room. 'The happy couple, whoever the groom will be, will appreciate them greatly. Their donors have been noted, and their generosity. As will the prowess of the men about to contend for her hand. Rest well tonight, my lords, for tomorrow the wedding games begin.'

He looks around the room – and his gaze finds me. 'Prince Odysseus, could you help an old man up the stairs?'

He's never needed such aid before, but now he's sick and weak, and I'm swift to go to him. As I help him leave, I can smell his sour, unhealthy sweat. But I'm pleased – and intrigued – that he's singled me out.

Get close to Tyndareus, Athena told me. *So far, so good.*

Castor, Polydeuces and Agamemnon join us in Tyndareus's private rooms, while Helen, giving me a burnished stare, departs to the women's quarters. No doubt her mother needs her. Leda has been a drunken wreck ever since Zeus's sordid seduction years ago.

The moment the door closes, Polydeuces rounds on me – he's only fifteen but he already towers over me, as tall as a full-grown man, and an exceptional one at that. He's more than just a theios: he's prodigiously gifted but he's still young and blind to all subtlety.

'What's this *pornos* doing here?' he demands of his ailing father. Castor steps in behind me, not a theios but still a mountain of muscle. Agamemnon watches with interest, and with a slightly bitter caste to his face: he too lacks theios gifts.

I'm wondering if I'll end up coming to blows with them, but Tyndareus intervenes. 'Settle down, my sons,' he says, in a weary voice. 'As I've already made clear, Odysseus is my ward and remains as a son to me. Theseus may have alleged that Odysseus aided him in taking Helen, but Theseus was a villain, and it was Odysseus who helped you rescue her. He will remain and he'll be heeded.'

'Thank you,' I say gravely, helping him into his seat and turning to face the two brothers. 'I really do have Sparta's best interests at heart,' I tell them, honestly. I glance at Agamemnon, who's settling into the other armchair. The High King just looks coldly amused by all this.

'Are you a suitor now, or an advisor?' Polydeuces grumbles.

'I'm a suitor, when it suits,' I tell him.

Tyndareus drums his fingers on the arm of his chair. 'Castor, Polydeuces,' he says. 'You must be hosts tonight at the banquet. I'm too tired to attend. Go now, and prepare.'

It's both a great honour, and a dismissal. Polydeuces is smart enough to recognise both, and they depart, grumbling. Once they're gone, I'm left alone with the two kings. *Time to learn their minds.* 'Did today go as you hoped?' I ask.

Tyndareus leans against the backrest. 'More or less,' he replies, his voice etched with exhaustion.

I shake my head. 'That gift-giving was a shambles,' I say, 'and it's infuriated a lot of people.'

'Hosting such a colossal gathering as this is costly,' Agamemnon retorts, 'though I suppose that someone coming from such a backward little kingdom as your father's would have little chance to understand such matters. That wealth will be used to pay the great number of mercenaries King Tyndareus has had to hire, as well as reward all his standard troops for the extra hours they'll need to work. And I can assure you, the more volatile suitors will see their gifts as an investment, a surety of good behaviour.'

So Polydeuces and Castor haven't been the only ones pressuring Tyndareus into this. 'I may choose to return gifts to the unsuccessful suitors later,' the king mutters, avoiding my eye.

Really? So why not tell them so?

'And there's another thing,' I add. 'Helen and her brothers seem to expect that *she* will make the final choice.'

'You shouldn't allow the girl even the pretence of a say,' Agamemnon says. 'Young women don't know their own hearts. As for this games nonsense...'

From which I gather he doesn't hold out much hope for Agapenor's success...

'You've proclaimed a *competition* for her hand,' I remind Tyndareus. 'If you backtrack on that, there will be a massive amount of trouble. Let this play out: the games might not mean anything in the end, but it'll allow the suitors to let off steam, instead of killing each other – or you.' I stare at Agamemnon as well as Tyndareus. 'I don't know what reports you've had from Cranae, but I firmly believe that Patroclus provoked and murdered Laas, whatever he claims. He saw him as a rival he could eliminate.'

Agamemnon gives me a warning look. 'Find a witness that says so. It was tragic, but these things happen when a man gets lost in his cups.'

He wants the Thessalians on his side, that's clear, so he's not going to turn on Patroclus. But Laas was Tyndareus's most trusted man. Even so, the Spartan king steers the conversation into more neutral waters, commenting on this or that suitor, and we converse civilly until Tyndareus becomes so tired he can barely sit upright in his chair. I call for Nassius to help the old man to his bed.

'Use your old room up here in the palace,' Tyndareus says to me as I prepare to go, an amazing offer in the circumstances. None of the guests bar Agamemnon and Menelaus are sleeping in the palace. 'I'd be grateful if you can attend the banquet, preferably to the end, and report back to me about anything untoward.'

I leave with Agamemnon, who turns to me as we pause outside the door. 'Menelaus is constantly pestering me to offer you a role in my council at Mycenae,' he tells me. 'Would that interest you?'

I'm taken aback, especially after his dig about my provincial status. Though it's nothing new for Agamemnon to deliver a blow with one hand and a caress with the other. Especially if he thinks he has something to gain. 'I didn't think you, er...'

'My brother is wet behind the ears, I admit, but you're clever,' the High King tells me. 'I've always known that. As for the business over Helen's baby – I'm grateful. It's given my wife some peace. You and I are ruled by our heads, Odysseus. But I also know you bring strange loyalties: Athena, Prometheus... I'm not sure what to make of that.'

'I'm for Achaea,' I tell him firmly. 'But I'm also heir to Ithaca, so I can't move permanently to Mycenae.'

'I'm not asking you to relinquish your position, though why anyone would cling to that meagre rock of an island escapes me. But perhaps you might become an informal counsellor to me, attending my seasonal high council? I need intelligent people around me, even if I don't always agree with them.'

'Then I'm honoured,' I reply. It's true – I am. And also intrigued. Perhaps Agamemnon was impressed by my display today – he's a calculating man, and devious, as I saw when he confronted Tantalus. Or rather, didn't confront him...

He gives what passes for a smile on his cold face. 'Excellent. Speak to my keryx about the dates.'

He wishes me good night and we part, him to the main guest suite and me to check out the small cell of my childhood, before I go downstairs. The upstairs part of the palace is quiet, but I can already hear the first guests arriving for the banquet, downstairs in the megaron.

The tiny, white-washed room is empty, except for a cot bed, already made up with simple covers, a small lamp on a shelf above the bed, and a stool by the window with a full water jug and a copper basin beside it. Under the bed, there's a pottery pot if I need to piss in the night. Even after five years away, the room still smells the same: linseed oil from the bed frame and the faint drift of lavender.

I'll have to head down to the feast shortly, but the day has taken more from me than I expected. I sink down on the narrow cot-bed for a moment – *just a moment* – and rest my head on the pillow, revelling in a sense of nostalgia when a crinkling sound has me sitting up again in a flash.

Someone has slid a folded sheet of parchment under my pillow. I kindle the oil lamp perched on a small shelf above the bed, and read. '*Odysseus,*' it says. '*Your life is in danger. Beware of the deepest shadows.*'

There's no name, and I don't know the hand. The letters are slightly inexpert, as if by someone whose writing skills are poor.

Who left the note? How did they know I would be using this room? How have they learned of this peril, and why won't they identify themselves? And how imminent is the danger?

My heart begins to beat double time, as all tiredness evaporates. I sit, listening to the growing swell of sound from the banquet below, and wondering what else the babble masks. Is that a stealthy footfall outside in the corridor? Is that really just the breeze that shifts the bushes far below my window? I let the lamp burn on, staring into the flame to steady my mind as my thoughts dart from one possibility to another.

And then my door-handle turns…

I've got my dagger out, heart thumping against my ribs, already on my feet even as the door swings open… and a shapely figure slips in and closes it again. It's a young woman with a lively face and curly black hair, and I recognise her instantly.

'Shh, it's just me,' she whispers – it's Actoris, Penelope's maid.

I blink in amazement. *How has she found her way to my room? How does she know I'm here?*

And then my brain, fuddled by surprise, finds the answers. She's Spartan, just like her mistress, and she will have visited the palace many times, before she and Penelope left for Delos. And my room? She'll know the servants well, being one herself, and whoever Tyndareus ordered to prepare my bed could easily have told her I would be staying here tonight.

Did she write the note? Has she come to warn me further?

But as she pulls off her cloak and starts to loosen her bodice, her real purpose becomes obvious.

'Not the weapon I had in mind,' she giggles, looking at my dagger with raised eyebrows. 'Are you all right?' she adds, hesitantly, when I don't react. 'Don't I please you?'

My mind is racing. Penelope has either organised this visit, to console me over Kyshanda's loss or, at the least, she's turning a blind eye to it. Did she not tell me herself that Actoris thinks of me fondly? And the girl is attractive, a little fleshy for my taste but pleasing to the eye. More importantly, I like her, and I was impressed with her on Delos last year for her loyalty and courage.

However, I've been raised *not* to sleep with servants, including other people's; my mother has drummed that into me many times. And right now, Kyshanda is still an open wound in my breast, and I'm still disgusted with myself over my coupling with the nymph, back in Arcadia.

But Actoris is here of her own accord, her face glowing in the lamplight with excitement and arousal. Am I going to punish myself for Fate's cruelty over my Trojan love? Am I going to spend the rest of my life looking backwards? Maybe Bria was right, about needing to let go of the past? In my heart and in my head, I know I'll never hold Kyshanda close to me again.

I go to sheath my dagger and realise I'm still gripping the parchment in my other hand. 'Did you write this?' I exclaim, waving it at her.

Actoris pauses, halfway through loosening her waistband. 'What's that?' she says, frowning. 'A love letter?'

'No. Quite the opposite,' I exclaim. I step over to the door, bar it and then close the window shutters as well before showing her the sheet. 'Is this Penelope's writing?' I ask and she shakes her head, puzzling over the symbols before look up at me in astonishment.

'"Your life is in danger",' she repeats. '"Beware the deepest shadows…" What does it mean?'

It's clear she knows nothing of it. *More and more strange.*

'Dear Actoris,' I say, gathering up her cloak and draping it over her shoulders. 'I'm really very flattered that you came.' And I am. But I'd rather disappoint her than risk us both being murdered as we roll amorously around on my cot. 'I think it's best if you leave now – if my life is really in danger, I'll not have yours imperilled as well.'

14 – The Games

> 'First of all, they challenged themselves with a foot
> race. The race stretched out from the very starting
> line, with all of them sprinting fast, stirring up the
> dust with their feet... Next they tested themselves at
> wrestling, that painful sport ... and at the jump ... and
> at discus ... and boxing ... for there is no greater glory
> for a man, as long as he lives, than what he might
> accomplish with his feet or with his hands...'
>
> —Homer, *The Odyssey*

Sparta

I escort Actoris along the corridor, my xiphos drawn and ready
and all my senses alert. But we meet no one, apart from the
guards at the top of the stairs down to the servants' quarters, and
I watch her head towards the kitchens and disappear. That done,
I make my way to the megaron, to do my duty by Tyndareus.

The banquet is something of an anticlimax. The king has
ordered the wine watered to a pale pink, and none of the suitors
wishes to talk to the others or to me. They're either guzzling
their food, as though making sure they are getting something
back for their extravagant outlay this afternoon, or pushing the
congealing meat around and around in front of them, staring
glumly at the tabletop, or glancing murderously around them.
The serious candidates aren't even present – they're getting
well-rested for the exertions of the morrow. Not long after the

meal has ended, the bard places his lyre back in its leather bag, and the swarms of servants wiping down the tables with wet sponges soon dampen whatever high spirits might have survived the dregs of the feast.

Back in my room, I check under the bed and bar both the door and the window again before settling down to sleep, my xiphos by my side. I wake the next morning to the quiet of dawn, alone and unassassinated, and struggling to free myself from a vivid and alarming dream.

I swing my legs over the side of the bed, taking a moment to ponder what meaning the dream might have. In it, I've been making love to Kyshanda, until I notice she has furry legs and cloven hooves, and when she reaches the height of her pleasure, she makes a bleating sound, like a nanny goat. I hear ribald laughter, and I find I'm surrounded by dancing maenads, their skimpy tunics baring one shoulder and splattered with wine. Behind them is Penelope, turning away in disgust...

They say dreams either issue through gates of ivory or of horn. The former are delusions, sent to deceive us; the latter give us glimpses of the truth. This one I'm scared to analyse at all.

I drag myself out of bed, feeling fragile, and thinly spread.

This is just a symptom of giving up Kyshanda, I tell myself. *I'll get over it... Soon...*

Or will I? I'm hardly an expert, I'm forced to confess to myself. After a few infatuations that went nowhere, followed by a pleasing but pale imitation of love with an Ithacan woman named Issa, what I had with Kyshanda felt pure as well as passionate, and it hurts to think that I may never feel that way about anyone else, ever.

But you will, the rational part of me insists. *You will love again.* Just the sort of advice I'd hand to someone else, all tidy and rational. But right now, my heart isn't listening.

I can't let myself be distracted further, though – I have a hard day before me. The competition is going to open with archery this morning, followed by a footrace this afternoon, wrestling tomorrow, and boxing the day after. Among the suitors are some of the mightiest men in Achaea. So I wash myself in the copper basin provided, put on a clean tunic and prepare myself mentally as best I can.

The archery competition is dominated by the famous Philoctetes, wielding the Great Bow of Heracles himself. He has a massive reputation as a master archer, and I've already heard that when he competes, no one even gets close to the standard he sets. Today is no exception, especially when Nassius, who is organising the games, sets up a variety of trick shots that make fools of most.

For my part, I don't use the Great Bow of Eurytus, despite having brought it with me. I'm sorely tempted but it would draw too much attention to me, when my role here is not to be a competitor but an instigator. And a spy for Tyndareus, alert to any trouble. That I have the famous weapon isn't widely known and I prefer to keep it that way. So with an inferior bow, and hiding my true abilities carefully, I fade early from the contest. A few people who know my skills, Diomedes and Menelaus amongst them, look at me curiously, but I shrug my shoulders, as if to say it's just not my day.

I'm also more than a little preoccupied with the parchment note. Everyone competing here is carrying a bow, and a stray arrow in the back might be easily managed to look like an accident. Unless the danger isn't coming from the Achaeans here, but from outsiders…

Philoctetes claims the prize, but that doesn't bother me: he's an arrogant, thin-faced reed of a man in his mid-to-late twenties, and despite a certain edgy charm, I don't think Helen's much taken with him.

The real contest will begin this afternoon, in the footrace. Our plan is to place Diomedes – handsome as Adonis and a warrior matched by few – right under Helen's nose.

A light midday meal is served for the suitors in the main palace courtyard. I've not long finished eating when I'm greeted by Bria, curvaceous and provocative in the body of Meli, and with the air of languid exhaustion that tells me her night was rather more eventful than mine. She sashays up to me, hips swinging. 'We have work to do,' she states, batting her eyelashes at me as though I'm longing to bed her.

'We both do,' I agree.

She takes my arm and puts her mouth to my ear. 'The best runners here are Aias of Locris and your mate Palamedes: nobble them, and Diomedes should win the race.'

'Nobble them?' I'm suddenly tense. These games and their rules are sacred: anyone who interferes with the natural outcome will be disqualified. And if they're suspected of deliberately using foul play…

'Trip the bastards up and bugger their legs,' she advises blithely. 'This is footrace as warfare, Ithaca.'

'But—'

'No buts. It happens all the time.'

'Not on my patch.'

She smiles at me sweetly. 'But your patch is so very, very small, Ithaca. And I know you'll be clever about it – it's rather important you don't get caught.'

That's the understatement of the year – deliberate interference at a contest as sacred as a marriage games can be punishable by death.

'I've met young Aias of Locris, and I know all about Palamedes,' I tell her, swallowing my doubts as best I can. 'Believe me, I'll have no trouble with motivation.'

'Mmm, it's no surprise that turd Palamedes is a good runner, is it? Think of all those bedroom windows he's had to flee through,' she sniggers. 'Good luck, Ithaca. Go out hard, and cut down those two arseholes so that Diomedes wins.'

She sways back through the courtyard, as the assembling suitors jeer or whistle. Then the giant Aias of Salamis sweeps her up and makes a show of kissing her, while the other men laugh or catcall, then he pats her behind and shoves her toward the courtyard doors. Bria gives him an over-the-shoulder look that almost has him following her out into the square.

I look around, checking who is and isn't here. The older men – Idomeneus, Menestheus, Polyxenos and a few others – are absent, disdaining the footrace. They know they won't win and have chosen to spare themselves the ignominy of working up a sweat in front of lesser men for nothing. Alcmaeon *has* shown up, but he's clearly drunk and out of shape. Among the younger men, I pick out those with a reputation for athleticism: Palamedes hasn't arrived yet, but Aias of Locris looks confident; and I know that Diomedes is no slouch. Nor am I, for that matter; my strong thighs are excellent in a sprint, though I tend to fade over longer distances, when runners with a more wiry build come into their own. It's the barbarians that interest me; Patroclus and Elephenor. Life in the north is no joke, and I suspect they'll have speed and stamina to burn.

Then Nassius orders a horn to be sounded, and calls us to attention.

'My lords, listen please! In a few moments, you will all parade through the central square in the town and out to the plain below, where King Tyndareus and his family await you. There, the race will begin – around the palace hill and the town three times, a distance of six miles. To the victor, the glory!'

That sets off a loud buzz of conversation – this is a longer race than any of us had expected. As I edge through the throng, seeking out Diomedes, I hear the unpleasant, rasping voice of the Locrian Aias. 'Once I get the little princess alone, I'll have her,' he's boasting. 'Once you grab a woman's pussy, they're meat in your hands. Never fails, I tell you.'

Whoever wins this, you're going to lose, I vow silently as I pass.

I find Diomedes, who seems well-rested and calm. I go over Bria's crude plan with him. 'I'll have to go out fast,' I tell him. 'Faster than I can sustain for long. Stay ahead of the pack, keep something in reserve, then once I've done my bit, push for the lead.'

Diomedes nods diffidently, his eyes on Patroclus. I nod. The Thessalian will be a big threat. 'Yes,' I say, 'keep an eye on that one. Those northerners can run, and he's a theios of Ares.'

213

Dio growls something under his breath, and goes into a series of stretches that make his impressive muscles flex and bulge. I do something similar, on a smaller scale. We watch the others as they watch us, everyone sizing up each other. Then Nassius calls us to move, and we all walk down from the palace through the town square and on down the hill. Most of us are silent, still limbering up as we go.

I know the track that we'll follow – Menelaus and I walked and ran along it many times, when I lived here as a youth. The start and finish line has been painted onto a cleared and flattened piece of ground at a crossroads, where the track around the base of the hill meets the main road. We ready ourselves, spreading out along the width of the line and warming up more urgently now, getting our blood pumping so that our muscles don't pull during the first, hectic sprint.

The whole town is here to watch, from house servants to craftsmen, to the sea of soldiers and servants who escort their masters. The kings, Tyndareus and Agamemnon, are now seated on a raised platform, along with Tyndareus's wife, Leda, and their three younger daughters, and Idomeneus and Menestheus and the other older men who have decided not to compete in the athletic contest. The royal party is surrounded by an array of priests and priestesses, representing every deity, in a sea of colour.

I glimpse Penelope's taut face and give her a brief wave, but she's talking to someone – a man. I feel a surprising twinge of jealousy, but when I look closer I see from her stance that she's not being at all friendly. And then I realise that it's Palamedes, her would-be suitor... and attempted abductor.

I bunch my fists and head toward them, but then her arm swings, open-handed, and Palamedes reels back, clutching his cheek. When he tries to face her again, a pair of Artemis huntresses close in on either side, and he's sent on his way.

Only then does Penelope see me – and her taut angry face softens into a wink.

Well done, you, I think warmly, following Palamedes with my eyes as he joins the runners. I drift in on his flank, unseen by my quarry, as Nassius calls us up to the starting line.

'Hey,' I growl in his ear. 'I told you never to talk to her again.'

He looks startled, then glances over my shoulder and decides he's got enough friends nearby to be brave. 'You don't have any call over me, you poison-mouthed runt,' he spits back.

'You're not so pretty with a red handprint on your cheek,' I tell him, and he flinches. 'Watch yourself.'

I back away – there's far too many Ares men around him and from what Bria's said, if I get caught up among them when the race starts, I'll be the one broken. Palamedes sneers as I edge away, but I'm not troubled. I know this racetrack very well – I ran it every day for years. My chance will come.

The crowd is thousands strong, chanting the names of their favourites. I hear Eurybates leading my lads in a rousing hymn to Ithaca, before chorusing my name, but that's just one drop of sound in a sea of noise. I wave to them and they cheer lustily as they wave back.

Then Helen arrives, flanked by her brothers and followed by a dozen Spartan warriors. The people go silent in awe as she ascends the platform to sit near her father, her demeanour alert, even eager. I wonder who she'll be cheering for.

Then Nassius blasts thrice on his horn, the first to warn us; the second time a few seconds later to ready us. At the third, we explode into action.

The first few hundred paces are brutal – Bria was right, this is war on the run. I'm not the only one here with an unsporting agenda, and not the first to strike either – I'm pushed and pulled, my feet are stamped on and several people try and trip me. Someone slams a fist into the small of my back and I almost go down. I'm wondering what the marshals are going to make of this lot – they can't disqualify us all, let alone execute us. So I give it back too, angry enough to ram my fellow runners with elbows flailing, fighting for space until I see a gap and explode through it, getting clear of the main pack and pelting along, now eighth in a field of over forty.

The seven in front of me must have gone out as hard as they possibly could to avoid the sort of melee I got dragged into, and they're strung out with the leader a distant twenty yards ahead – and it's Palamedes, as I feared. Elephenor and Patroclus aren't far behind him, then the giant Aias of Salamis, to my surprise. He runs gracelessly, but with real power. Diomedes is on his shoulder, with the archer, Philoctetes.

The nearest of the prominent runners to me is Aias of Locris, who has slipped into a steady, graceful lope, so I focus on him first. As we reach a low dip I know well, where the track is momentarily screened by willow trees, I close him from behind, ghosting in as he enters the shadow of the trees. He thinks he's pulled free of the carnage in the pack, running hard and freely, so he's not prepared when I lash out with my leading foot, clipping his ankles together. He cries out as he tumbles, rolling aside and rising in one fluid movement.

But I've veered to follow him, and as his snarling face turns towards me, I give him no time to react, slamming my fist into his jaw with a brutal running punch, and he goes down like a sack of meal.

I must admit to feeling a certain guilt and shame: this isn't how I was raised to race. But I've been given my mission and I'll see it through.

It all took seconds – I'm gone before the next runners enter the trees, and it's his word against mine that he didn't just trip, and we both know it. So I have no fear of retribution as I set off after the leaders, running as if this is the last lap. I need to use what strength I have as soon as possible; at this pace I'm going to blow out long before the finishing line.

I swiftly overtake the giant Aias, who is beginning to labour. He lunges at me as I dash by, but I'm ready for him and sidestep easily. Once I'm passed, some instinct has me glance back, in time to see him pick up a stone. As he hurls it at my head I dodge, and the missile whistles harmlessly past my skull.

He stoops to seek another, but the track is more open now, with a marshal positioned at the next bend, and he doesn't dare try again. I'm gaining on Diomedes and Philoctetes, when Diomedes puts on a burst that puts paid to the archer – he tries to keep up but soon blows out, gasping and swearing as he falls back towards the main pack.

We're out round the back of the hill now, with the eastern slopes rising sharply above us. I'm now shoulder to shoulder with Diomedes, who is only a few yards off the two northerners, Elephenor and Patroclus, with Palamedes not so very far ahead of them, running impressively. This stretch is lined with country dwellers, calling out encouragement as we pound by, with a few of Tyndareus's officials spaced out along the way, marking off names on wax tablets as we pass. I give Diomedes a nod and we put on another burst, to catch up with Palamedes before my stamina runs out.

I tear ahead, into a stony section with some awkward potholes and rock outcrops, overtaking Elephenor on a particularly nasty patch where any misstep would see me breaking an ankle, and haring past Patroclus, who throws me an incredulous look. 'It's three laps, not one, you idiot,' he pants, more amused than worried.

I ignore him, drawing as much air into my lungs as I can to sustain this last burst. Palamedes is only a dozen paces ahead of me now, his lean body well-suited to the task, his gait flowing as he eats up the yards. No wonder he's renowned for these damned long-distance races. But I'm not bad – even for something like this – I'm the best runner in Cephalonia, and have been since I returned home from my spell in Sparta, even before Athena claimed me. And this track was Menelaus's and my main training ground.

So yard by yard, I carve up the distance between us, so that when we burst back into the square and over the starting line, with the thronged citizens cheering themselves hoarse, I'm right behind him.

'*O-DY-SSE-US!*' my Ithacans are chanting. '*O-DY-SSE-US! O-DY-SSE-US!*'

I grin to myself and pour in more of my reserves. But I'm also conscious of a growing ache in my right thigh – the old wound sustained the day I became a theioi. It's been healed by both magic and time, but it's never been truly the same since that day. And now I can feel the deep scar tissue beginning to strain.

I'm up to just a few strides behind my prey though, and he knows I'm there. But the bastard keeps putting on a spurt, just as I'm about to catch him.

'I know what you're doing, islander,' Palamedes calls back. 'You can't catch me!'

He puts on another burst and now I'm really struggling, my face burning with heat, my lungs like bellows and every step jarring through my thigh as we sprint along the next straight stretch, the seductive shade of the willows at the end of it.

Nothing left… nothing left…

But somehow, I find more, veering toward a jutting boulder as we reach the crest of the dip and ricocheting off it, sailing through the air…

…and slamming into Palamedes's back, my left knee crunching into his buttocks as we collide and go head over heels down the slope, yelling as we tumble. He strikes the ground badly and flails to a halt at the bottom of the dip, clutching his left shoulder and screaming. I'm little better off, having ploughed into a clod of turf face first and bloodied my nose, so I'm lying dazed, only a few yards away.

I'm barely aware as Patroclus, then Elephenor and Diomedes in a duel for second, come rampaging past.

I sit up, testing out my thigh and wincing – a few more strides and something would have torn. Then I look across at Palamedes, who's glaring at me with absolute hatred on his face. But he's got a dislocated shoulder, and he's not much danger right now.

218

Job done. I stagger to my feet as more runners pass us, I tentatively put weight on my right leg – it's painful, and my run is over, but it'll mend quickly enough.

'You *fucking* cheat,' Palamedes snarls. 'I'll have you dragged before the marshals! I'll see you drowned for this! You *proctos*, you leprous piece of *pig* shit!'

All that profanity sounds funny coming from this snotty, lordlier-than-thou priapus.

'A pure accident,' I tell him, wiping blood from my face. 'I would never break such sacred laws as these. Do you want a hand getting that arm back into the socket? I know how to do it.'

'Go fuck yourself in Tartarus.'

'Whatever.' I leave him there as the rest of the field charges past, and gingerly climb out of the dip, heading back towards the town. If I amble along, making sure I don't strain my thigh, I should be back at the crossroads with plenty of time to see the finish.

As I set off, I can feel his eyes on my back, burning with pure malice. He is, I decide, not the live-and-let-live kind, but hey, we were already enemies. Nothing's changed except the intensity.

At this rate, my mysterious assassins will have to queue up for the right to kill me.

–

I make it back to the crossroads, hamming up my limp to reinforce the fiction I've withdrawn because of a serious injury. As the surviving competitors barrel past for the last time, I wave at them, putting on a woeful face. I find the watching crowd in high ferment as they await the end of the final lap. Eurybates and my Ithacan men are disappointed when I limp into their midst, after reporting to Nassius. We're commiserating when Bria slips her arm through mine.

'I love the smell of fresh man-sweat, Ithaca,' she purrs. 'How did you go?'

'Aias is out, and so is Palamedes. Last I saw, Diomedes was still duelling with the two northerners.'

'You should have stayed with him after doing the dirty on Palamedes,' Bria says tartly. 'He might have use of your talents yet.'

I give her a look. 'I just about liquefied my bones, catching up with Palamedes. And that old boar tusk wound is tearing again. You're lucky I can still walk.'

'Men,' she sniffs. 'Always boasting of their prowess, but never as good as they think they are. Let's hope Diomedes can do the rest by himself.'

'Yeah, "Thanks, Odysseus, you did great",' I mutter, but she's already gone, weaving through the crowd, while Eurybates and the lads give her dirty looks.

'You done good, boss,' one of my crew, stout Pollo, tells me. 'Don't listen to that stuck-up so-and-so.'

The lads have no idea who Bria really is. On our missions to Delos and Thebes last year, she was in the body of a Hamazan warrior woman. And 'Meli' is no warrior, and they've no reason to connect the two: they just think I have a penchant for cantankerous, mouthy women.

I clap Pollo's shoulder. 'I've got to attend on Tyndareus, lads. Cheer your lungs out for Diomedes, then go get a drink. I'll find you later, if I can.'

I work my way through the crowd, towards the royal platform where Tyndareus and Agamemnon are leaning toward each other in deep conversation. Castor, Polydeuces and Helen are huddled together, laughing excitedly about the race. The upturned faces in the crowd below them are just as reverent as the suitors', and suffused with excited joy, as if Helen's moods are infectious. Given her powers, they probably are.

I work my way to the side of the platform, where I'm recognised by the guards and helped up. I walk around the back of a dozen Spartan advisers and one priestess – who happens to be High Priestess Amphithea of Pytho – my grandmother. I'm expecting her to ignore me, but although her already hard face scowls, she deigns to join me.

'Grandson,' she says stiffly. 'You were unable to finish?'

'I chose not to,' I reply tartly. 'It must be annoying for you that footraces are so random, and the spirits can't foretell the winner. You could make a fortune that way, otherwise.'

'The spirits are not concerned with such paltry matters,' Amphithea sniffs. She's clad in a full robe, with her head cowled by a fold of her veil, her face wrinkled as she squints in the morning sunlight. 'They don't care.'

'But princesses do,' I note, indicating Helen, who is now straining her eyes toward the final stretch of road leading toward the finish line. 'And the outcome of this race could matter far more than the spirits might think.'

'Her choices will be made for her,' Amphithea says sourly.

'Do you think so? I rather believe that she will change the choices of those around her. That's part of her power.'

My grandmother has never forgiven me for being the son of Sisyphus, or forgiven my mother Anticleia for that liaison. Part of the reason is that she's stiff-backed and unforgiving; the other part is her allegiance to Hera, who hated Prometheus – as all the gods did, in the end. That's why he's chained up in Erebus being tortured, and why I have to constantly watch my back, even though I'm under Athena's protection.

'I see you've managed to inveigle your way into Tyndareus's confidence again,' she grumbles, but then with a visible effort, she unbends a fraction. 'I'm told we have you to thank for eliminating Tantalus?'

'I was involved. Athena wants the same things as Hera – to prevent Zeus's alliance with Troy from destroying Achaea…' I cast her a quizzical look. 'If that's still what Hera wants?'

Or is she continuing to seek her own accommodation with her 'husband' Zeus and his new eastern friends?

221

'That is still what she wants,' Amphithea says, glaring at me. 'But we were excluded from the attack on Tantalus. Agamemnon goes through the motions of worshipping Our Mother, but he's not asking my advice any more. Why is that?'

She knows nothing of my Dodona prophecy, that's clear. But she's the highest-ranking priestess of Hera in the world and she must be behind any overtures to renew the alliance between Hera and Zeus.

Do I reveal what I know...? I sense I can make gains here, so I lean in close and whisper, 'Why do *you* think you were excluded?'

For all her experience and guile, Amphithea's reptilian face flickers with anxiety. Is that because she knows that I know about her cult's duplicity? 'I suppose nothing is truly secret, is it?' she murmurs. 'I've heard a whisper too, that Dodona has been silenced, but Zeus denies it.'

The old game.

'Your whisper was correct – I went there myself and released Hera's priestesses, the ones Zeus had imprisoned beneath the shrine.'

Her eyes widen. 'Then you've done Hera a great service,' she says reluctantly. 'Did they prophesise for you before you released them?' When I smile knowingly, her face becomes hungry. 'What did they say?'

'This and that,' I tease. 'They pointed us towards Tantalus, for example. But they warned against involving you, lest you go straight to Zeus's people and share what you know with them.'

'We would *never* have done that.'

'So you say.' I look at her pointedly. 'But you're sheltering that viper Manto, the daughter of Tiresias, so why should I believe a word you say?'

We glare at each other – Manto and Tiresias almost killed me, and they've destroyed my sister's hopes forever: I'm not about to forgive anyone that shelters that sorceress.

'She's useful,' Amphithea says shortly. 'What matters is that the best Achaean candidate wins Helen.'

'It's not so important who wins Helen,' I reply, 'so much as who *doesn't*. As the field narrows down, we should unite behind one candidate – someone that Helen will accept, with the status and personal attributes to make her a good husband, one that pleases her. Diomedes, for example.'

She scowls again – Grandmother's default expression – but she's considering it.

'We'll see how things work out,' she says, peering out at the track as the noise of the crowd lifts. The leading runners have come into view, three of them strung out across the track, pelting towards us as the runners loom closer. We're forced to break off, for the noise has become deafening.

Elephenor, Patroclus and Diomedes have burst into a final sprint, the Argive prince in the middle with the other two trying to pincer him and trip him. Elephenor suddenly veers and sacrifices himself, trying to bring Diomedes down in a crash tackle, but Diomedes throws out a straight right hand and fends him off. The northerner goes down in the dust, and ironically, the extra thrust of the fend gives Diomedes enough momentum to surge up alongside Patroclus, right on the line.

'A dead heat!' Nassius pronounces, his massive voice rising above the roar of the throng. His announcement is met by boos, cheers and gaping mouths, as everyone swings round to see how Helen reacts. She's bouncing up and down on her feet, between her two brothers, clapping her hands together and squealing in apparent delight. It's all very endearing, and I'm sure she knows it.

All this blood, sweat, noise and effort, for you, darling Helen. It must do wonders for your ego.

I watch Diomedes and Patroclus square up on the finish line, their chests heaving and faces bright with exertion, and for a moment everyone fears – or hopes – that they'll come to blows, but instead the blonde Patroclus roars with laughter and throws his arms round the bemused Diomedes and hugs him.

'What a race!' the Thessalian bellows, thumping Diomedes's back. 'What a race!'

It's enough to make me wonder if I've misread the Thessalian, because his almost childlike pleasure in the contest and its even result seems genuine. But my mind goes back to the death of Laas, and I'm not convinced. There's something manipulative about the man, I'm sure of it. Diomedes, for his part, is initially taken aback, but then joins in the brotherly show, and it's with much mutual backslapping that they proceed to the platform.

Behind them, a lithe young man swarms past a limping, bloodied Elephenor to take third, and I notice that it's the Artemis priestesses who seem most delighted, including Penelope, who embraces the young man. I recognise him – his name's Eumelus, he's another from the north but he's a close friend of her oldest brother, a decent man, and a follower of Artemis, someone I've met in passing as a youth in Sparta.

I make a mental note to congratulate him, give a nod in parting to Amphithea, then make sure I'm near Tyndareus as the two winners are brought forward to be rewarded, both of them still sweating profusely – two prime examples of manly beauty. No wonder Helen looks charmed as they're introduced, their arms still around each other's shoulders as if holding each other up.

For the remainder of the day, the locals are going to be running their own footraces – hopefully less brutal. A number of Spartan families have taken their lead from the royal marriage games and have put their own daughters up to be wed to the winners, and there's a lively market for bets on the results, as well as dozens of food and drink stalls. An air of festival prevails, with music and laughter, a mood very different from that of the real competition.

On my way back up to the palace, several of Locrian Aias's mates try to get at me, but my fellow Ithacans close about me, and the scuffle breaks off after some pushing and shoving. I see other fist fights, and there's a general air of hostility – and the sense that scores will be settled in the wrestling and boxing contests that are to come.

But poor Palamedes won't be a part of that, I note wryly, as I see him being led away by his friends, still clutching his arm. Even a theios can't recover from such things that quickly. *Bad luck.*

But then I see Aias, the giant from Salamis, lumber past – he was well back in the field by the time he finished but he doesn't seem to care in the slightest. The wrestling tomorrow, he clearly believes, will belong to him.

I just hope I don't draw the big lug.

–

It's another gloomy night in the megaron, with the bard struggling to find any rousing song that doesn't depict some form of mutual violence. At one point, he begins a comic poem about Aphrodite's seduction by Ares, and the cuckolding of Hephaestus, but is soon shushed by Nassius. By now, the glum looks of last night have been replaced with more murderous ones but, though harsh words are spoken more than once, no blows are exchanged and no blood is shed.

They're probably saving that for the wrestling and boxing...

Once the dismal gathering has ended, and I've given my report to Tyndareus, along with a private recommendation of my own, I try to get some rest, with my door and window as firmly barred as before. But sleep is elusive and I end up spending too much time propped up, thinking about the day to come, and worrying at the slightest sound that seems too close to my door or window.

It's only now that I realise how stupid I have been today, running along the track around the town, where a killer could have lurked in any of the bushes I passed and dispatched me with ease. That dip with the willow trees would have been the ideal spot, not only for my own misdeeds but for my death. '*Beware of the deepest shadows*'... I'd assumed this means that I will only be attacked at night, and in the palace, but maybe not...

I'd been so caught up in our plans for Diomedes, I'd barely thought of it. That I survived does nothing to ease my nerves.

I have such a list of enemies here, it seems pointless to worry about who my intended assassin might be, so I try and think laterally.

Not many people in Achaea can write, but those who do, mostly kings, nobles and highly-trained bureaucrats, are well-practised, with firm characterful hands. This was written either by a child, still learning the craft, or…

The new possibility is so intriguing, it keeps me awake most of the rest of the night.

I rise before dawn, break my fast and then spend a good hour warming up down in the courtyard, ahead of anyone else, wondering if Tyndareus will have taken my advice. I'm eventually joined by a tired-looking Diomedes, who arrives in the courtyard wearing in the same clothes I saw him in at the feast last night, and reeking of alcohol. He's with the Thessalian, Patroclus, and they're laughing like they've known each other all their lives.

I'm instantly on guard. Patroclus is a little older than Dio, and a whole lot wiser.

'How was your evening?' I ask them both.

'Fine,' Diomedes mumbles, without meeting my eyes.

'Try not to get drawn to fight each other,' I advise them. 'It would be a shame to spoil a beautiful friendship.'

They don't even hear me.

I give my right thigh a good massage, to take some of the toughness out of the scar tissue, as the courtyard fills up – *everyone* thinks they can wrestle. Bria arrives, ignoring the men that call exhortations for her to come and give them a rub down.

'Want some good news, Ithaca?' she purrs. 'Your mate Palamedes has left town, after complaining to the keryx and being told that he could take his lies and piss off. He's screeching about collusion: if you listen carefully, you can still hear the whining noises echoing off the hills.'

'Nassius and I go way back,' I comment. *Good – one less person I need to watch my back over.*

Bria grins, then scowls as she sees Diomedes and Patroclus chatting. 'Why is Diomedes talking to that prick?'

'They seem to have bonded over dead heats and drink,' I observe. 'For an Ares man, that Thessalian seems to have way too much charm.' I think about Laas. 'No, not just charm… he can manipulate people.'

'Since their cults began to work together, some of the Ares men have been blessed by Aphrodite as well, where the potential exists,' Bria remarks. 'Not all of them just grunt and hit things any more – some have learned how to speak in whole sentences, it seems.'

'You think that bastard's trying to work Diomedes around to Ares?'

'I'd be surprised if he wasn't.'

'But Diomedes *worships* Athena,' I protest. 'Utterly.'

'I didn't say he'd succeed. Let's just watch them for now,' Bria says quietly. 'So, how are you at wrestling? Seeing as you won't wrestle me, I have no idea.'

I straighten up. 'As good as I am at sprinting. Or better. Best in Cephalonia.' It's true.

'*You?*' she says disbelievingly, running her eyes down my shorter-than-most frame. 'Really? Cephalonians must be smaller than I thought. I suppose you're Cephalonian boxing champion as well?'

I roll my eyes. 'Bria, there's a huge difference between the two. Wrestling is all about balance and skill as much as bulk and strength. And height can be a handicap. If you know what you're doing, being low to the ground gives you an advantage. I've won a lot of bouts like that. And I know what I'm doing.' *Short men have to work twice as hard to be regarded as half as good. I work hard.* 'Boxing depends on height and reach and bulk. You'll notice I haven't put my name down for that – there's no point in me being beaten to a pulp by some of these big thugs.'

'Well, you won't need to worry now. Haven't you heard the news?'

'What news?'

'Tyndareus is going to cancel the boxing.'

'Ah.' I give her a knowing smile.

'So you know about it, already?'

'I suggested it to him last night.' *So he took my private recommendation on board...* 'This lot...' I jerk my head at the other suitors, '...are getting a bit too frisky.'

'And it might spoil their pretty looks. Talking of pretty, Actoris, that maid of Penelope's, could well be a fan of your wrestling moves. She was giving you the eye all yesterday. There's a good chance she might have some interesting pillow talk...'

I had indeed felt Actoris's eyes on me – but I'd not given her anything back. 'I am not going to seduce a maid for petty gossip,' I tell her.

'You'll never make a spy at this rate, Ithaca.' Bria strikes a pose, one hand on her bosom and the other stroking her thigh. 'Perhaps you need some personal training?'

'I think we've had that discussion before,' I remind her. 'Why don't you check out the local goatherds, in case your Hermes friend shows up again?'

She's not put out in the least. 'What a splendid idea, Ithaca – your Arcadian girlfriend might be there too! We could do a foursome!' She snickers at her own wit, then changes the subject. 'So, wrestling, then,' she says with light, catty malice. 'Same plan as yesterday, Ithaca: Nobble some contenders so that Diomedes can win again. If you can last the distance. Unlike your running.'

She sashays off before I can think of a suitable riposte.

Midmorning, we're taken down to the central town square, where overnight Tyndareus's hardworking servants have created a circular wrestling arena, with a floor of hard-packed dirt. There's some space around it cordoned off to keep the crowds back, and a new royal platform directly overlooks it – we'll be fighting right under Tyndareus's and Agamemnon's nose, as well as those of Helen and her brothers.

Half of the contestants take one look at Aias of Salamis and pull out, so there's only two dozen of us entered. We're drawn by lot into threes, with each having to fight the other two in turn, and the overall winner progressing to a pure knockout. I'm drawn against Alcmaeon – who, once again, is as drunk as a maenad on a feast day to Dionysus – and, annoyingly, Menelaus.

My friend and I hug. 'I don't suppose you'd take a fall?' he asks, half-jokingly. 'Just for me?' He knows all about my wrestling skills – we grew up being tutored in the art together.

Unfortunately, the role Athena demands of me today won't allow for any such thing. 'I'm either fighting wholeheartedly, or going home,' I tell him. 'It would dishonour our hosts to do less.'

He sighs ruefully at the platform, where Helen's throne awaits her. 'Then I may as well go home myself.'

I eye him critically. 'You've filled out a lot since we sparred together, and you've always had the size and weight. You just need to be more aggressive.' I jab a thumb at Alcmaeon, and grin, 'Just direct it all at him, not me, of course.'

He laughs and slaps my shoulder. 'I think we'll both enjoy taking him on.'

Our trio are drawn to fight third, so we watch the first two – victories for brawny Elephenor in the initial rounds and the giant Aias of Salamis in the second. Then Menelaus and Alcmaeon are selected by lot to take the ring first, meaning I'll fight in the second and third rounds of our group. So I watch with pleasure as the aggressively drunk Alcmaeon has his face planted twice in quick succession by Menelaus, who certainly has picked up a trick or two.

I'm pleased for him, but Alcmaeon's whole demeanour is puzzling me. If you're here to win Helen's hand, why undermine yourself by getting pissed every night before the games?

Unless he can't help himself?

I've known many men with a drinking problem, and some are slaves to it. Yet, when we last parted, Alcmaeon was a cold-hearted, seething, revenge-obsessed killer, but no drunkard.

The next bouts fly by, as the crowds cheer and hiss their adopted heroes and villains respectively, while the royals look down, commenting loudly about technique, and the young women around Helen laughing behind their hands or cooing admiringly. Diomedes comes through his first round easily, and a few bouts later we're into the second round, and it's my turn.

I await the ballot, standing with a sweating, nervous Menelaus, and a reeking, silent Alcmaeon to see who I must fight: I draw Alcmaeon, which prolongs the agony of knowing I must fight my best friend. But I put that to the back of my mind and concentrate on the matter at hand.

We strip down to our loincloths, oiling our torsos and dusting our hands, then step into the ring on either side of the arena. Alcmaeon's swaying still, and as I size him up, I'm struck by two things – one, that in this state he's no threat; and two, something's really got to him, for him to be like this.

What happened? I know he's fathered a child on Manto – not a rape but a seduction, I'm told – but both she and the child have been snatched away from him. *Is this what has affected him so badly?*

I could almost pity him. Almost.

We stalk toward each other and face off. He towers over me and ordinarily he would be a real challenge, but not today. Nonetheless, I make little effort to slap away his attempts to get a grip on my shoulders, instead letting him bind as I grip him back. We contend like butting rams, shoving at each other with arms interlocked, low to the ground with legs wide. He's struggling for balance and I could have flipped him three times inside the first few seconds. But it's answers I really want from him, not empty success.

'What in Erebus is the matter with you?' I hiss.

Alcmaeon growls and snarls, tries to toss me and can't, despite his weight advantage, while I renege on two more chances to end it. Finally he groans. 'She's... damn well... here...' he mumbles.

The news staggers me. Manto must be with my grandmother's entourage… though Amphithea never told me, when we spoke yesterday. I curse softly.

Alcmaeon takes that for sympathy. 'I can't get her out of my head,' he moans. 'And now she's out there, looking at me as though I'm the lowest form of muck.'

No wonder he's in such a mess. From what I've seen and experienced myself, she can play with any man's head. And he's borne him a child, whom he's forbidden to see…

'Oi, Ithaca, are you here to chat, or fucking well fight?' I hear Bria screech from somewhere among the watchers. The crowd laugh and then they begin to jeer.

Fair enough.

I shift my footing while pivoting and twisting, and slam Alcmaeon to the ground on his back, locking up his arms and ramming a knee into his groin. He pukes as I rise, and shows no sign of being able to get up again. There won't be a second bout, let alone a third chance to throw him.

That wasn't nearly as much fun as I'd expected.

Manto's here… I rise, look for my grandmother, and then stare into the cluster of priestesses behind her.

Quite deliberately, the daughter of Tiresias lowers her veil and looks straight back at me, her regal, dark-browed face resolute and arrogant. Round her neck, she's wearing a magnificent necklace in the shape of a rearing cobra, and I catch a glimpse of her favoured scarlet clothing, beneath her cloak. She doesn't look like anyone's prisoner, but an honoured guest and adviser – which is exactly what she is, I'm sure.

Manto smiles coldly, and the golden cobra around her neck seems to move, as though it were real.

I wrench my eyes away, swearing under my breath as I stalk from the ring, leaving the servants to carry Alcmaeon out. Then I signal to Bria. She hurries toward me, her mouth open to give me a lecture – about faffing around instead of fighting, I expect – but I cut her off.

'Manto's with the Pytho delegation,' I rasp into her ear. 'Get Alcmaeon out of here, find him somewhere safe and sober him up. I want to know exactly what happened between him and that bitch.'

Bria's tirade dies unspoken. 'I'll see to it,' she mutters, patting my arm. 'You do what you must against your mate Menelaus. No more mucking round.' Then she's gone, waving to Eurybates to help her out. He shoots me a questioning glance, catches my terse nod and follows.

I look back at where Manto was standing. She's gone, but Grandmother is looking down at me smugly. I've half a mind to berate her, but I swallow my anger. *Pick your fights*, I remind myself.

My next one is with my best friend.

Menelaus and I walk out before the crowds together, with the sun approaching its zenith. The day had started on the cool side for early summer, but a cloudless sky and the press of the crowd mean that there's now a warm fug in the air, and we're both sweating already. As we turn to face the royal platform, I'm conscious that everyone here, apart from my small knot of Ithacans, is firmly behind Menelaus.

It's no wonder: he's tall, his hair is a mane of gold, and he's got a fresh-faced cheeriness that makes even strangers warm to him – and the local people remember his years in exile here in Sparta. Whereas I'm a just a short-grown islander, though there's no real hostility towards me. Some remember that I was here too, and that we're friends. There's some good-natured jeering, but mostly they just cheer for the beloved brother of the High King.

We bow to the royal platform, where the two kings have just clasped hands on a wager – shrewd Tyndareus knows that Agamemnon is compelled to bet on his brother, but that I know more about wrestling than Menelaus ever will. But I take a moment to focus on Helen, who is seated with her brothers. Castor and Polydeuces are of course barracking for Menelaus, and throwing me insulting gestures as if this were a tavern room brawl, not a contest for their sister's hand. But Helen's leaning back, appraising us both. She gives Menelaus a small, encouraging smile, and his face lights up. All his chivalrous instincts toward a vulnerable woman are there, plain to see. I watch his resolve double, then triple.

I'm going to feel wretched when I destroy his dream.

'Prepare,' Nassius calls.

We embrace, then go to our corners to dust our hands. I meet Menelaus's eyes across the ring, see resolve and pride – he won't ask for me to take a fall again, not in earnest. He's bigger than me, taller and maybe stronger.

I plant him on his face inside six seconds and win the first bout. The second takes twelve seconds.

'I'm sorry,' I murmur as I rise.

There's some good-natured booing, but a win's a win. I salute the kings, then Helen. Up so close, her skin is flawless, lustrous, and there's such glow to her that even somewhat disinterested as I am, I find myself holding my breath and staring.

'Aias of Salamis will break your spine,' Polydeuces sneers. 'I've asked him to cripple you, as a personal favour.'

I ignore him. 'I trust the princess is enjoying all this effort being expended on her behalf?' I ask the coolly-amused young woman.

'I always enjoy seeing big, handsome men working up a sweat,' she says, in a distant voice. Then she leans forward and whispers, 'But small, ugly, fishy-smelling men make me sick.'

'Have you made your choice yet?' I ask, just to see what she says.

'I don't see anyone worthy of me,' she replies with a tight little grimace, quickly disguised as a ladylike simper. 'Not in this barbaric backwater. But I'm sure my noble father will provide one.'

'There's so much more wealth in the east, isn't there?' I observe, watching her closely.

Her face tightens as she realises she's revealed more than she intended. But Polydeuces comes to her rescue. 'Accept your win and get out, Ithacan,' he growls.

'Yes, walk while you still can,' Castor adds.

'If I were permitted to compete,' Polydeuces adds, 'I'd kill you.' Given the blessings he's received as a theios, he might well be right.

I pretend for the crowd's sake that the princes are offering encouragement, and back away, sharing a smile with Tyndareus, who's just fleeced Agamemnon in their wager.

Menelaus is waiting for me, back on his feet now, dusty but nor really sweating heavily – I didn't give him time to work up a head of steam. His disappointment is palpable, but it's a measure of his friendship that he embraces me with genuine congratulations. He's a good man, and Helen could do worse – but I fear for him, getting entangled in her schemes. *Not that he'll have much chance for that.*

This is clearly all just a ruse. My growing suspicions have been confirmed – she's picked out her husband already, and he's not even a declared suitor: he'll be lurking in the shadows, waiting to claim his prize and take her away… to Troy.

15 – Wrestling for Leverage

'HESIOD: But what do righteousness and manly courage signify?

HOMER: To bring about a common advantage through private hardship.'
    —*Lives of Homer: The Contest of Homer and Hesiod*

Sparta

There are eight of us in the afternoon bouts, with the winner progressing from each fight. So in theory we're each of us three victories from glory. Over lunch, I seek Bria and Eurybates, hoping for reassurance rather than advice – I already know what I need to do but it's eating away at my courage. Neither of them are about; hopefully that means they've found Alcmaeon and are busy sobering him up. So I'll just have to face down my fears myself.

I eat with my Ithacans, keeping a wary eye on what I consume. Bria has yet to report back about the possibility that Tyndareus's ill-health is due to poisoning, and now I know Manto's here, I need to be extra vigilant on my own behalf, what with the assassin I've been warned of.

Imagine how much danger I'd be in if I were a serious contender.

As we march out to witness the draw, the crowds roar out encouragement for their favourites. The eight finalists are all theioi, though only those in the know realise – to the ordinary citizens here, we're just men with that little bit extra: 'Blessed by the gods' they would say, without realising just how blessed we are…

There's Diomedes and myself, for Athena. Those fighting for Ares, Heracles or Zeus are big Aias, Patroclus, Elephenor and Iolaus the Heraclid – an older man but as cunning as a fox. Finally, there's Penelope's brother's friend Eumelus, for Artemis, and Protesilaus, an impetuous Thessalian whose tokens are to Apollo. So far, he's been behaving as though this whole thing is a lark, but the fact that he's got this far gives the lie to that and I don't intend to underestimate him if we meet.

It's likely only Diomedes has any chance against Aias, and even that hope is slim. We need a favourable draw, and a lot of luck if our plan is to work.

'If we both lose, it's all over,' Diomedes murmurs to me, as we wait for Nassius to make the draw. 'Helen will be given to one of Zeus's cabal.'

'Maybe,' I reply. 'We still don't really know if the games are going to matter. Menestheus and the older kings are still trying to bribe Helen and her brothers with additional gifts, so Athena's other option may still be open.' I pat his shoulder. 'A cripple can't aspire to her, though.' I cast a meaningful glance at Aias of Salamis, remembering the threats Polydeuces and Castor made about getting him to maim me.

Diomedes follows my gaze. 'You think he'd do that?'

'Count on it.' I lean closer and whisper, 'I'll do what I can.' I'm trying to look brave, but inside my bowels are heaving, despite two visits to ease myself earlier. 'This is your chance, Dio. You drew the footrace. Win this and you'll be the crowd favourite, and that could carry you all the way to a wedding.'

He puffs up at that thought, as Nassius steps forth, and everyone goes quiet. The keryx removes the first clay tablet from the urn, and reads aloud.

'Diomedes, son of Tydeus, prince of Tiryns.' There are cheers, then a hush as he dips his hand into the urn again and pulls out another tablet: 'He will fight Iolaus of the Heraclids.'

The young tyro against the veteran – a classic encounter. The crowd cheers vociferously.

The next tablets are those of Elephenor and Patroclus. So one of the northerners must eliminate the other. But it also means that one must progress.

And it means I have a one-in-two chance of drawing Aias. I glance over at the giant, who's smiling up at the royal platform and the slender young princess, stripping her with his eyes as if he's already won her.

'Odysseus Laertiades, prince of Ithaca…' Nassius booms, and I catch my breath. '…will fight Protesilaus, son of Iphiclus, of Phylace.'

I exhale in a mix of relief and frustration. It's not what I've been praying for – well, wishing for – because praying is a waste of time. But I can't help but be pleased I don't have to face Aias yet.

Irrational, yes, but I've never claimed I'm perfect…

That means Aias will take on Penelope's friend Eumelus, and I throw a glance the young Artemis champion's way. He's gone pale, while Aias simply guffaws before venting a ferocious roar and flexing one of those giant, treetrunk biceps, playing to the crowd. They cheer him on, and like some performing clown he gives them more poses, bellowing like a bull in heat.

'Buffoon,' I mutter to Diomedes as we part. 'Good luck.' On impulse I pull young Eumelus aside. 'Go down early if you wish to avoid serious harm,' I advise him.

'But honour compels me—'

'Honour is for idiots,' I tell him. 'Do what you must but no more.'

He looks upset at that, but then he says, 'My friend's sister speaks well of you,' in tones that suggest that he's a bit smitten with her.

I reply by clasping his hand. 'Stay mobile, use your speed, and good luck.'

You'll need it.

I head for my little patch, where Eurybates is waiting. 'We've got Alcmaeon secure,' he tells me. 'Bria's found him a room in that tavern behind the old well – you know how persuasive she can be. She's with him along with Pollo and Itanus.'

They're two of my steadier lads. 'Good work,' I tell him.

I don't watch the two fights that precede mine – I'm stretching physically, preparing mentally, letting the crowd's reaction and Eurybates's breathless reports inform me. 'Diomedes took down Iolaus,' he tells me. 'Two bouts to one. The boy did well, after falling for an old trick in the first.' He smiles sadly. 'It was good to see a legend fight, but Iolaus is past his prime.'

That won't stop Iolaus trying to help Zeus in other ways...

The cheering tells me that Diomedes is a popular victor, and there are young women watching that burst into inchoate shrieking whenever they see him. I'm just relieved he's got himself out of that bout intact.

The next match-up is an interesting one: Patroclus defeats Elephenor with such ease that Eurybates is convinced the Boeotian took a fall. 'He's pretending he's disappointed, but he doesn't look too worried to me,' Eury growls. 'They'll be wanting to capitalise on Patroclus's efforts in the footrace, especially after Diomedes got through.'

'Makes sense,' I tell him, straightening and heading for the ring, as strangers slap my back and yell encouragement, advice or abuse. I'm not really listening. Protesilaus of Phylace is already waiting in his corner, and I've not really had a good look at him yet. But Menelaus has watched every bout the Phylacian has fought and he's giving me some good advice: 'He's about twenty-five, fast for a big man, left handed but pretends he isn't – he'll move opposite to how most men would. But he's all upper body strength. Go low, fight dirty.'

Hopefully the Phylacian's people have limited their appraisal of me to: 'He's short, so it should be easy.'

We salute the royal spectators, but this time I'm all concentration, and don't really take in the nuances of their expressions.

The crowd is a wall of sound and I shut it out, though I'm aware they're on my side this time – Phylace is a long way to the north from here – even further north than Elephenor's and Patroclus's kingdoms – and no one here wants their princess to marry a barbarian. I'm watching the way Protesilaus moves, over on the far side of the ring, planting both feet, hands on knees, breathing deeply. He looks calm, confident, and bloody big.

'Begin!' Nassius calls, and we advance, slapping away each other's initial attempts to grapple, circling left, right, seeking a misstep. He's wary, so am I, and those are muscular shoulders he's got. Then he steps in, and it's either dodge or grapple – I try to take him by surprise by hurtling into the clinch and we collide, as I drive up under him. He's forced back a few steps, but he twists and tries to throw, I hold on and we're both off-balance – we crash to the dirt, legs flailing for purchase, arms locking as we seek a choke hold. We're grunting at the exertion, skin to slippery skin. I'm working on locking up his right arm while he tries to trap my legs and roll on top.

Suddenly he gains the purchase he needs – as I find my lower leg pinned, he rears up and slams down, chest to chest and almost winds me. He's got the leverage now, gravity in his favour, then his forearm whacks the side of my neck and I'm chewing dust. I fight hard, but he's got the weight to pin me harder, harder...

'First bout to Protesilaus!' Nassius snaps, and the Phylacian rolls away, his intent face triumphant. I nod acceptance – he got me fair and square – and bounce back to my feet, cursing myself. There's time for water and to re-dust my hands, and then it's bout two, which I *must* not lose.

This time I go in more cautiously, feigning uncertainty as we circle, circle... Again it's Protesilaus who comes in – hard this time and faster than before and that's almost enough to outdo me – but as he rams into my chest I deliberately go with him, while gripping his weaker right arm, lifting and twisting, so that instead of finding himself on top of me and the victory all but won, we crash to the earth again. This time I'm on top with the better grip, wrenching his arm brutally round and rising to pin him, chest down beneath me. I could break his arm and there's nothing in the rules to say I shouldn't…

…but I don't, and the Phylacian recognises that. As Nassius calls the bout in my favour I rise and Protesilaus looks up and nods shortly, acknowledging what I did and didn't do.

'You're too nice,' Eurybates says, while handing me the water-skin. 'Bria will skin you for showing mercy.'

'My guiding principle is to be a better person than Bria in all things,' I tell him.

'Low hurdle,' he comments wryly. 'But aren't you trying to be a wrecker?'

'I'll win anyway,' I tell him, hoping I'm right. Otherwise Athena's likely to be as unimpressed as Bria.

It feels like no time at all before Nassius calls us to our third and final bout. The noise ringside is deafening as we step forward and size each other up. Whatever complacency either of us had is gone, knowing one slip will ruin our hopes – his to marry Helen, mine to wreck Aias's chances if I can. We close slowly, warily, crouched over with weight forward, moving almost in slow motion. He's trying to ensure I have no choice but to take him on, body to body, so that his superior weight can tell, while I'm trying to provoke him to lunge too soon, a little off-balance. He feints a charge, goes left, then drives in with his right shoulder…

I place my trust in Menelaus's assessment, and that saves me. Because this is another feint, designed to make me deploy my weight and balance to counter his right – but his feet shimmy and suddenly he's bullocking forward, leading with the left, but I've gone in lower than him, dropping to one knee and driving once again up under his shoulder as we slam together, chest to chest. He kicks off from his calves and thighs, tries to rear up over me again. I resist, resist…

…and then twist at the hips and wrench him downwards while sliding my arm from his right shoulder to his throat and pull him backwards onto me. He slips into a choke hold while my shorter legs lock onto his.

Protesilaus fights with all his power, trying to wrench his legs free and pull away, but I hang on, and as his first attempt subsides, I tighten my grip, forcing his back to arch. His face is scarlet now, eyes bulging as he tries to prise my choke hold free, battering at my forearm, pumping his hips up then back into my midriff, trying to knock the air from my lungs…

…but he can't get enough purchase to jolt loose, and it's his energy that gives out first. He's left clutched in my arms, writhing feebly as his face turns dark puce. In moments, he's slapping the turf in frustrated surrender.

'Bout three and victory to Prince Odysseus,' Nassius calls out.

I release my opponent slowly, because some men don't know when they're beaten, but the Phylacian rolls over and gives me a rueful grin, gasping for air. 'You fight well for a little man,' he pants. 'Too quick, too many tricks.' He offers me a hand, and when I grip it, we haul each other up and he gives me a grudging hug. 'Good luck, eh,' he mumbles. 'Especially if you fight that bear from Salamis.'

I'm led to the royal platform, still panting, where Agamemnon rubs his chin and tells me that he knew better than to bet against me this time. But Helen and her brothers are no friendlier.

'It's the dwarf again,' Polydeuces snickers as I salute them.

'We'll be peeling him from the turf next round,' Polydeuces adds.

I just focus on Helen. 'Princess, when royal children take up the mantle of their parents and become rulers, they must also embrace the dignity and honour of that role. For Polydeuces, that day is still far off, but for you it's only days away. I look forward to seeing the woman emerge from the child.'

She leans forward and beckons me close. 'I lost my childhood the day Theseus decided I was a gift he would unwrap,' she hisses, for my ears alone. 'He said you were involved, and he had no reason to lie.'

Same old, same old.

'I guided your rescue. Theseus was lying to get himself out of a hole.'

He didn't lie at all, but that's a truth that needs to die…

'You were serving Athena, and you were going to give me to one of hers,' she hisses back. 'Maybe you even thought to have me yourself? Was that your plan?'

'Theseus broke from Athena, and she aided your rescue – through me.'

That does nothing to allay her suspicion, but I can see she's unable to say categorically that I'm lying. Her lovely face takes on a sour, dissatisfied caste. 'How can I marry anyone I can't trust?' she asks quietly. 'You may as well withdraw now, because you're wasting your time.'

'If I thought that was true, I would,' I reply evenly.

Let her think I'm here for her, for a little longer.

I doubt she buys that, though – she's far from foolish. With minimal grace, she gives me another victor's bracelet: it's larger, and a purer silver – this trip is starting to turn a profit. I rise and Tyndareus gives me a friendly smile as I depart the platform – at least I have one true ally up there. If only I could win over Helen and her brothers.

I'm anxious to go and see what can be learned from Alcmaeon, but there's the small matter of the next round of the wrestling. Aias predictably flattens Eumelus, but the young man takes my advice and goes down swiftly, coming out with nothing worse than a grazed cheek and a bruised shoulder. I console him afterwards, and manage to share a smile with Penelope as she takes her battered friend under her wing. Behind her, Actoris gives me a half-wave. *Still keen… Ah, well.*

The four remaining champions – myself, Diomedes, Patroclus and Aias, stand before the kings for the semi-final draw. I'm desperate for the draw to provide me with what we need.

If Diomedes can win the final then, combined with his first-equal in the footrace, he's got a strong case for being awarded the overall honours for the games. *And there's only one way he can do that…*

The draw comes up with what I want, and yet I feel sick to the core as Nassius reads out the names. I'm on first, pitted against Aias of Salamis.

–

Little man, big man. Everyone knows how this one ends.

The gamblers in the crowd are restless because they can't find anyone to bet against Aias, so they start taking odds on whether I'm maimed, whether I'm conscious at the end of the bout or whether I survive at all. Aias is playing up to it, carrying skinny young girls round, one on either shoulder while pulling fierce faces.

But I've been thinking back to Thebes last year, and a personal duel between two champions – a hopeless mismatch, only accepted because of pricklish Argive pride. The favourite duly won, but he took a wound that made him vulnerable when he fought his next fight, and so he died.

That's my role here today. To somehow disable Aias badly enough that Diomedes – if he wins his bout – can beat this towering lug. The question is, how can I manage it? *Or am I about to have my head ripped from my shoulders?*

Let's find out…

I have Eurybates muttering in my ear as we make our way through the crowds ringing the arena – his last piece of advice is well-meant but substantially worthless: 'Don't die, she's not worth it.' Then he claps me on the shoulder as I enter the ring and the crowds cheer wildly: because Aias just entered on the other side, a shrieking want-to-be maenad on either shoulder. He kisses them both, nuzzles their cleavages then lowers them down and spanks their bottoms to propel them back into the crowd, before swaggering to the front of the royal dais.

Theseus without any brains at all…

Aias is almost seven foot tall. I'm five and a bit. He's got a rough-cast, broken-nosed face that speaks of many, many bouts and in terms of bulk, he's got perhaps double my body mass and it's all muscle. I've never seen a bigger man. I met him two years ago in the company of Heracles, up on Mount Ida, and the demi-god didn't make him look small. There's no obvious weakness, not even in speed. He's not noticeably one-sided, and his technique looks sound, if predictable.

But he's a cocky bastard, and though he plays the buffoon, I sense pride and a quick temper. I made a point of watching his bouts this morning, and he's no gentle giant; he enjoys dominating and humiliating others.

I join him before the platform, where Castor and Polydeuces are leaning forward avidly, while Agamemnon is offering Tyndareus double-or-nothing on the obols he lost on me earlier. I glance at Helen, but she's too intent on Aias's massive, oiled torso, where even the muscles have muscles, to bother with me at all.

We turn to each other, and Aias makes a show of looking over my head, then mock-starting as he looks down to find me. 'Oh,' he guffaws, 'there he is.'

'Why?' I retort loudly, as the crowd shushes to listen. 'Are you short-sighted as well as cross-eyed?'

The broad grin on his face dies, as he glares down at me in surprise.

'Tell me,' I add, 'was your father the hippopotamus, or your mother?'

His eyes bulge and he lunges for my throat, but I dance out of reach. 'You kopros-eating dung-beetle,' he snarls. 'Let's do this with swords!'

'Sure, let's,' I call back, as the crowd buzzes in disbelief. 'You're so slow, I'd kill you thrice before you drew.' I sense that all the royals are now leaning forward, but I don't take my eyes off Aias. 'The only question would be whether I could stab deep enough through the lard to find your vitals.'

It's not nice, it's not accurate and it's not even subtle – but niceness, accuracy and subtlety would be lost on him. He goes red and then purple and clenches his fists, wading towards me while Nassius roars that the fight will follow the rules – such as they are – and for Aias to be still. 'Wait for my—'

Aias doesn't wait: he shoves Nassius aside and charges, arms spread and face enraged – but I do the opposite to what he expects, and come toward him. As he rears up over me I slide in on my back, pretending I've slipped, and drive both feet upwards into his groin. They slam into his family jewels as he bellows in agonised fury, while momentum and my upwardly thrusting legs propel him headfirst over me... and his face ploughs into the dirt *over* the edge of the ring.

Technically, we haven't even started, but the keryx – furious at being pushed aside – shouts, 'First bout to Prince Odysseus!' and the crowd gasps, and then screams, a mix of excitement and outrage.

Aias peels himself off the dirt, bloody-faced and bent over, and tries to come at me again – it takes four armed guards to restrain him, while I provocatively stroll over to my water jug and my chalk bag. Eurybates joins me, while my other men fend off angry members of the crowd who want to take up my 'dirty, dishonourable tactics' with me first-hand.

'Good work,' Eury tells me, 'but the surprise element is gone, now. He's going to cool down, and start thinking again. Be ready for a real fight, my prince.'

'I will,' I tell him, flexing my hands and thinking hard. 'But he's not the sort to cool down that fast. I can still goad him.' I clap Eury's shoulder as Nassius calls for our return.

This time the crowd is hushed as we enter, though what cheering there is, is still for Aias, while I attract all manner of low hissing. Castor and Polydeuces are glaring at me with real anger, and Tyndareus and Agamemnon look uncomfortable, not wanting to be seen to condone what most see as cheating.

Helen though, seems a little amused by it all. *Well and good.*

I'm right – Aias has probably been given a strong talking-to by his men, but he's still seething. His huge fingers are twitching into a throttling position, and he's breathing through flared nostrils like a bull in mating season. He's actually pawing the turf with one foot.

'How was that, fat boy?' I ask him. 'Think you'll ever piss properly again?'

'I. Am. Going. To. Kill. You,' he snarls with slow menace.

'I do believe your voice has gone up an octave,' I comment loudly, and even Helen sniggers.

Aias begins to advance and Nassius – brave man – steps before him. 'This time, no one moves before I say,' he shouts, looking up at the not-so-gentle-any more giant with a steadfast expression. 'You will both await my signal.'

'Make it a clear signal,' I advise. 'This bloated ass I'm fighting isn't very bright.'

'Why you—'

'*Be still!*' Nassius barks. 'And be silent, both of you!'

'But I was hoping Aias could sing for us, now that he's a castrato' I reply, getting another laugh from the crowd. Aias splutters and the keryx glares at me.

'Prince Odysseus, do you wish to be disqualified?'

I wink at him. 'Not when I'm on the verge of victory.'

'You're on the verge of death!' Aias shouts. 'I'm going to smash you! I'm going to pulp your skull! I'm going to rip you limb from—'

'Prince Aias!' Nassius shouts. 'I have asked for silence!'

'…limb! I'm going to crush your—'

'Aias, shut the fuck up,' someone shouts from among his entourage – and all power to whoever he is, because Aias clamps his jaw shut, though he's still seething fit to burst.

'Thank you,' Nassius says tersely. 'Now, to your corners.'

I back away, and as the keryx leaves the ring, pitch my voice for Aias's ears. 'It's good that your friend knows how to control you. Does he cuddle you to sleep at nights?'

Nassius gives me an evil look, but he's clearly bluffing about disqualifying anyone. Instead he shouts, 'Begin,' and folds his arms, as if distancing himself from the carnage to come.

This time Aias advances slowly and crouched over – probably a good position to adopt, when you're nursing bruised nuts – and I do the same. A few yards in I begin to crab sideways, making him turn as he advances. He lunges at me cautiously, probably aware – assuming he *can* count – that one more mistake and he's lost. He keeps away from the edge though, giving me room to dart away, but all he has to do is turn and pursue, closing down the escape angles again.

It's a slow road to victory for him; eventually I'm going to run out of room – it's not sustainable.

'Not so fucking chatty now, eh,' he sneers. 'Come here, runt. Let's see if you can fight.'

He tries to hem me in, I evade again and as I go, I flash my hand in and tweak his left ear, making the crowd murmur and him snarl in frustration, turning and hurling himself at me, momentarily all his weight in the front foot.

I slam my heel into his leading ankle, as if it's an accident in passing.

If he'd been an ordinary man, it would have broken, I'd likely have been disqualified and we'd both have been eliminated – but he's a damnable freak and I just bounce off, land badly and almost get pinned. As it is I kick free, rise and spin, coming away as we both leap to our feet and then he charges me, grappling my shoulders before I can get away.

I offer token resistance, concentrating on staying up as he drives me backwards, then falling out of bounds before he can drag me to earth and do some serious damage.

''Bout to Prince Aias!' Nassius shouts and his stave slams into the turf beside our heads, to get our attention.

That prevents Aias from trying to break my neck, so it's a good thing.

One-one.

Reluctantly, Aias lets me go, getting up and glaring down at me. 'Thought so,' he sneers. 'You're all tongue.'

'Is that what you tell your boyfriend?' I ask mildly.

'*You—*'

Bang goes that stave again as Nassius calls, 'To your corners!'

Eurybates puts his arm round my shoulder as I return to my stool. 'Right choice to take the fall,' he murmurs. 'If you get caught again, do the same. Don't risk your life: if Diomedes wants the princess so very badly, let him take the rest of this.'

It's sound advice, though it's not what Athena will be wanting, and that low blow to his ankle was my best shot. I mightn't get another chance, and all I'm doing is alienating people right now. Achaeans love a winner, but we despise a dishonourable loser.

I go out there resolved to do this right, using my one possible edge: technique.

This time I pretend to repeat my earlier tactic, circling as if trying to avoid close quarters, but then I let him catch me, our shoulders lock as our arms entwine and he uses his massive weight to drive me back, but I fold and go under, buckling to one side then wrenching at his left arm as we roll over and forcing it up and back, while jamming my shin against his other arm as he tries to turn over, and for a moment I have the upper-hand.

We strain against each other, and though he's huge, I'm no weakling. The crowd hush, because they all know the sport well enough to see that I can win from this position. I bear down, rearing over him, and any other man would have buckled...

...but this huge bastard suddenly heaves and I go flying, barely staying in the ring, while he rises, roars in triumph and slaps his thighs.

'Come on, dwarf!' he shouts. But he advances with considerably more respect, as I scramble up and step away from the edge of the ring, circling again.

'Nearly,' I tell him, and he knows.

There aren't many rules – no punching, no headbutts, no elbows, no kicking – all the fun stuff like that is reserved for the pankration. My leg flip in the first bout was excused because I didn't actually kick him – technically he fell onto my upraised feet. So there's not many ways you can overcome such a mismatch. I circle, I feint and dart away. I slap away his arms, and once I even slap his already bloodied nose, making him yelp with pain, but I'm running out of space again. Sooner or later he's going to grab me, and then it'll be a case of survival before Nassius stops it.

He throws a move, left then right then lunge – but it's ponderous and I go in straight and hard, and for a moment I'm under him and pushing up, driving him back as he flails for balance. The crowd rise to their feet as they see this man-mountain toppling backwards, with the edge of the ring looming behind. Again, anyone else and they'd be gone…

…but his excess bulk allows him to crash us both down and we both flail desperately on the ground, seeking a hold, any leverage at all as we thrash against each other. I take a sly knee to the small of my back that almost numbs my spine, but I overcome the pain fast, throwing one arm over the back of his head and wrapping it round into a reversed chokehold while driving with both legs to force him to crash chest first into the dirt. His back is oiled and liquid with sweat – an expanse of bronzed muscle – but he can't throw me this time, and I realise that he's also *tiring*, his stamina flagging because none of his bouts have *ever* lasted this long. He strains, roaring to Ares for aid.

I squeeze tighter as he fights back but he's losing air. So he stops trying to break my hold and attempts instead to get up and drive me backwards. I can't stop him, because he's so fucking big, but *damn* I try, heaving with both legs, trying to hold back the wall of muscle, straining with all my strength as the crowd leaps to its feet again, and this time they're marvelling because the little guy is going toe-to-toe with the big guy and holding his own…

But then my right thigh muscle – the one shredded by the boar-tusk – rips yet again. I scream, give way and convulse in blind agony, my left thigh jerking upwards in reflex – and that's all it is – as Aias topples onto me... face first onto my left knee...

It breaks his nose, and the body that crashes down onto mine is utterly limp. But I'm seeing through a white-hot haze as I kick free and then crawl to an open space and just lie there, trying to hold back my howls of agony as I clutch my torn upper thigh and vanish into the pain.

When I regain enough vision and hearing to be aware of anything else, it's to find uproar: Aias's people want my head for my 'foul, dastardly false blow' – but Eury and my Ithacans are shielding me amidst the push and shove, while Nassius bellows for attention.

Finally the horns blast and there's something like silence. Soldiers separate my men from Aias's, and Eury helps me to my feet. I have to clutch his shoulder and hold on, as he helps me hobble into the space before the royal platform. Looking up through the haze of pain, I wipe my sweat-filled eyes and manage some kind of salutation to the kings.

Tyndareus and Agamemnon are looking at each other with quizzical expressions, not quite sure what to say, especially in public. A deliberate knee to the face is not permitted, but it was genuinely accidental and most knowledgeable observers would agree. Either way, Aias is still out cold and I'm not going to be fighting anyone for a long while.

It's hard-earned, but it's a win. I don't think even Bria could complain.

'Well, Prince Odysseus, it seems no one should ever bet against you,' Agamemnon observes, with wry amusement. He'll be pleased, I warrant, at least for Hera's sake – Aias was very much an Ares man.

Now my vision's cleared, I can read the crowd: they're in turmoil – their favourite is down, the villain of the piece has the victory and perhaps through underhand means – they aren't sure and opinions run both ways. But the small man beat the big man, and there's nothing a games crowd likes more than an upset.

'I learned all I know about wrestling here in Sparta, my lords,' I tell the kings, my voice raised so everyone can hear me, and that goes down very well. The crowd suddenly remembers that the victor is *one of them*, so this is a home ground victory.

Naturally, Castor and Polydeuces are sick to the stomach. But Helen is sitting back with arms folded, a faint smile on her lips as if all this *hurting* for her sake is a wonderful amusement.

I cast off from Eury's shoulder and somehow stagger up the steps, salute the kings again then kneel before her, wincing painfully as my poor right thigh spasms.

'Is that abominably painful?' she asks.

'My princess, you have no idea,' I tell her. 'I fear I won't be contesting the final.'

'Will you ever walk again?' she asks, with even more interest.

'I'll be fine,' I tell her, managing to sound debonair. 'Old wound, one that flares up occasionally.'

'Good.' She fakes a smile. 'It would be awful for Ithaca if you had to relinquish the kingship one day, because you were crippled. Though in such a backwater, perhaps that doesn't matter?'

What a treat *it would be, to be married to such a sarcastic, caustic puddle of bile.*

'Quite the opposite,' I tell her, suppressing my temper. 'To be King of Ithaca, the ruler of the Cephalonian Confederacy, requires considerable wit and vitality. And I am more than sufficient for such a task.'

She dangles another silver bracelet in front of me, which I accept with what good grace I can muster, before limping away, past her stewing brothers and the bemused kings.

Eury grabs my shoulder at the foot of the steps, and takes my weight. 'Get me to somewhere I can lie down,' I mutter in his ear.

'You don't want to watch Diomedes and Patroclus fight?'

'I don't give a shit,' I tell him. 'I've done my part. And the best bit is, I don't have to marry that foul-minded little *kunopes* up there.'

–

It's still daylight when I wake up – somewhat startled as I didn't actually know I was asleep. I'm in my room in the palace, the afternoon sun is seeping through the shutters and Eurybates is saying, 'Lady, I don't think he's awake...'

'I am,' I call in a husky voice, cough up some phlegm to clear my throat and say more firmly, 'Who is it?'

'Who were you hoping for?' a slim woman asks drily, entering my room with her head beneath a fold of her veil, then dropping it as she perches on a stool beside the bed.

It's Penelope.

'Lady?' I say, startled and somewhat aghast – I'm naked beneath a flimsy and badly-spread blanket. I try to sit up, but she raises a palm.

'No, stay there,' she tells me firmly. 'Your keryx says you have tissue damage to your leg?'

'I, er...'

'Actoris insists I tend you,' she says, in an ironic voice. 'Apparently she's quite worried about your inner thigh.'

I go scarlet, which she finds highly amusing, in her quiet, reserved way.

'I have some healing skills, as you already know from Delos,' she says briskly. 'Show me where it hurts.'

I struggle to pull the blanket up while keeping my private parts covered, utterly embarrassed but unable to refuse. My family equipment appropriately concealed, she probes my thigh – painfully – then applies a messy brown paste Then she closes her eyes and concentrates, her palms against my skin. A gentle heat begins to radiate, soothing and pleasant, and the throbbing pain starts to ease.

When I was awakened as a theios by Athena, the goddess applied a similar healing to the same thigh – it was swifter, but then, she's a deity. This is slower and less efficacious, but it's undeniably beneficial.

'Seer and sorceress. You're a theia of many talents,' I say appreciatively.

'One tries,' she says, a smile warming her coolly composed features. 'The paste is arnica-based, good for muscles and bruising. I would suggest complete rest.'

'Then you'd better warn your maid,' I say, remembering Actoris's little wave this afternoon.

'Don't worry,' Penelope replies. 'Actoris has plenty of good sense – when she's not mooching about, dreaming of you.' She leans in and looks me in the eye. 'I could use a break from hearing about your noble profile and kindly demeanour, though.'

'I'm not encouraging her.'

'You're her hero,' she says quietly. She pulls out a strip of gauzy fabric from her bag and begins to wrap it tightly around my thigh, to bind the paste to my skin.

'I'm not such a hero,' I reply, thinking about that last fight. 'The only chance I had against Aias was to goad him, but I prefer not to act that way.' For some reason, I don't want Penelope to think ill of me.

She pauses in her tasks, and looks at me with wise eyes. 'I've watched men wrestle, and as a huntress I've learned some of the art myself. I know what you were doing. And why.'

'I didn't know girls wrestled.'

'Only those brought into the arktoi, the "little bears" of Artemis,' she replies, smiling at the memory. 'Sometimes we all have to fight a little dirty to win. As you clearly know.'

'I'm having trouble picturing you wrestling,' I remark, colouring when I realise that I'm flirting.

'Good,' she says tartly, though her eyes glint with mirth. 'As a priestess of Artemis, I've moved beyond such things.' She pulls my blanket over my thigh and rises. 'Athena will be pleased with your efforts today, I suppose?'

'Only if Diomedes does his part,' I reply. Then I realise that I have no idea what time of the day it is, or even if it's the same day. 'Or has he...?'

'He had the victory,' she tells me. 'Two bouts to one in a close-fought match against the Thessalian, Patroclus. He's to be presented to Helen in private, tonight. I understand your grandmother the Pythia will chaperone them.'

Yes. I clench a fist triumphantly. *Well done, Dio.*

'Does it make any difference, though?' I wonder. 'Tyndareus still hasn't truly said how the groom will be selected. For all we know, Menestheus or Idomeneus... or someone worse... has bribed the king behind the scenes, and the games are meaningless.'

Penelope purses her lips. Then she leans towards me, close enough for me to smell the rosemary oil on her skin. 'I shouldn't tell you,' she murmurs, 'but Artemis's favourite avatar is part of our entourage. She's been fasting and preparing for the goddess top ossess her imminently. My high priestess, Sophronia, met with the Pythia not long after dawn, and your grandmother is adamant the real decision will be made tomorrow. She has confirmed what you've already guessed – the games are meaningless, and Hera will decide who will marry Helen.'

I sit up, forgetful of my blanket. This could be crucial. 'Tomorrow? And by Hera?'

'If I find out more, I'll let you know,' Penelope says, while her eyes stray to my bared chest and abdomen. Then she seems to remember that she's a virginal priestess, and with an awkward bob of the head, she exits the room.

I'm doing head-spins inside as her footsteps bustle away, wondering what in Erebus to make of all that.

16 – Alcmaeon

'Dionysus gave such gifts to men, both a pleasure and a burden of grief. Whoever drinks to satiety, the wine drives him out of his wits, ties his feet and hands up together with impenetrable fetters, along with his tongue and his common sense...'

—Hesiod, *Catalogue of Women*

Sparta

Penelope's ministrations do me wonders. After a short nap, I'm ready to get up and move about – I've been damaged often enough to know that letting an injury stiffen can be the worst thing to do. So, eschewing Eurybates's aid, I rise, wash my face and dress. I need to let Bria know what Penelope has told me about Hera, so I send Eurybates to her with a note, then join the throng in the megaron, to see if I can learn anything directly from Tyndareus.

But as I enter the hall, I see that the royal party hasn't arrived yet, and a servant tells me that Helen is due to see Diomedes right now. I chat briefly with Menestheus – he's about as much fun as a tax assessor – when a big hand falls on my shoulder.

I turn to face the chest of a giant, then look up.

Aias is glaring down at me, his nose straightened as far as such an already blunted appendage can be, but stuffed with wading. Both eyes are blackened and his lips are so swollen, they look like small sausages.

'Prince Odysseus,' he slurs, gripping my shoulder with fingers that could break a man's collarbone.

Once on Ithaca, I was out walking when a feral dog came up and put his jaws round my calf, its teeth about to break my skin. I went rigid, and just stared down at him. If I'd moved, the dog would have savaged me, but I remained utterly still, fixing him with a steady eye. He let me go and trotted off.

'Prince Aias,' I say, with exactly the same resolute calm.

My bravado knocks Aias off stride – but only for a moment. He's a theios and he's used to public displays of courage. 'You think you're something special, don't you?' he snarls, planting a finger on my forehead. 'But you're just a jumped-up squirt with a smart mouth. A dishonourable bastard, without any honour.'

'You know nothing about me or my honour,' I reply levelly, while those around us watch avidly.

'I know that you're a filthy cheat with the foul mouth of a goat herder,' he growls back. 'I'm the better man, and I'll prove that to you. That was just our first fight today, Ithacan. The second will make it even between us – and after the third fight, the loser dies.' He shifts his thick finger down to jab at my sternum. 'I swear this, on my honour, which is unblemished and the pillar of my existence.'

'*Pillar of my existence*', I think sarcastically. *No false modesty issues here.*

But this is no joking matter: he means it – two more contests, of who knows what, where or when, after which he'll seek my death, having proved himself the better man. If I best him, he will believe it his duty before the gods to take his own life. That's what honour means, to virtually every man in this room. And if I walk away, he'll decry me as a coward for the rest of my life.

That would undermine every piece of counsel I give, every alliance I offer, every undertaking I propose.

'I'll be waiting,' I tell him firmly. 'You're already one down – that's quite a knife edge to walk. And now, if you don't mind, I believe our host the King of Sparta wishes for my counsel.'

This may well be true – Nassius has just waved to me and is on his way through the press to speak to me.

Aias turns to the men behind him. 'You heard that,' he says. 'The islander runt accepts. He's mine.' He thumps his chest. 'Mark this moment. Him or me.'

That's two men named Aias who I've made a lifelong enemy of in two days. I wonder who else with a name starting with 'A' I can offend next. I limp away, to meet the anxious looking keryx.

'Prince Odysseus,' he greets me, 'You are a companion of the Prince of Tiryns? Do you know where he is? The princess is expecting him.'

I look at him quizzically. 'I assumed he was with her already. I haven't seen him since the wrestling this afternoon.'

He pulls a concerned face. 'He left with Patroclus of Thessaly after their bout, but no one has seen him since.'

'They left together?' I'm somewhat surprised – their draw in the footrace yesterday was one thing but the Thessalian doesn't strike me as a good loser, especially when there's so much at stake. Then I think about Laas and how he died, and I'm suddenly afraid. 'Is Patroclus here?' I look around, and see that Elephenor is talking to High King Agamemnon, but his fellow northerner isn't with them.

'Does Elephenor know where they are?' I ask, and Nassius shakes his head. I groan inwardly – despite Penelope's ministrations, my leg isn't up to dashing about just now. But I gamely volunteer my services. 'I'll find him for you.'

'Thank you,' the keryx says. 'I'll come with you.'

I'd really rather he didn't, but my lads aren't here and I may need someone to help me if we have to climb any stairs, so I reluctantly agree. I'd like to get my xiphos – no weapons are allowed in the megaron, apart from our eating knives – but there's no time to fetch it.

We make our way out through the citadel gates into the town. Dusk is creeping over the narrow streets and I'm vividly aware of the note under my pillow and its warning. So far, I've stayed inside the palace at night, either in the courtyard or the megaron or my room, trusting on the palace guards and my own instincts to keep me safe from my secret assassin. This is the first time I've ventured into the town after the day's end, and I'm feeling naked without a weapon. My skin is prickling with nerves.

Diomedes has told me who he's lodging with, a nobleman I know well from my years here in Sparta, and we find our way to the house without difficulty, and without anything untoward happening. Even so, I have a premonition of some looming disaster. We hammer on the main door, which is opened by a servant, who explains that his master is out, visiting a friend and won't be home this evening, but that Prince Diomedes is within. The man seems a little nervous, his eyes shifting to and fro.

When we ask if we can see Diomedes, he tells us to wait in the vestibule, a strangely inhospitable request – by custom, we should be taken into the main room, a smaller version of Tyndareus's megaron, and plied with wine and simple food. When we insist on seeing Dio, the man demurs, but after a few more attempts to fob us off, he admits that Dio is taking a bath.

'Up in his bedroom?' I ask, glancing apprehensively at the steep stairs up to the second floor.

'Oh no,' the servant says, in shocked tones. 'My master has a bathroom, properly plumbed and all.'

'That's all right,' I exclaim, pushing past. 'I've seen Diomedes stripped many times. He won't mind if I barge in.'

'He's been there half an hour or more. Said he didn't need me,' the old man replies, clearly uncomfortable. 'Didn't want to be disturbed.'

Perhaps Dio has simply lost track of the time.

Or...

My heart is thumping against my ribs by the time we reach the bathroom, at the back of the house. The door is shut and my sense of danger is now overwhelming, all my theios awareness at screaming point. Where is Patroclus? What evil revenge might he have enacted? Dio could be lying in there with his throat cut…

I shoulder-charge the door as best I can with my gammy leg. It's a flimsy thing and it bursts open immediately as the timbers splinter.

There are two naked bodies lying on the tiled floor. For one terrifying moment I think they're both dead. They're coiled around each other, top to tail, but as they jerk their heads up in alarm, it's obvious what they've been doing.

Diomedes and Patroclus… Oh, shit!

I look away, while Nassius backs out of the room, squawking. Patroclus looks murderous – but not repentant. As for Diomedes, he looks like he's waking from a dream into a nightmare.

Nassius stammers, 'Dear Gods…' then he grabs my shoulder and hauls me back into the passageway. The door, or what is left of it, slams behind us and I hear frantic curses and movement.

'You know he can't marry the princess now,' the keryx babbles. His face is a mask of horror, and his hands are fluttering about as if to swat away what's been going on in the bathroom.

'It's not a crime,' I try to protest, but he cuts me off.

'It's a damnable disgrace,' he rasps, gathering up his dignity.

That's the nub of it – not whether either of us condones what's been going on in the bathroom, but the insult it offers to Tyndareus and to his daughter. She's been stood up. It almost doesn't matter who Diomedes was making love to; the fact is, he preferred that choice over the honour of speaking with Helen.

And honour is the glue that binds Achaea together.

'I must tell Tyndareus. I have no option,' Nassius continues.

I seize his shoulders. 'Please, let me deal with this. I'll withdraw them both from contention – but I'll do it discreetly.'

The herald stares at me suspiciously. 'But I must—'

I place my face nose to nose with him. 'You make this allegation, *any* allegation about what they've been doing, and Patroclus will deny it – with his xiphos.'

His eyes jerk about, his forehead suddenly beaded with sweat. 'But you saw—'

'So you want to pay for this with your head? Or start a general bloodbath? The suitors are ripe for any excuse to carve each other up.' I shake him back and forth. 'Listen to me, and listen carefully. It was very steamy in there. I believe I saw one athlete helping another scrape the bath oil off his chest. That's what you saw, too.'

He nods. Or maybe his head's wagging because I'm shaking him so hard. 'Helen's honour is at stake,' he manages to gasp.

'Aye. And these men's honour is at stake as well,' I go on, through gritted teeth. 'And you know how warriors guard their honour.'

Honour – there's far too much of the damned stuff crammed into this town right now...

His face is ashen. 'Both of them, Prince Odysseus,' he says. 'I will be silent if you will swear that they will *both* be withdrawn.' Then he pulls away, and I let him go – I can hear the two men inside dressing hurriedly, and both have weapons. Nassius's life may be forfeit if I detain him any longer.

He's disappeared by the time Patroclus emerges, his face flushed. His tunic is damp, his long hair tugged into some kind of order and he has his scabbard slung over his shoulder but the blade thankfully is still sheathed.

I take a painful step into his path, and he looks down at me, eyes narrowing. 'Well?' he says coolly.

'I've persuaded the keryx not to speak to the king until I do. And the version I give will preserve your reputation.'

'You don't give a fuck about my reputation,' the Thessalian sneers. 'You're only concerned about your friend.' He places his hand on his xiphos hilt. 'Perhaps it's you I need to silence?'

I put my hand to where my own xiphos hilt should be – but of course, it's back at the palace. *Kopros!*

Diomedes appears at his shoulder, his face sickly. 'No one need be silenced,' he says. 'I will bear my shame.'

'No one's going to be shamed, if I can help it,' I tell them. 'And it's not about what you've been…' I'm about to say 'doing' which sounds crude and judgemental, and I don't mean that. '…sharing,' I conclude lamely.

If only I could be sure that Patroclus has brought the same open-heartedness to their love-making as Dio. But I'm not sure of that at all.

I can only imagine the fury Tyndareus will feel if he finds out why Diomedes has failed to keep his meeting with Helen. I'm sure the king knows that some men prefer their own kind – but if this got out it would mean public insult and humiliation to his family, with almost every important king and prince in Achaea here to witness it.

Thank the gods the servant didn't come back to the bathroom with us… One less tongue to wag…

'The keryx will only speak to Tyndareus if I don't,' I stress. Hopefully Patroclus will have enough sense to realise this means he'll gain nothing by skewering me. 'I'll think of some excuse for you both.'

But what?

The two men look at each other, a silent exchange so complex I can't begin to decipher it. Then Patroclus turns back to me. 'It's just pleasure,' he says. 'You know it makes no difference, with regard to the princess. She won't want for tupping if I win her.'

'Tyndareus won't see it that way.'

'Why not? Zeus's balls, pretty much every man alive has tried it at some point; it's a part of growing up.'

'Meaning, you *have* grown up?' I'm starting to lose my temper now.

'Oh, fuck off! You and Menelaus—'

'Are friends. *Real* friends, who would never risk the other's reputation at the most crucial moment of their lives. Which is what you have just done.'

This has nothing to do with seeing two men together. Several of my own soldiers have let a close friendship go further, and it's never overly bothered me, so long as it hasn't undermined the cohesion of the unit as a whole. They're all good men, and I'd trust them in a crisis – but not this snake.

'Listen,' I tell Patroclus, 'it's your own business who you lay with, but these games are for the hand of Helen of Sparta, who's been blessed by every god on Olympus. This is no ordinary wedding contest – for the safety of Achaea she must be happily married off to a loving husband, not someone who spends his time lusting after everyone else he can get his hands on, male or female. That's paramount, and it's why you are *both* going to walk away from this contest.'

I can actually feel Patroclus calculating – can he kill me and then overtake Nassius? But then he'd have to kill the servant too… And can he trust Diomedes to be silent, given that the young Argive has just demonstrated a strong weakness for public confession?

Somehow he comes to the right conclusion. 'Then we're in your hands, Ithacan,' he growls, and stalks away, without a backward glance, even at his erstwhile lover. Diomedes stares after him for a moment, waiting perhaps for some sign. When it doesn't come, he slumps against the door post, hanging his head.

I steer him back into the bathroom, though the shattered door is unlikely to give us much privacy.

'By all the gods, my friend,' I say. 'What came over you?'

He looks up, miserable as a prisoner in Tartarus. 'I'm sorry,' he blurts in a trembling voice.

I shake my head, still not really able to credit this. 'That bastard has blessings from both Ares and Aphrodite,' I tell him. 'Did he…' I wiggle my fingers in a vaguely 'magical' way.

'No… He just… It's always been there, inside me…' He hangs his head miserably.

'Bria is going to use your guts for harp strings,' I tell him. 'Which is nothing, compared to what our goddess will do. To get so close to victory and then let it slip through our fingers. Talking of whom, we thought you were in love with Athena!'

Diomedes sags onto the edge of the bathtub. 'I *do* love Athena,' he groans. 'I adore her so much…' He plucks at his tunic miserably. 'I want to *be* her, not this… this thing I am…'

Oh gods, I groan inwardly. I sit beside him, go to put a consoling arm round his shoulders – and then suddenly feel profoundly awkward about that, for the first time in my life. For the next few moments, I'm floundering. 'It'll be all right,' I finally say, my voice strained and unconvincing. 'No one need know. I won't tell Bria, *or* Athena.'

What exactly am I going to say to them, *let alone Tyndareus, to explain Diomedes's withdrawal?*

He nods, but he seems beyond caring. 'I'll pack my things,' he mumbles.

That would be a disaster in itself, but what if he decides to do something more drastic?

'No, you'll stay,' I reply, and follow it with an argument he can't disagree with. 'This whole business is bound to turn violent at some point, and Athena will need your blade.'

He falls silent. 'What will you say to Tyndareus?' he asks eventually.

Finally the solution comes to me. 'I'll tell him your heart is already given to another, a lifelong love.'

He gives me a pained look. 'I suppose I'll need to marry someone now, to prove the truth of it.'

'It would help.' This is very far from ideal, but the alternative is worse. 'Anyone in mind? It'll be useful if I can give Tyndareus a name.'

'King Adrastus has been nagging me about wedding his daughter. The youngest one.'

'*Aegialeia?* But she's your aunt!'

'And my cousin, depending on how you look at it. Our family tree is a little complicated.' He manages a wry smile. 'She's only a few years older than me…' His voice trails off.

'Do you like her?'

He shrugs. 'She's all right.'

'I'll tell Tyndareus you broke off a secret betrothal to come here,' I say, 'because you wanted the very best for yourself. But Aegialeia's heart is shattered and yours is not much better. And you apologise profoundly for the hurt you are causing Helen. Or something along those lines. I'll make it sound stirring and noble and *honourable*.' I give his shoulder a pat. 'Go upstairs and get some rest. We'll talk in the morning. I've been tipped off that something big is about to happen, and you can bet your life Athena will want us involved.'

That at least pricks his interest – to be ready when his beloved goddess calls. I see him to the foot of the stairs, sure enough of his mood that I no longer worry that he'll harm himself.

I *hate* Patroclus.

But regardless, I'm left to limp back alone along the streets of the town, staring into shadows and wishing I was armed. The assassin I've been warned of could be anywhere.

But I reach the palace unscathed, and when I enter the throne-hall, Nassius comes hurrying over and escorts me straight to Tyndareus's side. The old king looks at me impatiently. 'I'm told you found Diomedes?' he snaps. 'Where is he?'

I give him a regretful look. 'Alas, Prince Diomedes, after examining his conscience, has decided that he can't in good faith continue to court your daughter. The truth is, he has another love – a *lifelong* love for Princess Aegialeia, whom he left broken-hearted in Argos. He has tried to put his own feelings for her aside, but they will not leave him. So he apologises, and asks that you convey his regrets to your daughter.'

Tyndareus stares at me, astounded. '*Another woman?* Does he not know who and what my daughter is?' He rolls his eyes at the utter stupidity of the assertion. 'Has he lost his mind? I do believe Helen was warming to the notion of him, so taken was she with his prowess and bearing. He was champion of these games, the frontrunner for her hand!'

'Believe me, he is fully cognisant of all this. But sometimes a man's heart must rule his head.'

Tyndareus scowls, angry now on behalf of his family. 'Not if they aspire to greatness. This was the opportunity of many lifetimes. I cannot believe any woman alive could matter more to a man than my daughter!'

I'm tempted to remind him that she's not his daughter at all, and that she's already been spurned by Agamemnon, but that would be cruel and utterly counterproductive. 'I understand also that Patroclus has withdrawn, as he feels that the dishonour of losing the final of the wrestling discounts his claim. He's already leaving.'

Tyndareus looks up at the ceiling, silently berating the gods in his exasperation.

'What will you do now?' I ask him.

He rubs his chin wearily. 'What indeed? The gift-giving has been a disaster – it has caused more problems than it has solved – and now the games have also failed to reveal a worthy husband. I must consider and take counsel.' He pats my shoulder. 'Come, let us speak to Agamemnon, and determine a way forward.'

Although I'm anxious to see Bria now, and learn whether she has sobered Alcmaeon up and what tale she's managed to prise from him, this clearly takes precedence. While Tyndareus discreetly explains to Agamemnon that there's important news, I go to Nassius and tell him that both Diomedes and Patroclus have agreed to withdraw voluntarily, and that he should forget he knows otherwise. He's not stupid – he nods understanding and thanks me for my wisdom and protection.

I then follow the two kings, leaving everyone in the megaron somewhat mystified, though the passing remarks I hear as I leave tell me they're all thinking we're going to meet with Diomedes and Helen, in readiness for the big announcement.

We regather in a private room behind the megaron – thankfully there are no stairs to negotiate – and take our seats. A servant pours us wine as Castor and Polydeuces join us, taking in my presence with sullen resignation. Then the door flies open and Helen walks in, magnificent in blue and green silk, shining gold tassels swinging from the tiers of her skirt. Her eyes narrow as she sees me, but she offers no protest.

'What's this about?' she asks. 'Where is Prince Diomedes?'

'You tell her,' Tyndareus growls at me.

'Unfortunately, Diomedes has come to the realisation that his pursuit of your love is in vain, as his heart is already given to his cousin. He finds he must forgo happiness with you to honour his commitment to Aegialeia.'

Helen looks at me as if I'd just declared that pig shit was edible. 'You're saying he finds *Aegialeia* more desirable than *me*?'

'I'm just as surprised,' I remark – a little drily, perhaps. She gives me a sharp look, while her brothers make snide remarks about Diomedes 'not having the balls' to marry into their family.

But Helen doesn't look too upset. 'Then these stupid games have been an utter waste of time,' she complains to her father. 'Just as I said they would be. Why would I ever fall in love with someone on the basis of their ability to shoot feathered twigs at a bundle of straw, run round and round the town until we're all dizzied at the sight of it or – worst of all – grapple with other men? I told you, over and over again, but no one listens.'

Tyndareus slumps back in his chair, his face a mix of frustration and resignation. So I'm not in any way surprised when Agamemnon is the next to speak.

'It's not about love,' he growls. 'It never has been. It's about alliances and wealth and influence. At times, such a contest can reveal the right man, but I have always believed there to be better ways. To me, the games were always merely a means of keeping the suitors distracted while we make up our mind.'

Just as I thought, I congratulate myself ironically. *You, oh noble High King, have viewed this as your process*, your *choice*, all along. *You and Hera. I'm so delighted to have crippled myself just to help your orchestrated distractions.*

266

'What do you have in mind, my lord?' I ask him, politely. 'Or who?'

I see Castor and Polydeuces burning to interject, but even those two bull-heads know not to interrupt the High King. As for Helen, she sits back with deceptive disinterest, but I can tell she's listening avidly.

'I believe only the gods can choose for us now,' Agamemnon says slowly, eyes upturned as if he's receiving a divine revelation.

Does he really think we believe he's only just thought of this?

'I have just been approached by High Priestess Amphithea, the Pythia,' he goes on. 'She asks that she be permitted to perform an oracular seeing and pronounce upon the best candidate – for Achaea. With all other options discredited, I must trust in Hera and Pytho, who have always guided my line.'

He seems to genuinely believe that Amphithea means him well. And so much for Tyndareus's opinion. Amphithea gets to choose after all, with Manto looking over her shoulder and doubtless tweaking the result...

It all seems clear to me now: this is the position Zeus and his cabal wanted us to find ourselves in, all along. The winning candidate from the games has been sabotaged by an Ares man, and indeed, all the leading contestants are discredited, the richest kings have been sidelined, and now the gods – no, Zeus himself, with Hera as his gullible sidekick – can pronounce on their desired outcome.

I glance about the room. Castor, Polydeuces and Helen are neither surprised, nor perturbed. This is likely the outcome the two children of Zeus were promised anyway, and they've shared what they know with their older brother. And Tyndareus, who's tried to stave it all off, is grey-faced, too tired to fight it any more. He's as aware as anyone that this wedding contest has ended in disaster, with no clear favourite that everyone else can – even grudgingly – accept as the winner.

The longer this goes on, the greater the risk that it will turn violent, and on a large scale. And of course, the massive crowds of visitors are eating Sparta's granaries bare. If circumstances force him to return the gifts as well, he may end up without two obols to rub together.

The High King turns to me. 'Thank you for your counsel, Odysseus, but you're no longer needed here. In fact, none of us are needed – it's now a matter for the gods.'

–

Summarily dismissed, I start limping upstairs. It's glaringly obvious to me that the Patroclus-Diomedes liaison wasn't innocent desire – Patroclus took a fall for his side, in much the same way I took a fall for mine. The Pythia's proposal to Agamemnon to resolve this was pre-meditated, with the knowledge that the wedding games would be a farce.

That confirms that the Pythia's patron, Hera, is working with Zeus again, just as the Dodona oracle said. I could try to warn Agamemnon of this, but he won't believe me. They've lined up a mutually-agreed candidate for Helen already, and I can guess who that is. Achaea's fate is sealed. Unless…

It's now dark outside, with heavy clouds obscuring the moon. I need to find Bria, so we can get our heads around this issue before it's too late. We probably need Teliope too, and Diomedes if he has the heart for it, after all that's befallen him. I'm going to need my xiphos if I'm heading back down into the town tonight, so I head for my room.

I reach my little room to find Actoris leaning against the wall outside, waiting for me. She breaks into a broad smile as soon as she sees me.

'Odysseus, Lady Penelope said—' she begins, but I raise a hand.

'Actoris, it's a true pleasure to see you, but I'm only here a moment. I have to go out again immediately.' I fetch the key from my pouch.

She gives me a disappointed look. 'My mistress asked me to give you a message.' She brushes my hand with her fingers.

'That assassin note – nothing's come of it, has it? It must have been a joke, one of your funny friends. So I thought, maybe I could keep your bed warm for when you return? That's if your leg isn't too sore?'

After the day I've had, a little comfort would go a long way, but there really is no time for this, however sweetly meant. 'I have to go and meet someone,' I tell her. 'Honestly. And the threat of an attack still exists.'

Actoris looks hurt, which is vexing, and as I unlock I try to find the words to let her down while remaining a friend. I push the door open, distracted by her presence… but these days I never truly relax, so I'm instantly aware of a breeze coming from a window that I left shuttered and *locked*…

The room is unlit, but the light of the hallway illuminates it, and I see immediately that the shutters are ajar and that someone is perched on the windowsill. Light gleams on metal as I grab Actoris and hurl us both aside just as a bowstring snaps loudly in the silent, echoing space and an arrow slams into the doorframe, the bronze tip grazing my cheekbone as it whistles past.

I react instantly, hurling myself at the shutters, smashing them wide open and throwing the assassin off his perch. He gives a startled cry as he plummets two flights onto the cobbles below. I look out hoping to see him badly hurt, but he rolls as he strikes the ground and somehow staggers to his feet. It looks like he's broken his left arm, so he won't be plying his bow for a while. He casts me a furious, thwarted look before stumbling away.

I go to cry out, but stop myself. I've got a mountain of things to do tonight, and I can't afford to get bogged down with some pointless pursuit. At least he's not going to be a threat for a while now.

I turn to Actoris. She's crouched on the floor, staring mutely up at the arrow, which is still quivering in the wooden door frame. I pull it out – my name is inscribed on the shaft – before dropping to my knees beside her, my torn thigh muscle sending a savage flash of agony through my body.

'We're fine,' I tell her, as she clings to me, shaking all over and trying not to cry. 'The killer's gone. We're safe.'

But in my mind, I'm thanking my lucky stars – and whoever sent me that mysterious warning note when I first arrived. If I'd not been so wary, I'd be dead, and probably Actoris as well.

The glimpse I caught of my attacker has confirmed all my suspicions. His head was masked, so I could only see his eyes. But his legs were covered in slender tubes of cloth – eastern garb – and as well as his bow, he had a sword with a curved blade slung by his side. There's a known eastern assassin's cult that deals in weapons inscribed with their target's name. They operate out of *Troy*.

So the Trojans are here already. Most of them want me dead, which isn't so surprising. But one of them doesn't. *She* wants me to live, even though *she* knows I will try and thwart all their plans. And *she's* desperate enough to have bribed a palace servant to leave me a note, the handwriting awkward because it was written in what was to her a foreign script.

Kyshanda is still looking out for me...

I've forgotten Actoris's mention of a message, but she fumbles in a pocket of her gown and pulls out a small wax tablet. '*The town springs,*' it reads. '*One hour, come disguised in servile garb. Bring a rope.*'

'It's from Penelope,' Actoris adds, unnecessarily. 'Oh, and she's made up some more ointment for you; she thinks this one will work better than the last.' She hands me the vial.

I rub the ointment into my thigh muscles, ignoring Actoris's offers of help – she's a trier, I have to admit. Then I thrust the arrow through my belt and gather the few things I need together, along with my xiphos. My leg is already feeling much better as we exit the citadel, propping each other up like two drunks, as we head through the town – there are tipsy men with women draped over them everywhere, and we blend in well.

Once we reach the house where Bria has been sobering Alcmaeon up, I get Eurybates to take Actoris home, with Itanus and Pollo to escort them. Then I go upstairs to find Bria sitting slumped on a stool outside a bedroom. She looks up at me in annoyance when I appear.

'Ithaca! Where have you been? I did *not* come here all this way to nursemaid a drunken *mulas* of an Argive—'

'Save it,' I tell her. 'Diomedes blew it with Helen, so Tyndareus and Agamemnon have agreed to let the Pythia choose Helen's husband, through an oracular reading – which Manto will be manipulating. We've already lost, unless we can disrupt it.'

Bria gapes at me. 'Diomedes... what? Pythia... huh?'

It is *so good* to see her speechless. I just wish it happened more often.

I give her the heavily edited highlights of the afternoon and evening – without mentioning at all what happened between Diomedes and Patroclus. Instead I pretend that Diomedes and Helen argued, blaming it on the girl. 'She clearly wanted this to happen all along,' I tell Bria. 'The wedding contests were just a ruse.' This last part of my story has the advantage of being true. 'And I'm supposed to meet Penelope in less than an hour, hopefully to discuss whatever the Pythia and Manto have cooked up.'

Bria takes it all in swiftly, and claps me on the shoulder. 'So, the game moves on!'

'Oh, and a Trojan assassin just tried to kill me,' I throw in, just to knock her further off balance.

Her eyes widen for a fraction of a heartbeat, and then she shrugs, as though this is the most normal, natural thing in the world. 'You're clearly still alive.'

'Thank you so much for your concern. The timing is significant, don't you think: just after I left my meeting with the kings, and learned what they propose for tomorrow? The Trojans are not only here, they knew immediately what I'd be told – so they have active spies in the palace. They obviously fear how I might use that knowledge.'

'If your enemies don't want to kill you, you're not screwing with their plans properly,' Bria replies offhandedly. 'It's to your credit that they finally see you as a threat.'

'Lucky, lucky me.'

'Quite. Well, why don't you take a turn with Vomitface Alcmaeon, while I find Teliope. Then go and meet your Artemis priestess at the Springs and see what you can get out of her.' Bria grins evilly. 'I'm presuming she doesn't just want some of what her maid is after?'

'Penelope isn't like that,' I retort, more hotly than intended.

'Oh, but perhaps you wish she was?' Bria says archly, deciding she's found a chink in my armour. 'Play it right and maybe you'll nail them both. At once, even!'

'Off you go!' I tell her firmly. Then I pause. 'I don't suppose you found out if someone is really poisoning Tyndareus?'

'Nothing conclusive,' she admits, her face souring. 'But that doesn't mean it's not happening.' She claps me on the shoulder, then hurries away toward Teliope's lodgings.

I'm left alone to check on our guest. Alcmaeon's asleep on the bed, and the air is thick with the vile, syrupy stench of wine-vomit. I take the half-full bucket beside the bed downstairs and empty it on the midden, rinse it out, and bring it back.

Then I sit on the stool, taking a moment to remind myself of all I know about the snorting, snoring prick stretched out on the cot beside me. The key fact is that, like so many other men here, he hates me.

Alcmaeon led the Epigoni – the orphaned sons of the famous Seven who perished at Thebes – in a revenge attack on the city, ten years later. I helped them, because Thebes was planning to provide a beachhead for a Trojan invasion. But he and I fell out, in particular because he wanted to torture the seer, Tiresias, and rape Tiresias's daughter, Manto. I just wanted both dead, because they'd blighted my sister's life, tried to murder me and betray all of Achaea. In the end I had to settle for giving Tiresias a clean death, and arranging for the priestesses of Pytho to take the already pregnant Manto off Alcmaeon's hands.

Alcmaeon has never forgiven me for that, and he's an important, dangerous man: the heir apparent to the throne of Argos. And he's here, drunk as a satyr, not for Helen's sake but for Manto's.

I nudge him awake. He comes to, rolls over and spews. I have the bucket ready, wait until he's done, and feed him water until he's aware enough to realise who it is that's caring for him, and that he loathes me.

'You,' he growls. 'You can *fuh... ugh... bleurgh...*'

Again, the bucket saves the day.

'Good evening, Prince Alcmaeon,' I greet him evenly. 'Are you done yet?'

'Aye...' he mumbles blearily.

'You're welcome.'

He catches the *hint* of sarcasm in my voice. 'If you think this makes amends for what you did—'

'I never considered the possibility,' I tell him. 'I want to know what happened between you and Manto after I left Thebes.'

'You can go...' he starts. But then his eyes narrow. 'Why should I tell you anything?'

At least he's thinking again. 'Because if I help you, you might help me.'

'Help me how?' he growls.

'Help you get what you want. Or *who* you want.'

That snags his attention. 'You *know* who I want,' he rasps. 'But *you* want her dead.'

'I've changed my mind,' I reply, not quite honestly. 'Tell me what happened between you and Manto at Thebes.'

He fixes me with a cold, sweaty stare, his face working through various permutations of disgust, contempt and disdain, before settling on some kind of hopefulness, blended with outright suspicion. It's a very odd mixture indeed.

'When you *fled*,' he begins finally, 'I took her back to camp. I fully intended to cut her throat when I had done with her...'

273

His voice trails off, and I start to think that's all he's going to tell me.

Then he moans, as if in pain. 'But the thing was, I couldn't get done with her. Gods, I've had women, but never, *ever*, anyone like her. The passion, all she brought out in me... the sheer heart pounding excitement of riding that storm... You have no idea. We're kindred souls, she and I. We were made for each other, enemies or no. We *must* be together. But then those *interfering bitches* from Pytho came for her, and they persuaded Adrastus. We fought – damn, I must've nigh shouted the walls of Thebes down, what was left of them – but they all turned against me...' He buries his head in his hands. 'They took her away.' His voice trails off, then he mumbles, with naked honesty, 'I've not been sober since.'

'And you have a child by her?'

He gives me a haunted look. 'Aye, a son... she birthed him in Pytho, nine months after she was taken from me. She's called him Amphilochus...'

'Your brother's name,' I remind him. 'Why would she do that?'

Alcmaeon rolls over to face the wall. 'You'd have to ask her,' he says in a desolate voice. 'Can I have a drink?' he adds, in a deathly whisper.

'I think not,' I tell him.

Am I sorry for him? *No*. He was and is a thoroughly arrogant, dislikeable and violent man. But I pity anyone who lets Manto get her fangs into them. And right now, she's the problem, not him.

I have a seed of an idea, and I think, looking at the drink-ravaged mess on the bed, that it will find fertile ground. But time is running short. And Alcmaeon, I realise as his breathing changes, has fallen unconscious again.

I leave the surly sot to sleep it off.

I have the chance, perhaps, for one last try at jamming a spar into the spokes of Zeus's wagon. So I tuck my hair under a wide-brimmed hat I've brought with me, throw on a shapeless grey mantle over the pack that holds the rope, and pull a fold over my head. Muffled in my new disguise, I'm ready to meet Penelope at the town springs.

17 – A Secret Olympus

'How is it indeed, that when I learnt of such things, I came here, instead of respecting the oracle of the god? Because Hera is far greater than any divine oracles and would not forsake me.'

—Euripides, *Children of Heracles*

Sparta

There's a cloaked figure standing beside the low wall that surrounds the town springs, waving to me through the crowds. Penelope's composed face peers out from a fold of her priestess mantle as she looks me over. 'Do you think you can climb if you have to?' she asks.

'My leg's much more comfortable now, thanks to your new ointment,' I tell her. 'I can manage most things, as long as it doesn't take too long.' I look around me. 'Why, what do we need to climb?'

She gives me a conspiratorial look. 'I'm not sure yet. But there'll be something. And thank you for protecting Actoris. She's very lucky.'

'We were both lucky.' I hesitate then add, 'I don't know how to refuse her without hurting her feelings.'

'You're not used to refusing women, then?' she says wryly. 'I'll have a word with her, to spare your feelings and hers.' She indicates the direction of the lower town and adds, 'Come.'

I find I have to hurry to keep up. *Just as well my leg is feeling better than it was…* 'Where are we going?' I ask after a couple of blocks.

'I want to break into a shrine,' she says, slowing down enough to face me.

I stare. 'Um, good, but why do you need me?'

'Do I look like someone who knows how to break into anywhere?' she replies.

'No, but…' We're friends, good friends even, but our goddesses are hardly allies. 'Why send for me? You have theiae in the Artemis cult who could do just as well.'

'Yes, but I'd have to persuade them to do something against their scruples.'

'You think I *don't* have scruples?'

She pauses, a smile playing about her lips. 'I'm sure you do, but they're not the usual set. Listen.' She drops her voice so we won't be overheard by any passers-by. 'Sophronia has been summoned to a meeting in the house of Dionysus's local high priest, but I've not been invited. You know I have doubts about my patron's place in Zeus's new order, and I want – no, *need* – to hear what is being said. To do so, I need the help of someone outside my cult, and the only person I know with the skills and local knowledge who'd be willing to help me, is you. Or am I wrong?'

I'm never going to refuse that offer. 'I'm your man,' I reply – with an inadvertently flirtatious smile.

'I've sworn off men, remember?'

'I've not forgotten. It's mankind's great loss.'

'Flattery will get you nowhere.' She suppresses another smile. 'I'm hoping you know the house.'

'Indeed I do – Menelaus and I used to steal his ceremonial wine.'

'Excellent. Come on – we'd better keep moving.'

I take the lead as we hurry on down through the town, making sure we avoid the deeper shadows, even though the

Trojan assassin is hardly likely to be a threat at this point. The streets are still busy, torches on street corners and outside taverns creating small pools of light in the gloom. Boisterous laughter comes from the overflowing taverns, but the locals appear surly, probably already sick of the strangers and interlopers. Those who look at us do so incuriously, perhaps seeing a man and wife hurrying home. Although it's early summer, the air is cold. Eventually I steer her through an alley that I know will take us to the rear of the priest's house. I press Penelope against the wall as we reach the end of the alley, and creep forward, peer around the corner and then return.

'There's a guard at the rear entrance,' I whisper.

'I assumed there would be,' she replies, with quiet anxiety. 'But you must know another way in if you—'

'Nicked the votive plonk.'

'Quite. We'll need to hurry though – the meeting will be about to start.'

'Don't worry – it won't take us long. Menelaus and I used to break in here at least once a week.' I smile at the memory. 'The wine wasn't too bad, either – not that we cared too much about vintages in those days.'

I take her to the rear of another, smaller building with a relatively low, flat roof, and help her clamber up – silently, as there's a family living inside. Their roof butts against the wall of a two-storeyed house which yields just enough toe and fingerholds for us to scale it. That done, we tiptoe over to a vantage point overlooking the Dionysus priest's house, just a few yards away on the other side of another narrow alley.

On this side of the house opposite us, there are no windows and more importantly, no doors, and therefore no guards. It's a modest building, with a few bedrooms upstairs that open off a narrow internal balcony that surrounds a large, central, covered light well. Below, there's a single room that occupies the whole ground floor. If you were being grand, you'd call it a megaron, but it's not that big. There's an altar in the middle instead of the customary hearth, so it's freezing in winter – presumably you don't feel the cold if you've drunk enough votive wine. Thirty people at the most could pack themselves around the altar, if they stood shoulder to shoulder, but it doesn't happen that often. Dionysus's worship is a minor one in Lacedaemon, and most of their rites are secret, ecstatic and take place out in the fields and wilder places.

Penelope moves well, like the trained huntress she is, but now our cloaks will be a nuisance. 'Leave your mantle here,' I whisper in her ear, 'so you can move freely. This next part's the hardest.'

We shed our cloaks, and I pull out the thin, tough cord I've brought with me and tie a loop at one end, using a slipknot. I wait until the guard comes around the corner on a cursory sweep before returning to his position, out of sight. If he's kept up the habits of years ago, there'll be a small brazier and a flask of wine back at his usual station and he won't budge from there for a while.

All's clear…

There's a wooden beam jutting out from the edge of the roof opposite, with a sturdy vertical pin near the end, the twin of a beam on our side. The men who build houses round here use such beams to secure a pulley, so they can haul up roof tiles and other building materials. I send the rope snaking over the alley, and loop it over the peg on the first attempt – it's satisfying to find I haven't lost the knack after all these years.

I pull the cord as tight as I can, winding it around the peg on this side and tying it off, coiling up the slack that's left. With Penelope watching open-mouthed, I step onto it, as much to make sure I still have the skill as to test the strength of the rope. 'Have you ever walked a tightrope?' I whisper, after returning to the solid footing of the rooftop.

She gives me a panicky look. 'No.'

'Then I'll make it easier for you.' I tie another loop several feet along the slack and reach down to hook it over another bronze peg below us. Menelaus and I put it there all those years ago for this very purpose, and a sharp tug on the rope reassures me that it's still firmly wedged into a joint in the massive timber framing that supports the wall.

Once that's safely done, I stand and, with the coils of the remaining slack in one hand, tentatively place a foot on the upper rope, spreading my arms.

'Are you insane?' she whispers, incredulous.

'I've done it before,' I whisper back, and step fully onto the tightly strung cord. Then very, very carefully, I walk, one splayed foot after the other, across the empty space and onto the opposite roof.

Okay, it's not quite that straightforward. In fact at one point I nearly fall and only my good balance enables me to steady myself. But I make it.

Once there, I stretch down to hook the last of the slack around yet another peg, the twin of the lower one opposite, drawing it as tight as I can before tying off on the beam at roof level. Penelope can now hang onto the upper rope while walking along the lower one, just as Menelaus was able to do, back when we went on our wine stealing expeditions.

She's got the strength and nerve to make it across without mishaps, and a few moments later, we're huddled together on the roof of the priest's house. I pat her arm in appreciation of her efforts thus far.

'Do we have to do that again when we leave?' she asks, pressing her mouth to my ear. Her breath on my skin is sweet and I have to fight the impulse to reach out and stroke her face – this is the first time I've been so intimately close to her. I wonder how she feels about being near to me.

'If the alarm is raised, we'll be running out one of the doors,' I tell her. 'Otherwise, yes.'

'Then so be it,' she replies, her voice regaining its usual calm. 'What now?'

I'm very impressed with both her composure and her athleti- cism. Clearly her confined island life hasn't prevented her from staying fit and lithe. And though she's clearly stressed, she's maintaining her alertness, and hasn't succumbed to fear.

She's a diamond, I realise. *A kindred soul.*

'There's a suitable vantage point inside,' I whisper. 'We can climb in through the light well, and onto the balcony overlooking the ground-floor room. We'll have to move silently but the worst is over – it'll be much easier than the tightrope.'

I lower myself down into the light well, hanging by my hands so that my feet are dangling not far above the balcony rail. This is tricky too – if I misjudge it and miss the rail, I'll make too much of a racket landing on the balcony floor, at best, or fall the other way to crash down onto the altar, at worst.

Just a few yards below me, there's a hum of conversation and the shuffling of feet as people assemble – enough, along with the clatter of votive bowls and jugs, to mask the muted thud I make as I land neatly on the rail. I check that no one has heard me, before stretching my arms up to catch Penelope's legs and lower her down. I can't help noticing that her behind is pert and shapely as it slides through my hands…

Stop it, I tell myself, as I slide off the rail and crouch down beside her, out of sight but well within earshot.

We're barely settled when I hear my grandmother, the Pythia, speak, just a few yards below us and clearly audible. 'Welcome, Sophronia,' she announces, in a cold, formal voice.

'Greetings, Amphithea,' the high priestess of Artemis responds coolly.

'No doubt,' my grandmother goes on, 'you'll know some of these others—'

A familiar male voice interrupts her, one that makes my skin creep. 'I'll speak for myself,' it says, in a strong eastern accent. 'I am Prince Skaya-Mandu of Troy. With me is my half-brother, Prince Parassi, and my sister, Kyshanda. We speak with the authority of the king and queen of Troy on all matters.'

Kyshanda… My poor heart feels such pain, I almost groan aloud. My face must have betrayed my anguish, and Penelope, *bless her*, covers my hand in hers and squeezes. I twist my hand over and squeeze back, straining my ears to hear my lost love speak.

But the next voice is new to me, a gravelly, resonant Achaean one, with an aged burr to his tones. 'My name is Carnus, a seer in service to Hyllus and the Sons of Heracles, and an initiate of the Order of the Sphinx.'

I know both the name and the reputation: he's a prophet who has always stood in Tiresias's shadow, but he's well known for his cunning and wisdom. The Order of the Sphinx are some kind of cabal operating throughout Achaea and Egypt, in service of Zeus. I'm doubly thankful to Penelope for asking me to come here with her. Our eyes meet in the half-dark, hers shining with nervous excitement.

The following voice I know only too well. 'And I am Manto,' the Theban prophetess says, 'daughter of Tiresias and the great Heracles.'

I tighten my grip on Penelope's hand. *Oh for my bow, and a quiver of arrows!*

'And I, Melampus, priest of Dionysus, will be presiding over this gathering tonight,' a light, musical male voice adds. *So... the local priest isn't good enough – they've even imported the top Dionysus priest in Achaea.* 'Are we pleased with the progress of the wedding games thus far?' Melampus asks.

'I am,' Carnus says gruffly. 'Apart from one matter: why is the damned Prince of Ithaca still breathing? He disrupted our ploy to buy the girl's hand, and then he wrecked the chances of three of our main contenders in the games. If I hadn't instructed Patroclus to destroy the credibility of Diomedes, we may yet have had one of Athena's men crowned as victor, and been forced to give him the girl.'

He's only confirming what I already suspected, but it doesn't stop me feeling an almost uncontrollable anger. I glance across at Penelope, who's listening with a bitter, distasteful look on her face.

'Tyndareus should have been compelled to hand her over to a candidate of our choosing from the start,' Sophronia declares in a querulous voice. 'This whole wooing has been a farce.'

'The death of Tantalus and the sudden declaration of the wedding caught us all off guard,' my grandmother Amphithea complains. 'We were working on Tyndareus, but this acceleration of events could not be foreseen.'

'Your grandson was behind that disaster too,' Carnus growls.

'Ithaca is no fortress,' she replies. 'You know where to find him if you wish to eliminate him.'

Thank you, Grandmother, I think. It's obvious the blood in her veins is no thicker than water. I'm grateful for Penelope's sympathetic glance at me, and another small tightening of our hands. Right now, I have no objection to holding her hand for the rest of my life.

'We have assigned an assassin to deal with him, this very night,' Skaya-Mandu puts in tersely. 'Korakis, one of the best in the business. I'll hear from him presently, I don't doubt.'

Perhaps, but I don't think you'll enjoy his report.

'Good,' Sophronia says. 'I'm weary of finding the phrase "Man of Fire" in my readings. Now, what of tomorrow?'

'Very simply, this,' Amphithea responds. 'I shall go before King Tyndareus and proclaim that Zeus and Hera themselves command that this matter be resolved. I will tell him that, in the sacred shrine at the heart of the palace, where all the gods are honoured, I will grant him a special oracular pronouncement. It is an ancient place, and with a blood sacrifice and Manto's help, I can enter a trance that will open a path to the spirits.'

'But how will you ensure that you utter the right words, when the prophetic fit overcomes you?' Carnus asks. 'We all know that we are helpless when walking the Serpent's Path, and we must speak as we are compelled.'

'Manto's father Tiresias found a way to control the visions,' she replies, causing a stir among her audience. 'Didn't he, dear?'

There's a murmured acquiesce from Manto.

'Manto also has this skill,' Amphithea goes on. 'We will arrange it that she uses her powers to channel and manipulate the spirits, and I will speak the agreed phrases. Through easily interpreted symbolism we will point the king in the direction of Prince Parassi, alongside a prophecy of shared prosperity for Troy and Achaea. Once Tyndareus and Agamemnon hear our words, they'll have no choice but to surrender Helen to us.'

'And I'll finally get the woman I was promised,' a confident eastern male says. It's Parassi himself – I recognise the tone of his voice from the gathering on Mount Ida two years ago, though he's dropped the fake 'country-bumpkin' accent. 'She's grown into quite the beauty. I can fully believe she really is the most beautiful woman in the world.'

'And with her at your side, as she desires, Agamemnon's attempts to unify Achaea will die stillborn,' Carnus says. 'When the moment comes, resistance will be paltry. Polydeuces will usurp his father as King of Sparta, and be made High King of Achaea, as a client of King Piri-Yama of Troy, and the new Trojan empire will finally take shape.'

And what does Kyshanda think? She's staying very quiet…

Penelope and I look at each other. I'm silently swearing that this will not come to pass, if I can possibly help it. From the grim expression on her face, she's feeling the same. She notices suddenly that we're still clutching hands and shyly releases mine, her face colouring. I miss her touch instantly.

'And of course, Hera will be given full dominion here,' Amphithea puts in imperiously. 'As well as being honoured in Troy alongside their queen-goddess, Hanwasuit. This must be pledged.'

'I have the authority to give that pledge,' Carnus says firmly. 'I am both seer and avatar, and call now upon the Skyfather to attest this.'

There's a sudden shiver in the air, like a wind that surges over all my skin, and then a deeper, darker male voice resonates. Penelope and I stare at each other in alarm…

Carnus has taken on the spirit of Zeus himself...

'*I, Zeus-Tarhum, King of Olympus, do testify that Hera, my Queen, shall be known in the East as Hanwasuit, Queen of Thrones, and given worship throughout the kingdom of Troy and its adherents. Let this sign be my pledge.*'

Far off, we hear a rumble of thunder, and suddenly the sky above seems to crack as a thunderbolt explodes above us, making every timber quiver, once, twice then thrice in rapid succession, the lightning piercing the gloom and bringing light and shadow into stark relief. Penelope's mouth has fallen open and I put my hand over it to prevent her crying out in surprise.

'By the Huntress,' she whispers, when she's calm enough to remove my hand. She looks petrified, yet utterly alive – which is exactly how I feel.

There's complete silence below us, broken by Carnus's weak cough. It seems Zeus only entered him very briefly, leaving him breathless. It takes him a few moments to recover enough to speak, and when he does his voice is still shaking. 'Lady Amphithea, does that suffice?' he asks.

'It suffices,' my grandmother croaks. She sounds shaken.

'Under my rule,' Prince Parassi puts in, 'Achaea will be purged of the gods that have not stood with the Skyfather. Athena and Hephaestus will be the first to go. By the end of summer, with the help of Hyllus and his Heraclid followers, our soldiers will occupy every kingdom and every island to enforce our rule. Existing royal families will grovel before us, or be put to the sword.'

To hear it stated with such certainty, and such imminence, is chilling. Their plans are much further advanced than we feared, if they're so confident that Hyllus and Heraclids will march to their drums...

'Then we are agreed,' Kyshanda says, speaking for the first time. I feel my whole body crumple in anguish when I hear the resolution in her voice. 'Tomorrow, just before noon,

Amphithea will go to Agamemnon and Tyndareus. It's essential you Achaeans keep control of the shrine and the palace. Even with our divine blessing, you must remember that most of those present will be hostile to our Trojan party, and there may be active resistance to our appearance. We must be given the princess, and safe passage from Sparta.'

How cold and how certain she sounds. I want to cry aloud in denial. *My lover*, my heart pleads…

My once-lover…

Penelope presses her forehead to mine. 'Be strong, Odysseus,' she murmurs. Somehow her words, her presence keep me grounded as I face the hideous, unarguable fact that Kyshanda has now become my enemy. *The last act of love she offered me was to warn me of the assassin.* But from now on, we are utterly sundered.

Penelope's presence anchors me, the touch of her forehead to mine the most real thing in the world. I wrap my arms around her and she does the same. Our faces press closer as each of us grieve – me for lost love, and her for a goddess that has betrayed her faith. Our cheeks press, skin to skin and in our despair, it's as if we have no skin, that we're trying to burrow into each other's souls. For all we've lost and are losing, and with the doom of our cause being stated so certainly below us, we seal a silent alliance.

Were it not for the gut-wrenching need I still feel for Kyshanda, standing just below us, I might already be in love with this precious woman I hold. But it's too soon, and that wave of emotion hangs above me, poised but not yet breaking.

And of course, I have no idea how she feels, nor can I ask.

But if Kyshanda was like a forbidden dream, Penelope is an earthy grounding in all that's wholesome. There's a sense of rightness to everything about her, from her scent to the texture of her cheek as it presses to mine, that insists that she, not Kyshanda, is the true mate of my spirit.

I slowly become aware that they're still talking, below us, and reluctantly, painfully, I open my eyes and so does Penelope.

We stare into each other's souls, almost forgetting to breathe as we hold each other tight. My mind is a turmoil; everything I thought I knew and wanted has been turned on its head.

Then another reality intrudes. *I'm holding an Artemis priestess.* There are legends of such transgressions being punishable by death. Theiae of Artemis have been known to hunt down men that have seduced one of their priestesses and leave their bodies pierced with so many arrows that they look like porcupines. I pull back, mortified.

Penelope, her face stricken, shakes her head, as if denying our moment of oneness. But the voices below intrude, taking our immediate attention.

'What did you say?' Skaya-Mandu has just blurted.

A new voice, a male with a Trojan accent, replies. 'I was unable to make the kill,' he says. 'The Ithacan eluded me.'

'You failed,' Skaya-Mandu says numbly. He's slow, when he's thwarted.

'I'm sure you did your best, Korakis,' Kyshanda says, and her voice sends a shiver through me, because I know it well enough to detect *relief*. 'Will you try once more?'

'Even if I could,' and here there's a pause, presumably to show them his broken arm, 'it is not wise for me to make another attempt immediately. I have been seen and my purpose is known. Security will be increased and the quarry wary. One seldom gets a clear second chance.'

'Try again anyway,' Skaya-Mandu snarls. 'Your right arm is whole and you can still use a blade. I want him dead.'

Kyshanda sent the warning note. She still cares. But my heart has no idea what to do with that information any more, and nor does my head. Because everything tells me that what she and I shared was something we stole, against all odds, and that anything lasting is impossible. Our nations, our causes, have already torn us from each other's arms, and though war might be averted, I doubt we'll ever find union. She's already a phantasm, an illusion that's fraying in the cold blast of reality.

But Penelope is here, and real. Possibly just as unattainable, but unequivocally on my side.

'If the Ithacan still lives, then we must move with greater urgency,' Carnus growls. 'Don't wait until midday – go to the king at dawn, and convene the seeing as early as possible. I will send my chosen theioi and their men to hunt down Odysseus on some pretext. He has to die.'

They bustle into action, footsteps departing with varying urgency, until the space below us is empty. I can hear Carnus talking with someone out in the vestibule – the local Dionysus priest, who has otherwise been silent. But there's no time to waste. Any moment, the two priests will finish their conversation and one or both will come inside, presumably to sleep. Which means, they'll come upstairs...

We climb onto the balcony rail and I lift Penelope up so that she can grasp the edge of the light well. With her safely on the roof, I leap, catch the lip and hoist myself out into the fresh air just as footsteps start up the staircase from the ground floor room. Even then we can't relax. When we're sure the other conspirators are all gone and there are no guards in sight, we repeat the acrobatics of our rope-walk above the alley, though this time Penelope seems a lot more at ease, physically. Once she's across, I dismantle the lower rope, repeat my tightrope exercise in reverse, free the final stretch of rope and slowly reel it in. In less than a minute, the entire coil is in my hands.

I turn to face Penelope. 'Holding you so close was wrong,' I mumble, trying to confront the problem head-on. 'Heat of the moment. I apologise.'

'Nothing happened,' Penelope replies tersely, her composure still clearly frayed. Head warring with heart? Or perhaps it's just confusion at having been forced into intimacy with a man – any man – when she's pledged celibacy. But her expression is of self-recrimination, and when she speaks again her voice is gentler. 'Odysseus, I have to think, and pray. I've never questioned my vocation, but the Artemis cult is changing into something I no longer understand. And Delos is killing me. I can feel my brain atrophying with every blank day... I don't think I can endure the place much longer.'

'Then don't. Leave.'

'You don't understand. I'm like a trained puppy to them now. They don't care about my needs, they just record my words and gather my weaving every night, and I never see or hear of either again. I'm going to die having never lived.'

Instinctively I go to hug her, but she stops me.

'No,' she says softly. 'You've grown into an extraordinary man, Odysseus of Ithaca. In another life...' Abruptly she turns to make her way back across the roof top and I have no alternative but to follow her meekly, as we clamber down and into the alley.

Once we're back at the town springs, with the earlier crowds dispersed, we exchange urgent words, planning our next moves. She needs to return to her quarters as soon as possible, before she's missed. But we must somehow find a way to disrupt Zeus and Hera's plans, before Helen is given to Parassi, and the Trojan invasion, with all its bloodshed and rapine, becomes a forgone conclusion.

'Will you be included in Sophronia's delegation tomorrow morning?' I ask her. 'It'd be good to have someone on the inside.'

'I'll do all I can to be there,' she tells me. 'And you?'

'I'm going to try and rouse resistance to this,' I tell her. 'I think I have a plan...'

18 – In the Eyes of the Gods

'Seeing such a great crowd of [suitors] Tyndareus was
frightened that, by deciding in favour of one, the rest
would erupt into violent disagreement.'

—Apollodorus, *The Library*

Sparta

There'll be no sleep for me tonight...

I'm unable to return my room, not with Carnus's *theioi*
hunting for me. With so many enemies here, he'll have no
shortage of volunteers. But I have a plan and I know these streets
and palace grounds like a local – if that local happens to have
spent half his youth out on midnight jaunts, as I have.

I slip right past all the hunters, and seek out the people who
can really help me now: Bria and Eurybates – and Teliope –
we're going to need her even more than we thought. Diomedes
is probably too much of a mess to assist us, but I ask Eury
to see if he can talk some sense into him. My main focus
is to smuggle my way undetected into the palace, and seek out
the person who has the rank and reputation to be the public
mouthpiece for my idea, now I can no longer act freely and
openly: Menelaus.

He's up for it, of course. Together we creep back down into
town, evading groups of men who are quite clearly hunting for
me.

By now, it's after midnight, but we're both wide awake, stimulated by the danger. It's a cold, clear night, with a waning half-moon giving us enough light to find our way into the sea of tents outside Sparta town. There are two temporary villages which have grown up during the wedding games; the one we're heading into houses those suitors and their entourages who live in the Peloponnese and the southern mainland – the pure Achaeans, in other words. There's another one on the other side of the ridge that houses mostly Thessalians and other north-erners – the men of Zeus and Ares and their cabals. It's been raucous in both camps every night, and even now there are still men lined up outside the whoring tents, or sitting round drinking and dicing. It reminds me of an army on campaign.

I take Menelaus to the pavilion of Menestheus first. We rouse and brief him before moving on to Idomeneus and then Euryalus of the Epigoni, and so on and so on. We tell them that Tyndareus is planning to betray and rob them all – that's not altogether fair on Tyndareus, but we need to keep the message simple – and ask them to gather at the edge of the town half an hour before dawn, and to pass the word.

I use the remaining time to prime Menelaus as to what to say. He's a good speaker, so long as he's well-rehearsed; and everyone knows him as someone who wears his heart on his sleeve.

What he says and does next could change Achaea's fate, or seal it.

–

'They're not going to give back the gifts! They're not going to recognise the victor of the games! And they're going to marry Helen to a Trojan!'

Menelaus punches the air, his voice hoarse with outrage. His words catch fire among the hungover, dog-tired and hugely disgruntled suitors. We're perched on a rock outcrop, a natural speaking platform, just outside the edge of the town and my

Ithacans have massed behind us, to ensure no one tries to bar the gate into the main street. There's also a crowd gathering of disgruntled locals, roused from their houses and workplaces by the hubbub. As they listen, they're beginning to get as worked up as the suitors.

'They only invited us here to fleece us!' he goes on. 'There was never any real competition! It's a farce! Are you going to let them get away with it?'

As one, the men begin to shout, 'No! No!'

Menelaus flashes me an anxious look. 'How am I doing?' he mutters, his handsome face flushed with excitement and worry, and the exertion of shouting.

'You're doing well,' I reassure him, from my concealed position at his feet. 'Now talk about the Trojans again. Show them the arrow.'

'There was an arrow fired inside the palace compound last night!' he shouts. 'A Trojan assassin with an inscribed arrow, bearing the name of my friend, Odysseus of Ithaca. That assassin is still out there, lurking around waiting to murder good Achaeans, right under our noses – and make off with Princess Helen!'

'Death to the Trojans!' shouts Itanus and my Ithacans, and the call is readily taken up. The suitors are all warrior-born, all armed and armoured, a menace to anyone; and, with every word, they're growing angrier and angrier. It won't take much now to push them into action.

I love a good rabblerousing.

'Tell them about Carnus being here,' I remind Menelaus. There is no one more hated and feared in Achaea than Hyllus, son of Heracles, and anyone associated with him attracts the same opprobrium.

'I have it on good authority,' Menelaus shouts – *Damn, he's doing this well* – 'that the seer Carnus, who serves Hyllus, the man who ravaged the Peloponnese and lusts to do so again, is here, right now! He's up there, at the palace shrine, plotting to kidnap our princess, the daughter of Zeus, and hand her over to our enemies! Are we going to let him?'

'Fuck, no!' roars an Arcadian champion. 'Let's go get that piece of shit and tear him apart!'

The whole crowd starts bellowing, a sea of heads and open mouths, lit by blazing torches held aloft, sparks flying up into the night sky as they're shaken about. The men are fully primed now, ready to surge through the town and up to the palace. Just like that, our work here is done.

I rise and clap Menelaus on the shoulder, keeping a fold of my cloak over my head 'Go on, take the lead,' I urge him. 'Keep them focused, and angry. I'll stay hidden in the crowd for now – there are still men hunting me.'

He gives me an anxious grin. Menelaus is a decent and conservative young man and this kind of wild near-riot is anathema to him. He also loves Tyndareus. But he believes in me and what I've told him. He really does fear for Helen and for Achaea, and rightly so – leaving aside the fact that Helen is complicit in all this plotting with Troy – a small detail I haven't yet shared with him.

Our mass of angry Achaean warriors goes bullocking through the town, joined by scores of excitable Spartan men equally inflamed by Menelaus's words. I scamper along in their midst, huddled close to Eurybates as we exchange information.

Bria has gone ahead – she has a vital mission right now, a move that might just turn the tide our way. Eury reports that the small band of Ithacans he sent off earlier have been partially successful, and returned with one of their targets to join our rearguard.

It's not all good news: Diomedes has ruled himself out – he's too humiliated to show his face, and perhaps that's for the best, given his moment of weakness could be used against him – and us.

Worse, word comes from a runner that the other suitors' camp – the one made of mostly Thessalians and other wild northerners – has been warned, and they're also on the move, surging into town through another gate. Those local people not already joined with us are barricading themselves into their homes. If this goes badly, the bloodbath Tyndareus and I have feared could easily come to pass. It's a huge gamble with people's lives, which I will be responsible for. I'm desperate to prevent such a bloodletting, despite the hornets' nest Menelaus and I have kicked here – our plan *has* to succeed.

'We *must* get to the palace gates before the other lot,' I tell Eurybates, and he hurries off to urge Menelaus – now at the head of the mass of men – to redouble his pace. We are striding out now, and I disperse my Ithacans to flank the column and provide early warnings. There's danger in the air, and the taste of blood.

But we started first, and we reach the palace before the Northerners. Tyndareus has barred the gates – not at all surprising in the circumstances, but he's nowhere to be seen on the battlements above us. Over beyond the Parnon mountains in the east, there's just the faintest hint of dawn light. The ceremony in the palace shrine must be about to begin, if it hasn't done so already.

There's a guard commander fretting above the gates, and I imagine it looks terrifying from his perspective: a sea of angry warriors breaking against the rock he's perched upon.

But the citadel has walls twelve feet high, lined with guardsmen, bows and spears at the ready. If this really turns bad, he's got all the advantages. Already some of the men behind Menelaus are aware of this, and the energy of this march is starting to dissipate. And the mainland camp – all those damned Northerners – are starting to arrive behind us. We're about to be caught between a rock and a very hard place indeed.

That's where sending Bria ahead pays off, because she appears atop of the gatehouse – with Agamemnon.

I'm too far away and there's too much of a din for me to hear anything, but the gestures and body language are quite clear. Agamemnon, resplendent in purple and gold, is ordering the guard captain to stand down and open his gates, and the captain is maintaining that he's answerable only to Tyndareus.

Agamemnon raises his voice at this point, so that even I can hear him, down in the baying crowd. His message is basic: he's the High King and Tyndareus's overlord, so *every-fucking-body* is answerable to *him*, and does the captain wish to be hurled from the gatehouse right now?

That threat – and Agamemnon's hallowed status, a reverence for lineage and blue blood, all the stuff that gets ingrained into every Achaean from birth – cause the captain to back down… indeed, *crawl down*… pretty damned fast. Just as the chanting that Menelaus is leading is beginning to falter, the gates are thrown open, and Agamemnon joins Menelaus at the head of the column that spews into the palace grounds, and pours upward to the royal shrine, at the centre of the citadel compound.

And the gates get slammed shut again, in the faces of the Northerners.

Nice touch, that.

At this stage, I decide that the safest place in the world is right behind Agamemnon, so I elbow through the crowd as best I can, and so I'm virtually treading on the heels of the High King and his brother – who look more pleased with each other than I've ever seen – as they burst into the sacred gardens and interrupt my grandmother's little gathering.

The shrine is a colonnaded garden with a statuary icon of every Olympian god, one beneath each column, and an altar in the middle piled high with offerings and votive candles and oil braziers that never go out. The greatest statues are of Zeus and Hera, at the head of the rectangular space, flanked by Ares, Aphrodite, Dionysus, Apollo and Artemis on one side; and Poseidon, Hades, Hephaestus, Hermes and Athena on the other.

No Leto, of course. This is the heartland of Lacedaemon and the Peloponnese, where old tales die hard. The Apollo statue is especially new, and the least garlanded.

Before some of these statues of the divinities are poised their primary servants. Carnus – a balding man with a thick, bushy grey beard and the build of a warrior – has placed himself before the Zeus icon; my grandmother Amphithea is positioned before that of Hera. Sophronia, High Priestess of Delos, stands before the Artemis icon, beside an easterner I don't know, languid in coloured silks beside the Apollo figurine. A burly man in furs is stationed before the Ares statue, next to a shapely young woman representing the Aphrodite priestesses. A rather handsome grey fox of a man is before the Dionysus statue, presumably Melampus. No others: no Athena, Poseidon, Hades, Hephaestus or Hermes servants – just seven of the twelve Olympian gods. Zeus's new inner circle.

They all have extra attendees – I see Manto among those people gathered behind my grandmother, and right now they're all seething with indignation at being interrupted – but it's more than indignation. I read fear and frustration, shock and bravado on their faces in equal measure.

Tyndareus and his family are also here – not just Helen, Castor and Polydeuces, but also his once-beautiful, once-vibrant wife Leda, whose life has been destroyed by a longing that turned to drunken despair, in the aftermath of her one night of divine love with Zeus. Even Tyndareus's younger children are present, three prepubescent daughters, Timandra, Phoebe and Philonoe, who are clutching their mother in bewilderment and fear. They're in the middle of the garden near the altar, a place of honour. But, huddled together, they look more like hostages.

Agamemnon and Menelaus pause at the edge of the shrine, and the mob behind us pipe down, straining to hear. The High King draws himself erect and opens his mouth…

…and for once Menelaus speaks ahead of his brother. 'Tyndareus!' he shouts, in a stricken voice – he's doing this just the way I told him – 'How can this be, that you harbour the counsellor of Hyllus, the ravager of this kingdom, in your sacred shrine?' He thrusts an accusing finger toward Carnus, while turning his head to address Agamemnon, 'There he is, brother; the man whose invective unleashed Tartarus-on-earth upon our people!'

Carnus is visibly shaken, and begins to cast his eyes about, seeking escape routes. But with our crowd of armoured suitors beginning to spill out around the shrine, those options are fast disappearing.

Make a run for it, I silently beg him. *You too, Amphithea – back down now, and make this easy for us...*

I must say this for my grandmother, though: she's not one to allow being caught in the act of betraying her people to shut her up, or even cause visible embarrassment. She's impressively brazen, as she steps forward. 'High King Agamemnon,' she cries in a high-pitched, imperious voice, 'I am here at *your* invitation, to make clear the will not only of Hera, but of all the gods!'

'You're here by your own bidding,' Agamemnon retorts crisply. 'King Tyndareus called the greatest men of Achaea to contend for the hand of his daughter, many of whom are gathered behind me. They wish to see a just settlement of his obligation to them.'

'Aye, Tyndareus,' Menelaus adds, at a nudge from me, lurking right behind him. 'We are the suitors for Princess Helen. You made us give magnificent gifts to woo her which you still hold. Until you return them, that contract binds you! You promised us all an equal opportunity to contend for Helen's hand, through proving ourselves in the games held in her honour. Yet here you are, in secret, deciding the matter without us! Where amongst you is the richest suitor? Where is the champion of the games? You've not played us fair, Foster Father, yet I know you are a fair man. Indeed, you are he who sheltered my brother and myself when no one else would, and restored my brother to his rightful throne. I don't understand! Why should we now be excluded by...' he sweeps his hand around to indicate the assembled priests and priestesses, '...some under-hand trickery?'

Tyndareus visibly groans, casting his eyes from the lines of men that now surround his shrine, to the lordly but now defensive figures stationed in front of the colonnades. And to his children – I see clearly that he fears for their lives, in this tense, fraught setting.

Is he a part of this conspiracy? Or its victim? Or has he been manipulated? How will he react now that all the hidden hands are being revealed?

I'm about to nudge Menelaus again when something happens, something which I haven't planned for, which I could never have anticipated.

Carnus steps forward, his weathered features changing as he advances down the garden. His face becomes smooth and lordly, his stature seems to grow by two feet or more and his robes turn a shining silver-blue. '*Then you shall see this matter resolved!*' he pronounces – and every man present shudders.

I'm among the closest, so I see the illusory form take shape. Those further back probably don't see it in detail, but they all sense something, because a wash of fear ripples back through the assembled men, strong enough to penetrate their anger. Illusions must reach out to the observers, and alter what they see: the more people present, the harder it is to make this work. But to me and those in the front ranks of the watchers, it's clear: *Carnus has called Zeus into his body again.*

The Skyfather glares about him, his eyes gleaming and his voice breaking over us like thunder. '*I call upon the Pythia of Pytho to come forth, to walk the Serpent's Path, and reveal the man chosen by the gods to wed my daughter, Helen of Sparta!*'

There's an audible gasp among the crowd as those watching and listening take this in – especially the words 'my daughter'. The rumour that Leda was seduced by Zeus has never been publicly confirmed, though it's well known in theioi circles.

Poor Leda drops to her knees. 'My lord,' she cries, 'My lord! I've stayed beautiful for you, my lord, I'm here!' She drops to her knees before him, opening her arms to him, her plump body and bloated face scarlet and quivering, as she implores him to take her up again.

Zeus doesn't even look at her.

Tyndareus, openly weeping, kneels down and gathers his struggling wife to his arms, pulling her face into his chest and pinning her there as the Skyfather walks straight past them.

'*We, the gods, will decide this matter,*' Zeus thunders. '*Let the Pythia make her pronouncement!*'

We're all mind-numbed, almost paralysed; those who can see are in awe of the sight and those behind are milling in confusion. I confess, I'm completely stunned – of all the ways this might play out, I never imagined Carnus invoking his god in public like this. Menelaus and Agamemnon look as helpless as I feel, all our brave initiative stolen away from us.

A trice later, the priest of Ares and the priestess of Aphrodite start to shimmer with light: clearly they're also avatars, because they grow in size, radiant with power and beauty respectively. Those men close enough to be affected by the illusion gasp in wonder; as Ares glowers about him, his gaze enough to make everyone take a step back, while the glorious visage of Aphrodite is enough to freeze the brain.

Amphithea seizes the opportunity to take full control once more, with a vengeful glance at me. She steps to the side of the Skyfather, claps her hand and a black horse is led forward, already painted with symbols and garlanded in readiness for sacrifice. Before our stunned eyes, an axe, wielded by one of her guards, slams into its skull, and its knees buckle. Tyndareus cries out in agonised protest – it's his favourite horse.

Normally, with a sacrifice, the animal's throat is slit, the blood is collected to offer to the god, then attendants discretely remove the body, to be dissected somewhere out of sight. But here, the axeman keeps hacking at the horse in a bloody frenzy, blood spurting everywhere, while Amphithea invokes Hera, her voice rising and falling in a pulsating chant. As she does, the blood fountaining from the horse's body gathers and forms a

299

spiral pattern on the flat cobblestones, a spiral only too familiar to me from my own experience of walking the Serpent's Path.

This garden has been transformed into a sacred oracle, where prophecies may be taken by a theios-seer.

My heart lurches as my grandmother steps to the beginning of the spiral pattern, and behind her, Manto lifts her arms in supplication and preparation, just as they spoke of last night.

I can't let them do this without at least trying to prevent it.

So I step forth, from behind Agamemnon and Menelaus. 'I challenge this desecration!' I shout.

My grandmother whirls at the sound of my voice, her reptilian face contorting in fury; but worse is the visage of Zeus-Carnus, which is instantly inflamed with a terrifying wrath. He raises his hand and I am suddenly, absolutely aware of one of the most central beliefs concerning the Skyfather – that he can destroy a man with a thunderbolt.

Among the gods, in a sacred place, belief is reality.

He shouts aloud, and I am certain that I have overstepped – fatally. Time seems to freeze as lightning crackles across the sky. I am about to be destroyed.

Prometheus, save me, I whisper – no, *scream* – inside my soul.

An image flashes into my mind, of my tortured greatgrandsire, hanging by a manacle on a cliff-face, naked and bleeding. His face is twisted and distorted by agony, his mouth emits a howl of perpetual torment, but his eyes are still clear as they see me, and the bravest smile I've ever seen transfigures his face.

Odysseus, he says, inside my head. *I am with you.*

Instantly, I sense something like a burst of energy envelop me.

Zeus shudders and Carnus almost loses his grip on his deity; and although Zeus then reasserts himself, the energy required drains away the forces he'd conjured. There's no thunderbolt, and I breathe again.

My link to Prometheus tells me there wouldn't have been an actual thunderbolt – not one that mortal eyes could have seen

– but I would have collapsed from a massive heart seizure, and the moment would have been utterly lost.

But I haven't. The presence of my supernatural patron lingers within me; and Zeus-Carnus lowers his hand, sensing the countering power, and – extraordinarily – he's now uncertain.

Maybe even afraid.

Prometheus is bound in Hades's Realm, but perhaps that's because they can't *kill him? Perhaps containing him is the most they can do...*

Before Zeus can recover, I seize my chance. 'We're here to adjudicate about a marriage,' I shout. 'The Pythia has denied a good man – a prince, a king in waiting – his lawful bride. This woman, here.' It's not Helen I'm referring to; my accusing finger is thrust at Manto, who stares at me, at first in stunned disbelief and then contempt which turns to disgust as Bria shoves Alcmaeon through the crowd, and out to the front to stand with me. 'This is Prince Alcmaeon of Argos,' I declare, 'who has fathered a child with Manto, daughter of Tiresias. Under law, that child and this woman now belong to him. She has left the guardianship of the Pytho shrine, and is therefore subject to the laws of Achaea.'

This is a law I've argued against many a time, a horrible, one-sided statute that has condemned many an unwilling woman, often the victim of rape, into a marriage that is little more than slavery. When I am king of Cephalonia, I will abolish it in my kingdom if it's the last thing I do.

But right now, although the law is an ass, it's my ass...

Few people here understand why I'm doing this. To most, this gathering is all about Helen and they're completely dumbfounded as to why I'm suddenly invoking common law about someone else.

But Zeus-Carnus knows, and so do Amphithea and Manto herself.

Manto shrinks away as Alcmaeon advances toward her, his face twisted with desperate, uncontrollable want. It's piteous, but his lust is something she's conjured up and fed, until it has penetrated his very marrow. *She is responsible for what he is; she made him this way...*

I'm waiting for her to try some trick, even to invoke some sorcerous spell that will avert this fate, but her face has changed from disgust to something more calculating. There's even a glimmer of hope there. Perhaps she's not Amphithea's ally after all? Perhaps she's her slave, and this is a way to escape, even if it's into a different kind of bondage. But knowing her, she won't be in bonds for long...

She throws me a look that's supposed to be of utter loathing, but she can't hide a gleam in her eye that just might be gratitude. *She'll hate herself for that.* All this is intensely ironical, because I was the one that suggested she be taken to Pytho in the first place. And now I'm freeing her from their clutches.

These are tangled webs I've woven, and it's not the first time I've had to fight to undo my own schemes. Just ask Theseus and Helen.

'Are you, legally, the wife of Alcmaeon of Argos?' I demand of her.

'Yes,' Manto snarls, before Amphithea can open her mouth.

So I guessed right... The sorceress rushes to Alcmaeon as though he's her every dream, falling to the ground and clutching his knees, wailing her thanks to the gods. Tears course down Alcmaeon's cheeks as he bends down, sobbing, to embrace her and pull her to her feet. She responds by stroking his chest and gazing adoringly into his eyes... *and likely reasserting her control...*

Alcmaeon has no further interest in this gathering – he pulls her away, and she lets him. As they leave the courtyard, they pass close by me and she shoots me a truly terrifying look, instantly covered by a simper. 'I thought you wanted me dead,' she murmurs.

'Being married to him will do just as well for now,' I whisper back, while Alcmaeon just gazes at her with the blank need of a poppy juice addict.

'This isn't over between us,' she threatens, fixing me with those bewitching, scary eyes.

'I know.'

That's all we have time for – Alcmaeon rouses himself from whatever erotic reverie he'd lost himself in and pulls his reclaimed wife impatiently away. The crowd parts and closes again behind them.

I really, *really* don't ever want to see either of them again. But I'm seldom that lucky.

I turn back to see how Amphithea likes having her prop snatched away.

Rewardingly, she's not taking it well. Her face is suddenly naked – and fearful. Yes, she can still walk the Serpent's Path: but without Manto there to pervert the voices of the oracle she knows what the spirits will say about Helen's marriage. Phrases like 'the doom of Achaea' and 'the inexorable rise of the Trojan stallion' won't sound too good in front of an angry mob of armed Achaean warriors.

Got you, I think silently, hoping that's true.

Zeus-Carnus's illusory face is wavering. This hasn't played at all according to his plans, and now he's caught between Scylla and Charybdis.

'The omens are not… amenable…' Amphithea says weakly. 'I cannot… not today…' She feigns weakness, as though on the brink of a fainting fit. Should I allow her to retreat, or insist on her seeing it through?

But what if she prophesizes something so dire it breaks all of our hearts?

I've almost resolved to let her back out, when the matter is taken from my hands.

A wiry young man, wearing a traveller's wide-brimmed hat and a dun-coloured tunic, emerges from behind the previously deserted colonnade dedicated to Hermes. As he steps forward, he transforms into the god himself, with winged sandals and a gleaming skull cap. '*I desire to hear the words of the spirits on this matter*,' he proclaims, his glowing eyes passing through every hue of the rainbow.

Zeus's face is thunderstruck. As for Hermes, he doesn't exactly wink at me, but something in his stance tells me that this may well be the fruit of our bargain in Arcadia. He will be looking for signs of double-dealing on Zeus's part, especially any that concern the unleashing of Hyllus upon the Peloponnese. My heart begins to thump again.

'*I too desire this reading,*' says the avatar-priest of Dionysus, changing, as he speaks, into a beautiful youth clad in a leopard skin robe, with grapevines laden with fruit in his hair.

The crowd recoils in awe, and so do I. This is escalating into something even more unpredictable.

'*As do I,*' thunders a massive figure with a broad, bare chest and seaweed in his hair, who steps from the shadows to plant his feet before the Poseidon icon. He's joined by a silent, dark-haired, pallid deity with cavernous eye sockets – Hades.

Teliope joins them, calling Athena into her body, a bronze helm atop her piled up hair, and a shrieking owl on her wrist. '*I too would hear the fate of this young princess,*' she declares coolly. I glimpse Bria near her – she gives me an apologetic shrug, of the 'what could I do about it?' kind.

The easterner representing Apollo backs away, looking this way and that, as if to escape. Suddenly his whole body trembles and he changes into a gloriously handsome man with golden skin and hair. '*Do not permit this, Great Father,*' he tells Zeus. '*There are malign influences here.*' He's looking at me. '*The spirits will not speak truly.*'

Sophronia is looking terrified. Either she's not an avatar, or she's too scared to summon Artemis into this fraught situation. She's backing away, her eyes darting to and fro as she searches for a way out.

Interestingly, no one appears to speak for Hephaestus at all, his colonnade remaining unattended. His era is indeed at an end, his cult dying away.

I've been so mesmerised by what is happening before us, I've failed to realise there's a cluster of people at the far end of the garden, huddled behind the statues of Zeus and Hera. Their identities are masked by the shadows and the folds of the cloaks they've dragged over their heads, but I suddenly realise from what I can see of their clothing that they must be the Trojan party – Parassi, Skaya-Manu and their men... and *Kyshanda*, here to collect their prize, but now trapped in a situation that's escalating out of control. My pulse begins to race, and my throat goes sticky and dry.

And on my left flank, behind the defiant avatars of Ares, Aphrodite and Apollo, the northern champions are beginning to appear; led by Iolaus the Heraclid, with Patroclus, Elephenor and Locrian Aias at his back. They've somehow found another way into the citadel, by persuasion or by force; they're heavily armed and they look angry and ready for violence if needs be.

What will Hermes make of this? I glance at the god, but his face is inscrutable.

The reek of the sacrificed horse's blood fills our nostrils. I swallow, very hard. This has become a meeting of all the Olympians, and it's happening right before our amazed eyes.

Tyndareus is awestruck, and his wife Leda's eyes are red and swollen as she drinks in the sight. She'll never recover from this. Maybe none of us will. But Castor and Polydeuces are gaping at each other, alive with excitement – they probably think of the gods as family anyway.

As for Helen... she's watching avidly, her lips parted and moist. After making all the great kings and heroes of Achaea fight for her, now she's about to watch the gods contend as well.

She seems to regard it as her due.

Zeus rallies at Apollo's words. '*I do indeed see malign influences,*' he thunders, wheeling back and pointing at me. '*The last bastard Promethean, for one. Give him the same fate as his father!*'

Only a few of the people here know or suspect who my real father is – Sisyphus, who seduced my mother then died on the streets of Corinth, his body left to the dogs. The rest have no idea what Zeus is talking about. But Aias of Locris draws his sword and Patroclus, Elephenor and a dozen of their cronies follow suit, weapons bared in a sacred place. The watching priests among the crowd clamour protests, but no one's listening.

My Ithacans have stepped up, protecting my back, and now everyone's got a weapon out, as the Northerners urge on their men, and Menelaus and Agamemnon's guards array to protect their masters – not me. Suddenly, terrifyingly, we are teetering on the edge of the bloodbath I have feared all along.

And the War-God is here, in the flesh… Ares stalks toward me. '*Be still!*' his voice rings out.

I feel the soldiers around me go rigid with fear. The ground quivers as he approaches, his gleaming bronze xiphos rasping from his scabbard. He's eight feet tall, he's built like a bull and nothing my brain screams at me can unlock my limbs. I try to reach inside myself to find Prometheus again, but it's as if there's some inner barrier around me, and I can't reach him.

I look to Athena, but Ares shoulders her aside as she tries to intervene – they might both be deities of war, but I've just glimpsed the relative might they wield. Ares lifts his blade, and no one – least of all myself – can stop him from hacking me down.

Who do you pray to when your own goddess has just been swept aside?

Then someone emerges from the crowd and interposes his blade between me and death.

Diomedes.

Ares roars, and swings anyway, but the Argive prince's sword, wielded two-handed, slams into the space between the arcing blade and my neck, and with the deafening clang of metal on metal, god and hero strain against each other.

'Get out of my path, you cock-sucking weakling,' Ares snarls, and Diomedes flinches.

But he doesn't give way. He's struggling, though, his muscles bulging and his joints twisting under the stress. But his intervention has unlocked my limbs and those of my men. We prepare to do something really stupid, something that will almost certainly end in our deaths…

'Enough!' Athena shouts, and suddenly she's right there, her spearhead against Ares's neck. 'My champions have my protection, and this is a holy place. Respect that, if you're capable.'

Ares goes rigid – because avatars can die, and when they do, their patron gods had better not be inside the body, if they don't want to be crippled and cast into the void for a very long time. There's even a chance he might never recover – especially if the tale becomes gospel – that Athena, War-Goddess of Attica, slew mighty Ares.

Half of me wishes she'd just do it, and damn the consequences.

But she doesn't, because there's too much at stake here, and she, like Ares, is far from invulnerable when inhabiting a human body. It takes several seconds to both call and release a divinity's spirit, moments in which they are as mortal as you and I. So, like two great predators that come face to face in the wild, they snarl and show their teeth… and then back away.

My skin is slick with sweat, my heart is racing and my very bones won't stop shaking. But somehow I summon the strength to grip Diomedes's shoulder. 'Thank you, brother,' I manage to gasp, as Ares stalks backwards, mouthing his fury but unwilling to take the fatal step.

'You kept my disgrace a secret,' Diomedes whispers. 'I owe you… brother.'

There's no time even to embrace – over on the other side of the garden, Zeus, Ares, Aphrodite, Apollo and Dionysus are now arrayed with their priests and seers, with the northern champions on one side and the Trojans on the other. A moment later Hermes joins them, but his eyes meet mine as he does so, with a faint shake of the head that could mean anything.

Poseidon and Hades are watching with open interest, neither obviously taking sides; and their dread presence is somehow enough to quell the spread of violence. For now.

So that leaves the only one actively arrayed against them as Athena, alone and defiant.

Interestingly, Hera, like Artemis, hasn't possessed her avatar…Perhaps the goddess has some compelling reason not to appear? I think I know what it is: while this was a secret meeting in which a pre-arranged mockery of a prophecy would be delivered – one that made marrying Helen to a Trojan prince seem like the will of Olympus – Hera could claim to be working for the Achaean people.

But now their subterfuge is in the open, she's afraid to show, knowing that any prophecy that emerges from the Spiral Path will be uncontrolled, and delivered before a volatile crowd of Achaeans, all of whom have been fantasising about murdering each other for days. If someone or something lights the tinder, the whole of Achaea will go up in flames. *Today*. That will suit Zeus very well but it most certainly doesn't suit Hera, because why on Earth would Zeus honour his promises to her of post-invasion sovereignty, if her people have butchered each other in a civil war first?

No worshipper, no worship. And without worship, no goddess.

Zeus's promise to her, last night, is worthless.

I'm breaking out in a cold sweat, because I can see that Zeus, our great Skyfather, is raising his hand, in preparation for the prophecy, waiting to unleash all-out war…

And then a slender figure steps into the open space by the altar. '*I shall walk the Serpent Path!*' she cries out.

It's Penelope – but her face is alight with a strange, divine radiance. I want to rush over to her, to support her, but before anyone can react she shrieks, as an invisible current of energy slams through her. She flings her arms wide, shaking to and fro like a rag doll caught in the fist of a gigantic, invisible hand, her hair billowing about her as she wails, arms reaching up to beseech the heavens. She sweeps around, lowering one arm to point a finger at Amphithea, who has instinctively blocked her way to the spiral of blood on the ground.

'Begone!' Penelope cries.

The Pythia tries to defy her but she's swotted aside by an unseen force, sent sprawling on the bloodied paving stones and staring up at Penelope in bewilderment. Around me, hardened fighting men are simply staring, mesmerised, their weapons slack in their hands, eyes stretched wide, mouths open. My own heart is pounding, terrified for Penelope and for what her actions may spark – and also from wonder, because I've never seen her look so unearthly and potent.

I steal a glance at the Spartan royal family. Tyndareus has drawn his wife and daughters close around him, all of them kneeling on the ground; even Castor, slack-jawed and frightened, has followed suit. But Helen and Polydeuces are standing erect, staring now at Penelope, now at Zeus. They must be wondering if the promises made them are about to be ripped from their grasp. Helen wants a vast eastern empire to rule; and Polydeuces has been pledged the High Kingship of Achaea. All that now stands in doubt.

'*Who are you?*' Zeus bellows, over the rumble of thunder, his robes lit by the jagged glint of lightning through the clouds gathering above.

Penelope's eyes roll back as she drops to her knees and plants her splayed hands in the horse's blood. Then she stands, holding her palms aloft once more before ripping her tunic open and smearing gore over her face, breasts and belly. The path of blood on the cobblestones realigns, as though issuing from her feet, and begins to glow, droplets rising weightlessly around her like a mist. A trio of voices, a blend of youth and age, bursts from Penelope's throat. '*WE ARE THE MOIRAE,*' they proclaim.

The Moirae… The Fates…

I recoil at the impossibility of it, repulsed by the very concept of fate, of inescapable destinies for myself and my nation. I would rather deny the Moirae's existence – but at this moment, perhaps, they're our only hope. So like everyone else here; from the children of Tyndareus to the warriors and priests and kings, to the gods themselves, I just stare in amazement...

Penelope begins to tread the bloody path before her, her eyes white orbs, her feet lightly placed but sure, moving with a fragile, beautiful grace. The horse blood covering her breasts and belly has writhed into a glowing spiral that matches the path she's treading. At last she reaches the very centre of the path, and the three voices of the Moirae screech from her throat once more.

'THE BLADE TURNS, AND THE DANCERS TREAD ITS EDGE! THE FLOCK SCATTER, THE SHEP-HERDESS LOST, AND THE HOOVES OF THE STAL-LION PAW THE GROUND! WOE TO EARTH! WOE TO THE LAND!'

I want to save Penelope from this, to pull her from the grip of the Serpent's Path and cover her blood-smeared body. But my rational brain is saying: *No, this must be heard.* I look across at Athena, but she's as transfixed by this display as everyone else. Does she know the Moirae? Or is she just as shocked as the rest of us?

'THE SEVENTH WAVE ROLLS OVER US, TO LEVEL THE WALLS AND TOWERS, SCOUR THE LAND! NOTHING CAN STAND, FOR THE NAILS HAVE BEEN STRIPPED FROM YOUR HOUSES OF TWIGS AND LEAVES! WOE TO YOU, O LAND!'

I groan inwardly. Achaea has no hope, that can be the only interpretation.

'WHITHER THE BUILDER? WHITHER THE SHEPHERDESS? LURED AND LOST! WHITHER THE BEACON, THE SCEPTRE, THE CHALICE, THE WINE OF HOPE? GIVEN AWAY! BETRAYED! DIVIDED! SCATTERED! WHITHER THE SHINING BLADE? GIFTED AND GONE! WOE TO THEE, OH LAND!'

I'm certainly not the only one able to interpret this, and I'm probably not getting all the nuances that better-trained seers can, let alone the gods. But I can see the effects – Zeus, Ares, Aphrodite, Dionysus, Apollo – they're lapping it up. Achaea is doomed, and they are vindicated in fleeing her, and seeking to become the gods of the victorious Trojans. Hermes's face has turned a sickly grey as he tries to conceal his horror.

Meanwhile Athena is ashen-faced, and even Hades and Poseidon look haggard, like trees lashed by a rising storm wind. And my grandmother Amphithea is on her knees, head in hands. Because she is for Hera, but she is also for Achaea, and the promise of Hera being dominant in a post-invasion, Trojan-dominated Achaea is being exposed as a lie.

'*TAKE UP THE SCEPTRE, TAKE UP THE CHALICE, TAKE UP THE BLADE!*' the Moirae cry through Penelope's tortured throat. '*FIND THE BUILDER, FIND THE SHEPHERDESS. BIND YOUR THREADS, YE WEAVERS! LIGHT A TORCH, MAN OF FIRE! TAKE UP THE BLADE! TAKE COURAGE, OH LAND, FOR THINE ONLY HOPE IS HOPE!*'

Abruptly, the Moirae are gone, and Penelope is left, half-naked and smeared in blood, kneeling in a bloody puddle next to the horse's sprawling body in the centre of the courtyard, surrounded by the gods. Beyond them are the watching priests and warriors – almost all of us Achaean, and most if not all of those theioi present will have understood what we just saw.

We've just heard the doom of Achaea pronounced.

It's as if I'm the only one whose limbs still work. I race forward, unpinning my cloak and wrapping it round the bloodied, disoriented Penelope, pulling her to her feet and against me. She looks up at me blearily.

'I… I heard…' she groans, 'I heard… from far… away…'

She sags against my shoulder, so exhausted her legs are giving way, and I have to loop an arm under her armpit to hold her up. To have done what she just did must have taken a reserve of strength beyond my imagination.

'It's a prophecy of disaster,' someone wails – a priestess from among Hera's retinue.

'No,' I shout out. 'It's a message of hope!'

Zeus turns to face me, his majestic face livid to find me still underfoot, still defiant. 'How so, mortal?'

'"*Find the builder, find the shepherdess, bind the threads, light the torch*",' I reply defiantly. 'The Moirae exhort us to unite! The Fates are not Trojan or Hittite gods – they're Achaean, like us! "Woe to the Land", they cry, for it's their land also! They are telling us that our only hope is unity!' I throw out a hand – pointing straight at Helen. 'There is the Chalice!' And then Polydeuces: 'And there the Shining Blade! Will we give these precious talismans away – to our enemies the Trojans?'

'No!' shout a few voices – led by Diomedes, Menelaus and Bria. But soon they are joined by a swelling chorus: the suitors and the Achaean priestly retinues on both sides of the shrine – people both of the Peloponnese and the North. '*NO!*'

Iolaus the Heraclid is silent, though, his eyes fixed on Zeus, as though waiting for some sign. I glance across at Hermes. Has he noticed? Is this enough, subtle as it is, to convince him of the nature of the betrayal the Moirae just spoke of?

'Where is the Builder and the Shepherdess with her sceptre?' I ask. I look up, right into the eyes of Zeus the Skyfather, challenging him, and then glare at my grandmother, who has regained her feet but looks like a corpse. 'Have they gone over to our enemy? Or are they still with us?'

Renounce your path, or renounce us.

Zeus knows – he sees exactly what has happened. His over-arching authority has been challenged by the Moirae. And I've just given him both an ultimatum, and a way out – right here where his human avatar is vulnerable.

He could just depart his avatar and run. But surely it's too soon to abandon Achaea completely. Even though he's now in Troy as Zeus-Tarhum, if he abjures us, he'll risk becoming just another minor deity in the overcrowded pantheons of the east. Here, he's the big dog. Can he afford to abandon us yet?

But that means backing down and at least pretending to side with Achaea. It means abandoning Helen to an Achaean wedding: a setback to his Trojan allies, and a failure to be marked against him in their eyes.

I spare a glance for the others behind him. Ares is sullen and watchful – he understands. So too does Aphrodite, whose glittering, divine eyes want to burn me to ash. Apollo is seething, his impossibly handsome visage contorted with hate for Penelope and me.

Hermes is watchful, calculating. But he doesn't act, despite all he's just seen and heard – the Moirae, the presence of the Trojans and of Iolaus. Is the Messenger God still in Zeus's hands?

Then, after what seems like an eon but can only be a few heartbeats, Hermes sidles up to Zeus and whispers something in the Skyfather's ear, and the King of the Gods nods slowly, his expression falling into blank resignation.

'*I am the Builder*,' Zeus says in a thick, menacing voice. 'I am your Father, Achaea, and I give you my daughter, Helen of Sparta, in token of my love for thee, Oh, Land.'

Hermes finally meets my eye – momentarily – before kissing Zeus's hand, the loyal keryx advising his master. But whatever he's said may just have spared Achaea from disaster, and given us back control of our fate.

'*And I am the Shepherdess*,' a woman calls – the avatar of Hera, transformed at last into her goddess, finally taking sides now the outcome is known. She strides down the centre of the garden, through the blood of the sacrificed stallion. '*I am the Goddess of the Earth, and of the Land. I shall never abandon my people.*'

Bravo, I think scornfully. Though her skill in conspiring for war then switching sides, just in time to take credit for peace, isn't to be sneezed at, I suppose.

With all the pomp and grandeur Hera can muster, she takes the hand of her unwilling 'husband' and raises them both high. '*It is time for unity, among the people of Achaea. We the gods are as one, watching over you all.*'

'*Aye!*' calls Athena, her grey eyes glinting.

'*Aye!*' the other gods chorus, in voices laced with false triumphalism.

Even golden Apollo and too-pretty Dionysus, the most eastern of them, feel compelled to follow the lead set them. They have little choice – their small Trojan retinue is standing mute and helpless – and the avatars containing them must surely be close to exhaustion by now. One day the gods may emerge to battle openly for supremacy, but it won't be here and now.

Zeus glances at me again, and he whispers into my mind, '*I will punish thee for the rest of time for this. I will nail you up beside Prometheus and watch you scream for all eternity.*'

Then suddenly the avatars are all emptied, a row of mere men and women, utterly drained by their efforts. The gods have gone, not just because their avatars can't be possessed any longer. They can't risk tarnishing their golden auras of infallibility by remaining amongst us. And, I am absolutely certain, they simply can't stand to be with each other a moment longer, either. But as their avatars reel in the aftermath, it's as if the air has been sucked out of all our lungs and we're all left gasping for breath.

Penelope stirs beside me, giving me a quick smile as she regains her balance. 'Thank you,' she says, with firm assertive-ness. 'I'll be all right now. I must stand alone.'

I'm still concerned for her, and very doubtful that she's half as recovered as she pretends. But there's still a touch of the Moirae about her, and I do as bid, though I allow myself to hover at her shoulder, just in case. Inside the cloak I've loaned her, she's visibly trembling.

Those around me look as though they've just been shaken out of a coma, such is the intensity of being in the presence of the gods. Tyndareus is clutching Leda, who is weeping with renewed loss. Polydeuces is gaunt-faced, one hand grasping his brother Castor's arm with whitened knuckles and staring into the void. And Helen – gorgeous, ramrod-straight and sharp-eyed Helen – is slumped like a discarded doll, emptied of volition, defeated, her dreams of empire broken before her eyes.

Agamemnon and Menelaus are sharing a shaky, incredulous look, chests heaving in relief. Amphithea is crouched by Hera's colonnade, too frail and broken to stand unaided. Even Bria looks pale, and if there's anyone who's seen it all, it's her.

In the aftermath of the gods, we mortals struggle to cope with our own reality. And in moments of bewilderment, often it's the person that speaks next who wins: I make sure it's me.

'My King,' I say loudly, directing my words at Tyndareus, 'The Gods have spoken. Will you choose a good Achaean husband for your daughter?'

The King of Sparta looks like he's too confounded to think. *That's fine, I'll do it for him.* When he nods vaguely, I turn that gesture into words, turning to face the shrine and shouting, 'Thank you, Great King. Let us take counsel together, and choose Helen a husband, here and now. I nominate—'

I break off, because a figure has just emerged from the crowd, a Trojan with a javelin, and before anyone can react, he hurls the weapon with its gleaming, wicked-looking head.

I see his face, in the instant that he throws: it's the assassin, Korakis.

But the javelin flies not at me, but at Princess Helen.

'No!' I shout, turning in horror as the shaft hurtles past me…

…and skids across Menelaus's armoured shoulder as he throws himself at Helen, bearing her to the ground and covering her with his body.

'*Take that man alive!*' I shout, but I'm too late. Blades are already drawn, and the closest men lunge in. Swords flash up and down and Korakis is dead in an instant, hacked, slashed and stabbed, before being cut almost in two by the giant Aias of Salamis.

Then they turn their swords on the watching Trojans.

'*No! No!*' I shout, terrified for Kyshanda. '*No more killing!*'

Thanks be, this time I'm heeded – along with those others that take up my cry, principally the local priests that have just seen their holiest shrine desecrated with human blood. That doesn't prevent the Trojans from being seized and dragged roughly forward, then thrust to their knees before Agamemnon, who takes charge.

'Unmask them,' he shouts, and their cloaks are pulled away from their faces.

There's a dozen of them; most just soldiers, I deem. But Parassi, Skaya-Mandu and Kyshanda are known by a few here. All three have cast their eyes down, but now Kyshanda raises her head to look at me – standing oh-so-close to Penelope.

Her eyes well up, and tears run down her face. I can only blink my own away.

Why Helen? Why did Korakis attack Helen, and not me?

Logic answers me: I might be a nuisance, but Helen is the Sacred Bride, the woman whose husband will rule the Aegean. Korakis tried to kill her, to prevent any Achaean from possessing her. *Possess the twain and rule.* If a Trojan couldn't have her, no one would. But did he come to that conclusion alone – or did Skaya-Mandu order it?

Or did Zeus himself inspire the act, out of spite? The more I think on that, the more it seems likely…

I wonder if Helen realises.

But right now, Kyshanda and her retinue face execution, and though our love might be broken, I can't allow her to die here.

'Behold! Two princes of Troy and a princess also,' Agamemnon declares, as I wrack my brain for some way to extricate her. 'Why are you here?' the High King demands.

Parassi remains sullenly silent, but Skaya-Mandu raises his head, defiant, arrogant as ever. 'My brother is the eldest son of Piri-Yamu, a man who one day will rule you all. He was promised a bride, a daughter of the gods, and he will have one.'

Some theioi really do believe in their own immortality. If Agamemnon hadn't raised a hand, Aias of Salamis would have taught the stuck-up twat his error by beheading him.

I cast a look at Menelaus. He's helping Helen up, and she's clearly aghast. I'm sure she knew there was an assassin in play, but she never thought he might be turned on *her*, the absolute, golden, immutable centre of her own universe. She's deadly pale, her beauty almost ghostlike – and Menelaus's protective nature and weakness for those he sees as helpless means that he can't let her go, can't look away.

Helen will get over her shock in a moment, no doubt, but right now, she's at least a little more manageable than she might have been…

Agamemnon stalks down the line of kneeling Trojans, each with a blade to their throat, then pauses beside me to throw me a searching look, one eyebrow twitching upwards. I'm surprised and gratified: he needs my counsel.

In answer to his silent question, I shake my head faintly. While I would happily see Skaya-Mandu and Parassi dead, the act would certainly precipitate an immediate war with Troy. *We're not ready for that yet.* And Agamemnon would have Kyshanda killed also, or raped and enslaved, and I don't want that at all.

Just looking at her, the sword blade sketching a faint red line of blood across her throat, is a torment. 'Killing them would oblige Troy to attack us,' I murmur to Agamemnon. 'We need more time to prevent that, or to prepare.' I raise my voice a little, so that the people around us can hear. 'It is said that a great king shows his power through his mercy. Perhaps these people can carry a message to Troy, one that tells of Achaean unity?'

Agamemnon weighs that up. He's cold-hearted enough that I still fear for Kyshanda's safety; but then he inclines his head.

'This is a sacred place,' he declares. 'There will be no more killing. These people were brought here by the Skyfather, who has blessed us with his divine presence, and shown his love for Achaea. Let us not dishonour his hospitality.'

There's some dissatisfaction among the men holding swords to the Trojans' throats, but we all know that Agamemnon is not someone to question, let alone oppose. It's his Atreiades blood – the knowledge that he'll go further, longer and bloodier than anyone else, to avenge a slight.

The armed men all back away – though Aias of Locris, who had his blade at Kyshanda's neck, pulls her to his feet and whispers something in her ear, leering down at her breasts as he does. She tosses her head and spits in his face.

He wipes her spittle off his cheek and raises a hand to strike her, but Diomedes grabs his wrist and the Locrian backs down. For myself I'm livid, my urge to skewer this rampant *pornos* almost overwhelming.

Aias sees the look on my face, and smiles evilly. He touches two fingers to his eyes, then points them first at me, then Kyshanda, and licks his lips. He yanks his hand from Diomedes's grasp and stalks away.

If he touches her again, I will *kill him.*

'Attend her if you must,' Penelope murmurs. But I shake my head. I've already let Kyshanda go. Now I have to live with that decision.

Agamemnon assigns trusted men – his own Mycenaeans – to take the Trojans away, as Tyndareus's 'protected guests' under the ancient laws of guest friendship. He strides to the altar, and looks around the circle of priests and priestesses and pallid-faced, sagging avatars. Someone's helped my grandmother up, but she and her entourage look devastated. *Their illusions have been destroyed and they're still reeling.* So too are the priests of Zeus, Ares, Aphrodite and Apollo. They're here, but reduced to passivity – for now.

Agamemnon swiftly recognizes the opportunity, turning to the crowds and raising his voice.

'Yea, here we are! You have haggled, you have given generously, you have competed with the bow and you've run and wrestled. All for the love of a young woman, for the right to marry her, to honour and protect and love her.'

Very occasionally, someone speaks as well as I do – not often, mind. Seldom is someone better at seizing the moment, but Agamemnon is doing that now – and I have a horrid feeling where he's heading and I don't like it at all.

But do we have any alternative? It's as though we've all been caught up in an avalanche, flailing about and now it's coming to rest, with our bodies tossed about and jumbled together in the most unlikely combinations…

Agamemnon gestures grandly to Helen, who is still being held by Menelaus, although her head is now high and her lips tightly pursed. 'I could elaborate about the need for the leading suitor to be of noble birth,' the High King continues. 'For him to be whole of limb and fair of face, great-hearted and gentle, a warrior and a leader. The type of man who can rally men behind him and challenge wrongs. A man for whom being a husband and father is his greatest and longest held dream.'

My heart sinks as my guess becomes a certainty. Agamemnon doesn't need to name names, when his brother fits all these criteria.

'It might even help if the princess knew this man, had known him all her life, and forged bonds of love and trust with him already,' says Agamemnon in that pompous but compelling voice of his. 'That, instead of a stranger, she could be easy of heart knowing that for them both, marriage will be an extension of the friendship they share. And for her to know that in a moment of supreme danger, her husband is the only one present whose first and only thought was for her safety.'

My mind is full of fear and doubt. I'm terrified for my friend. But we need to keep Helen in Achaea, we need her married and safely guarded. Who has the strength to clasp such a viper to his breast? Because I know in my heart that Helen can be another Manto, someone who breaks those around her. Who could hope to contain her?

But hope, the Moirae have proclaimed, is the one weapon we have.

Then I realise that I'm thinking about this the wrong way. We shouldn't be trying to *contain* her. She's a complex young woman who's been through terrible things, and had all manner of evil whispered into her ears, of superiority and domination. Caging her will further ruin her… but love, real and uncon-ditional love, might redeem her, and unleash her incredible potential – a woman blessed by all the gods, a queen, not a tyrant.

Can Helen become that person? Can she open that cold heart of hers to be warmed by the love of a decent, caring man? If anyone can reach her with kindness and loyalty, it's Menelaus. No one else sees her as anything other than a prize. But he feels her pain, and he wants to heal it. Not even Diomedes is capable of that. Might unquestioning love be the only thing that can reach her and give her back the innocence and happiness Theseus ripped from her?

That I helped him rip from her?

I watch, torn and confused, as Menelaus beseeches her with his eyes. Even Agamemnon dare not speak now – my eyes meet his and I can tell he, like me, realises that this marriage will never work unless Helen herself makes the final decision.

Although nobody utters so much as a whisper, I'm almost deafened by the sound of my blood, hissing and surging in my ears.

What's the tipping point? I don't think she's capable of true gratitude – even Menelaus throwing himself in front of death to save her is probably something she just *expects* lesser mortals to do. But maybe – hopefully – she sees in the eyes of my best friend something she instinctively knows that she needs.

For a moment I think I glimpse her real self – a still-unformed girl, too privileged to feel empathy, but possessing tremendous resource and potential. Then the mask slams down, and she's the girl the audience wishes to see, the princess seeking love. She smiles tremulously, murmurs something only he can hear, then kisses my friend's mouth with all the passion and intensity that a beautiful young woman can summon.

The groom has been chosen.

No one else need speak, and no one does: until Agamemnon claps his hands together, and all those round us burst into a ragged cheer that is as much relief as it is joy.

19 – The Oath

'HESIOD: And what, above all, is the most excellent thing to pray to the gods for?

HOMER: To be ever at peace with oneself and with everything around one.'

—*Lives of Homer: The Contest of Homer and Hesiod*

Sparta

This business isn't finished though. There's something we must do, to try and seal the fragile unity we so badly need, in order to make it real. It's not prophecy or divine knowledge that tells me so, but instinct. We're flesh and blood and we need tangible symbols to remind us of the intangible. I wrack my brain… and an answer begins to form.

Penelope goes to return my cloak just as Bria joins us, only to realise for the first time what state she's in underneath the heavy folds. She hurriedly covers her blood-smeared body and ruined tunic again, struggling to keep her discomposure hidden and failing dismally. 'Oh Gods, did I…'

'I'm afraid so, honey,' Bria says cheerily. 'Nice tits, by the way. I'm sure Ithaca thinks so, too.'

Penelope collects herself enough to raise her eyes skywards, before huddling deeper than ever into the cloak.

'We need to have a nice long chat about the Moirae,' Bria adds.

'I have to go back to Delos. My place is with the cult of Artemis—'

'No way,' Bria drawls. 'You're your own cult now. You don't belong on that bloody rock, and after what you just did, you're not safe there anymore.' Then she gives Penelope a mischievous look. 'On the bright side,' she adds, 'I don't think all the Fates are virgins.'

Penelope gives her a steadier look than I would have been capable of. 'You must understand, I've never wanted to be anything other than a priestess of Artemis, before...'

Before... My heart thuds at the implications of that word.

Her eyes flicker to the knot of Artemis priestesses and huntresses, staring at us with hard eyes. 'But I fear you're right,' she adds, her voice cracking as she contemplates a life in which all past certainties are gone.

'We'll protect you,' Bria tells her, in a voice that is for once devoid of irony or sarcasm.

'Yes, we most certainly will,' I put in. 'But there's something I *must* do, right now.'

The two women look at me quizzically, but I turn away, as my plan takes shape. I think it's a good one. Brilliant, even. Right now everyone is standing around, in a mostly stunned silence, but I can already see a few disgruntled faces. This harmony isn't going to last long.

Light the torch, Man of Fire...

I go to the near end of the colonnaded garden, and climb onto a handy bench so everyone can see me, and pitch my voice for all to hear. 'You are witnesses to the fate of Achaea,' I shout, stretching my arms out as everyone turns to hear. 'You heard the seeress speak: of a land whose very soil will be scoured, if we do not provide the nails to hold it together. A land that would give away those very things it needs to keep us safe, its chalice and its blade. A land which almost lost its builder and its shepherdess.'

The listening men nod anxiously, as I confirm their own interpretations.

'The seeress spoke of hope,' Eumelus calls – Penelope's friend.

I give him a nod of thanks. 'I believe the spirits gave us a warning, not of what is and will be, but of what will become of us if we do nothing. They showed us what we need, to save ourselves. And, as soon as they spoke, our needs began to be met. Great Zeus vowed to be our builder, the unifier who will keep us together and strong. Great Hera promised to be our shepherdess, and drive away the wolves that divide us.'

'Aye,' a few men reply, the mood of the gathering lifting.

'So let us bind ourselves to that promise of hope,' I tell them, pointing to Helen and Menelaus. 'We have all contended for the hand of Helen of Sparta, sometimes rancorously. Aye, we have fought, some of us like dogs. We've made enemies, I'm sure.'

Too bloody right we have.

'But the matter is settled now, and we need to put it behind us,' I tell them. 'No more contention! The decision is made and must be respected, if we are to go on in fellow feeling. Such friendship is the bond that will keep Achaea whole. The Moirae have spoken – telling us we need to be *united*. From Thessaly in the north down through Attica and Euboea, from the Peloponnese to the islands of Crete and Rhodes and beyond – we must all find a common bond. I offer you this one: that we will unite to preserve the marriage we have declared today. That any enemy of Menelaus and Helen, any man that drives them apart, is the enemy of us all.'

I leap down off the bench and stride into the middle of the shrine, where Tyndareus's poor dead stallion lies in bloody pieces. I don't admire the cheap posturing most orators use, but I sense that these men will be more easily swayed by some dramatic gesture. 'This is a sacred place, a holy place. The gods and the spirits are listening.' I place my right foot on the butchered horse's shoulder and cry out, 'Hear, O Gods. Hear me, Tyndareus, in whose name I invoke these words, hear me Lord Poseidon, master of horses, whose puissant power fills the bloodied pieces at my feet. I, Odysseus of Ithaca, pledge to preserve the union of Menelaus and Helen. He who comes between them is our enemy, and I will unite with you, my brothers to strike any and all of them down!'

I mean any and all of these suitors – but perhaps *they* think I mean Parassi and Skaya-Mandu and their arrogant claiming of Helen. Regardless, after some sideways glances, they begin to come forward, and for no reason other than my example, they decide that placing a foot on that poor horse's remains makes the oath more solemn and binding.

Perhaps it does, because whatever Amphithea did to that horse's blood, I can sense the spirits that fuel the oracles straining to listen. They see everything we do, it's said, but some moments are more significant than others.

The web is woven and cast over us all. I step away, wondering what it is I've really done. Bria's frowning, but she gives me a nod of approval – and Penelope is gazing at me, and I can see that she too approves.

That's all the acclaim I need.

-

Two days later, as evening gathers, I'm sitting on a bench, watching musicians play and supping ale. All round the camp-sites, men are feasting, drinking, gaming, wrestling – for fun and or to prove a point – and generally forming the sorts of bonds that are easy in peace time but can be the glue that keeps an army together in war. We're even mingling – islanders and mainlanders, north and south, men from every corner coming together to boast, laugh, and just perhaps become a nation.

The Oath of Tyndareus, as the promise I encouraged them to take is being called – named for the man we all swore it to – is binding us together in common cause. Achaea, perhaps more than in any previous time, is one nation, under one High King.

I did that.

A few hours ago, Amphithea married my best friend, Prince Menelaus, to Helen of Sparta, the most beautiful woman in the world. She looked radiant and utterly composed – or was that resigned? I don't trust her, I still believe she's a menace to our entire nation, but if love has any power, perhaps Menelaus's might change her heart, and bring her to love her people?

As for Menelaus, he looked delirious with joy. I wish them every happiness, clinging onto that vision of hope the Fates have held out to us. *This has to work.*

At this moment, up in Tyndareus's palace, they're alone together, working through the beginnings of what it means to be married, and to be the symbol of Achaean unity – with our gods and with each other. It's a behemoth of a burden, not one I'd want.

'Hey, Ithaca,' Bria drawls, swaggering up and throwing one leg over the bench. She drains my ale, then loudly calls for more. 'Thought you'd be off somewhere with the priestess of the Moirae,' she teases.

'Penelope and Actoris set out this morning,' I tell her.

'For where? Not that bloody rock in the Aegean?'

'No, not for Delos. She's left the cult of Artemis, but she's still on hostile terms with her father. She's going to stay with an aunt, somewhere on the other side of Mount Taygetus.'

Bria pokes my arm. 'Thought you'd have something to say about that?'

'I will have something to say,' I admit, 'when she's ready. But she says she has to relearn who and what she is. She expected to serve Artemis all her life, and now she has to find a new path. She has to think it through.'

'I always think better after a nice long fuck,' Bria comments, in her usual charming way. 'Anyway, won't her prick of a father – Icarius, yes? – just peddle her off again to the highest bidder, like some *dromas*.'

'She says no,' I say, though I'm not so sure of that.

Bria grins wickedly. 'Did you give her something to remember you by?'

325

'A bracelet,' I tell her.

'A *bracelet*!' She rolls her eyes, then jabs her thumb in an easterly direction. 'So what about Her Royal Nibs – Kyshanda? Are you seeing *her* off?'

I sigh. 'No. It's better we don't—'

'Bullshit,' Bria guffaws. Two fresh mugs of ale arrive, care of Eurybates, and she scoops one up. 'Come on,' she says, handing me the other. 'You owe it to her. Or are you a gutless slug that's scared to say goodbye?'

Put like that…

The ale downed, we wind through the town, to the house of a rich man whose home has been commandeered – with compensatory payments – by Agamemnon to house his 'guests'. As the sole woman in the Trojan party, Kyshanda has been kept isolated, and to Agamemnon's credit, well-guarded.

Bria and I are shown into a small room downstairs, where Kyshanda mopes by a window. Her lovely, lively and sensuous face is downcast and miserable – but when she sees me it comes alive with hope.

'Odysseus!' She leaps to her feet and hurries toward me.

Bria steps between us. 'Uh-uh, sweet-cakes. We're here to talk business. Do you know who I am?'

'You're Bria,' Kyshanda says warily, looking past her at me. 'Odysseus? We have to talk.'

Bria grins. 'Perhaps – but you and I will speak first.' She jabs a finger into the middle of Kyshanda's chest. 'Lay it on the line, Princess! Were you ever sincere about wanting to prevent war between Achaea and Troy?'

Kyshanda's narrow face lights up with urgency. 'Yes, yes, I swear—'

Bria jabs her again, harder this time. 'I know when people lie, bitch.'

'I'm not lying, I'm not. I swear it's true—'

'Did you screw Ithaca here, because your mother, Queen Hekuba, told you to?'

'I didn't… we didn't—'

Bria opens her palm as if to slap her. 'I told you, I know when people lie!'

Kyshanda looks past her at me. 'I swear… I do love Odysseus. My love is true…'

'*Knew it,*' Bria grunts in satisfaction, holding up a hand to prevent me from intervening. 'But you still want to enslave our people, don't you, Princess?'

'No, I want peace. Honestly. *I swear.*'

Peace? Only on Trojan terms. I heard her say it, the other night at the secret gathering. Which she doesn't know I overheard. The only place I could find in her love would be at her feet.

Though, maybe, she was playing a role, in the Dionysus priest's house. If you want to be in the game…

'So much swearing, but no cussing,' Bria snickers. 'Prissy, highborn bitch.'

'That's enough,' I tell Bria. 'Kyshanda, I loved you too. But our people are enemies.'

Loved… I just said 'loved'.

She understands the implication instantly, and turns away, clutching at her face. 'Go away, I don't want to talk,' she croaks, looking back at me. 'I don't want to talk to *you*. I don't want to see you. Just go.'

Bria doesn't relent. 'Not yet, Princess,' she says, grabbing Kyshanda's shoulders. 'You say you wish for peace, but what are you prepared to do to make sure that peace is what we have?'

'*Everything!*' Kyshanda screeches, struggling helplessly in Bria's grip. '*Anything!*'

'Good,' Bria rasps. 'Because your lot have been coming to Achaea, visiting our oracular sites and learning our ways, but we know little or nothing of yours. Our traders can enter your harbour, but foreigners aren't permitted in Troy itself. And we know nothing of what your mother, the greatest seer in Troy, is told by the spirits.'

'I would never betray my family,' Kyshanda says hoarsely.

327

'I'm not asking you to betray your family, but preserve them, by undermining the impetus to war,' Bria says cunningly. 'Do you know about the Palladium?' she asks.

I frown – it's not a word I know. But another name for Athena is 'Pallas'…

Kyshanda does know it. 'It's an idol we keep in the Achaean Shrine, a trophy of war from an older age. There are a few Achaeans living in Troy and they pray there.'

'Aye – and do you realise that the Palladium is an idol to Athena?'

Kyshanda bits her lip, then nods. 'Yes. But my mother says it's powerless.'

'Hekuba doesn't know what it can do,' Bria says smugly. 'It can open the Serpent's Path, for example. Learn to use the Palladium, and you'll gain your very own prophesies, independently of her. And furthermore, you'll be able to communicate with any other Athena seer walking the Paths at that time. Me, for example, or even Ithaca here – his training is coming along nicely.'

Kyshanda gulps, looking back at me, a shy hope burning again in her face.

And my heart still palpitates. Half of me only sees this wondrous, enchanting Trojan princess. But the other half yearns for a self-composed, calm, brave, resourceful woman who may well be just as impossible to build a life with.

Don't come to me for advice on matters of love.

'But to use the Palladium,' Bria goes on, 'you'll have to pledge wholeheartedly to Athena.'

Kyshanda's eyes widen. 'And if I refuse?'

'You're free to,' Bria tells her, in a tone I don't trust. She's just told her about the Palladium's hidden powers – if Kyshanda refuses, just how important is that secret? Is it worth killing for?

Kyshanda drags her gaze from Bria's face to mine. 'That other woman… it was Arnacia, yes?'

'Her name's Penelope now,' I tell her.

'Penelope…' I hate the way her face crumples as she repeats the name. Then she regathers her pride. 'Then you won't wait for me? For a time when peace truly reigns between Achaea and Troy?'

Dear gods, my parents have been nagging me to marry, the whole damn world expects men of my kind to do that. But the marriage she proposes is impossible, and the time she speaks of may never come.

And where once she owned my heart, now it is split in two.

'I can't,' I reply, hating myself but knowing it's the right thing to say.

Kyshanda shudders, closing her eyes and gathering her hands to her breasts. 'Then neither can I,' she croaks. I expect her to refuse Bria's demands now, and damn the consequences, but instead, with a convulsive sob, she says, 'Aye, I will swear to Athena.' She looks up at me. 'Please, go. I'll do this with Bria alone.'

I want, urgently, to go to her, then think better of it. What possible good will that do? Numbly, I turn and leave the room, as a future I'd longed for, ever since I first saw her, disintegrates before me.

I know better than to look back.

But I'm also scared to look forward, to an unknown future without her. But that's the fear I must confront.

Ithaca, 2 months later

'Come on, you lazy prick – carve it up,' Bria rasps, from her perch on a rock in a secluded bay some miles north of Ithaca town. It's far enough from my father's farm, which occupies a good part of this northern end of the island, to avoid prying eyes, but close enough to borrow the necessary equipment. She's taken over the body of Hebea – the slender serving girl is off-duty, and probably unaware of what Bria's doing to her –

which is to fill it with more wine than is probably healthy for a teenage girl.

'Move!' she shouts again. 'We need to be done by sunset.'

I have a farmer's plough – the sort a pair of oxen would be harnessed to, to drag round a field and break up the turf before planting. I have an ox on one side of the yoke, with the other side taken up by an extremely bemused and recalcitrant ass, making the plough very lopsided. I'm steering this strange contraption up and down the beach, just out of reach of the waves. I'm blindfolded, too, just for good measure – that's apparently to help my concentration.

Why? Because I'm learning how to prophesize. Bria says I have the gift, and what's now needed is to find the medium for unlocking it. Some oracles use symbols on wax or parchment, to be melted or burned; others use cloud shapes or the flight of birds or pig entrails or wine lees or a hundred other routes to inspiration or madness. But after all kinds of tests and false turns, Bria's decided that what might work for me is the sand and sea, farming implements and this peculiar combination of animals. 'It's because you're an islander,' she tells me. 'And you don't fit into any conventional mould. Worth a try, anyway.'

I think she just likes humiliating me in bizarre new ways.

'Repeat the questions,' her voice reminds me, accompanied by a slurping sound.

I wince and resume my low chanting, repeating over and over as I steer the plough in whatever direction feels right. '*Will we have peace? Does Troy still plan invasion? Will the Skyfather remain true to Achaea?*' and under my breath: '*To which woman should I give my heart?*'

It's the latter question that's really exercising me, because it's one thing for my head to know that it's over between Kyshanda and me, but hearts take longer to give up on love. Part of me still believes, with a faith that defies reason, that our story isn't over.

There's an afternoon sea breeze blowing, sending the occasional sharp gust to whip the sand up and sting my shins. After a while, I lose track of time and direction, walking back and forth, the two animals plodding and farting along in front of me and the plough tip catching on buried rocks and bits of driftwood. No answers are coming to me, either from the hissing waves or the whine of the wind around my ears. I've pretty much given up when Bria shouts, 'Right, finish!'

I pull off the blindfold and blink at the sight: in the fading light, I see that I've carved line upon line of furrows in the sand and gravel, just above the water line – but the wind is getting stronger, driving the waves further up the beach. As I watch, a larger one rolls in, and the surging water covers the lines closest to the shore.

When they recede, some of the furrows have been smoothed away, while other parts remain in traces that have been distorted by the water.

I catch the shapes of three letters, in syllabic Achaean script. I cry out in astonishment. 'Look...' I sound it out: '*Eirēnē: binding together; unity... peace.*'

Bria comes dancing down the beach to meet me. 'I think we've unlocked your prophetic gifts, Ithaca,' she crows. 'Ha, ha! I'm the best damned tutor in the whole bloody Aegean! You're so lucky to have me, boy!'

I'm not sure I feel lucky, especially when she whacks me with the wineskin.

But I do feel somewhat awed, as the next wave creates an image that just might be a bridle – the Stallion restrained? And then I'm sure I see a pair of identical male faces in profile, each facing away from the other. Zeus is torn still... *The danger hasn't passed...*

Bria slaps my back, snorting with delight. 'I knew you had it in you, Ithaca!'

She thinks we're done and turns away, so she misses the last image, which the seventh waves creates then erases: *a loom* – for the weavers, for the Moirae... *for Penelope.* My chest tightens, and I feel a painful sensation, like a needle plunging into my chest, dragging a thread of fire through my torn heart – sewing it back together. It's not mended, but now my head is clear.

Thank you, I whisper to the spirits. *Thank you*.

'Come on, Ithaca, that's enough for today,' Bria says cheerily. 'Is Hebea old enough to get laid? I haven't had a good pumping in weeks and I'm getting frisky.'

'No,' I tell her firmly. 'Why don't you sod off to somewhere else, now we've got this worked out. I'm sure the goats of Arcadia would welcome your company. Telmius would, anyway.'

She thrusts the wineskin into my hands. 'Brilliant idea.'

A moment later she's gone, leaving Hebea staring blankly up at me. 'Oh, gods... Not again,' she stammers, clutching her stomach. She's looking a little sick and the wineskin in my hand feels surprisingly light...

'It's all right,' I reassure her. 'She's left us, and we're heading home. Nothing bad happened.' I heft the plough and with the ox and the ass trailing behind us, we set off back to the farm.

Hebea's anxiety subsides – she can trust me, and she knows it. After a few minutes of idle chat, she feels well enough to go skipping ahead, while I lumber after her up the hill, enjoying her giddy delight in life.

Somehow, a sense of well-being steals over me, and I indeed feel at peace.

In part, this is because a fragile truce still holds in my father Laertes's home, where he and my mother try their best to forget her infidelity and restore the love they once had.

Peace also resides in Achaea: for now. High King Agamemnon reigns unchallenged, and his newly wedded wife Clytemnestra is already with child by him. Hyllus and the Heraclids might still be plotting vengeance, but they are quiescent for now, and every kingdom gives the High King his rightful due, from here in Cephalonia to Attica through Boeotia, Argos, Euboea, Lacedaemon, Elis, Phocis, Locris, Aetolia, Messenia, even Thessaly, and all the larger isles of the Aegean.

That includes Arcadia. Agamemnon, having thrust his new puppet Agapenor forward to gain Helen's hand, decided he had overreached himself and resorted to the oldest trick in politics – divide and rule. He's split the kingdom in two to lessen its power, bequeathing the west, ruled from Pisa, to Agapenor and the east to Echemus, one of his most loyal men. Tyndareus helped tie the alliance tighter by proposing the marriage of his third daughter, Timandra, to Echemus – he's the younger, untested man and Tyndareus's support will help him resist Agapenor if the latter becomes too feisty.

So, although no Achaean kingdom is more than a tenth the size of mighty Troy, we are many and now we're united. The Stallion is bridled, for now.

And hopefully, peace reigns in the house of Menelaus, as he learns love with divine, damaged Helen. May they never be parted, and may the oath I made for them – 'The Oath of Tyndareus' – never be invoked. May Menelaus's gentle kindness quell the venom in her veins, the thread of bitter heat she can't control.

The Wedding of Helen is already being distorted by the storytellers into something I barely recognize. Those tale-spinners weren't present of course, and in their ignorance of the real issues, are turning events into a predestined love affair between Helen and Menelaus. The presence of the Trojans, the near outbreak of war, even the appearance of the gods, are being glossed over or ignored: it's turning into a golden-clad romance, and I'm happy with that. But deep down I worry that Helen still dreams of empires and vengeance. Healing her might be a lifetime's work.

My role in these wedding stories seems to be one of comic-relief: turning up with no gifts and insisting on everyone swearing an oath while standing on a dead horse. I'm not too unhappy over that, though: better funny than dead.

I still don't believe in Fate either, that some overarching, immutable destiny binds our every act and hope. Are the

Moirae, the Fates, anything more than just another set of hungry spirits, preying on mankind's fears? I don't know, but they have their own priestess now. I think about Penelope every day, and wonder if she thinks of me.

I still fear for Menelaus – indeed I fear for us all. Parassi and Skaya-Mandu are not, I judge, ones to leave another's wellbeing alone. Troy still grows fat while strangling the trade routes – grow or die, is the imperial imperative. Despite all that, I pray that peace will also reign in the giant palace of Piri-Yamu, far across the Aegean Sea. Let them grow strong, so long as their eyes no longer turn our way.

And may peace reign in Kyshanda's heart, as I hope one day it will reign in mine.

My prayers whispered, I glance back at the sea, now far below us, as the sun goes down, setting on the westernmost kingdom of Achaea. The glow of orange and red behind the hills and limestone peaks of my small island is a sight of beauty to lift any heart. In a spirit of optimism, I pray that the gods keep faith with us, as we keep faith in them. Like for like, this for that. May they, one day, be worthy of the reverence we give.

It's something to hope for.

Acknowledgements

Cath: Many thanks to Heather and Mike, our agents, Heather doubly so for her beta reading skills. And to the rest of the reading team – Lisa and Kerry and Paul. Extra thanks to Sofie Wigram for making sure my translations of all our Greek quotes don't go off the rails. To Alan, my husband, for his continuing, unquestioning support. And last but not least to Canelo, Elizabeth and Patrick especially, for believing in our wild adventure into Ancient Greek mythos, and working hard to share it with our readers.

David: Thanks as always to our test readers Kerry, Heather, Paul and Lisa; and to Canelo for their faith in this project, especially Elizabeth for the editing, and Patrick for the awesome covers. Much gratitude to our agents Heather and Mike for putting the relationship between writer and publisher together, and their constant support and advocacy. Thanks most of all to Kerry, for putting up with having a writer for a husband, and all your support and encouragement – I love you always.

Hello to Jason Isaacs. Tinkety-tonk and down with the Nazis.

Glossary

General terms, names and places

Achaea, **Achaean**: The whole of Greece. While 'Achaea' is also a minor kingdom on the north coast of the Peloponnese, 'Achaean' is a common term in Homer's *The Iliad* for all Greeks, who were united by a common culture and whose mostly-independent kingdoms owed allegiance to a High King. Hittite documents dating from around the time of the Trojan War refer to 'Ahhiyawa', as one of the great political powers they interacted with; 'Ahhiyawa' is now widely believed by scholars to be their word for "Achaea".

Adonis: A wildly handsome mortal lover of the goddess Aphrodite.

Arktoi: The little 'bears'; young novices of Artemis.

Avatar: A **theios** or **theia** who has the ability to allow their god to enter them and take over their body, so that the god, who is otherwise invisible to all but the **theioi**, can be seen. The god may appear in the form of the avatar, or in their own mythic form.

Axeinos: The Ancient Greek name for the Black Sea; the literal translation of Axeinos is 'inhospitable'.

Cerberus: The monstrous hound that guards **Erebus**, allowing the dead souls in, while keeping the living out.

336

Daemon: A spirit, without connotations of good or evil. The term can also refer to a lesser deity, but can also describe the major gods.

Dromas: A whore, specifically a street prostitute, from the Greek word for 'racecourse'.

Eirēnē: Peace, binding together, unity.

Elysian Fields: Also known as 'Elysium'. A place of eternal happiness in **Erebus**, the Underworld, reserved for the Blessed Dead – heroes, and others who have won the blessings of the gods for living a virtuous and noble life.

Erebus: The Underworld, where the souls of the departed go after death.

Hamazan: Amazon, a member of one of the woman warrior cults in the nomadic (Scythian) tribes who live by or near the **Axeinos** or Black Sea, at the outer edges of the Greek known world.

Hubris: Wanton disregard for the feelings or rights of others; overbearing arrogance; a spirit of wanton violence; excessive and foolish pride, especially in defiance of the gods.

Keryx: A herald serving a royal master, discharging important public functions such as making proclamations, undergoing missions, summoning assemblies and conducting ceremonies.

Kopros: Dung, shit, dunghill. **Koprologos:** shit-gatherer.

Kunopes: Bitch, shameless one, slut (from Greek 'kuon': a dog).

Labyrinth: A confusing complex of pathways through which it is almost impossible to find one's way.

Labyrinth of Minos: The original **labyrinth**, built under the palace of King Minos, of Crete to house the Minotaur, a monstrous half-man, half-bull which was slain by the Athenian hero Theseus.

Laertiades, Sisyphiades, Atreiades, Heraclid etc: These are patronyms, the equivalent of our modern surnames, except that they always refer back to the father's given name. They translate as 'son of Laertes', 'son of Sisyphus', 'son of Atreus' and so on. This form parallels Scandinavian and Scottish names like 'Anderson', which initially meant 'Son of Anders'.

Magus: A sorcerer; a **theios** or **theia** with magical powers, who can bend reality.

Megaron: The main hall of a palace or important stately house. It is either broadly rectangular or square-shaped, with a large circular hearth in the middle surrounded by four pillars, and is often reached via a large vestibule and perhaps a porch opening onto a courtyard. A royal megaron will have its throne against one wall and will have brightly painted walls, ceiling and floor.

Mulas: A cock-sucker.

Mycenaean, Mycenae: On a specific level, it refers to the kingdom, city and people of Mycenae, seat of the Achaean High King, in the north-eastern corner of the Peloponnese. The term is also used nowadays by archaeologists to describe the whole of Late Bronze Age Greece and its culture.

Nymph, naiad, dryad: Female **daemons** associated with nature, presiding over various natural phenomena such as springs, clouds, trees, caves and fields.

Obol: A unit of everyday currency. Before coinage was introduced in the 7th century BC, an obol was a bronze skewer which was used as a form of exchange. A 'fist' of six obols was as many as a grown man could be expected to hold in one hand, and was called a drachma, after the Ancient Greek word 'to grasp'. Later, obols and drachmas became coins.

Olympians: The select group of powerful Greek gods who dwell on the mythic Mt Olympus. The physical Mt Olympus is in northern Greece.

Oracle: A seer or seeress capable of delivering prophecies.

Pankration: A form of unarmed combat sport, using a mixture of boxing and wrestling. Almost anything is allowed, apart from biting and eye-gouging.

Pantheon: This word translates literally as 'all the gods'. In later times it was also a building, which we anticipated in its basic form and function by many hundreds of years in Book One of the *Olympus* series, *Athena's Champion*, by creating an open-sided building in **Erebus** with a roof supported only by pillars, intended as a meeting place for the **Olympians.**

Phallos, (pl.) phalli: Penis, prick.

Ploistos: A festival celebrating the start of spring; the name of the first sailing month of the year, after the winter storms.

Pornos: Male prostitute.

Priapos: Penis, prick.

Proktos: Arse hole.

Pythia: The high priestess and prophetess of the oracular shrine of **Pytho**. When prophesying, she sits on a stool straddling a deep cleft in the rock from which vapours arise, sending her into a prophetic trance.

Pytho: A major oracular site high on the slopes of Mt Parnassus, and later known as Delphi. It has been sacred to a series of Earth goddesses – Gaia, Themis and now Hera.

Satyr: A male **daemon,** a nature spirit associated with fertility who consorts with nymphs, naiads and the like.

Scree: A steep mountain slope made up of small stones or rock fragments.

Serpent's Path: A prophetic process or 'journey' undertaken by an **oracle**, a person with oracular powers.

Signet: A small, lens-shaped object, often of gold or silver but also of agate, chalcedony or a similarly hard stone. These are carved with intricately-detailed images – ritual or combat scenes are common – and are used as seals, creating the reversed image in relief, to identify a particular person in the same way a hand-written signature would.

Suagros: A person with a romantic attachment to wild pigs; a pig-fucker.

Theios, theia, theioi, theiae: A human who has some measure of divine blood; the Greek word translates literally as 'god-touched'. They are born of a union between a god and a human, or of a union between their god-touched descendants. A man or boy is a 'theios', a woman or girl is a 'theia', and the plural forms are 'theioi' (m) and 'theiae' (f). A person's theios nature is latent until it is awakened; this awakening can be carried out either by their ancestral god or by another god whose nature is in tune with that of the latent theios or theia, allowing gods to claim the descendants of other gods. In rare instances, a theios or theia can have affiliations with more than one god. Theioi, once awakened, can switch their allegiance to another god, but this is perilous, for it invokes the extreme anger of their original awakening god and usually leads to their death.

There are four types of theioi: seer, champion, avatar and magus. The seer has prophetic powers; the champion has superior physical strength and talent; the **avatar** can become the physical vessel of their god, who is otherwise invisible; and the **magus** is a sorcerer, with magical powers. Sometimes a theios or theia can be more than one type, though usually one aspect is dominant, and generally each aspect is weaker than it would be in a theios or theia who has only one attribute. In later generations, theios blood can become too diluted to give theios powers to new offspring. How long this takes depends on the power of the ancestral god, and on the mutual theios strength of the theios couple who produce the child.

Wraith: A ghost, phantom or spirit.

Xenia: The sacred **Ancient Greek** customs of guest friendship: the respect and ties of obligation between host and guest, which not only bind people who share that relationship, but their family and their descendants as well.

Xiphos: A sword. Achaean swords of the Late Bronze Age, around the time of the Trojan War, were broad, straight and relatively short. They were made of bronze, as were all weapons of the time.

The Gods

Around 1300BC, religious worship in the western Aegean region is dominated by the gods of the **Achaean** peoples. They are worshipped throughout Achaea (geographically equivalent to modern Greece); and their influence has recently begun to extend as far as the kingdom of Troy, on the Anatolian coast (modern western Turkey).

These Achaean deities are divided into the **Olympian** gods (those aligned to Zeus, the Skyfather and head of a **pantheon** of allied sects); and the unaligned gods whose worship is independent of the Olympic pantheon.

However, in Troy, a client-kingdom of the Hittite Empire (modern central and eastern Turkey), worship is dominated by the Hittite gods, with some Achaean influences through settlement and trade. As Troy's influence grows, so too does the influence of their gods; especially Apaliunas (known in Achaea as Apollo).

Zeus is the senior god of the Achaean peoples, but his worship has spread well beyond the **Achaean** kingdoms. As a sky god, he is actively aligning himself with other such deities as his priests seek to make his worship universal. The Zeus cult is now questioning their alliance with the primary Achaean goddess, **Hera**, whose worship is limited to Achaean lands.

Hera is **Achaea**'s strongest goddess, aggressively absorbing other fertility goddesses (such as **Leto**, Gaia, Themis, Hestia and others) into her cult to increase her worship. Most of her followers are women, though she is still the dominant deity at the Achaean High King's capital of Mycenae, and her priestesses control the main oracular site of Pytho. As a purely Achaean deity, her cult faces challenges in a changing world.

Athena is a lesser goddess whose cult promotes wisdom and skill in war and peace, and whose primary power base is Athens, capital city of Attica. Outside that kingdom, her cult is in conflict with **Ares** the traditional war god. Like **Hera**, she is worshipped only in **Achaea**, and is even more vulnerable if Achaean culture were to fail.

Ares, an Achaean god of war, personifies the belligerent warrior culture of **Achaea**. Recently, his sect has joined forces with that of **Aphrodite**, the goddess of love; a deliberate alignment to match the cult of **Ishtar**, the Trojan/Hittite goddess of love and war. Ares is the particular rival of **Athena**, who inhibits his worship in Attica.

Aphrodite, the **Achaean** goddess of love, promotes an alternative view of femininity to the **Hera** cult, idealising beauty, love and marriage in an outwardly submissive context, compared to Hera's traditions of strong womanhood. The cult of Aphrodite is in the process of breaking from the failing cult of the smith, **Hephaestus**, and partnering with that of **Ares**, leading to a spate of new 'legends' that depict Hephaestus as being a crippled lecher. Aphrodite's cult follows that of her new ally Ares in seeking alignment with **Ishtar** (in the hope that they will usurp the eastern deity in due course).

Hephaestus is the smith-god, harking back to an earlier time when smiths were community leaders venerated for their 'magical' skill in metal-work. But society has changed, the smith is now just an artisan, and their cult is in decline. Tales now portray this failing deity as crippled and cuckolded; the first step in a process designed to erase him from human worship.

Apollo is revered already by the Trojans as their patron god **Apaliunas**, and his cult is aggressively expanding into **Achaea**, aligning him with the Achaean hunter goddess **Artemis** to capture the next generation. He is worshipped by the Trojans as a source of light, which brings him in conflict with **Helios**, the Achaean god of the sun, whose cult is collapsing in the face of his more sophisticated rival.

Artemis, the Huntress, is the traditional goddess of young **Achaean** maidens, and for centuries has dovetailed with **Hera's** cult, though in a subservient role. However, threatened by Hera's dominance, the cult has aligned with that of the new shooting star, **Apollo/Apaliunas**. The next generation, they believe, belongs to them.

Leto, like Gaia, Themis, **Eileithya** and Hestia, is now a minor goddess. Her cult is seeking to regain their earlier influence by putting her forward as 'mother' to **Apollo** and **Artemis**, hoping to be instated as **Zeus's** consort if or when the Skyfather's cult renounces that of **Hera**.

Hermes is a nature deity from the **Achaean** mountain region, Arcadia, whose cult has been subordinated by that of **Zeus**, and is tolerated by the Skyfather's priests as it gives them access to the Achaean heartland. With Hermes personified as Zeus's herald, his cult exemplifies masculine cunning, in the grey area where skill morphs into trickery, and functions as a 'political' wing of the Zeus cult.

Demeter is an **Achaean** goddess of fertility and harvests, the latest to find her cult overwhelmed by that of **Hera**. To survive, the cult of Demeter has built an alliance with **Hades**, god of the Underworld, personified by the figure of her 'daughter' **Persephone**, a subordinate deity 'married' during winter to Hades. As an Achaean alliance, it is threatened by eastern expansion, but believes the universality of death will enable it to survive any circumstance.

Dionysus is god of wine and the intoxicating power of nature. His cult has – like that of **Apollo** – pushed westwards into **Achaea** from the east. While appearing to align with Apollo and **Zeus**, the core rites are highly secretive, and the cult's true allegiances remain unknown.

The Unaligned Achaean Deities

Prometheus is a Titan who aligned himself with the Olympian gods in their battle against his fellow Titans, but was punished for stealing fire, which – out of pity for their miserable state – he gave to mortals against the wishes of the gods. For this, he was chained to a rock, where, every day, an eagle rips out his liver; the liver then grows back so that he can be tormented all over again. Known as a clever trickster, he also gave mankind the gift of metalwork and other skilled crafts. 'Prometheus' translates as 'forethinker'.

Poseidon claims mastery of the sea and as a result gains worshippers throughout **Achaea**, primarily those involved in sea-born trade and travel, a vital part of life in such a mountainous, sea-girt country. His equivalent god in the mostly-landlocked East (Aruna) is a minor deity, so any foreign invasion of Achaea will diminish Poseidon's cult. As a result, he is in potential conflict with **Zeus**, but his cult believes his worship is universal and unassailable.

Hades is the Achaean god of death and the afterlife, conceived by **Achaeans** either as an eternal limbo or as a reward or punishment, as appropriate. This universal concept affords the cult great durability, but *dread* of death is not *worship* of death: the cult has therefore limited influence in daily life. As a consequence, it has sought alliance with **Demeter**, goddess of fertile life (as personified by a 'marriage' to Demeter's "daughter" **Persephone**), as a direct challenge to the **Zeus**/**Hera** hegemony.

Persephone, a seasonal harvest deity, has become 'daughter' of **Demeter** and 'wife' of **Hades**, enabling followers of both sects to bridge the divide between life and death, fecundity and sterile extinction, and make their worship more universal. Persephone's worship is growing as this duality of life and death in harmony gains appeal in **Achaea**.

Helios, the ancient god of the sun, has suffered from the growing worship of **Zeus**, who claims dominance over all the heavens; and more recently by the emergence of **Apollo**/**Apaliunas**, the Trojan god of light. As a consequence, the cult of Helios is collapsing almost unnoticed.

Eileithya is the **Achaean** goddess of childbirth, appealed to by pregnant women, and by men who fail to get their wives with child. Once a much-worshipped fertility goddess, she and other primal goddesses have seen their worship eaten up by **Hera**, whose worshippers now claim she governs every aspect of an adult woman's life, from unmarried virgin through to wife/mother and aged crone.

Eros is a primal god of procreation. Recently his worshippers have been increasingly lured away by **Aphrodite**, forcing the cult of Eros to subordinate itself to the rival cult to survive.

Hercules was originally a powerful 'theios' – a god-touched human gifted with extraordinary powers. Such was his strength and ruthlessness that he has become a subject of worship among **Achaean** warriors after his death; which has seen his spirit ('**daemon**') elevated to godhead by the **Zeus** cult. He is now seen as a powerful figure in Achaean religion, closely aligned to Zeus – and a potential rival to both **Athena** and **Ares**.

Hecate is a goddess of magic, a personification of the mysteries of womanhood and born of a time when women's cults excluded men and handed down secrets and traditions only to their own gender. Hecate is therefore primarily a 'household' deity with few temples, but with widespread allegiance among women.

The Moirae: The Fates, three daughters of Nyx, Goddess of Night, who spin people's destinies from birth onwards, and supposedly even the gods cannot overturn their decisions. 'Moira' is the Greek word for a share or portion.

Notable Trojan and Hittite Gods

There are many Hittite and Trojan deities – these are the ones who impact on this tale (so far).

Tarhum is the Trojan sky god, the most important deity in the Hittite pantheon, who is placated to gain favourable weather and therefore crops. The priests of Tarhum foresee the dominance of the Hittite Empire over the entire Aegean region through their client kingdom of Troy, and are more than willing to merge their cult with that of their **Achaean** equivalent **Zeus**, to undermine the Achaean people and extend their own dominance.

Ishtar is a goddess of love and war, who personifies a union of warrior-man and fecund-woman that has captured the imagination of the Trojan and Hittite peoples. This powerful notion has forced the Achaean cults of **Ares** and **Aphrodite** to seek alignment: the priests of Ishtar are happy to swallow up both, and foresee a time when they, not **Zeus-Tarhum**, dominate the Aegean.

Apaliunas is the patron god of the Trojans, who worship him as a source of light. In **Achaea**, he is now called **Apollo** and revered as the son of **Zeus** and **Leto**, and the brother of **Artemis**.

Kamrusepa is goddess of magic, the equivalent of the **Achaean** cult of **Hecate**: her cult however enjoys the powerful patronage of many influential women in the eastern kingdoms, especially Queen Hekuba of Troy, and is therefore a powerful cult among women.

Lelwani is the Hittite and Trojan goddess of death, believed by her followers to preside over the Underworld in much the same way that **Hades** rules over **Erebus**. Her priests also attribute her with the power not only to induce sickness but the ability to heal it.

Hanwasuit: The 'throne-goddess' of the Hittites.

CPSIA information can be obtained
at www.ICGtesting.com
Printed in the USA
BVHW081932271220
596494BV00001B/218

9 781788 638500